# Soul Seducer

by

Alicia Dean

*Reapers of Boone, Book 1*

**Soul Seducer**


Contact Information: info@thewildrosepress.com

Cover Art by *Lisa Dawn MacDonald.*

The Wild Rose Press, Inc.
PO Box 708
Adams Basin, NY 14410-0708
Visit us at www.thewildrosepress.com

Publishing History
First Edition, 2021
Trade Paperback ISBN 978-1-5092-3580-3
Digital ISBN 978-1-5092-3683-1

*Reapers of Boone, Book 1*
Published in the United States of America

She whirled. The blond…Gaylen…stood there, looking…well, radiant. His posture was relaxed. The beautiful, white-toothed smile was in place. A satisfied glow emanated from him. He appeared ready to break out in song. She glanced back to Dimitri, who stood with his fists clenched at his sides, his teeth showing in a feral snarl. "What do you want, Gaylen?"

The calm tone Dimitri had used with her altered. He growled the words, his body tense, as if holding itself back from pouncing.

"I think you know." His eyes moved to Audra. "Pleasure to finally make your acquaintance. Properly, that is. I'm Gaylen." He bent at the waist in a bow.

Screw this. Did he expect her to curtsy? "What do you want?" she repeated Dimitri's question.

Gaylen smiled and flicked a glance at Dimitri. "I want to disprove whatever nonsense he's fed you. I only want to be friends, to get to know you." His amber eyes darkened to a burnished gold. He lowered his voice, and a shiver worked through her insides. "I've waited a long time for this."

"Don't believe him, Audra. He only seeks to destroy."

She looked from one being to the other. Dimitri's angry, ready-to-battle stance. Gaylen's amused, calm, confident posture. Was she actually being asked to choose between two *reapers*?

She remembered the creepy costume Jaxon had shown her at the mall. The ghostly white mask…the black hooded robe…the deadly scythe. Somehow that image of a reaper now seemed a hell of a lot less scary. That was only a costume…a myth. The creatures here with her now were all too real.

**Praise for Soul Seducer:**

"Alicia Dean sucks you in from the very first page and holds tight with characters who are flawed and fascinating. Readers will reap an all-encompassing emotional experience in this fast-paced, emotionally charged, paranormal tale. With a hero who wasn't always heroic, a villain whose twisted journey has made him truly terrifying, and a passionate heroine willing to sacrifice everything for those she loves, Ms. Dean has built a world where life and death hang in the balance—with choices and consequences that truly matter. This one's a keeper." *~Bestselling author Robin Perini*

~*~

"A spellbinding tale of dark designs, passion, and heart-rending love." ~ *Author Claire Ashgrove*

~*~

"From a cold knot of fear to the flash of hot passion, Alicia Dean evokes every emotion in this supernatural suspense—the tale of a battle between good and evil and the woman caught in the middle. *Soul Seducer* is an electrifying and satisfying read." ~ *Author Silver James*

~*~

"Dark and steamy, *Soul Seducer*, seduces you from the first page." ~ *Author Denise Grover Swank*

~*~

"Alicia Dean serves up a steamy concoction of supernatural with a peek on the other side of Death. Her Reapers are an exotic breed of alpha male that create their own brand of dark and delicious." ~ *Mel Odom, multi-published award winning author*

## Dedication

To my mother. Thank you for the encouragement you've given me—for the unconditional love you show your family—and for your caring, selfless nature. I love you so much.

## Acknowledgments

Thank you to my friends and family for your support, my OKRWA and HERA groups, my critique partners, Natasha, Janet, Betty, Christy, Sheila and Kelly. I'd also like to thank Winona for her guidance on the nursing details—I had no idea where to even start. Thank you, R.T. Wolfe, for your beta read. And thank you Claire Ashgrove—a talented author, my friend, critique partner and sometimes editor. You totally rock.

## Chapter 1

"Lady. Hey, lady! Are you okay?" The man's voice barely penetrated Audra Grayson's tormented mind.

She groaned, and agony screeched through her entire body. Panic rose to her throat. *No, please, no more…*

But wait…she remembered…this man wasn't one of the attackers. His arrival had scared them off. Thank God…

Hands touched her—gently this time.

"Call 9-1-1."

Audra opened her eye, the one that wasn't swollen shut. A middle-aged man knelt over her. He wore a brown coat with hair the same shade. Unfamiliar. Relief trickled through her, but it was soon overpowered by the pain screaming through her body.

"An ambulance is coming. Is she alive?" This voice belonged to a female.

"Yeah, but God knows how." Another gentle touch, on the tip of her shoulder, as if he was afraid to touch her anywhere else. "Hang in there, lady. Help is on the way."

She squinted in the dim lighting. A woman a few years younger than the man stood behind him, wearing an expression of horror combined with sympathy.

Movement ten feet away, at the mouth of the alley,

caught Audra's attention. Two men. Not close enough for her to see, yet she could see them clearly. How could that be?

Even though she couldn't lift her head, couldn't actually *see* them, their images played out in her mind. One man was tall, handsome, the streetlights making his golden hair glow like an angel's. The man next to him had dark hair and wore a leather jacket.

The angel smiled, but the other man scowled as he stared at her, his chest rising and falling with ragged breaths. His eyes were an odd shade of blue, reminding her of something… Yes. She remembered. The Caribbean. Standing on the boat, looking out over the water, marveling at the many colors of the ocean. The most vivid, startling blue had been the one on the horizon, just below the setting sun. His eyes were that same hue.

"She's mine," the blond said.

"Like hell she is," the dark one growled.

"You think you're going to take her?"

"You can't have her. I got here first."

Audra frowned. Surely, she was hallucinating. At this distance, in the state she was in, how could she see and hear the two strangers so clearly? And what were they talking about? Take her where?

The man leaning over her seemed unaware of the figures in the background. His attention was focused on her, until the wail of sirens split the night.

He looked over his shoulder, then back down. "They're here. You're going to be fine."

She wished she could share his optimism, but she was an RN. She knew she was in a bad way. She'd probably have known, even if she hadn't been a nurse.

There was nowhere on her body that didn't scream with agony.

Still at the mouth of the alley, the blond man started toward her, but his companion shot out a hand, gripping his arm. "I said you can't have her."

The blond halted. His angelic features took on an expression of fury.

Were they Heaven and Hell, battling for her soul?

If so, she didn't care who won the battle, as long as they made the pain stop.

## Chapter 2

Audra opened her eyes and turned her head, sending a sharp pain through her jaw. She swallowed and briefly squeezed her eyes shut, fighting back nausea. When it eased, she once more moved her head, taking in her surroundings.

Machines beeped next to the bed. An array of vases holding flowers rested on the windowsill. A border patterned with brightly colored seashells ran along the wall. She was in St. Anne's, the hospital where she worked.

Outside the window, a light smatter of rain fell in a dusky sky. Evening then, but what day? Why was she in the hospital? She drew her gaze away, to the opposite side of the room. Her friend, Riley Sullivan, sat next to the bed, head bowed.

"Hey." Audra made a croaking sound but wasn't sure if the word actually formed into something coherent. That little bit made her entire face hurt, so she didn't attempt anything further.

Riley lifted her tear-streaked face. "Hey, back," she said. "How you feeling?"

"Hurting. Wha' happened?"

Riley shook her head, her silvery hair shimmering like a disco curtain. She opened her mouth as if to answer, then clamped it shut, turning to look over her shoulder.

Audra heard what Riley must have heard. Someone coming into the room. With difficulty, unsure why such a small thing should take so much effort, she lifted her head.

Dr. Jaxon Maroney, her ex-husband and lifelong friend, stood just inside the room, clipboard in hand.

"Hey," Audra said, the only word she could manage.

"Hi. How are you?" Jaxon moved to her bed. Riley scooted back to give him room.

"Feel…funny." Audra struggled to speak. "Wha' happen'?"

"You don't remember?" Jaxon smiled, but worry hovered in his soft brown eyes.

She scowled, trying to recall. Nothing. She shook her head. The motion sent a shock wave of agony through her face. She held her breath until it subsided.

He stared down at her, his expression solemn, the perpetual dimples disappearing. "You don't remember the attack?"

Her scowl deepened. "Attack?" The memories started crowding in, along with the fear. "Maria. Needed help." She wasn't sure how many of the words actually came out. Her mouth was numb, dry. "They…they…" The fear intensified. She remembered it all. Arms grabbing her from behind. Dragging her into the alley. Three men, maybe four. "Oh, God…th-they… beat me. Why?"

"Shhh. It's okay," Jaxon soothed. "You're safe now."

"When did—" She frowned. She had no idea how long she'd been here.

Riley came closer to the bed, taking Audra's hand

in hers. "It happened last night. I've been here since, waiting for you to wake up."

"Sadie?"

Sadie was Riley's five-year-old daughter. She'd never been away from her mother for this long.

"Brent is taking care of her. I didn't want her to see—" Riley broke off, but Audra knew what she was going to say. The way Audra's face felt, she could only imagine what it must look like.

"Where's Maria?"

Jaxon looked at her questioningly. "Maria Bellafonte?"

Audra nodded, slowly, painfully. "Scott was…out of his mind. Where…is she?"

He shook his head. "I don't know. She was nowhere around when they found you."

Her stomach knotted with worry. "Got her. Maybe…killed her."

"Was Scott one of the men?" His jaw clenched.

Scott and Maria were frequent visitors at the hospital. Maria as a result of the beatings Scott administered, and Scott from one altercation or another—a knife fight, a drunken brawl, an equally drunken fall from one of the roofs he repaired on the rare occasions he held down a job.

"Not Scott," she told Jaxon. She hadn't recognized any of her attackers. They'd caught her unaware. It had been dark. The beating started before she could make out anyone's features. But she'd have known if one of them had been him.

"Then maybe it had nothing to do with Maria." Jaxon said. "Maybe she's safe, and you're worrying about her for nothing."

The pain was swelling, coming on full force. Her ribs had gone from aching, to a piercing pain that nearly cut off her breath. Her face was no longer numb but had started tingling with unbearable sensation. She sucked in a breath.

"The pain's coming back, isn't it?" Jaxon asked, frowning.

She managed a nod.

Riley patted her hand. "We'll get you something for it, sweetie."

"I'll be right back," Jaxon promised.

Audra watched him leave and caught a glimpse of two men—one blond, one dark—hovering in the hallway. As quick as the flash came, it was gone. One second the men were there, then they weren't. She recognized them, though. The men from the hallucination she had while waiting for the ambulance. Why would the same hallucination return now?

A disquieting sensation filtered through her soul. Not a hallucination. They were real. She knew they were.

"Just hold on," Riley soothed. "Jaxon will be back with something for the pain."

Audra nodded, not telling her it wasn't the pain that was causing her consternation, but rather bewilderment and an abiding fear that something in her world wasn't right.

"I'm okay." Audra paused to cringe as a shaft of pain ripped through her mid-section. "Tell police. Maria…"

"Shane's waiting outside, so you'll have a chance to tell him yourself, but here's an idea. Why don't you worry about *you* right now? Maria's been with that asshole for ten years. She knew the risks."

"Doesn't deserve—"

"Please. Don't try to talk," Riley interrupted. "You need to save your strength. I didn't mean she deserved to get hurt. I'm just saying that she's not the one in the hospital right now. Let's focus on getting you well, then we'll worry about Maria."

Audra didn't reply, but she thought maybe Maria wasn't in the hospital right now because, instead, she was dead.

Before that unsettling thought could take hold, Jaxon reappeared, administering pain medications into her IV.

"This will make you sleep. The police are waiting to speak with you, but I'll tell them you'll talk when you wake, okay?"

She nodded, already feeling her limbs and mind relax. In seconds, the room faded away, and she drifted into oblivion.

****

Some hours later, Audra pulled her eyes open to find Riley and Shane Dunham standing next to her bed. She'd gone to school with Shane. He'd moved away right after high school, but had returned a year ago and was now sheriff of Boon Springs. They'd dated in high school, but Jaxon and a lot of years had come and gone since that time.

"Audra, you feel up to answering a few questions?" Shane asked.

She managed a nod. Shane's deep brown eyes held concern, although he smiled reassuringly. Sprinkles of grey dotted his dark hair and character lines creased his tanned face.

"I don't think she's up to it, Shane," Riley said. "She can barely talk."

"I'll be brief." His tone was gentle. "The sooner I can get information, the sooner I can run these assholes down."

"S'okay." Audra made herself smile at Riley. "I'll talk." She didn't want to do it, but she wanted it done. She wanted the assholes found.

Riley sighed reluctantly and moved to one side so Shane could take her place.

"Try to answer the best you can. Just nod or shake your head on the yes or no questions, okay?" He pulled out a notepad and pen. "Did you recognize your attackers?"

She shook her head.

"Did they say anything to give you a clue as to who they were?"

Audra swallowed painfully. "Water."

Riley picked up a cup from the tray next to her bed and put the straw to Audra's lips. Audra sipped, then lay back against the pillows. "Nothing. I was…meeting Maria. Laundromat. They grabbed me." She sucked in a breath. "Dragged me…alley." Panic swam in her chest as she recalled the terror, the pain. "Beating. Hitting. Kicking."

Riley moved closer and placed a comforting hand over Audra's.

"How many were there?" Shane asked. "Don't try to talk, just lift up the number of fingers."

Her head was woozy. Her hand felt disconnected from her body as she lifted it and held up three fingers, then four.

"So, it was three, maybe four?" At her nod, he

continued. "Is there anything you can tell me about them? Anything familiar at all?"

She thought for a moment, then shook her head again.

"Did they threaten you? Tell you why they were doing it? Did they take anything, like your purse? Money? Jewelry?"

"Geez, Shane. Slow down," Riley admonished. "Give her time."

"Right. Sorry." Shane gentled his voice. "Just answer as succinctly as you can. If you don't know, shake your head. Only speak if you have information for me."

"Didn't take anything."

"Did they give you any clue why they attacked you?"

Audra started to give him another headshake, then remembered something. A very small something, but it was something. "Said I should learn to…" she drew in a breath before continuing, "…mind my own…business."

Shane scowled. "Did that mean anything to you? Do you know what they were referring to?"

Audra thought about Maria. Her husband would damn sure think Audra should mind her own business. But Scott hadn't been one of the men. She was sure he'd *like* to beat the shit out of her, but it hadn't been him.

"No." She lifted her pleading gaze to Shane. "Check on Maria."

"You think she had something to do with this?"

Audra frowned in irritation. "Hurt. Could be hurt."

"Okay. Sure. We'll check on Maria. If you were going to meet her, she might know something about what happened. I'll go talk to her when I leave."

Audra sighed wearily. She was worn out and hurting all over.

"Do you know the couple who came to your rescue?" Shane asked. When she shook her head, he said, "I spoke with them. They're not from here. They were heading back to their hotel room when they heard the men shouting, cursing at you. When they ran into the alley, the assailants fled."

"Tell 'em…thank you." The words seemed so insignificant. Those men had likely saved her life.

"I will." Shane flipped his notepad shut. "I'll let you get some rest while I check a few things out. I'll be back to talk to you in a few days, okay?"

He patted her hand and left.

"They'll be in soon with your pain meds." Riley moved back to her bedside. "Are you feeling any better at all?"

Audra thought about the rundown Jaxon had given her on her injuries. Her ulna was fractured, necessitating a wrist brace. She had several contusions, a couple of bruised ribs, and a dislocated knee. Nope. Not much better. She didn't expect to feel better for a long while. For Riley's benefit, she forced a smile and a nod. All in all, she was grateful. She could be dead. Probably would be if her rescuers hadn't shown up and scared off the attackers.

"Yes, better," she lied.

After a dose of pain meds, she drifted off and woke a while later, with Riley standing next to her bed.

"How you feeling?" Riley asked for the thousandth time.

"Better," Audra said, although she wasn't

completely convinced of the fact. “Maria?”

Riley rolled her eyes. “Shane called. Maria was at home, unharmed. She claimed she knows nothing about what happened to you. Apparently, Scott was in jail last night. He’s still in jail.”

Audra nodded, relief sweeping through her. Maria was okay. At least for now, until the son of a bitch was released from jail.

Riley turned and retrieved something from the nightstand next to the bed. She lifted a large pink Teddy Bear toward Audra.

“A volunteer brought this in. It was delivered downstairs. It’s cute, but the neck is ripped.”

“Too bad,” Audra replied sleepily. “Coulda given it…Sadie.”

“Yeah, too bad. She only has about a zillion stuffed animals as it is.”

Audra smiled.

“There’s a card.” Riley silently read the message. Her eyes widened, her face losing color.

“What?”

“Nothing.” Riley put the card behind her back, as if Audra would lunge from the bed and snatch it from her.

“Tell me.”

“We should call the police.”

Audra lifted a hand for the card. Reluctantly, Riley held it out to her.

Audra read the words, fear clutching her heart as she realized, the bear’s neck wasn’t *accidentally* torn. Its throat had been cut.

The words on the card confirmed the intended threat.

*Next time, you die.*

****

Three days after the attack, Audra lay in her hospital bed, somewhere between sleep and wakefulness, her limbs heavy, her body relaxed from the medication. Rain pelted her window, perfect background music for an early evening nap.

"Good news!"

Jaxon's too-chipper voice made her start. Her eyes flew open, and a fresh wave of pain shot through her body. Since being gifted with the nearly decapitated Teddy Bear, she'd been as skittish as a deer at a firing range.

She scowled, allowing the pain to ebb before she replied. "Yeah? What's that?"

Her jaw was still sore, but it didn't hurt as much to talk, or to breathe since they'd taken out the chest tube from the punctured lung, and her ribs had started to mend. Her mind had also apparently mended. The apparitions hadn't been back.

"At the rate you're healing, it looks like you can go home tomorrow."

Unexpected dread spiked her blood. "Tomorrow? So soon?"

Jaxon studied her in silence, a troubled frown marring his brow. She tried to mold her expression into something resembling happiness but knew she didn't succeed when he reached out and gently stroked her arm. Her heart did the tiniest bit of a flutter, signaling something she'd known all along. She still wasn't over him.

Fat lot of good it did. Granted, if Jaxon could ever love a woman, she was sure it would be her. That was the problem, though. He could never love a *woman.*

She'd accepted that long ago.

"Is something wrong?" he asked softly. "You don't seem happy about leaving. Are you frightened?"

"A little." *Actually, I'm a crybaby, chicken shit, and I'm afraid to leave this room in case the big bad men come after me again.* She forced cheerfulness into her voice. "I'm happy about going home. I just didn't expect it to be this soon."

"Physically, you're doing remarkably well. We'll talk about it tomorrow and see if you feel ready to be released."

"Any updates on the case?"

"Dunham is outside waiting to speak with you. I told him I'd see if you're up to it before I send him in."

"I'm up to it."

He gave her an affectionate smile. "You need anything? How's the pain?"

She chuckled. "You know, I've asked patients that same thing a million times and didn't realize until now how stupid it sounds. The pain's awesome, thanks for asking."

"You know what I meant." Jaxon grinned. "Is it manageable or do you need something before you talk to the sheriff?"

"I'm okay for now. Thanks."

"I'll send him in."

As soon as Jaxon left, Shane entered. He wore a troubled frown, and the lines around his eyes seemed deeper.

"Did you find out anything about where the bear came from?" she asked before he was fully in the room.

He shook his head. "'Fraid not. It didn't come from the gift shop downstairs, and I couldn't find any others like it around town. We're expanding the search, but I've got a feeling it wasn't purchased here. It was delivered to the information desk downstairs, but no one saw who brought it. We checked hospital security cameras but found nothing."

She choked back a rush of terror. Exactly what she'd feared. They'd been to the hospital. Or, at least one of them had. Didn't take a gang to deliver a Teddy Bear. Not like it did to beat the shit out of a woman.

"So, you have no leads? You're not even close to catching them?"

"I'm sorry, Audra. You know we're doing all we can." His jaw tightened. "Can't imagine what kind of sick bastards would want to do this to you."

"Can't either." What kind of sick bastards would do this to anyone?

"A witness saw four men running from the area that night. She didn't get a good look at them, but she said one wore a hoodie with some kind of emblem on it. I thought if you'd gotten a look at the emblem, could identify it, it could help us track him down."

"No," Audra whispered, dejected. She couldn't recall a damn thing. The cowards had blind-sided her, and once the beating started, everything became a blur. Her voice shook with fear and frustration. "They attacked so fast. So viciously, out of nowhere. It was dark…"

"I know. It's okay." He awkwardly patted her shoulder. "If you think of anything else to tell us, anything that might give us a lead, you be sure to give me a call." He smiled, his brown eyes kind, concerned. "Or, you can give me a call if you just want to talk, okay?"

"Okay. Thank you."

Shane left, and she was once more alone. For the first few days, Riley had been at the hospital most of the time, but she had a job and a child. She couldn't stay twenty-four/seven. Selfishly, Audra wished she could. When Riley—or anyone for that matter—was with her, she didn't feel so alone…so scared.

"Damn you," she muttered to her unidentified assailants. She'd gone from being an independent, take-charge woman to a sniveling wreck.

She comforted herself with the possibility that she'd get over her fear and things would go back to normal once she was home, then finally able to go back to work. Surely, that would be the case. It had to be. She refused to live like this, waiting for danger and pain and death to strike.

Of course, there was always a chance the bastards would make good on their threat and finish the job. That would certainly put an end to the paranoia and the whole 'living in fear' thing. Put an end to it for good.

Shaking off the morose thought, she reached into the nightstand drawer for a *People* magazine. Maybe the problems of the rich and famous would take her mind off her own.

****

Later that night, Wilton Starkley, one of the aides, came into her room.

"How are you?" Wilton was a chunky, nerdy guy whose reddish brown hair always looked as though it needed a comb.

"About as good as can be expected," Audra said.

He handed her a plastic cup that held antibiotics. His face colored. "I was supposed to bring these a few hours ago. You won't tell Nurse Ratched, will you?"

She grinned at the nickname he'd given Mary Lou, the charge nurse. She berated him non-stop, looking for reasons to discipline him. Then again, Wilton was kind of a screw up, so it wasn't difficult to find a reason.

"I won't. I promise." She swallowed the pills, grimacing as a twinge shot through her ribs. She hadn't had pain meds in hours. If she was going home tomorrow, she needed to toughen up and ride out the discomfort.

After Wilton left, Audra turned off the light above her head and slid under the sheets, shifting until she was as comfortable as she could get in the hospital-issue bed. One thing about it, after this, she would likely become a better nurse. Or, at the very least, one who was more attuned to what her patients had to deal with.

Later, somewhere amidst a deep, restful sleep, the pain came back with a vengeance. Agony stabbed through her ribs, moving like a rocket through her fractured wrist and into her shoulder. Eyes still closed, she moaned loud enough to wake the entire floor. Tears squeezed beneath her lids as she grimaced, waiting for the pain to ease enough that she could hit the call button and request a big dose of morphine.

She felt the merest flutter of a touch at her hairline. A voice said, "Shhh…it's going to be okay."

Her heart thudded, and her eyes flew open. One of her hallucinations—the blond—sat next to her bed, gently stroking the bangs off her damp forehead.

She gasped. "What the…?"

"I can make it go away." His voice was mesmerizing, hypnotic. His golden eyes, the exact same shade as his hair, gleamed in the semi-darkness. His teeth were perfectly white and straight, his skin as smooth and flawless as ivory. "I can take away all your pain."

*Take away my pain?* Oh, yes—

"No!" A harsh voice rang out, and Audra jerked her gaze to the foot of the bed. The dark specter was there, too. He scowled, his arms folded over his chest. He still wore the leather jacket from when she'd seen him in the alley. "She has to work through the pain. That is how it must be."

*Asshole.* If she were going to hallucinate, why couldn't she hallucinate *two* nice guys instead of only one?

She focused her attention on her angel of mercy. Dimly, she realized that while she could see him stroking her forehead, she couldn't really *feel* his fingers…only the odd sensation of a near touch.

"How?" she whispered. "How can you make it go away?"

A beatific smile lit his face. "She can see us," he called over his shoulder, keeping his gaze on Audra.

"No. That can't be," the dark one said.

"You can see us, right?" Angel's golden eyes looked hopefully into hers.

"Of course I can." She smiled. Something about the wonder of this mirage seemed to take the edge off her pain. "You're beautiful." She turned a scowl on the other figment of her imagination. "You're hateful."

The blond threw his head back and laughed, a sound both melodic and haunting at the same time. "I believe she prefers me over you." He glanced toward his companion. "And you were wrong. She *can* see us."

The realization seemed to delight him as much as it infuriated the other. The dark one strode to her bedside, his blue eyes glittering dangerously, his jaw set as he glared down at her. A tremor trickled through her body.

Why was he so angry with her? What had she done? They were the ones invading her room…her dreams.

She turned to Angel, ignoring the other. "How can you make it go away?"

He smiled and opened his mouth to answer, but the mean one cut him off.

"He can't. Don't believe his lies."

"Now, now," Angel said. "Testy, aren't we? At least let her hear me out."

The dark one cast a baleful look at the blond, then turned back to Audra "You never saw us. We were never here. Call for someone to bring you the chemicals that will ease your pain and forget all about this."

"You think that's going to work?" Angel sounded amused. "What's done is done."

The leather-clad apparition shook his head, a hank of dark hair falling over his forehead. "No. She's out of her mind with pain. They've been pumping drugs into her for nearly a week. She'll never remember this. Never believe it happened if she does."

Now she was coming more fully awake, and the pain was increasing, as was the fear. This kind of fear had nothing to do with dying a horrible and painful death. Now, she was afraid for her sanity.

"Go away," she rasped. "Just go away and leave me alone."

Angel lifted his brows. "A moment ago, you were—"

"No!" She screwed her eyes shut, blocking out his perfect features, his tempting, sympathetic tone, his promise of nirvana. With it, she knew, surely came madness.

"I told you," he murmured softly. "I can give you peace. Please. Just look at me, my sweet."

"Leave it alone." Without opening her eyes, she knew the dark one spoke again. She recognized his harsh, raspy voice, such a contrast to the soothing tones of the blond.

She fumbled blindly for the nurse call button. When it landed in her hand, she opened her eyes to find the dark one leaning over her. His fingers brushed hers in that same, strange almost touch before he released the hard plastic into her grip.

For a brief moment, their eyes locked, and the blue flames of his stole her breath. How long the moment lasted, she couldn't be sure, but suddenly he straightened, backing away, and it was over. She suffered a twinge of inexplicable disappointment.

She pressed the call button for the nurse. Almost as if the device were some kind of cosmic eraser, the phantoms vanished.

"Can I help you?" Kyle, the ward clerk, said through the speaker.

"Can I get something for the pain?" Audra gasped.

"I'll send your nurse in."

As Audra waited for the dose of narcotic candy, she wavered between believing the men were real one second, to being certain she was losing her mind the next. She wasn't sure which scenario was more frightening. Regardless of which proved to be true, she realized she'd missed a golden opportunity to quiz them.

*Who are you? What are you? Why were you in the alley? Why the hell am I seeing you?*

Of course, if their existence was all in her head, they couldn't answer with anything more than she already knew, so the interrogation would have been futile.

Victoria, a cheerful petite brunette nurse, bustled into the room, carrying a small plastic cup. Audra swallowed the pills, then lay back, letting the questions slip from her mind as she waited for the morphine to take effect. Before long, bliss flooded her system.

*Ah, sweet, blessed relief.*

As the pain meds lulled her back into sleep, one last thought flitted through her mind. *Real or not, please don't ever let me see them again.*\

## Chapter 3

*Six weeks later*

Audra brought a hand to her eyes to shade them from the sun as she searched the sea of grade-schoolers until her gaze landed on a bobbing silver-blonde head. She smiled. From a distance, Sadie's pageboy haircut made it look as if she wore a silver cap.

Today was Audra's last day of sick leave before going back to work. Riley, a lawyer, had court, so Audra offered to pick Sadie up and hang out with her until her parents got home. There wasn't much she'd rather do on her last day of freedom.

The child's face lit with delight when she saw Audra. Her slow, plodding gait became a full on sprint.

"Audra! Hey Audra!" she shouted, waving her hands to get Audra's attention, even though they'd already made eye contact, so she had to know Audra had seen her.

When Sadie drew near, Audra squatted and took her weight full into her body for a tight hug.

"Hey, kiddo." Audra stood and ruffled her hair, taking the stack of skewered papers from her hand. Unzipping the nearly empty denim backpack, she placed the papers inside. "How was school?"

Her small shoulders lifted. "It was okay."

"Just okay? What did you—" Audra paused when

she saw what Sadie wore beneath her coat. “Why are you wearing your shirt wrong side out?”

“They made me.”

A slow burn started at the thought of kids picking on her, playing cruel tricks. “Who made you?”

“The princ-ta-pal.”

“Why would the principal make you turn your shirt wrong side out?”

“So I wouldn’t have to go home and change.”

Audra took a deep breath. The kid was a nonstop chatterbox, but sometimes getting to the pertinent information was a slow and winding process. “Why would you have to go home and change?”

“’Cause she said my Chucky shirt isn’t ’propriate for school.”

Audra halted. “Wait. Your Chucky the killer doll shirt?” She laughed. “Hmmm. I wonder why she didn’t think it was appropriate.”

“’Cause it scared some of the kids.”

“Oh, I see.” Audra nodded as if her comment hadn’t been facetious.

“They’re a bunch of babies.”

“I can’t believe your mom let you wear that to school.”

“She didn’t know. She left early, and my dad took me.”

That explained a lot. Brent was a good man, a good dad, but not the most attentive parent in the world. Sadie was a little twisted when it came to her likes and dislikes, which weren’t the usual five-year-old fare. Her parents allowed her to watch scary movies, and Sadie loved them. They didn’t keep her up nights, didn’t make her have bad dreams, and she was one of the happiest, smartest, most well-adjusted kids Audra had ever seen. Perhaps they weren't damaging her psyche too much.

Audra took Sadie's hand and led her out of the schoolyard, keeping her stride short to match Sadie's. With the limp she'd acquired from the beating, it helped to pace herself anyway.

Leaves crunched beneath their feet, and a brisk fall breeze blew as they made their way along the sidewalks leading toward downtown Boon Springs. Halloween was just over two weeks away and nearly every house they passed displayed an assortment of decorations—pumpkins, scarecrows, and various other creatures of the season.

"Hey, want to go to Sally's Sundries?" Audra asked.

Sadie lifted her face, squinting up at Audra. "Yes! Can we really?" She bounced up and down. "Please, can we?"

"You betcha."

The bouncing turned to skipping, and Sadie tugged Audra along behind her.

Sally's Sundries was a combo ice cream parlor, coffee house, and gift shop that was only a ten-minute walk from the school. The original owner, Sally Wright, had died forty years earlier. She'd been found hanging by a rope in her attic. Her hands were tied behind her back, so suicide had been ruled out. Later, her husband—seemingly a normal, loving man—confessed. He was tried, convicted, and put to death.

Some blamed the town's tragic history for Calvin Wright's murderous act. Twenty years before Oklahoma became a state, a group of settlers had stopped to make camp. A band of outlaws attacked, murdering them all. Boon Springs was built on the site and superstitions had it that, due to the horrific beginnings, the town would be seeped in tragedy forever. Judging from some of the incidents that had happened over the years, Audra wasn't sure it was too far-fetched.

Sadie kept up a steady stream of chatter during the walk to the shop. She didn't slow down when they arrived, other than to exclaim, "Can I get mine in a cone?" as Audra opened the door, inhaling the fragrance of potpourri, candles, and espresso.

At the counter, Audra ordered chocolate Swiss while Sadie chose rainbow sherbet. Once they had their ice cream, they slid into a blue plastic-upholstered booth.

Audra glanced around, unable to shake the lingering fear that she was still in danger, even though nothing had happened since the night of the beating. There had been no more threats, no more mangled gifts. The best the police could conclude, the men—teenagers, boys, whatever they'd been—had chosen her randomly, decided to have some evil fun and stretch it out a bit with the Teddy Bear, and had then gotten bored and moved on.

The concern in Shane's eyes when Audra last spoke with him indicated he wasn't entirely convinced, but with no leads, no clues, there wasn't much more he could tell her. He promised they'd keep working on it but didn't seem optimistic they'd solve it. Neither was Audra. So, she'd made a determined effort to put the attack behind her, even though the scar running along her jaw line was a daily reminder.

"Look at you, you're a mess." Audra smiled, using a napkin to wipe the colorful liquid streams dribbling down Sadie's chin.

"Mom and Dad never let me get cones," she complained. "They make me get a cup with a lid."

"That's because you're usually driving home after, and they know you'll get ice cream all over the car."

"Yeah. We hardly ever get to stay here and eat. Or walk home like I do with you."

"I live closer than your parents."

"I like your house. It looks like Hansel and Gretel's. It's a lot better than ours."

"*Your* house is a mansion." Audra laughed. Riley earned a healthy salary as an attorney, and Brent was an executive for a computer software company. Two houses the size of Audra's small bungalow would fit into theirs. "You're a very lucky little girl, you know. You have great parents and a beautiful house and lots of people who love you."

Sadie frowned at her cone and darted her multi-hued tongue out to take a lick. She seemed to be considering whether to lament further about her parents or accept that they weren't such bad people after all.

After taking another couple of swipes at the sherbet, she said, "So, how come you don't have a little girl of your own?"

"Well…" Audra swallowed as she searched for an answer. Sadie's question took her by surprise and made her heart ache just a little. In a too-cheerful tone, she said, "Because I have you. I don't need my own."

Sadie smiled, showing a space between her teeth where a sliver of white enamel was just starting to poke through the gum. "So, you're my second mom?"

"Something like that. If I had a little girl, I'd want her to be just like you." *Minus the penchant for serial killers,* she added silently.

"Momma said you don't have a kid because you need a daddy first and you don't have one. You had one but y'all got 'vorced."

Audra pushed her cup of ice cream aside, the last bite she'd taken sitting like a lump at the base of her throat. "Yes. You can have kids without daddies, but it's much easier if you have one."

"Why did you 'vorce Jaxon?"

Jesus. How had the conversation turned from ice cream and real estate to the complexities of marital relations?

"We had some differences."

Actually, they had more similarities than differences. They both liked men.

Sadie zipped straight into another topic—her upcoming dance recital and the sparkly red-and-black costume she would wear. Audra let her prattle, relieved that her personal life was no longer the focus of the discussion.

Listening with half her attention, she glanced around the room. She'd gotten in the habit of being ultra aware of her surroundings. A small part of her—and sometimes a not-so-small part—still expected another assault. She'd also become diligent in watching for reporters. For the first few weeks after the attack, she'd been bombarded by media hounds. Granted, the media in Boon Springs was comprised of two wannabe journalists, but still, hounding was hounding.

Audra sucked in a breath when she glimpsed a familiar figure. "Stay right here, Sadie."

"Huh? You're leaving me?"

"I'll be close. Just wait here."

Audra made her way toward a row of shelves that held jars of apple butter, jams, and every kind of food that could possibly be pickled.

"Maria?"

The woman turned, her eyes rounding, then darting from side to side as if searching for an escape route. Audra hadn't spoken to her since the attack, but it wasn't from lack of trying. She'd attempted to get in touch with her several times, but it was obvious Maria was avoiding her. With Scott in jail at the time of the attack, and Maria's assertion she knew nothing about the incident, there was little need for the police to pursue the interrogation. Audra, however, wanted some answers. She wanted to make sure Maria was okay and find out why she'd changed her mind about leaving Scott.

"Hello, Audra." Maria's voice quivered, and she wouldn't meet Audra's eyes. She was delicate-boned, with dark hair and haunted brown eyes. Two of her three children were with her. They both had Maria's dark coloring. The oldest had her fragile frame, while the younger child was tall and stocky like their father.

Audra smiled at the girls. "Brooke, Stacy, how are you?"

"Fine," they said in unison.

Audra turned her attention back to their mother. "Is everything okay? I haven't heard from you since that night we were supposed to meet." Her gaze darted to the children. "Did…anyone…do anything to make you…uh…change your mind?"

"I realized I was making a mistake." Maria

replaced the candle she held with shaking hands. "Scott is a good man. He's out of jail now, and he's trying really hard."

The bastard had threatened her, no doubt about it. Audra searched her face for bruises but saw none. Perhaps he'd delivered blows in places that were hidden by her clothing. In the past, he hadn't cared to hide the abuse, but maybe he'd guessed Maria came to Audra and decided he should be more cautious. Or, and she fervently hoped this was true, maybe his stint in jail had frightened him, and he wouldn't beat her anymore.

*Yeah, right.* He was about as harmless as a rabid pit bull.

Audra brushed back an errant strand of hair and moved so she could keep an eye on the table where Sadie munched on her cone. She said to Maria, "So, you're okay? You sure?"

"Scott's my husband. He loves me."

*Yeah, and love hurts like a son of a bitch.* "I hope he's really changed." Audra glanced at the girls once more. "You know, someone could end up getting badly hurt."

Maria's face colored and, as if remembering Audra's injuries for the first time, she said, "Are you okay? I heard what happened. I was going to come see you but…"

Audra waited, but Maria didn't come up with a reason why she hadn't visited.

"I'm fine," Audra said after an awkward silence. "Much better. I'll be back at work tomorrow."

"That's good. Scott was in jail, you know," Maria said almost defiantly.

"Yes, I know." In Audra's peripheral vision, she

saw Sadie climb from her seat, tugging her book bag off the back of the chair "I have to go. Take care of yourself. Call me if you need anything."

"I will," Maria promised.

Audra headed back to Sadie, her mind going over the conversation with Maria. Why had she felt the need to mention Scott's whereabouts on the night of the attack? And why had she seemed so wary, so defensive?

****

Dimitri leaned against a porch column at the house across the street from Audra's. The front door opened, and she appeared. His throat closed. A trickle of warmth moved through the cold recesses of his insides. The glow from the porch light crawled over her olive skin, giving it a golden hue. Her thick mane of dark hair lifted in the breeze. She rounded the side of the house and took hold of the trash dumpster, dragging it to the curb. Even such a menial, normally unprovocative task, was a pleasure to watch when it was performed by Audra.

Her limp was more evident when no one was around. She'd become adept at hiding her imperfections, her weaknesses. The gesture tugged at him, evoking an emotion he didn't want to experience.

He shook his head. What was wrong with him? No use asking, really. There was no answer. He'd questioned himself multiple times about the unnatural fascination this woman held for him…had held for nearly thirty years, since the night her mother died. Back then, his interest had been admiration at such intelligence and bravery in one so young. As she'd grown into womanhood, his feelings had become something different. Something as uncomfortable as it was futile.

*Reapers have no business mingling in the human world. Stay away, serve your sentence, get through the remaining fifty years so you'll finally have peace.* He damn sure never had peace in life. But then, that was his own doing.

Pushing away from the post, he meandered closer. Audra knelt in the flowerbed beneath the front window, pulling weeds from the ground. As he reached the curb across the street, she froze, lifting her head.

He halted, dread settling in his gut. Had she sensed him? Surely she hadn't really seen them in her room that night? Couldn't still see them? If so, that would be disastrous.

He was debating whether to test the theory by approaching her when he felt a familiar pulling at his mind. The sensation seeped downward to his chest, growing until it was almost painful.

Damn.

He was being summoned. Someone was in jeopardy. He wouldn't know if they were to be taken until it was over, but he had to go. Had to be there in case Gaylen got any ideas about making an appearance. He backed away, keeping Audra in his sight for as long as possible.

He let the sensation lead him to a small motel room. Not exactly a five-star one from the looks of it.

The room held two occupants. The girl was young, maybe in her late teens, although admittedly it was becoming more and more difficult for him to guess ages. After being dead for over two hundred years, that was to be expected.

A man crouched over the girl. Dimitri could only see the back of him, but he appeared to be older than she. His hair showed hints of gray, and his damp T-shirt was molded to rolls of fat. The bottom of a tattoo was visible beneath the sleeve of his shirt. Was that a dragon? A dinosaur? Dimitri squinted. Maybe Godzilla. It was definitely some kind of monster. Fitting.

The man cut the strap of the girl's pink, lacey bra. She screamed, and he clamped his hand over her mouth. Mascara-smeared eyes wide with terror, she fought against his grip, but she was no match for the man's strength, or for his frenzied excitement.

The girl's pale, pink-streaked hair clung damply to her cheeks as she wept. Skimpy clothing lay discarded on the floor. A prostitute, perhaps? Or maybe just a foolish runaway who had no idea what kind of danger she'd gotten herself into when she took to the streets. She certainly had an idea now.

No light filtered in through the curtained windows. The room was nearly dark, save for the glow of the muted TV. The screen flickered with images of people at a party, drinking, laughing, while on the bed in the room that reeked of sweat, old food, and fear, the girl struggled for her life.

Dimitri positioned himself at the side of the bed. He could now see the man's face. A goatee sprouted from his chin. The skin on his forehead was slick with perspiration. Older, just as Dimitri had guessed, but how much older he couldn't be certain.

The pink scrap of material now lay in tatters next to the terrified girl. Still holding the knife with one hand, the man squeezed her bare, exposed breast with the other. His fat jiggled as he pounded into the girl, his grunts of pleasure nearly drowning out her pain-filled cries.

After a few moments, he collapsed on top of her, his hand sliding away from her mouth.

"Let me go, please," she whimpered. "I won't tell anyone, I promise."

The man roused and stared down at her, blinking rapidly as if unsure who she was or what had just happened. "Sorry. Can't do that."

"But, you don't have to hurt me. I don't know your name, don't know who you are. I can't tell them—"

"Shhh," he interrupted, his whispered voice gratingly loud in the small room. "Really. You have to stop babbling."

"Okay. Anything you say." Her round gaze now reflected a glimmer of hope.

The man's brows drew together, and he studied her for a moment. Then, as casually as he might have changed the channel with the remote lying nearby, he lifted the knife and slid it across her neck.

Her eyes widened further, and her hands flew to her throat. She made a gurgling noise, blood pumping from the gaping wound in her neck.

The man wiped the knife on the sheets, then slid off of her. He stood, retrieving his pants from the floor and tugging them on. After zipping up, he slipped on a pair of gloves, then went around the room, wiping surfaces and searching for items he might have left behind.

Dimitri turned his attention back to the bed. A nearly transparent twin of the dead girl rose slowly from her lifeless body. The spirit whipped its head from side to side, the features showing almost as much fear as they had in life.

Dimitri stepped forward and held out his hand. “Come.”

Tears brimmed in her eyes, and she looked down at the figure on the bed, then at him. She shook her head vigorously, not acknowledging the only living creature in the room—her killer—who now stood at the door with his gloved hand on the knob. He cast one last, triumphant, lascivious look at his victim and cracked the door open, sliding out and letting it fall shut behind him.

“It’s okay.” Dimitri kept his voice low, soothing. “You’ll be okay. Just come with me.”

Her head shook even more vigorously, and she backed away, stumbling over her own body, falling off the bed and onto the floor in a heap. She sprung to her feet and looked around wildly, making no sound, although Dimitri could hear the keening of her soul as she wailed in despair and terror.

He moved closer and took one of her hands in his. He put his other on her cheek and turned her face up until she was looking into his eyes.

“I promise you,” he said softly. “Everything will be okay. Just come with me, please. There’s nothing here for you now.”

He didn’t know if it was the realization he was right, or the comfort of his touch, but she nodded, then looked once more at her former self and let him lead her away.

They moved through the walls out into the evening air. Dimitri could feel the coolness of the night breeze. He’d been in this state long enough that he’d started to experience a few of the sensations he had when he’d been human. The girl, however, no longer felt anything.

They walked for a few moments before Dimitri halted. He nudged her gently on the back. She looked over her shoulder and offered him one last, shy smile before moving away, her footsteps silent as she became dimmer and dimmer until she disappeared altogether.

****

Jaxon slapped the chart on the desk and rested his elbows next to it as he leaned toward Audra. Altering his normal tone of voice, he said, “This is the worst fake I.D. I've ever seen. You realize you made yourself sixty-eight.”

His mouth spread from one corner of his face to the other as he waited for her answer. It was a game they’d played since childhood. Growing up, they’d been obsessed with movies and had taken to challenging one another in the movie quote game. Every wrong answer cost the guesser ten bucks. By Audra’s calculation, she owed Jaxon roughly a million dollars, give or take a few hundred. She loved movies as much as he did, but he retained more details than she.

“What’s with the big, goofy smile?” she asked.

“Just guess the movie. Are you trying to get out of owing me another ten bucks? You don’t know, do you?”

“As a matter of fact I do. Just curious why you’re grinning like a big dufus.”

He reached out and chugged her chin with his bent forefinger. “Because. I’m really glad you’re back.”

“Yeah?” She returned the smile. “Me, too.”

“Now, what movie is it from? Need me to repeat the quote?”

“Doctor Maroney. Good morning.” A strident

voice interrupted them, and Audra turned to the source. Her co-worker, Tonya, had joined them and stood, staring at Jaxon like he was the last chocolate in a box of empty wrappers.

Jaxon shot Audra a look and, while he didn't roll his eyes, his expression said he wanted to. "Hello, Tonya."

Tonya was short and rotund. Her hair was a riotous mop that had been every shade of red in the universe during the six years Audra had known her, including a short period where an inept hairdresser had created an unfortunate blend of yellow and mauve.

In spite of Tonya's lack of physical appeal, she was popular with the male species and had bedded at least half of the men who worked at the hospital. She'd been gunning for Jaxon hard, not knowing she waged a fruitless battle. He followed the 'don't ask, don't tell' policy. He thought his reputation and trust might be compromised if people knew he was gay, so he kept it on the down low.

Audra could have saved Tonya some time and trouble, and saved Jaxon some stress and frustration, but she'd made a promise to Jaxon years ago that she wouldn't reveal his secret. Besides, it was a lot more fun to watch him squirm.

"So, Doctor Maroney," Tonya said, her voice lilting hopefully. "Are you going to the hospital Halloween party with anyone?"

The party was a few days before Halloween. There was no way they could have it on the actual night. Nearly everyone on staff would be working. Halloween was one of the busiest nights of the year.

Jaxon turned his petrified gaze to Audra. "Well,

I...actually..."

Smiling mischievously, Audra said, "I need to go check on Ms. Chapman. I'll leave you two alone to chat."

Ignoring the pleading in Jaxon's expression, she gave a little wave and headed around the desk. She didn't feel the least bit guilty. Served him right for being so smug about the huge lead he had on her in the movie quote game.

Which reminded her...

She paused and glanced over her shoulder to see Tonya was now the one leaning on the desk, and Jaxon was bent backward in an effort to distance himself from her.

"Hey, Doctor Maroney," Audra called.

"Yeah?" he asked, his voice sounding almost as hopeful as Tonya's had.

Audra shoved her hands in the pockets of her cranberry-colored scrubs and gave him a smile. "*The Breakfast Club*."

His face fell, and she chortled, heading down the hall to Ms. Chapman's room.

Although morning, the sun had yet to rise. The room was coated in darkness, save for the lights from the machines pumping next to the bed, aiding the frail woman who clung to life.

Ms. Chapman lay still, eyes closed, chest rising and falling almost imperceptibly. Audra checked the readings on the monitor, then turned back to the woman.

"How you doing, sweetie? You about ready to get out of here?" She smoothed a wisp of gray hair off the elderly woman's forehead. "I bet those men down at

Sunnyview are lonely without their best gal."

Audra let out a sigh. It was unlikely Ms. Chapman would be going back to Sunnyview Retirement Center. Poor thing. Her heart was weak. She'd had a triple bypass a few days ago and was here for post op care. Her condition was worsening. At her age, it was difficult to recover from major surgery.

Sensing movement behind her, Audra whirled. In the shadowed corner of the room, she could make out the figure of a man, although she couldn't distinguish his features.

Visiting hours weren't until ten a.m. And even then, only family members were allowed in this wing of the ICU. Audra had met each of Ms. Chapman's relatives, and this man wasn't one of them. She could tell by his body type and height. The only male in Ms. Chapman's immediate family was her son, and he was short and stocky.

"I'm sorry," she said, her voice hushed. "You can't be in here."

He looked behind him, then back at her. "You can see me?"

She frowned in puzzlement. "Of course."

"You saw me that night. Both those nights."

Her frown deepened. "What nights?"

He moved from the gloom, drawing closer. Her instinct was to back away, but she forced herself to remain in place.

As he left the shadows behind, his features emerged, and part of her brain recognized him, but she wouldn't let the terrifying thought solidify.

He wore faded jeans and a form-fitting black T-shirt. His pectoral muscles and biceps would rival a male model's. They were tight and well-defined, not overly bulky like those of steroid-enhanced body builders.

Reluctantly, her mind acknowledged she'd seen him before. He'd been part of her hallucinations. Her worst nightmares were becoming a reality.

Somehow not as frightened as she should have been, she stared into his icicle blue eyes as he continued to move slowly toward her. She waited, holding her breath in expectation.

Why did she feel this tingly sense of excitement? This glimmer of anxiousness mixed with fear? Why did she feel like she might explode with anticipation?

He halted a couple of steps in front of her and lifted his hand, brushing it along the scar on her cheekbone, causing a shudder in the pit of her stomach. A current moved in the air, like a burst of electricity.

"The first time was the night you got this." His words were a whisper along her skin, as was his touch…almost as if his caress was the hint of a sensation, but not actual contact. Her eyes drifted shut, and she swayed toward him. Her nipples tightened. She swallowed back a moan as heat seared between her thighs. She wasn't even dismayed at her sexual response to his nearness. It felt so right…so deliciously right. One slight move forward, and she could touch him, press her aching breasts against his chest. Biting her lower lip, she just barely held back from giving in to the urge.

Softly, she murmured, "That night—I—you…" The only words she could form were incoherent drivel. Her heart pounded, her belly clenching with the strangest feeling she'd ever had. She lifted her lashes, staring up at him, wanting to lose herself in his glittering blue gaze. Wanting to feel his hands on her body…his full, sensual lips on hers. Wanting to be swept away in whatever madness this was. It felt so strange, yet at the same time, exhilarating, compelling, irresistible…*dangerous.*

*Yes, dangerous.* Gulping in a breath, she stepped back. His touch fell away, breaking the strange hold he had on her.

"You! It was you there that night. In the alley…" Her breath came in short gasps as the odd yearning was replaced by fear. "Then again, at the hospital." She shot her gaze around the room. "Where's the other one? The blond guy? Who the hell are you?"

Her voice had risen, and she glanced at Ms. Chapman. Audra had almost forgotten she was there, but of course, the woman hadn't heard a thing. She had remained oblivious to the world around her since the surgery.

Audra turned back to the man…her hallucination. Now so real she could almost feel his touch.

*I've suffered brain trauma. Dear God. There's something seriously wrong with me.*

He gazed at her, his expression a mixture of concern and unhappiness. "I hoped this wouldn't happen. I didn't want you to—"

The heart monitor's slow, steady beep turned into one, long monotone. Ms. Chapman had flat-lined.

Whirling from the stranger, Audra pressed the emergency call button and grabbed the bed board from beneath the bed. As she was sliding it under the patient, the code team—Jaxon in the lead—burst into the room with the crash cart. Audra took position at the patient's head and placed the Ambu Bag over Ms. Chapman's nose and mouth. She began squeezing in five second intervals to help the woman breathe, while each of the other team members assumed their roles.

Heart racing, knowing it was unlikely she could save her, Audra continued her attempts to resuscitate. Jaxon and the others moved with efficiency and speed born of practice as they administered aid to the rapidly fading Ms. Chapman.

From her peripheral vision, Audra was aware the apparition was still in the room. He reached his hand out toward the elderly woman in the bed. Audra shivered.

*Ignore him, concentrate on Ms. Chapman. He's not there...he's not real.*

## Chapter 4

That evening, Audra filled a tub with hot water and tossed in some bath beads she'd received for Christmas a few years back. They'd been part of a relaxation gift pack that included a bath pillow and a CD with the sounds of the ocean and a rainforest.

Of course, all the bath beads and relaxation pillows in the world wouldn't bring Ms. Chapman back. Nothing would.

Audra let out a heavy sigh. She'd never become accustomed to losing a patient. Never. Over time, the pain and feeling of hopelessness lessened, but it was always difficult…heart wrenching. Mary Lou had been sympathetic as Audra turned in her incident report, but all the sympathy in the world didn't ease Audra's feeling she should have done more.

Sure, she knew all the platitudes. *Ms. Chapman was old, she'd been ill for a while, she is in a better place, blah, blah, blah.* Truth was, she was gone. Hard as she and Jaxon and the others had tried, Ms. Chapman was as dead as if they hadn't done a thing.

Shaking her head to rid her mind of the dismal thoughts, she stripped and slid into the hot, scented water. In a matter of moments, the gentle sound of rain and the soothing scent of vanilla enveloped her.

She rested her head on the bath pillow and closed her eyes, trying not to see Ms. Chapman's sweet face, or hear the drone of the heart monitor as it mocked their efforts to save her. It just wasn't fair. Not fair at all. Death was so sudden, so final. One second you were there, the next you just…weren't.

She took a long, deep breath, trying to visualize a tropical rainforest. Green thick, leafy trees…a drizzle of moisture falling gently…monkeys chattering…

The muted sound of the doorbell cut through her solitude, and she startled awake. She had no idea how long she'd been dozing, but now the water was tepid. Standing, she reached for a bath towel, shivering when the cool air licked her skin.

As she limped down the hallway, she attempted to dry her body, slip on a robe, and make her way to the door all at the same time. She was only marginally successful with the drying.

Through the peephole, she saw Riley standing on her porch.

When she swung the door open, Riley lifted a bottle of Chablis toward her like a presenter at an awards ceremony. "I brought wine."

Audra smiled, stepping back to allow Riley inside. "I can see that."

As Riley brushed past, her gaze took in Audra's attire. "Already in your robe? It appears I'm just in time. You're not allowed to be pathetic tonight. Grab some glasses."

Riley wore black sweatpants and a Packers sweatshirt, and had her hair pulled back in a ponytail, which, in Audra's estimation, only put her a few rungs ahead of Audra on the wardrobe ladder.

Audra forced a small smile. "You know, you don't have to bring alcohol every time I lose a patient. I'm sure you had better things to do tonight."

"Trust me, I wanted to come over. Sadie's with Mom, and I had nothing to do."

"Where's Brent?"

She grinned. "At home. And that's the third good reason for me to be here."

Audra laughed. "Have a seat," she said, taking the bottle. "I'll get the glasses."

While Riley settled in the living room, Audra searched the kitchen for the corkscrew. Following a brief struggle to remove the cork, she filled two glasses and joined Riley, bringing the bottle with her.

"Thanks," Riley said when Audra handed her a glass, then settled cross-legged on the sofa.

Audra set the bottle on the coffee table and sat next to Riley. She clicked the remote and turned the television onto the Elvis Presley music station. "Long Black Limousine" was playing. Sadness filled her heart as Elvis sang the haunting lyrics of a hearse carrying his lost love. Just the kind of song she needed to hear, the mood she was in.

Riley took a sip from her glass, then tilted it toward Audra. "We'll call this a combination mourning and celebration. I settled a case today, and my client got almost everything we asked for."

Audra scowled. "Somehow, celebrating divorce just doesn't seem right."

"I don't *celebrate* divorce, but if there is a divorce, I celebrate my client not getting screwed over. Better?"

Audra thought about it for a moment and shrugged. "Sure. Works for me. Here's to success." She lifted her glass, and they toasted.

"You okay?" Riley studied Audra with narrowed

eyes.

Audra shrugged. “You know how it is. You never really get used to losing a patient, failing to save someone’s life.”

“No. I don’t know how it is. I can’t imagine having a job where I knew, every day, there was a chance I’d watch someone die.” Her voice lost its former joviality, and Audra knew she was thinking about Steve.

Riley and Brent had separated a few years back. Riley met Steve and fell in love, but, for the sake of her daughter, she went back to Brent. A little over a year ago, Steve was killed in a boating accident.

Riley never showed the impact his death had on her, but sometimes Audra would see her stare off, her face clenching, her eyes clouding with grief, and she’d know Riley was thinking about him.

Audra had always wanted to ask her if she regretted staying with Brent, but that probably would have been a stupid question. Had Riley married Steve, she’d be a divorcee, and now a widow. But then again, maybe if they’d gotten married, Steve wouldn’t have died. Who knows what would have happened if Riley had left Brent for Steve. Funny how one change could set someone’s life on a totally different course.

“It’s not easy. Thank God it doesn’t happen every day.” Audra refilled her wine glass, then Riley’s.

“Anything new with the case? Any lead on your attackers?”

Audra shook her head. “Nothing. Doubtful there ever will be. I’ve put it behind me.”

Riley grimaced. “Whoever did this is still out there. Don’t you think you should be more cautious? Stop walking everywhere you go? You have a car, you know."

Guilt stabbed her. "I told you I was sorry about walking home with Sadie. It won't happen again."

"It's not just Sadie I'm worried about. Those guys could come back and hurt you again."

"I figure if they were going to come after me, they would have already."

"I hope you're right." Riley gestured to Audra's empty glass. "Pass that over here." Audra complied, and Riley split the last of the wine between the two of them, then set the empty bottle on the coffee table. "If it were me, I'd still be a little creeped out."

Audra thought of the two apparitions who'd haunted her since the night of the attack. *You want creeped out, I've got something that can top those amateur thugs.*

She hadn't told anyone, but if there were anyone she could tell, it was Riley. Suddenly, she felt the need to unburden herself.

"Listen," she said. It came out sounding a little like 'lishen.' The Chablis was working its magic. "If I tell you something, will you promise you won't think I'm crazy?"

"Well, I always think you're crazy." Riley's eyes twinkled with mirth. "But go ahead, try me."

Audra set her glass down on the table. She tried to work out the words in her head before she spoke them, knowing no matter how they came out, she'd sound like a lunatic.

Twisting her hair around her forefinger, she said, "Actually, that's part of the problem. I think I might be a little crazy." A frisson of trepidation moved through her. She picked up her glass and took another sip before continuing. "I…uh… Well, since the attack, I've been…seeing things."

"Things? Like what kind of things?"

"This is going to sound bizarre, but I've seen these two men. Several times. The first time was right after the attack, before the ambulance came." She described what they looked like, and about seeing them again in the hospital.

"Seriously? You keep dreaming these same men over and over? That's a little freaky." Riley took a drink of her wine.

"It's not a dream. I've been awake. Or, at least for the most part. Today, I saw one of them when Ms. Chapman…" The lulling effects of the wine fled, and she shuddered, remembering how real he'd seemed, how *there*. How she almost felt his touch. Or maybe she had felt it. "I'm not sure if I suffered some kind of brain injury or what. I don't know whether I should consult a neurologist or a psychiatrist. What do you think I should do?"

"Wow, you're really serious."

"Yeah. I am."

Uncurling her legs from beneath her, Riley scooted to the edge of the sofa. "Well, I'm not a medical professional, so it seems you'd be in a better position to decide what you should do. Now, if you end up marrying one of these hallucinations, and you need a divorce, I'm your gal."

Audra flashed back to the intensity in the dark one's blue eyes, the sizzle of air when he'd touched her skin. The sensual pull as her nerve endings crackled with the yearning to feel his hands on her bare flesh. Her face burned, and she tried to hide it by lifting her glass and gulping wine.

Riley's brows rose. "Oh, my God. You're blushing. You have a thing for one of these guys or what?"

"For God's sake, of course not. It's just all so insane." Audra gazed solemnly at Riley. "Am I crazy?"

The humor left Riley's expression. She patted Audra's knee. "No. Of course not. I mean, if you were crazy, you wouldn't dream up *hot* ghosts, right? You'd dream up a couple of smelly old fat bald guys."

Audra forced a laugh. Riley smiled back, but Audra could see concern lurking in the depths of her green eyes.

****

The next evening, just before Audra's shift ended, Shane called and asked her to meet him for a drink. She and Jaxon had planned to watch a movie together that night, but Jaxon now had to work late, so she was free. When she suggested The Red Door, a bar down the street from the hospital, Shane readily agreed.

On the drive, she mulled over his invitation. Was it a date or an update on the case? Whichever it was, she was looking forward to it. She hadn't had either in a long time.

Audra entered the club and peered through the haze of cigarette smoke. She searched for Shane, and in a few moments, spotted him straddling a barstool.

He smiled as he watched her approach, studying her with frank appraisal. She flushed. Maybe she should have changed out of her pale blue hospital scrubs and into something more alluring. She at least wished she could tug the ponytail holder from her hair to let it hang loose, but that might be too obvious.

"It's good to see you," Shane said. A glass filled

with clear liquid sat on the bar in front of him. She guessed it was club soda or water, rather than something alcoholic. Shane wore his uniform—a Khaki color that suited his dark good looks—and was therefore probably still on duty. So, maybe this wasn't a date.

The bartender, Ron, winked at her when she settled on a barstool next to Shane. Ron was broad-shouldered and squarely built with a shaved head, a skull tattoo on his neck, and a soul patch. He looked like a biker or ex-con—and she had no idea if that were the case—but she did know that he was an excellent bartender.

Without asking, he slid a glass of Chardonnay in front of her. "How's it hanging, Audra?"

"Not bad. Thanks." She sipped the wine, then twisted the stem between her fingers as she looked up at Shane. "Did you learn anything?"

"No. I'm sorry." He shook his head. "Sorry if I got your hopes up. I just wanted to see if you'd thought of anything to add. Remembered anything new. I know it sounds unlikely, but sometimes, even after this much time has passed, victims start to recall details they didn't remember before."

She tried to hide her disappointment by taking another sip of the wine. "No. Nothing new."

"I know it's frustrating. Scary."

"I try not to think about it."

He reached out and placed his warm hand over hers. "I'm here if you need me. Don't hesitate to call."

She swallowed and cleared her throat. "I'll keep that in mind. Thank you. There is one thing you could do for me."

He leaned slightly forward. "Name it."

"Could you keep an eye out for Maria? I mean, I know you can't put police protection on her or anything, but maybe just be aware. Her husband has a violent temper. He's hurt her before, and she was meeting with me that night to finally go to the police."

"Sure. I'll check it out. It's kind of you to be so concerned about her."

Audra didn't tell him that her reasons weren't totally altruistic. Maria reminded Audra of her mother. Not because they looked alike, but because Audra's mother had also been the victim of domestic violence. Although she'd died when Audra was very young, the memories of the fear and pain her mother endured would be with her forever.

By the end of the night, Audra still didn't know if she and Shane had been on a date. He took her to dinner, then followed her home to make sure she was safe, came in for coffee, and gave her a chaste, friendly peck on the forehead before he left.

As she dozed off to sleep that night, she thought about their evening and decided she didn't care what it had been. She'd enjoyed his company, and he'd given her a brief respite from the crazy her life had become. For the time being, that was enough.

****

Any doubt that Audra was losing her mind was now totally erased. She was most definitely insane. Otherwise, why on earth would she agree to accompany Jaxon to the mall on a Friday night, two weeks before Halloween?

He'd convinced her to come with him to help pick out a costume for the hospital Halloween party. After being jostled by more people than even *lived* in Boon

Springs, they'd made it to Spencer's Gifts and were now sifting through costumes.

Jaxon turned to her, holding a black-hooded robe in front of his body. In his hand, he held a white mask and a semi lethal-looking scythe. The fact that that the weapon was made of plastic lessened its intimidation factor.

"What do you think?" he asked.

She smiled. "The Grim Reaper? I get it. It's ironic because you actually *save* lives."

"Bingo."

He replaced the costume, choosing another and holding it up for her inspection.

"Elton John?" Audra laughed. "Not quite as ironic."

"Guess not," he said with a rueful grin.

Jaxon continued to peruse the costumes, intermittently presenting one for her opinion.

She groaned after what had to be the tenth costume. "Come on. You better pick something quick, or I'll die of starvation. Don't forget you promised me a giant pretzel."

"Yeah, yeah." He sighed. "Let's just go with the gladiator."

"Good choice. Makes you look sexy. Tonya will be all over you."

She'd tried to say it lightly, but the truth was, it made him look *extremely* hot. With his sun-tanned surfer-boy handsomeness, the touch of gold in his sandy brown hair, and the warm glint in his brown eyes, he was the epitome of a warrior hero come to life.

He rolled his eyes. "Maybe it's not the best idea."

"Hell, you could wear that." Audra grinned and

pointed at a giant baby costume, complete with over-sized diaper and baby bottle. "And she'd still be all over you."

Jaxon grunted and snatched up the gladiator costume, heading to the register.

Once he made his purchase, he put a hand on the small of her back, guiding her through the throng of people to the food court. The place was a teeming mass of bodies. Nearly every one of the food stands circling the tables had a line as long as a football field.

"I'll find us a table." Audra took the shopping bag from his hand. "You find me a pretzel."

"Yes, ma'am." Jaxon saluted and made his way through the crowd toward Sweet Annie's Pretzels.

Audra scanned the seating area. At one of the long tables, two sullen teen boys sat at one end, while the remaining chairs were empty.

She limped over and raised her voice to be heard above the din. "Mind if I take these seats?"

She got an almost shrug from one and a disinterested stare from the other, so she took it as permission and plopped her purse and the bag on one of the chairs, then dropped into the one next to it, giving a long, relieved sigh to finally be off her feet.

Glancing over to the pretzel line, she spotted Jaxon. He'd moved surprisingly far in a short amount of time. Good. She was starving. And thirsty. Had she also told him she wanted a Diet Dr. Pepper? Surely, he'd get her one, he knew—

A crash and a scream sounded over the noise of the crowd.

Audra shot to her feet and stared in the direction of the commotion. At a gyro stand near where Jaxon stood, a small group of people had started to move frantically, some in one direction some in the other. Between the sea of bodies, Audra glimpsed a toppled chair and the prone figure of a man.

A male voice shouted, "Give him room, people. Back off. Someone call 9-1-1."

Jaxon rushed over to the source of the uproar, and Audra grabbed their belongings, heading to join him as quickly as she could, although her progress was slowed by her limp and the rush of people. Several had vacated their seats and were also moving toward the action, trying to get a glimpse of what was taking place.

Keeping an eye on her target, Audra was pushing her way closer to Jaxon and the hubbub when she spotted the blond ghost. She halted, her breath stalling in her lungs. What the hell?

He was closer to whatever was happening than Audra was. She peered through the mob and, just as she feared, the dark stranger was there, too. He moved through the crowd easily, which was no surprise. After all, ghosts weren't hindered by mere solid objects. Anger contorted his face, his dark brows drawn over his piercing blue eyes. Forgetting the potential victim for a moment, Audra changed her course and headed toward the dark man, who was nearer to her than the blond. Once and for all, she would get some answers.

When she was within earshot, she shouted, "Hey, you!"

He whirled at the sound of her voice, his eyes momentarily widening in surprise, then he turned away and continued his course.

"Stop!"

Some of the people nearby cast her puzzled

glances, probably wondering who she spoke to, but most of them were focused on the drama unfolding next to the Gyro stand.

She was almost upon the man now. "I said stop. You have some explaining to do."

He barely spared her a glance. "I can't talk now," he bit out, still striding toward where Jaxon was administering aid to the ill man.

Before he'd covered half the distance, he came to a sudden halt, his fists clenching next to his sides. "Son of a bitch!"

Audra followed his gaze, and her brow creased in confusion. Through an opening in the crowd, she saw Jaxon crouched next to the fallen man, giving him chest compressions. The blond stood just behind Jaxon, his arms outstretched. Even from this distance, Audra could see an expression of complete rapture on his handsome face.

She looked back at her companion. Unlike the blond's, his expression held abject despair, his shoulders slumped in defeat.

"Son of a bitch," he muttered again.

"Someone," Audra whispered next to him, "had better tell me what the hell's going on."

He didn't answer. Instead, his attention riveted on the scene unfolding near the gyro stand. When Audra looked again, she saw the blond man reach out his hands in a beckoning gesture, a white-toothed smile spreading over his face.

She shifted her gaze back to the dark one, whose features tightened in a mixture of revulsion and grief so intense, she could actually feel those same emotions move over her flesh, through her body. She shuddered as she turned her attention to the tableau unfolding nearby.

Still, all she could see was the gorgeous, smiling ghost, reaching out as if welcoming a long-lost loved one into a hug.

Obviously, the dark-haired guy was seeing a hell of a lot more.

****

Gaylen trembled with euphoria as he watched the man's spirit writhe and twitch, fighting release from its body.

Chuckling, he stretched his hands farther toward his victim. "Come," he intoned softly. "You can't win. Let it be."

The spirit's head jerked toward him and shook violently back and forth, the mouth stretching into a frightened grimace. Then, it lifted partially away from the upper body and doubled over, clutching its stomach. A keening wail screeched through the room, magnifying until it became a blood-curdling scream.

A tingle of electricity shot through Gaylen's body. He shuddered, nearly crying out in joy.

*Power.* This was power and ecstasy and *life*, and no one would deprive him of it.

Although his focus was on the man, he was aware of the people around him. Most of them had gone silent, watching and waiting while the doctor made a futile attempt to save the man's life. From the periphery of the food court, voices rose and fell as oblivious shoppers went about their shopping. The doctor knelt beside the patient, muttering, "Come on, come on. Dammit, come on."

Dimitri was nearby. Gaylen could feel him. But he

was too late. Gaylen had gotten here first. *And this one is all mine, asshole.*

Still clinging to its earthly body, the spirit rubbed frantically at his arms, his face, his torso, trying to rid himself of the pain, but he couldn't. The pain was in his mind, part of the early exit program. The man would have to suffer through it. Every delicious second of it. In the meantime, Gaylen would simply enjoy.

Images flashed through Gaylen's mind. Images of things the man would never do, never see. The birth of his first grandchild. The retirement he'd worked so hard for. The illness that would give his family a scare, followed by his survival that would make them all realize how lucky they were to have him.

Gaylen smiled as he flashed forward to the best one. The man's thirtieth wedding anniversary. Only two weeks away. Even now as his dying body lay on the ground, a small jewelry box rested in his pocket. Diamond earrings for his wife. He'd been saving for a year.

Gaylen first saw the 'would have been' picture. The wife's face as she opened the box, emotions chasing across her expression, a blending of surprise and love and gratitude at the many years they'd been together.

Then, the true picture. The woman holding the Zale's box. Tears leaking from her eyes. Body shaking with sobs. Her children trying to comfort her, but there was no comfort to be had. The love of her life was gone. Forever.

*Yesssss.* Gone forever. Because of Gaylen. Because of his power. He felt his face stretch in a blissful smile.

"Come!" he shouted, impatience making his voice

harsher than it had been earlier.

The spirit turned its frightened expression to Gaylen, the eyes begging for mercy. Gaylen shook his head. There would be no mercy. Gaylen was hungry, weak. A shadow of his true potential. He needed this. Even now, he could feel himself growing stronger, feel the power of reaping a soul before its time reviving him, renewing him, giving him the surge of potency he craved.

Tensing, Gaylen concentrated with all his might. The spirit jerked again as if unseen hands yanked at him. Another wail, this time culminating in a pain-filled roar. The face contorted in agonizing despair.

Gaylen groaned with ecstasy. There was no feeling better than this, nothing else that could give him this pleasure, this satisfaction—with one exception. Audra Grayson.

Gaylen lowered his arms. His happiness was dulled by the realization that this man was a poor substitute. No one could ever measure up. She was so beautiful, so strong, so determined to conquer death.

He recalled that moment in the hospital when their eyes met. She'd seen him, he was certain. That made it all the sweeter. She would see him coming, see his power as he ravaged her soul from her body.

The most exciting caveat was that she would be bound to him forever. Audra had the rare gift of communicating with reapers. When a reaper took a soul with that gift before their time, the soul belonged to that reaper forever. Audra would be his eternal mate. He could only imagine…Audra by his side for eternity. What an astounding gift that would be.

First, he wanted the chance to taste her breath. It

had been so long since he'd had the opportunity to enjoy the sweet elixir of human breath. And Audra's would be the most delicious of them all. *Yes.* He would have her. Audra Grayson would be his. She was meant for him. He didn't know when or how, but she would be his. Never before had he reaped the soul of a human he'd connected with. The thought brought a wave of heady elation.

Most satisfying of all, he would snatch her right out of Dimitri's clutches. He would bring the smug bastard to his knees, once and for all.

Dimitri was besotted with the woman. He'd watched over her, coveted her since the first time they'd seen her. Gaylen should have had her then. Fucking Dimitri.

A thrill of awareness skittered through him. She was here. Somewhere nearby. He closed his eyes, savoring her presence.

Thoughts of Audra made this paltry substitution almost not worth his time. *Almost.* But an opening act was still entertaining, even if it didn't have the star-power of the main attraction.

Tiring of the game—as much fun as it had been—Gaylen moved closer to the spirit and once more lifted his arms. Tendrils of electricity shot through him, warm currents of power and energy. The spirit cried openly now, sobbing, begging with his eyes. Against its will, it tore completely loose from the body. Moving toward Gaylen in a slow, pain-staking stumble, it shook its head. Its expression was that of someone facing execution.

Gaylen allowed himself another grin. If the thing had any idea what was in store for it, it would pray for a fate as humane as execution.

****

Audra's gaze shifted back and forth between the blond and the man standing next to her. The blond appeared to be gleefully leading choir practice, while the dark-haired one acted as though he were watching a horror flick. He flinched. Raising his hands, he scrubbed them over his face and shoved them through his hair.

"What's happening?" Audra demanded, keeping her voice low. Whatever this apparition was, she was the only one seeing it. She didn't want her fellow mall patrons to think she'd lost her mind.

The man shook his head, not bothering to look at her. He stumbled back a few steps, then turned, heading away from the food court.

*He was ignoring her?* The hell he was.

She weaved through the crowd, fighting jostling bodies as she followed him. By the time she escaped the throng, he was well ahead of her. She broke into a run.

"Hey! Come back here. I have to talk to you."

He ignored her and kept walking.

"Damn you!" Her angry shout turned into a desperate cry as a sob caught in her throat. "Damn you to hell."

The man paused. His shoulders squared, then dropped. He slowly turned to face her. Waiting.

She halted a few feet in front of him. The air around them was cool, yet sizzled with a current of electricity. Just like she'd felt in Ms. Chapman's room.

He didn't speak as he stared at her.

"Who are you?" she asked breathlessly. "What just

happened?"

He glanced around. Shoppers passed them, some oblivious to their presence, a few others casting puzzled glances at Audra.

"I'll explain everything. But not here." The corner of his lips tilted in a half smile. She caught her breath. It was the first time she'd seen him looking anything but pissed. "They'll think you're nuts. Meet me outside this exit." He gestured toward the glass doors next to JC Penney's. "There's an alcove with an emergency door. We should have relative privacy there."

"Meet you? I'm coming with you now. I'm not letting you out of my sight."

"Aren't you forgetting about your friend? You're just going to disappear on him?"

*Jaxon.* Shit.

"Right." She shoved her hands through her hair. "I'll be there in a few minutes." Lifting her head to stare directly into his face, she said, "Don't screw me over. You'd better be there."

His eyes glinted with amusement. "I wouldn't dream of *screwing* you over."

Audra held his gaze, trying to decide if she were missing a sexual subtext. Who knew with supernatural beings?

She gave a quick nod and backed away, keeping him in sight for a few moments before turning and hurrying back to the food court.

Would Jaxon still be there? Would he wonder what had happened to her? Was that poor man dead?

Paramedics were lifting the victim onto the stretcher when Audra pushed her way through the crowd to the scene.

She found Jaxon standing next to the man, overseeing his care.

"Hey, is he okay?" she asked quietly.

He gave an almost imperceptible head shake. "I'm going with him in the ambulance." He fished his keys out of his pocket. "You take my car. Okay?"

"Sure."

"Sorry about the pretzel."

She smiled. "You'll do anything to get out of treating me, won't you?"

He reached out and tugged a lock of her hair. "You know me too well."

Impulsively, she gave him a quick hug. "I'll see you soon. Call me when you're done and I'll come get you."

He nodded. The stretcher was now moving quickly toward an emergency exit, and Jaxon followed.

Audra turned and went back the way she'd come. Her heart raced in fear and anticipation. Was she really on her way to meet some kind of supernatural being? Some creature whose existence she could neither confirm nor explain? She would soon get the answers she needed. Would those answers ease her anxiety, or send her spiraling into insanity and terror?

## Chapter 5

He was there. Waiting where he said he'd be, leaning against the wall, his hands shoved in the pockets of his jeans. A light above the emergency door illuminated the alcove, allowing Audra to make out his features clearly. His crystal blue eyes glittered as he watched her approach. He didn't speak when she reached him.

"Okay," she said breathlessly, staring up into his face. "Tell me who you are and what the hell has been going on since the night of my accident." Blood pounded through her veins, rushing loudly in her ears as she waited for his reply.

He chuckled, taking his hands from his pockets and straightening.

A flash of anger shot through her. "What's so damned funny?"

"Nothing. It's just that, this hasn't been going on 'since the night of your accident.' It's been happening since the beginning of time."

She threw her arms in the air and let them drop to her sides. "Great. All the shit I've been through, and I get riddles. You think you're a Batman villain or something?" She moved closer and jabbed her finger toward him. "I want some straight up answers. Right. This. Second."

He lifted his hands in surrender. "Okay, okay.

Calm down. I'll tell you, but it's going to be difficult to believe."

She gave a humorless laugh and crossed her arms. "Everything that's happened lately has been difficult to believe. Try me."

He took a deep breath and let it out in a long sigh. "My name is Dimitri. I'm a reaper."

She waited. She couldn't have heard him right, so ran the words over in her mind. What else might he have said? It sounded like he said he was a *reaper.* But that wasn't possible. That was utterly ridiculous. Of course, all of this was utterly ridiculous.

"Did you just say you're a reaper?"

"I did."

"And what exactly is it that you reap?" She'd play along. See where this led.

"Souls, Audra. I reap souls."

*Right.* She impatiently brushed a lock of hair back from her forehead. "So, you're a reaper as in, *Grim* Reaper?"

A grin played over his full lips. "I can't say I'm fond of that adjective. *Grim.* Sounds sort of…repugnant. I'm just a reaper. Plain and simple."

"Plain and simple? A *reaper* is plain and simple?" She shook her head, stalking away from him, then back. "You're telling me you're *death*? You take people's souls? You're a killer?"

He scowled. "A killer? Absolutely not. I'm not a killer."

"Well, pardon me. Then why don't you tell me how the hell this works."

"It's very complicated. There are rules and procedures—"

"Oh, so it's like a job? You mean your job is to *reap*?" A bubble of hysteria worked its way up to her throat.

Was she really having this conversation? Had this guy actually just told her he was a reaper? Then again, would a ghost or a demon or whatever else she'd imagined be any easier to believe? Could this really be happening?

Wait. Maybe it wasn't happening. Maybe she'd died the night of the beating, and she couldn't move on because she hadn't accepted it yet. Maybe nothing that happened since then had been real. Her body sagged with the realization.

He reached out as if to grab her but let his hands fall.

"Am I dead?" she choked.

He shook his head. "No. No, you're not dead."

"I didn't die the night of the beating?"

"No. You survived."

A chill went over her flesh that was only partly due to the bite of the frigid air. She pulled her jacket more tightly around her. "Then why can I see you? What has happened to me?"

His shoulders lifted, then fell. "Certain people are more attuned than others. They have some extra sense that allows them to see us."

"But why haven't I seen you before?"

"You wouldn't, until you had a near death experience."

She was aware of people passing, hurrying through the cold night to their cars, paying her little mind, but she still kept her voice low. "What?"

"When you were beaten in the alley, you almost

died. You were conscious long enough to become aware of our presence. That, combined with your…gift…made you able to see us."

"This is all so craz— Wait. Us?" She squeezed her eyes shut. "The blond. You were both there that night." She looked up at him. "You were trying to take me."

"Yes, he's a reaper, too. No, I wasn't trying to take you, he was."

"But you said, *I got here first*, or something…" She concentrated, trying to remember the details, what was said. But she'd been delirious, or thought she was. Now she didn't know what the hell she'd been.

"Right. I got there first, so he couldn't take you."

She rubbed her hand across her forehead. Her head was starting to hurt, a dull, throbbing pain. She was so confused, so utterly baffled.

Suddenly, a thought occurred to her. She raised her head to gaze at Dimitri, a smile forming on her lips. She was an idiot, a complete fool. What evidence did she have that this wasn't just some guy one of her friends or co-workers had put up to screwing with her? Most of the odd visions she'd had of him were when she'd been out of it from pain or medication, or both. It would be easy to screw with her under those conditions.

"Why are you smiling?" he asked, his tone wary.

"You're not a reaper, not a ghost, not a dark angel, or anything of the sort. You're just some asshole who's screwing with me."

"What?"

"You're just a man."

He frowned, considering for a moment as if waging an internal battle, then said, "No. I wish that were the case. I'd like to let you believe that, but the truth is out.

Gaylen's not going to leave you alone. I have to make you understand the facts."

She chortled. "Right. You and the blond are a couple of reapers." She turned to leave. "I'm out of here. See you around." She'd only taken a few steps when his voice stopped her.

"Wait. You can't go. You have to understand what you're dealing with."

She looked back at him. "A couple of asshole practical jokers."

His lips tightened, and he took a step toward her. "No."

She took a step back. "Yes."

Another step. "Touch me."

"What?" She shook her head. "No. No way."

He came closer. "Prove it. Once and for all. Touch me."

She shivered, meaning to back away, but found herself unable to move. When he stood a few feet from her, that same cool electricity filled the space between them.

He slowly closed the distance, coming within inches of her body. So close, she could see nothing except the black material of his T-shirt stretched over his pectoral muscles.

"Touch me," he whispered.

"I—I can't—I don't want to—" But she did want to. Blood pounded through her ears, and it seemed to be saying, *do it, do it. Touch him…feel him…*

She started to lift her hand, then stopped, shaking her head. "I can't."

"Okay." He moved again, closer to her, until there was no way he could get any closer without…

She gasped as his body made contact with hers but didn't actually make contact. A surge of electricity, a cool shiver combined with an odd heat, then he became a part of her…stirred inside her…

Her breasts tingled as fire licked over her skin, spreading downward. She had an urge to thrust her hips against him, to satisfy the twitch between her thighs. She moaned, savoring the delicious feel, the impression that his body was a part of hers…*in* hers. The yearning built, aching and trembling through her. *Yes. There. Stay there and let me feel you...just let me...*

The sensation abruptly fled. He was gone. A small cry escaped her.

"Here."

She whirled to find him standing behind her. For the love of God. He'd just literally walked through her. Shame heated her cheeks. She'd almost had an orgasm because of some wacked out supernatural bullshit that should have frightened the living hell out of her. Now that the disturbing, sexual contact was broken, she *was* frightened. What the hell was going on?

"Now do you believe me?"

Tears filled her eyes, and she lifted a hand to her mouth. She shook her head, even as her words acknowledged the facts. "It's true. You're really a…a reaper? This is actually happening?"

He nodded slowly, sympathy showing in his eyes. "I'm sorry. I didn't want you to find out. Never wanted you to be able to see us. Now that it's done, we have to deal with it."

"Deal with it? How do I deal with something like this? What's going to happen now? What am I supposed to do?"

He pursed his lips. "You have to be very careful. Now that Gaylen can communicate with you, he'll use you however he can. He'll get close to you, find your weaknesses. He'll take more souls simply by the connection you've opened with him."

"Take more souls?" she scoffed. "You take souls, too. You took Ms. Chapman, didn't you? You were there, in her room. Then she was gone."

"Yes, I took her."

"So, why are you so much safer than he is?"

Silence followed the question, broken only by the sound of a train wailing in the distance. A gust of wind blew a strand of hair over her mouth, and she brushed it away.

Finally, he spoke. "I only take souls when it's their time. Gaylen is bent on destruction, on evil. He wants to take as many as he can, *before* their time. Violently and painfully, with no regard to the natural order of things. He's a monster."

She opened her mouth to respond but halted when the expression on Dimitri's face changed. He looked over her shoulder, his mouth tightening, his eyes turning a dark sapphire.

A voice behind her spoke. "You're not painting a very flattering picture of me."

She whirled. The blond…Gaylen…stood there, looking…well, radiant. His posture was relaxed. The beautiful, white-toothed smile was in place. A satisfied glow emanated from him. He appeared ready to break out in song.

She glanced back to Dimitri, who stood with his fists clenched at his sides, his teeth showing in a feral snarl. "What do you want, Gaylen?"

The calm tone Dimitri had used with her altered. He growled the words, his body tense, as if holding itself back from pouncing.

"I think you know." Gaylen's eyes moved to Audra. "Pleasure to finally make your acquaintance. Properly, that is. I'm Gaylen." He bent at the waist in a bow.

Screw this. Did he expect her to curtsy?

"What do you want?" she repeated Dimitri's question.

Gaylen smiled and flicked a glance at Dimitri. "I want to disprove whatever nonsense he's fed you. I only want to be friends, to get to know you." His amber eyes darkened to a burnished gold. He lowered his voice, and a shiver worked through her insides. "I've waited a long time for this."

"Don't believe him, Audra. He only seeks to destroy."

She looked from one being to the other. Dimitri's angry, ready-to-battle stance. Gaylen's amused, calm, confident posture. Was she actually being asked to choose between two *reapers*?

She remembered the creepy costume Jaxon had shown her at the mall. The ghostly white mask…the black hooded robe…the deadly scythe. Somehow that image of a reaper now seemed a hell of a lot less scary. That was only a costume…a myth. The creatures here with her now were all too real.

****

"What a night, huh?" Gaylen flashed a smile.

She didn't answer. Her eyes narrowed, and her brow furrowed. Her hands shook, either from the cold—or maybe because of him. Whatever the cause, he liked it.

Yes. This had been quite a day. He'd feel as though he'd died and gone to Heaven if he weren't already dead. And, if this weren't so much better than anything Heaven could offer.

An evening that had begun with a successful harvest had culminated in being with Audra. Actually conversing with her. Like regular people. She was here, only a few feet away. He could sense her…smell the energy, the life emanating from her.

God. This was the moment he'd been waiting for.

The only thing that would make it better would be to touch her. Move closer…reach out a hand…taste her breath…He nearly groaned aloud. It had been so long since he'd tasted human breath…the nectar he craved with a painful, physical urge.

Dimitri craved it too. He was just too self-righteous to acknowledge it. To give in to it. Gaylen would have no problem taking it if the opportunity arose…taking it until there was no breath left. But there was only one way to do that, and he wasn't willing to take the risk. He'd just have to continue to fantasize.

How would it feel to stroke her skin? To hold her throat between his hands, to feel it pulsing with life, like a butterfly beating delicate wings against its cage? How would her breath taste? So sweet and warm as he drew it in…

"Get away from her!" Dimitri's harsh command snapped him back to reality.

Son of a bitch, the guy was a killjoy.

Dimitri stormed toward him, his hands clenching and unclenching, no doubt with the urge to throttle him. Gaylen's smile widened. The only thing better than being close to Audra was knowing Dimitri didn't want him to be.

"Chill, man." Gaylen lifted his hands. "I'm not going to hurt her."

"Damn right you're not."

Audra's beautiful hazel eyes filled with confusion and fear, but she hadn't tried to flee. Curious little kitten, wasn't she?

Gaylen forced his face into a trustful 'I only want what's best for you' mask.

"Audra," he said gently. "Please don't let him convince you I mean you harm. I'd never hurt you. Dimitri's a little—" He gazed heavenward, searching for the right word. "He's a little paranoid, a little melodramatic."

Audra laughed without amusement. Her full, silky lips pulled back in a sneer. "You think I'd trust you?" Her eyes shot to Dimitri, then back to Gaylen. "Either of you? You're *reapers*, for God's sake."

"Yes, but that doesn't mean we're evil." Gaylen took a step toward her, and she backed up.

"Stay away from me. Both of you."

She panted, her breath puffing like smoke in the chilly wind. Gaylen's chest tightened. He met Dimitri's eyes. He'd seen it too. Had also been affected by the urge. Cocking his head, Gaylen licked his lips and winked at Dimitri. Dimitri started toward him, but Gaylen moved closer to Audra.

"Hey, now. You don't want anything to happen in front of our new friend here, right? She's frightened enough as it is. Look at how her chest rises and falls as she struggles for air. She's panting so hard you can literally see her breaths. Sorry, Audra. The grouch and I have a history. We go back a long way, and we weren't all that chummy then."

She snorted. "Why not? Did you fight over who was going to club the women over the head and drag them into your cave?"

Gaylen howled with laughter. Even Dimitri's mouth twitched. Perhaps a sense of humor lurked somewhere beneath all that rage after all.

"Cavemen," Gaylen said. "I get it. No, Audra. Not that far back, but it was a very long time ago. Hundreds of years."

She frowned. "Literally hundreds of years? You two have been alive…" She shook her head. "…existed, for hundreds of years?"

"I think tonight has held enough surprises," Dimitri barked. "We'll leave you alone, Audra. We have no business interacting in your world. I'm sorry. I'll do my best to make sure he doesn't—"

Dimitri halted in mid-sentence, and a pained expression crossed his face. He lifted a hand to his chest.

*Fucking A*. He was being summoned. He shook his head in a quick, vigorous motion, like that would make it go away.

"You'd better go," Gaylen said, trying to keep the satisfaction out of his voice.

Dimitri glared at him.

"Or…" Gaylen cocked a thumb over his shoulder and lifted his brows. "I could go for you. How about that? Want me to go in your place?"

A sound between a growl and a snarl came from Dimitri. Gaylen couldn't make out what he said, but would have guessed it was something other than, 'Sure, it's very kind of you to offer.'

Dimitri's expression darkened, reflecting his internal battle. Stay or go? Perform his beloved duty or rescue the damsel? Gaylen knew what he'd choose. For a conformist like Dimitri, not going would be unthinkable.

Predictable as always, Dimitri let out another frustrated growl and turned to Audra. He moved close to her, so close Gaylen thought he was going to merge with her.

"Be careful," he said quietly.

"Careful? How the hell am I supposed to do that after you two death mongers have entered my life?"

Dimitri stared at her, but didn't speak. After all, what could he say?

He slowly backed away, shooting Gaylen one last, parting look. "I'd tell you to stay away from her, but I know how pointless it would be."

"So, don't bother. Just run along. Audra and I want to get acquainted."

Dimitri scowled, but continued to retreat. He made his fingers into a vee, pointed them at his own eyes, then toward Gaylen. The message was clear. *I'm watching you...* And then he faded into the darkness.

Gaylen turned back to Audra. "Alone at last. Thought he'd never leave." Her lips parted, and a puff of air escaped. Excitement surged in his chest. "Now, where were we?"

****

Audra skirted around Gaylen, keeping an eye on him, but maintaining a safe distance. She didn't trust either of them, but she damn sure didn't want to be alone with this one.

"Are you leaving?" he asked in an injured tone. "I thought we were having fun."

"Listen, I don't know what either of you want, and I don't care. You stay the hell away from me."

He crossed his arms and moved slowly toward her. His eyes dropped down her body. "Your limp." He moved his gaze upward, settling on her cheek. His eyes glittered. "That scar. I was there that night. I saw it happen. You were so helpless, so close to death."

"Too bad for you and your buddy I survived, huh?" Audra's stomach quivered. Her heart pounded a loud, fast rhythm that seemed to say *flee, run, get away...*

"I thought so, but I kind of like you this way, too. Talking, breathing, spitting fire. It's cute."

He moved closer. A wave of fetid, warm air enveloped her. An unpleasant energy reached out to her, something inhuman and despicable. It was different from the aura Dimitri carried. Although she was loath to admit it, Dimitri's caused her pulse to race. Gaylen's, on the other hand, made her stomach heave.

"I'm leaving now. Please don't follow."

He rubbed his hands together, chuckling. "I don't have to follow you. I can just…appear…any time I want. Why are you being so standoffish? I want to be your friend. I tried to help you that night in the hospital, remember? I wanted to take your pain away. I'm not your enemy. Would an enemy do that?"

She frowned, trying to remember the details of that nocturnal visit. He'd said, *I can take your pain away* or *I can make it go away,* something like that. "Dimitri stopped you. He didn't want you to help me. Why?"

He rolled his eyes. "The guy is such a stickler for rules."

"Really," she scoffed. "Somehow he doesn't strike me as the law abiding type."

"Oh, yes. He's all about rules now. In the days before he became a reaper, things were different." His eyes took on a faraway look. His face contorted in what almost seemed to be a human emotion. "Back then, he was a cold-hearted bastard. He made his own rules, and what he wanted was all that mattered. To hell with the consequences or who he hurt along the way."

One part of her wanted to hear the story, but the other wanted to run like mad, to get as far away from this monster as she could. "I'm going," she said. "Stay away from me." She backed away. "Don't either of you ever come near me again."

"What? You're not having fun?" He feigned injury.

"Just stay away," she choked out, then whirled and hurried toward her car.

His voice echoed behind her. "No point in running. We'll always be around. Me, Dimitri, you. Together forever. The fun is just beginning."

Even as she reached Jaxon's car and thumbed the unlock button on the key fob, she could hear his laughter, following her, mocking her.

****

Barney sat in his car, his gaze searching up and down Main Street in downtown Broken Arrow. It was after midnight, few people around, but he needed *zero* people around.

Well, maybe not zero. *One* was more like it. The one sitting no more than twenty or thirty tantalizing feet away.

At the moment, she wasn't alone. A couple of teenage boys were coming down the sidewalk, smoking cigarettes and engaging in a shoving match, playfully shouting *mother fucker* and *fuck off* at one another. If they kept walking, he was home free.

While he waited, he flipped down the visor, then slid the cover back from the mirror and stared at himself.

Facial hair in place…check. Green contacts…check. Friendly smile…check. All was good to go.

"Barney," he whispered, trying the name aloud.

Although he'd used it several times, he still wasn't used to it. *Barney* didn't really fit him, but it worked. What other name would evoke as much familiarity with a generation that grew up watching the lovable purple dinosaur?

He'd chosen the name for multiple reasons. He'd recently read a novel featuring a character he'd admired named Barnabas Silent. And, who could forget the ever-lovable, classic vampire from Dark Shadows, Barnabus Collins?

Yep, he couldn't have chosen a name that would mean so much to him, yet at the same time, inspire such trust in his young, impressionable, barely-out-of-childhood prey.

He waited a few minutes after the boys had disappeared before climbing from the car and heading toward the lone figure sitting on the curb.

Smoke rose from her cigarette, dancing in the glow from the streetlight before dissipating. She was maybe sixteen. A white girl, but her hair was in a bunch of little tight braids all over her head. Not an attractive look.

"Hi there. Is everything all right?" he said as he

approached her.

She looked up at him with a face that had once been pretty, but was now gaunt, the green eyes devoid of hope. “What?”

“I said, are you okay, you need help?”

She shook her head. “I don’t need help.”

The look of wariness was there, as it always was with these street kids. Poor things.

“My name is Barney. I won’t hurt you. I’m just concerned. It’s dangerous out here.”

Her eyes slid away from his. “I’m waiting on my mom to pick me up. She’ll be here any second.”

He smiled. “Come on, we both know that’s not true. You’re on the streets. I don’t know if you ran away or were kicked out, but I’ve seen it too many times not to recognize it. I can help you.”

“How?” A twinge of hope glistened in her eyes

“I’ll get you a motel for a few nights. Something to eat. Then, we’ll figure it out from there. If you want to contact your parents, go to a shelter, whatever. Your call.”

She frowned suspiciously at him.

He held out a hand. “I want to help you.”

“I—I don’t know.”

“Look, if I wanted to hurt you, wouldn’t I do it here?” He glanced behind him. “There’s no one around. I could do whatever I wanted right now. I just want to help you.”

She sighed and swiped a hand over her face. “I wouldn’t say no to some food.”

“All right. Come on, then.”

She slowly rose, but didn’t take his hand. Good enough. She was coming. That was all that mattered.

"My car's right over here."

She followed obediently. Once they were inside, he started the engine. "You in the mood for burgers, pizza, tacos, what?"

"I can have anything I want?" Her voice lilted with delight, the child she'd been not so long ago surfacing.

"Sure. Name it." He tried to regulate his breathing, tried to ignore the soft flesh of her neck. His fingers nearly ached with the urge to slide around it…gripping…squeezing…

He shifted the gearshift into drive, but hesitated when a sharp pain hit his heart. He let out a grunt and grabbed his chest.

"Hey, you okay?"

"Yeah. Fine. Just didn't take my medicine."

He'd been so excited, he'd forgotten. That happened a lot more often than it should. He had to be cautious. Take better care of himself.

He retrieved a bottle from his jacket pocket. Shaking out a couple of nitro pills, he swallowed them dry. In seconds, the pressure subsided. He smiled at his passenger. "All better."

He eased the car out onto the street. Reaching over, he turned on the radio. "Put that on whatever kind of music you like."

The girl pointed at his arm. "So, what's that tattoo? I can only see the bottom part. Is it a dragon?"

## Chapter 6

Audra rubbed her temples, trying to ease the pounding in her head. Her eyes were raw and dry, as though they'd been scrubbed with sandpaper. She'd barely slept last night and now, she was paying for it. The normal rhythm of hospital sounds—pages over the speaker, rolling carts, chatter of her coworkers, beeping of machines, sounds that were always just background, comforting even—now ate at her brain like termites on a tree.

She took in a deep breath and let it out slowly. *Just get through the day, put them out of your mind. You can do this. You* have *to do this.*

She sat at the nurse's station, studying Trevor Rosdale's chart. Poor kid was admitted this morning. His leukemia had been in remission, but now it was back. Death reaching its greedy fingers out to…

She shivered. Death now had a face, a name.

Make that *faces* and *names*, plural.

Had she actually met two Grim Reapers last night? There had to be another explanation, but no matter how hard she tried, nothing occurred to her. Not after everything she'd witnessed. What she'd felt when Dimitri had been…inside her. She shuddered and closed her eyes. That had been the strangest sensation she'd ever experienced. She hoped to God it never happened again.

"Hey."

She jerked her head up at the sound of Jaxon's voice. Her heart stilled, then raced like it might leap out of her chest.

*Calm down, Audra. Get a grip.*

"Hi." She forced a smile. "How are you? I'm sorry about what happened last night."

The man he'd treated at the mall had died. Heart attack. Maybe if she'd helped Jaxon instead of chasing after a phantom, who turned out to be a reaper, who turned out to have an accomplice…

She shook her head. *Stop thinking about that. Stop it.*

Jaxon peered closely at her. "I'm okay, but I'm not sure about you." His mouth turned down at the corner. "You look like shit."

His words sent a sharp pain through her heart. "Oh yeah?" She choked out a laugh and jumped to her feet, clutching the chart to her chest. "Not exactly the revelation of the century. You don't find me attractive when I look my best, so what the hell, right?"

A pained look came into his eyes, and for a split second, she regretted her words. But only for a second. She'd had a helluva couple of weeks, a horrific night, and she was in no mood to make apologies. He could just suck it up.

"Excuse me. I need to check on Trevor."

She rounded the desk and brushed past him, not checking to see if he still had that hurt, puppy dog look in his eyes. He'd get over it. She'd earned being a little pissy to him once in a while. After all, she'd gone along with marrying him, helping him in his quest for a straight, 'normal' life—something his father and the staid citizens of Boon Springs wanted more than he did—and in doing so, she'd given up Shane.

To be fair, she hadn't been in love with Shane. She'd loved Jaxon. But, who knew what might have happened? She could have ended up falling in love with Shane.

Of course, if she were honest, her actions hadn't been completely selfless. She'd been so in love with Jaxon, she'd hoped she could somehow make him realize their marriage was the path he wanted to take, the life he wanted to live. In the meantime, she'd lost her chance at something real, allowed Shane to leave, hurt, because she'd chosen Jaxon over him

"Hell of a wise choice, Audra," she muttered as she stalked down the hallway.

Her anger abated when she went into Trevor's room. She found him sitting up in bed, his face pale, his shoulder blades protruding like knives beneath his hospital gown. All in all, a nice-looking kid, but it wasn't easy to see with his shaggy hair hanging in his face, hiding his pretty blue eyes. The hair wouldn't be a problem for long. Not when the chemo treatments started again.

Wilton, the nurse's aide, stood next to Trevor, adjusting his bed, helping to make him more comfortable. Wilton looked up when Audra came in, then said to Trevor, "All set, dude?" Trevor nodded. "Then I'll leave you in the capable hands of Miss Audra. Later."

When Wilton left, Trevor looked up, flipping the hair back with a jerk of his head. His fingers kneaded the blanket, and he glared at her, tears swimming in his eyes. He sniffed and swiped angrily at his face.

"Morning," she said brightly. "I heard you were back with us. Couldn't stay away, huh?" She gave a cheerful smile, although neither of them was in the mood for gaiety.

Seventeen years old. Last year of high school. So much to do, so much to live for, yet so little chance to live it. Or, at least, so little chance to live it without trips back to the hospital, suffering through weakness, pain, nausea, depression, lost hope. It sucked like hell. The vile, despicable disease took over a person's body with no regard for age, no regard for the bright future they could have, or for the people who loved them.

"It's back." His voice was accusatory, as if she'd invited the leukemia to return. "I was supposed to try out for Varsity on Friday. *Fuck.*"

She put a hand on his. "I'm sorry, Trevor. We'll do the best we can to get you better."

He jerked away. "Yeah, but your best isn't very damn good, is it? I thought I was cured the last time. You said the cancer was gone!"

"I said it was in remission. The doctors—"

"Fuck the doctors! They all suck, and so do you. Leave me alone."

"I have to start your IV. Please try to calm down. Let me help you. This will ease your pain."

She was surprised at how much his diatribe hurt. She was used to crabby patients, used to being blamed for their discomfort and pain, but Trevor had been in and out of the hospital several times, and she thought they'd bonded. But then, who could blame him for his anger? If she were in his shoes, she'd be a raging bitch.

He glared at her, then turned his head away. "Yeah, you can take the pain away, but the poison will still be there. What the fuck, right?"

She let out a breath. Talking to him would do no good while he was in this state. Once his medications started working, he'd feel better. Physically and mentally.

She tied the tourniquet around his arm and swiped his hand with alcohol pads. "This will sting a little, but I'll be quick." The needle trembled as she moved it toward his vein. She paused. Damn. What was happening? She'd never had trouble starting an IV before. That was one of her specialties. She took a deep, calming breath and tried again. The needle refused to be still.

Trevor snorted. "Right, you'll help me. No wonder I'm dying. The people in this hospital suck."

Unexpectedly, tears stung her eyes. He was right. She sucked. She'd hurt Jaxon's feelings, and now she couldn't even help a sick boy who needed her. Those assholes had taken over her life and rendered her a useless mess.

"I'm sorry," she whispered. "I'll get someone else to do it."

"Yeah, you do that." His bitter words followed her out of the room. "Get someone else to prolong my misery. Why the fuck can't you people just let me die?"

****

Dimitri filled a glass with scotch. Holding it up in front of his eyes, he swirled the amber liquid, watching it catch light from the flames in the fireplace. This was just what he needed. This, and solitude.

Thank God Veronica wasn't here. Her incessant chatter, her clingy, needy whining might send him over the edge. For God's sake, you do your duty, mentor a reaper, and you're stuck with her for fifty years. He'd mentored other reapers and they'd gone their own way. Hadn't followed him home like a stray dog.

Of course, he *was* sleeping with her. That may have given her the impression he didn't mind her hanging around.

"Big mistake," he muttered, then downed the liquor, letting it burn where his heart once beat.

On top of that mistake, came the Audra slip-up. Fucking Gaylen. He'd screwed everything up. The last thing they needed was for a human to know about their existence. Audra would end up getting hurt. He knew it as sure as he knew Davy Crockett hadn't fared well at the Alamo. And he'd had a front row seat to that.

Other people would get hurt too. He had more to worry about than just Audra. Letting her take over his mind would be disastrous.

He lifted the decanter to refill the glass but halted when he sensed someone enter the room. Without turning, he knew who it was.

"Pour me one, would you?" Gaylen said from behind him.

Dimitri filled his own glass and set the decanter down. Turning, he tilted the glass toward Gaylen in a mock toast, then brought it to his own lips, swallowing half the contents in one drink.

Gaylen laughed. "You're not the most gracious host in the world." He moved to the decanter and poured a glass for himself.

Dimitri stepped away from the bar. "You're not exactly an invited guest."

"We're not vampires. We don't have to be invited in."

"What do you want?" Dimitri swallowed more of the liquor, but this time it stuck at the base of his throat.

As reapers, they could still drink, eat, have sex, pretty much do all the things they did as humans. But it was nothing more than mimicking their past lives. They could go through the motions, they just couldn't achieve the same effects. The tastes, the sensations were dulled. Like they were experiencing it all through a filter.

Gaylen sipped from his glass. "Just a chat. A little bonding, reminiscing, what have you. It's been too long."

"I'm not in the mood for your games."

"Oh?" He cocked a brow. "What kind of mood are you in? I'll tell you what kind of mood *I'm* in. Did you see Audra's breath drifting in the night air?" Gaylen moved closer, his grin making Dimitri want to smash his face in. "Can you imagine how it must taste? How sweet her breath would be?"

"Shut up."

"Come on. I know you've thought about it. Wanted it. We're not that different, you and I."

"I'm not like you."

"No, no you're not *like* me. You have no sense of adventure. No idea what you're missing by being such a Righteous Randall. But, you still want it. You still crave human breath—crave Audra's above all. Am I right? I know I do."

Dimitri smirked. "Yes. I know you do too. But you'll never have it, will you? You're afraid to do the one thing it would take."

"Not afraid. Just cautious."

"Right. Because you know, the moment you turn

human, I'm there. And I'll tear you to pieces."

"You're forgetting. You'd have to turn human, too."

Dimitri shrugged and set the glass down on the table. Although it would take gallons of the stuff to get him drunk, he was tempted to give it a shot. He'd welcome the escape. But it was best he didn't. He couldn't afford to let the alcohol muddle his thinking, slow his reflexes. Now that Gaylen had made contact with Audra, he'd be even harder to control.

A shudder ran through him. "I'm not forgetting. Unlike you, I'm willing to take that risk. I'll do whatever it takes to stop you, Gaylen."

Gaylen laughed. "Yes, but therein lies your problem, my friend. Just what will it take to stop me?"

****

Audra parked in the Maroneys' driveway and climbed out of the car. Jaxon's parents were in Florida for the winter. Their large, two-story Victorian house was empty. It didn't matter, though. The house was not her destination. She headed around back to where the yard fed into woods that she and Jaxon had played in as children.

Sunlight glinted through the trees as she moved toward the creek. She'd thought the workday would never end. If she had to listen to one more complaint, get bitched at by one more doctor, empty one more bedpan, she might explode. Not that she could blame anyone for the complaints. She hadn't been much of an asset today. She hadn't even been able to place an IV. Those monsters had taken over her thoughts, her life, keeping her so distracted she couldn't think about anything else. And now, every waking moment—and most of her moments had been 'waking' since she'd discovered what they were—she was terrified.

She heaved a sigh when she came to the tree that had been hers and Jaxon's sanctuary, their secret world. It was a humongous oak that had fallen across the creek years ago. She and Jaxon had actually seen it happen. A bolt of lightning had severed it from its roots, sending it crashing across the creek…a bridge created by nature's fury.

It was Audra's fault they were outside during the storm. She'd been upset over her father's reappearance in her life. At ten years old, she'd hated her dad with an intensity as great as the tempest brewing around her. Yet, stubbornly, a part of her loved him.

After her dad's phone call and his promise—threat—to visit her that evening, she'd taken off. Jaxon ran after her, even though his mother was calling, her voice panicky as she shouted for them to come back, to seek shelter in the cellar.

Jaxon caught up to Audra by the creek. Torrential rain mixed with her tears, but did nothing to dilute the hate she felt toward herself for wanting to see her worthless father.

"Hey," he'd soothed. "It's okay." At twelve, Jaxon was two years older than she, but ten times more mature. He'd been like the brother she never had, the father she never had…and eventually, the lover she would never really have.

"Okay?" she'd railed at him. "You have two parents who love you. Not a dead mom and an asshole for a dad."

Jaxon usually smiled when she said swear words. He wasn't brave enough to say them himself, but thought it hilarious when she did. This time, he didn't smile. He gazed at her with sympathy.

A few seconds later, there was a rush of wind louder than a freight train, and a crack like the world was splitting apart.

Jaxon looked past her, and his eyes rounded. "Audra, watch out!" He grabbed her arm and jerked her off her feet just as the huge oak toppled and fell over the creek. They tumbled to the ground together. When she was able to catch her breath, she raised halfway, resting back on her hands, gaping at the tree.

"You saved my life," she said in wonder. She already had a tiny bit of a crush on Jaxon, and now that he'd made like a superhero, it bloomed into full-blown love. Or, at least as much love as a ten-year-old could feel.

Since that time, this had been *their* tree, a symbol of the miracle of life, the bond of friendship.

She trudged across the wet ground until she could grip a branch. Putting one foot on the trunk, she pulled herself up and tightrope-walked across the trunk until she reached her favorite spot—the forked branches that seemed to have been created for her to nestle in. In the colder seasons, she didn't hang out as long, but somehow, coming here and just *being* in this place brought her peace, comfort.

She lay back and wrapped her coat more tightly around her. Closing her eyes, she listened to the wind sigh through the leaves above her head. Before long, winter would take away the leaves and open up a view to the sky. Nighttime was the best, when she could stare at the stars, make wishes that would never come true.

"I thought I'd find you here."

She jerked, nearly toppling into the water as she rose to a sitting position. “Jaxon, you scared the shit out of me.”

He was coming toward her, already on the trunk, and she hadn’t heard him approach. What could those reapers have done while she’d been so distracted? Hell, they could probably do whatever they wanted, even if she was on high alert.

“Sorry about that. Sorry about earlier too.” He settled across from her, straddling the tree trunk. “I didn’t mean to upset you.”

A lump rose in her throat. “No. I’m sorry.” She reached out and squeezed his forearm. “I was a bitch for no reason.”

“When you’re a bitch, there’s usually a reason.” He grinned. “Tell me what’s up, and I’ll make it better.”

She sighed. Releasing him, she rubbed her fingers over her forehead. “Don’t think you can make this better, but I appreciate the offer.”

“Can’t you tell me? We tell each other everything. Guy trouble?”

She shook her head.

He smiled. “Girl trouble?”

She laughed and slapped his arm. “Wrong again. I guess I’m just having problems adjusting. You know, being back at work, Trevor’s leukemia coming back, knowing those assholes who attacked me are still out there.” Truth was, she’d almost forgotten about the beating. She had much scarier assholes to deal with now.

“Hey, it’ll be okay.” Jaxon scooted closer and pulled her in for a hug. “Dunham’s on it. He cares about you. Marshall Dillon will ride to your rescue, save the day, carry you off into the sunset. All that hero in a white hat stuff. You'll see."

She returned the hug. "Thanks, Jaxon. I feel better already."

He rubbed her back and squeezed tighter. "That's what I'm here for." Still holding on, he murmured in his movie quote voice, "I never had any friends later on like the ones I had when I was twelve."

"We've known each other longer than that," she said.

"Do you know the movie or not?"

She leaned back to look him in the face. Smiling, she said, "*Stand By Me*."

****

Gaylen crept through the trees, keeping behind Audra. The gay-doctor-ex-husband couldn't see him anyway, so no need to stay out of his line of sight. But he didn't want Audra to spot him right now.

He'd show Dimitri who was in control. Did the asshole think he could take any woman he wanted? Did he think Audra was his to claim? Even if Audra wasn't aware of it yet, she was succumbing to Dimitri's charms, whatever the hell those were.

Personally, Gaylen didn't see it. But Audra did. She'd given Dimitri a certain look. Gaylen had seen the same look in Louisa's eyes. A look that said, although she knew she shouldn't, she wanted the bad boy. That had been right before the bastard had stolen Louisa from him. Not long before Dimitri killed her.

Gaylen wouldn't let things end that way again. Wouldn't let Dimitri win.

He was about to unleash a whole lot of hell on everyone in his path.

Of all the people Audra loved, who should he take first? Whoever his choice, they had to be in jeopardy, of course. But there were ways to bring that about.

Audra and her ex-husband broke apart, and she leaned back into the crook she'd occupied a few moments ago. Gaylen moved behind a tree, just in case she caught him in her peripheral vision.

A breeze blew the scent of her to him, and he inhaled deeply. *Yes.* So delicious. He had to have her.

Soon.

What to do, where to begin… Should he start with the doctor? The best friend?

An image of the tiny blonde girl with whom Audra shared a mutual worship formed in his mind. What was her name? Sandy? Sadie? That was it. Sadie. He chuckled, pushing away from the tree and heading back the way he'd come. Ah yes, the sweet little girl, Sadie.

But he wouldn't start with her. Someone Audra wasn't quite as attached to would be better. After all, when you start at the top, there's no wiggle room, nowhere to go with negotiations. He needed an example to show her he meant business. If he didn't get her attention with that, he'd move on to bigger—or should he say, smaller—things.

## Chapter 7

"Oh, God. I'm dying," Riley moaned, shouting above the sounds of clanging weights and music blasting from the gym speakers.

"Quit whining." Audra scowled. "This was your idea."

Riley pursed her lips and blew a breath out. "Yeah, well. Next time, shoot me. We should have taken the Zumba class." She twisted the handles of the treadmill like she was revving up a motorcycle. "At least they play peppy music while we're being tortured."

"So true." Audra panted. "I say we take it down to a leisurely stroll." She slowed her machine to 'cool down.'

Riley did the same, then took the towel hanging on the handle of the treadmill and used it to blot the perspiration from her face. "Nice. This is more like it."

Across the room, a woman wearing a tight pink sports bra and black workout Capri's did curls in front of the mirrored walls, grimacing in concentration. Sweat glistened on her tanned flesh, and her Jean Claude Van Dam-like biceps jumped with every repetition.

"Wish I was that dedicated," Audra said, motioning with her chin toward the woman.

"You want to be built like a man?"

"Well, maybe not *that* dedicated." Audra grinned.

"We haven't talked much the past few days," Riley said. "How are you? How has it been, being back at work? You seen much of Shane lately?"

"Geez. Are you interrogating me, counselor? How about one question at a time?"

"Okay. The Shane one." Riley slid her a look from the corners of her eyes.

"I saw him once." She didn't mention the drinks and dinner. Riley would grill her like she was on the witness stand.

"I think he still likes you. You should go for it."

Audra rolled her eyes. "The man's been back in town for two months, and you think I should pounce on him?"

Riley nodded vigorously. "Pounce the hell out of him. He's gorgeous."

"I'm absolutely not looking for a relationship. Things didn't exactly go great the last time."

"That was almost fifteen years ago. You're divorced. He's back. Kismet."

Audra let out a sigh. Kismet. Right. The man had suffered some terrible tragedy in Cincinnati, moved back to his home town to heal, and Kismet wanted Audra to circle him like a vulture. "Can we talk about something else?"

"Sorry. Just think about it, okay?"

"How about I at least wait until he shows some interest?"

"You haven't noticed the way he looks at you?"

"You mean like a concerned cop looks at a victim? Come on, Ri, you're reaching."

"Speaking of victim. Guess who came to see me today?"

"I have no idea."

She blotted her face again, then draped the towel around her neck. "Maria."

"Maria? What for?"

"About a divorce. We filed a petition."

Audra dialed down the treadmill until it stopped. Her legs felt like they might fall off.

She turned to face Riley. "No way."

"Yes way."

"Wow. After all this time." She chewed her lower lip. What had Scott done to send Maria to a divorce attorney? If beating the hell out of her weekly wasn't enough, what was? "So, you think she'll go through with it?"

Riley stopped her treadmill. "Let's take a break."

They stepped off the machines and dropped onto the hard wooden bench that lined the wall behind them. The smell of sweat and tanning lotion hung in the air. A Lil' Wayne song played from the speakers in the ceilings, punctuated by occasional grunts from the weightlifters.

"Ahhh. This is more like it." Riley leaned her head back. "I thought for a minute I would pass out. Next time Sadie's at dance class, let's go to a movie or something. This working out thing sucks."

"You were saying about Maria?" Audra prodded impatiently.

Riley shrugged. "I can't say much about our consultation. Now that she filed, it's public record, but I can't give you details. I just wanted you to know because I'm worried."

"Worried? Was she hurt? What did he do to her?"

"She was fine. I'm worried about you. That asshole

husband of hers has it in for you just for trying to help his wife. When he is served with the papers, there's no telling what he'll do. He'll blame you, I'm sure."

Audra waved a hand dismissively. "I'm not afraid of him."

"Well, you should be. I wouldn't be surprised if he had something to do with what happened to you."

"He was in jail."

"So. He could have put someone up to it. Nothing he did would surprise me."

"I just hope Maria finally gets away from him."

"She's taken the first step. We'll see." She raised her brows at Audra. "Any more of those hottie ghost sightings?"

Audra's heart jumped. "What?"

"The ghosts you saw after your accident. Still seeing them?"

In an effort to avoid Riley's gaze, Audra bent to re-tie her shoe.

Maybe she should tell Riley the truth. The door had been opened, why not let her walk through?

Because, knowing the truth could possibly put her in danger. And, there's no way in hell Riley would believe her, anyway.

"No more sightings," she answered, sitting back to face Riley as she told the lie. "Guess it was just the trauma of the accident and the lingering effects of the pain meds. The apparitions are gone."

Riley slowly nodded. "That's good, right? Means you're not losing your mind."

"Right."

Instead, she was faced with a reality more frightening than insanity could ever be.

****

Trevor's mother, Cheryl, sat next to his bed. She was in her late thirties, short and round. Her bright pink fingernails caught the light from above as she twisted and kneaded a wad of tissue. All the times Audra had seen her before, her blonde hair was poofy, teased at the crown. The past few days, it seemed to have wilted, hanging limp and lifeless around her plump cheeks. The desperation in her eyes was evident. She wasn't even pretending to think her son would live.

"How you feeling today, Trevor?" Audra came over to stand beside his bed. He'd grown paler and thinner than he'd been only a few days ago. Was it the illness or his lack of hope that was taking such a toll?

The young man dragged his gaze from the ceiling and turned his sullen expression on Audra. "Like shit."

"Trevor, please. Language," his mother admonished.

He whipped his head toward her. "Really, Mom? You're upset that I said *shit*? I have poison eating me from the inside out, and you're worried about my language?"

Cheryl dropped her head and pushed a hand against her mouth. A sob wrenched from her, but she didn't speak. Trevor cast her an irritated look, then returned to staring at the ceiling without apology.

*Teenagers.* Most of them had attitude problems, but this was beyond the norm. In all his trips back and forth, Audra had never seen him this bitter. Maybe he knew, like she did, that this could be his last visit. She blinked back tears as she checked his IV. The tape was damp. He'd been sweating…side effects from his medications. She took a roll of tape from her pocket and tore off a few strips, then began re-taping his IV.

"I was finally going to have a shot to make Varsity," he said quietly. "Starting fullback. Two practices are all I made. Then it came back." He sniffed and tried to hide it by gritting his teeth and crying out, "Watch what you're doing, okay? That hurts."

Audra smoothed the tape over the needle and gently rubbed his arm. "I'm sorry," she whispered, locking gazes with him.

His lips tightened, but she could see them quiver as he tried to hold back tears.

The silence in the room was oppressive. He and his mother didn't seem to converse much. Audra hadn't seen any friends stop by. Poor guy was probably lonely, bored, not to mention, scared out of his mind.

"So, tell me what's been going on besides football," Audra said while she charted his vitals. "You have a girlfriend?"

Trevor's laugh was filled with bitterness. "Right. A girlfriend."

Cheryl lifted her head. Her expression was as bitter as her son's. "Trevor had a girl he was seeing, but—"

"Tell me something, Miss Perky," Trevor cut his mother off, glaring at Audra. "Would you want to go out with some dude who's too weak to carry the equipment when there's a field full of healthy, able-bodied guys?" His voice rose to a shout. "Would you, huh?"

"Trevor—" his mother began.

"It's okay." Audra took a step back. "I understand. It was stupid of me. I shouldn't pretend everything's normal in your world."

Trevor jerked a nod and bowed his head. He was

on the precipice of being a man, but death was looming and made him a scared little boy. Suddenly, an image of Gaylen or Dimitri taking him away came to her. They would rip his soul right from his body and—

"Audra? Hey, Audra?"

Trevor's voice penetrated, and she shook off the images. He looked at her curiously. "You okay? I said, like, ten things to you but you were totally zoned out."

"Sorry. A lot on my mind. So, what were those ten things?"

He gave a small smile. "Maybe it wasn't quite ten. And only one is worth repeating. I'm sorry."

She smiled back. "It's okay."

Over Cheryl's shoulder, a shadow flickered. Dimitri materialized, and Audra gasped involuntarily. She opened her mouth to speak, but he lifted a finger to his lips, gave a brief headshake, and pointed to Cheryl and Trevor.

Of course. What was she thinking?

"Hey, what's wrong?" Trevor asked.

"Nothing. Sorry. Everything's fine." She tugged his blankets, smoothing them over his legs. "You need anything?"

"No."

"Call me if you do. I have to go check on some of my less charming patients. I'll let you visit with your mom."

"A couple of my friends are stopping by after school."

Audra grinned at the hopeful lilt to his voice. "That's great. See you soon."

She headed toward the supply closet, assuming Dimitri would follow. He was obviously here to talk to her. Unless…Trevor.

Dear God, surely it wasn't his time this soon. Dimitri couldn't take him. Panic gripped her heart. She whirled, intending to rush back to Trevor's room, to try to talk some sense into Dimitri, to beg, plead—

If he'd been solid, she'd have run right into him. He was there, behind her, close enough that she should have felt that cool spark of electricity, even when she hadn't known he was there.

He lifted his brows. "What's the matter?"

She let out a breath. She couldn't answer him, not in public like this. She turned and continued to the supply closet.

Once they were inside, and the door was shut, she still kept her voice low. "What are you doing here? Are you…reaping someone?"

His lip curled. "Not today."

"Not today at all?"

"Well, not right now. Not at this moment. I never know when duty will call, but that's not why I'm here."

"Why are you here?"

"I wanted to check on you. Sorry I had to leave so abruptly the other night."

"No problem. I'm sure you had someone to kill."

"I don't—" He shook his head, not finishing the sentence.

"This is all just so crazy." Her voice quivered, and she swallowed hard. *I will not cry in front of a reaper.* "Why did you come here, really? If it's not to take someone, why?"

He moved closer, staring down at her.

The cool sizzle reached out to her, and for a moment, she couldn't breathe. She flinched and drew back, stopping when she made contact with the shelf behind her. What was wrong with her that this creature could incite sexual longing every time he was near?

"Something the matter?" he asked softly.

Ignoring the understatement of the century, she said, "Why do you always have to get so close?"

"Sorry." He lifted his hands and backed away. "My bad. Sorry."

He hadn't answered her question, but at least he'd given her some breathing room. "Again, why are you here? The real reason."

"I told you. I wanted to see if you're okay. I regret having to leave you with Gaylen."

"Oh yes, the *dangerous* harbinger of souls. As opposed to the safe one. Wouldn't want that."

He grinned. "What did he say to you? He didn't try to..." He trailed off and frowned. "Well, no. He couldn't have really harmed you at that time."

"Why? What do you mean, at that time?"

"He can't take someone unless they're in jeopardy."

"Jeopardy? As in, they're going to die anyway?"

"Not necessarily. They can be ill, injured, any kind of momentary peril that they'd normally recover from. If Gaylen gets to them while they're in that state, he can take them."

"That night in the hospital. When you two...visited me. He was trying to help me. Trying to ease my pain."

"He wanted to take you."

"Kill me?"

"Yes. Don't be fooled by his charming ways. It's all an act."

"How do I know it's not all an act with you? That

you're not the one who's trying to kill me?"

He shrugged. "I suppose you don't." He held her gaze. In the depths of his blue eyes, she saw a flash of something. Was it malice? Regret? Desire?

She shook off the thought and looked away. If she wasn't careful, he'd hypnotize her, brainwash her…God knows what kind of things he could make her do.

"Am I going to start seeing reapers, ghosts, whatever, all the time?" She thought of the little boy in *The Sixth Sense*.

*I see dead people…*

"You have the ability to see reapers," Dimitri told her. "There are many in this area, so the odds are good you'll run into them from time to time."

"Why in this area?"

"Reapers are drawn to places where death is prevalent. I think that's why you're more attuned to us. Others in this town likely are, too, but they haven't yet suffered a near death experience where they connected with a reaper. The history of your town, the tragic beginning, has attracted a greater number of reapers than other places do. Although they're around, most of the time, they won't bother you. You probably won't even know they're reapers. Most of the time," he repeated.

"I don't get it. How can this be possible?"

Dimitri sighed. "It just is. That's all. Like the air you breathe. You can't see it, but it's there and you believe it's there. You accept it."

She laughed without humor. "I think this is a little more than I'm prepared to accept."

"You have to. And you have to be aware. At all

times. Don't let Gaylen get to you. Now that he's able to communicate with you, he'll use it to his advantage."

"How?"

"You're around sick people all the time. He'll sweep through your life and snatch up anyone in his path. I'll do my best to stop him, but I won't always be around."

"Couldn't he have done that before I could see him?"

"He could have stumbled across your patients, yes. But your connection with him has opened a door to your world. It's hard to explain, but he was more or less drifting on the peripheral before. He could watch you, check in on you from time to time, but he had other…hobbies, so to speak. Now, his fascination with you is amplified, and he'll spend more time around you. Around you and your sick patients."

"And have more opportunity."

"Exactly."

She wrapped her arms tightly around her body. Tears crowded her throat. "Is there anything I can do to stop him?"

"No, nothing. It's my job to stop him."

"Is there anything you can do to stop him? Permanently?"

His jaw clenched. Heaving a weary sigh, he said, "I've been trying for nearly three-hundred years. What do you think?"

****

Audra stood at the counter in Riley's kitchen, slicing a large white onion. The smell of chicken sizzling on the stove fought for dominance over the onion's odor. The onion was winning.

Sounds of a video game carried from the living room as Brent and Sadie battled it out. Most fathers would let their little girl win, but Brent competed fiercely. Sadie still beat him most of the time.

"Jesus," Riley muttered. "You'd think for one night they could forego X-Box and maybe watch TV. Something educational." A loud exploding sound came from the living room, followed by an unintelligible shout from Brent. Riley cringed. "Something quiet."

Audra laughed. "Guess if you wanted that, you shouldn't have married a man-child."

"Touché."

The doorbell rang, and Audra looked at Riley through onion tears. "Expecting anyone?"

"Who me?" Riley's eyes rounded. "Could you get it, please?"

Brent called, "I'll get the door, sweetheart. I need a break. This kid's killing me."

"No!" Riley shouted. "Audra will get it."

Audra frowned curiously. Obviously, Riley was expecting someone.

Riley smiled. "Please?"

"Okay." Audra dropped the knife on the carving board and wiped her hands on a paper towel. "Weirdo," she said over her shoulder as she left the kitchen.

In the foyer, Audra opened the front door to find Shane standing on the porch.

"Shane? I'm surprised to see you here."

"Riley invited me."

That, however, didn't surprise her.

"Great." She stepped back. "Come in."

He held out a bottle of wine as he passed. "I wasn't sure what we were having, so I went with Merlot." His smile made the corners of his dark brown eyes crinkle.

He was out of uniform, wearing worn, faded jeans and a button-up burgundy shirt. The flecks of gray in his hair glinted in the light from the setting sun. He looked really, really good. She owed Riley one.

"This is perfect." She took the wine and closed the door. "You can join Brent and Sadie in their vicious video war or help Riley and me in the kitchen."

He seemed to weigh his options for a moment. "How about the kitchen? Knives sound safer."

She grinned. "You're right. Must be the cop instinct."

They stopped in the living room to say hello to Brent and Sadie, but barely received an acknowledgment. Brent was leaning forward on the couch, staring intently at the television screen, and Sadie sat cross-legged, her small face scrunched in concentration as her fingers flew over the control.

Shane laughed. "The kitchen is definitely the better choice."

When they entered, Riley turned from the stove. "Shane. Hello. So glad you could make it."

"Thanks for inviting me. Smells great."

"Lemon chicken. Hope you like it." She put down the spatula and moved over to him. Placing her hands on his arms, she tiptoed to plant a kiss on his cheek. "I have some things to take care of in the other room. You two have it from here, right?"

Audra's mouth twisted with amusement. "No problem, Captain Obvious. We got it."

Shane chuckled, and Riley gave a finger wave as she left the room.

"What can I do?" Shane asked.

"Riley has the chicken simmering in the skillet. Keep an eye on that, please." Audra moved over to the sink and began snapping asparagus stems. "I'm on vegetable patrol. Don't do meat."

"You don't do meat at all?" He wiggled his brows. "Thanks for the head's up."

Audra's mouth twitched. "Not exactly what I meant."

"So, you're a vegetarian."

"No, I'll eat it once it's cooked, just can't stand to touch raw meat." She shuddered. "It's slimy and disgusting."

"But you're a nurse, and you touch God knows what every day. Probably more disgusting things than I've seen as a cop."

She waved a stalk of asparagus in the air. "I'm an enigma. What can I say?"

"Yeah. Well, I'm a cop. Figuring out enigmas is one of my hobbies." He winked, and her heart pitter pattered. She took a deep breath, switching her attention back to her task. Not a good idea to flirt with Shane. Not with the way her life had been going lately.

Just when she had her heart rate under control, he moved to stand beside her, close enough that she could smell the light, citrusy cologne he wore.

"How have you been?"

"I'm good. Everything's fine."

He rested his hand on her arm above her elbow. She turned to face him.

"You sure you're okay? No more threats? I've been worried about you."

She thought of the reapers. Would Shane consider that a threat? How would he handle it if he knew? How does one kill a reaper? Not easy to do, considering they were already dead.

"No more threats."

His hand gently slid down her arm until it gripped her fingers. His touch was warm and slightly rough. Manly. Alive. A tingle moved over her skin. Not the same as that otherworldly icy crackle Dimitri evoked, but the tingle was definitely there. What was happening here?

She took a moment to steady the mounting tension. Shane was attractive, but she hadn't really thought about him that way in a long time. He caught her gaze with his. The look in his eyes said he *had* thought of her that way.

She sighed. Now was a really bad time to start a relationship. Especially to rekindle an old flame that hadn't been a raging success the first time.

Her mind weighed the pros and cons for a few seconds, then she smiled up at him and squeezed his hand. What the hell. She had a couple of reapers hovering around her now.

Life was short.

Possibly getting shorter by the day.

****

Dimitri sat up on the edge of the mattress and retrieved his pants from the floor.

"Come back to bed," Veronica purred. "I wasn't finished with you."

"Can't." He didn't look at her as he dressed.

"So, you just use me and that's it? No cuddling?"

He glanced back to where she knelt, naked, on the bed, opening her legs just enough to expose her feminine flesh. Her auburn hair hung thick and luxurious over her shoulder, falling over one perfect breast, leaving the other exposed. She'd maneuvered her full red mouth into a sexy pout. Still, he had no desire to crawl back under the blankets with her. His libido didn't so much as stir, not the way it did every time he even *thought* of Audra.

Stir, hell, it practically did backflips. But looking at Veronica? Nothing. Nada. She was right. He was done. "I have somewhere to be."

"You weren't summoned. Neither of us was. Come on, Dimitri. Where do you have to be?" She reached out and gripped his shoulder with her claws, digging her nails into him.

Sometimes he wished reapers weren't solid to one another. Wished they were amorphous beings, like they were to humans.

"I said I have somewhere to be. You need to pack up. The Wilsons will be back from their vacation tomorrow."

"We could still stay here. It's kind of fun to hang out when a family occupies a house. Remember how we used to do that in the old days? Fuck with their lives?"

"That was then. I'm not into those games anymore."

"Yeah, you're not into a lot of things." She slid from the bed and stalked over to him. "Well, you're into *one* thing. But then, you've been into that for a while."

"What's that?" he asked, even though he didn't give a damn.

"That bitch, Audra."

His shoulders tensed, but he didn't respond.

"Now that you're in contact with her, your obsession will be out of control."

"Why the hell do you and Gaylen insist I'm obsessed with her?"

"Because you watch her every chance you get. You make sure that she, above all others, is protected."

"I'm doing my job."

"*Your job*. Right. That's all she is to you. That's why you've thought of nothing else for thirty years. Why your eyes spark like fireworks when her name is mentioned." She gripped his shoulder and turned him to face her. "I don't get it. You can't even touch her." Staring at him from under her lashes, she grazed her fingers over his chest. He moved her hand aside, buttoning his shirt to prevent access. "You can't feel her. Can't fuck her. She can't give you what I can."

"Knock it off, Veronica. I won't have this discussion with you."

He moved away, but she stopped him with a hand on his arm. "Don't make the mistake of thinking I'll always be around. There may come a time when I make you choose. Me or her."

He grinned and leaned in close, tapping her nose with his finger. "That, my dear, is an ultimatum you don't want to issue."

# Chapter 8

Bert Neufeld was Audra's least favorite patient. Maybe in her entire career. The man was rude, abrasive, and unclean. When he was admitted two days ago, an acrid, sour smell had emanated from him, as if he hadn't bathed in a week. She'd forced him into the shower that first night but, judging from the lack of improvement in his odor when he came out, she doubted he'd bothered to use soap. Since then, he'd refused to shower again. Now, he was refusing to go to the restroom.

"Mr. Neufeld," she said gently. "Let me help you to the bathroom. Your bowels haven't moved since yesterday."

"I'm a grown man, missy. I know when I gotta go, and I ain't gotta go."

He punched the remote over and over with his thumb. "Is that all the channels you got?" He flung the device, and it slung out on its coiled cord, then bounced back to hit the bedrails.

Audra took a deep breath. "Sorry. Just basic cable. That's it."

"The money I'm paying for this rat hole, you'd think you could at least have something decent on TV."

"Your insurance company is paying, Mr. Neufeld."

His face contorted in anger. "You better watch that smart mouth of yours. I'll have your job."

Her brows rose. “Somehow, I can’t picture you being a nurse, but if you really want my job, go for it.”

He lifted his upper body like he was going to leap at her, then settled back onto the bed, breathing hard. “You can’t talk to me like that. I’m in pain.”

A twinge of guilt pricked her, and she sighed. “I’m sorry. You’re right. Just please try to be a little more pleasant to the staff, okay? You had the aide, Wendy, in tears this morning.”

“Pleasant to the staff?” he bellowed. “Can’t you people understand I could die? You’d think I could get a little more sympathy.”

“You’re here for gall bladder surgery. I’m sure everything will be fine.” She tried to breathe through her mouth to keep from smelling him as she handed him his medications. “How about I get you in the shower again tonight so you’re feeling fresh and clean for surgery tomorrow?”

He swallowed the pills, then his gaze dropped to her breasts, and his mouth stretched into a leer. “How about you give me a sponge bath instead?”

The guilt fled and anger replaced it. Freakin’ pervert.

“Mr. Neufeld, if you insist on saying inappropriate things, I’ll ask to be removed from your care and replaced with a male nurse.”

“Ain’t no sissy man-nurse gonna come near me.” He paused, obviously mulling over her warning. Finally, reluctantly, he said, “I’ll behave.”

“Okay, one more chance then. Are you sure you don’t want me to help you to the bathroom before I go?”

“If I gotta go, I’ll go. I ain’t a baby.”

True. Babies were cute and easier to care for and smelled much better.

"Call if you need anything." As if she had to tell him that. The man constantly "needed" something.

Not five minutes after she returned to the nurse's station, the patient board lit with Mr. Neufeld's room number.

Kyle pressed the button. "Can I help you?"

Neufeld's voice came through the speaker. "I need you to send Audra back in here. I shit the bed."

"Are you kidding me?" Audra bit out, her blood pressure spiking. "I just begged him to let me help him to the bathroom."

She stalked down the hallway to deal with Mr. Neufeld. Entering his room, she flinched and held her breath at the nauseating odor. She just *thought* he couldn't smell any worse.

****

Barney roamed through the motel room, checking for any clue he'd been there. Nothing. He wasn't worried about fingerprints so much. Motels had more fingerprints than Ethiopia had hungry people. As long as he continued to keep his activities away from his home town, no one would ever know.

He surveyed the dead girl lying on the bed. Her red hair partially covered her face. The blanket rested just below small, pert breasts. Her brown eyes were closed now. He'd done that, given her that one last sign of dignity. He wasn't an animal, after all.

He sighed. Such a sweet young body. Shame he had to end her, but that was part of the pleasure. He chuckled. Who was he kidding? That *was* the pleasure. Not a damn thing they could do about it, either. They were all so weak, so fragile, so vulnerable.

Not innocent, no. Their innocence died the moment they took to the streets. Only a matter of time before the body followed. That was where he came in.

He experienced a moment of concern. The girl—Whitney? Winona? What was her name?—had been the second in four days. He usually tried to pace himself. His growing need could be a problem.

"No," he said in a whisper. "You leave no evidence. You're miles from home. They're only street girls. No one's even looking that hard. No pattern established since they're all in different towns. You're golden, my man."

He felt much better. It was nice to have friends. Nice when someone had your back. Someone you could always count on to reassure you.

He made one last sweep through the motel room, tugging a pair of gloves on before he touched the doorknob. He'd let the girl open the door coming in, but she couldn't help him with that little task now. That would be a place where fingerprints might get him. Forensics would focus there.

His head swiveled to the bed as he gave his latest achievement one last perusal. Then, he slipped out of the room and headed back to Boon Springs.

****

Audra slapped Neufeld's file on the desk. "Disgusting. The man is disgusting and hateful and piggish. I can't say I'll be sorry when he's gone."

"You shouldn't have cleaned him up," Tonya said, not lifting her head from the keyboard where she was charting patient notes. "Should have let him lay in his own filth all night."

"It would serve him right, but when Rosalie comes on, she'd have to deal with it." Audra picked up the card-ex notebook, flipping through, documenting orders that had been changed on her patients.

Tonya shrugged. "Better her than you."

Audra raised her head from the notebook, and something down the hall caught her attention. At first, she wasn't sure what it was. Nothing unusual that she could see; a few patients meandering along, hospital employees bustling about, performing their tasks by rote.

Then, she spotted something that was definitely out of the ordinary. A figure outside Mr. Neufeld's room. Entering without opening the door she'd shut behind her. Walking right through solid wood.

Fear seeped into her chest, growing into panic and settling in the pit of her stomach. She skirted the desk, starting down the hallway, her speed increasing to match her heartbeat. She barely heard, didn't acknowledge Tonya's shouted, "Hey, Audra! What's up? Everything okay?"

She reached Mr. Neufeld's room and entered—using the door like a normal person.

Only moments before, she'd wished the man gone. Now he was. But she hadn't meant it this way. His vacant stare pointed to the ceiling, his arms outspread, lying limp at his sides.

"Mr. Neufeld?"

No response. Although she didn't have to check to know, she rushed to the bed and pressed her fingers against his wrist, then to his neck.

Movement from the corner grabbed her attention.

Gaylen leaned against the wall, smiling, his golden

eyes feral with excitement. She opened her mouth to speak, but her throat froze, and no words came out. Didn't matter anyway. Gaylen gave her a wink, then faded through the wall.

Just like that.

He was gone.

****

Walnut pews upholstered in red and gold lined either side of the aisle of the large church auditorium. Inset into the walls, from floor to ceiling, were stained-glass windows depicting crosses, the Virgin Mary, and various other religious symbols.

A tall, slender man stepped gracefully off the stage and came toward Dimitri. Gray flecks like sprinkles of sugar glinted in his dark hair. A trimmed beard shadowed his black skin, broken by the smile that spread over his face.

"Dimitri. Welcome." He reached out a hand, and Dimitri took it in a firm shake.

"Good to see you, Samuel. When did you get into town?"

Samuel was the gate-keeper between the reaper world and beyond. He and Dimitri had known each other for over two-hundred fifty years, since the day Samuel had reaped him.

"I arrived a few days ago. Let's go to my office." He put a hand on Dimitri's arm and gestured toward the alcove.

*His* office wasn't entirely accurate. Samuel had acquisitioned the church as his dwelling. It was a wise choice. Other than an evening or two a week, and twice on Sundays, he had the place to himself.

Samuel offered him a drink, but Dimitri declined,

taking a seat across a wide oak desk while Samuel settled behind it.

"How have you been, my friend?" Samuel lit a cigar and leaned back in his chair.

"Not bad. But I doubt you called me here for chit chat. What's up?"

Samuel studied the smoldering tip of his cigar. "Just curious about some of the recent events. What's happening with the Grayson girl?"

Dimitri blew out a breath. "Oh, that."

"She can see you? You've spoken with her? You know how dangerous a development such as this can be."

"Of course I know. But the damage is done. She's one of those rare individuals with the ability to see us. She suffered a near death experience. I was there. Gaylen was there." He shrugged. "Well, I'm sure you can guess the rest."

"Yes. I can guess. Now the best we can do is damage control."

"I'm working on that."

Samuel tapped the ashes from his cigar in a crystal ashtray. "Will she tell others?"

"I don't think so." Audra didn't want to admit what was going on, even to herself. Didn't want to acknowledge Dimitri's existence. It was unlikely she'd share the news with anyone else.

Samuel narrowed his eyes, peering closely at Dimitri. "Tell me something. You, of all reapers, deserve your reward. Why do you continue to do things that only delay it?"

When a reaper broke the rules, time was added to their sentence. Dimitri's original hundred years had turned into three-hundred. “I haven’t in a long time.”

“True. But I see it coming with the girl, Audra.”

“No.” Dimitri shifted in his chair. “Not again.”

“You risked your life, your eternity, to save my wife and daughter. I haven’t forgotten that.”

“It was instinct.”

Samuel smiled. “No. It was bravery and morality. Maybe a little foolishness, too.”

Dimitri returned the smile. “Probably mostly that.”

“You’ve done everything you were called to do. I want you to finally get the peace you crave.”

“As do I.”

“Then keep that in mind. Even if the girl is in trouble. Remember, you’re not her protector.”

“I realize that. My only aim is to do my duty. Abide by the rules. Serve my sentence. Finally die and find peace.” He scrubbed his hands over his face. “I’m afraid we have a different matter to be concerned about. Gaylen’s behavior is spiraling out of control. His urges rule him.”

“Yes. And, unfortunately, he’s not the only unstable reaper prowling the area.”

“I’m staying on top of it.”

“You have less than fifty years left on your sentence. Don’t extend it trying to be a hero.”

“The last thing I intend is to be a hero.”

Samuel smiled and puffed on his cigar. “That’s the thing, my boy. A hero seldom intends to become one.”

****

Audra rushed toward the wall, hand outstretched. “Gaylen,” she whispered loudly. “Come back here. What have you done?”

She waited, but he didn’t reappear.

She turned back to the bed. Mr. Neufeld shouldn't have died. He was here for a routine surgery. Sometimes, things went wrong in surgery. Patients died from anesthesia, their heart stopped, surgeons made mistakes. But not this. Not a cantankerous, pain in the ass, pervert with a bad gall bladder just expiring for no reason.

Fucking reapers.

She pressed the emergency call button. Over the intercom, Kyle called out the Code Blue. In seconds, the code team was in the room, each with their own role to play in trying to revive Mr. Neufeld. The next few moments were a blur of feverish activity…fruitless activity.

Dr. Singh pronounced the patient dead, and the flurry slowed.

"Audra, are you all right?" he asked in his East Indian accent. He was her same height, making his dark brown eyes level with hers as he studied her. "You seem a little pale."

"I'm fine." She nodded jerkily, not trusting herself to say more, afraid she might blurt out that she knew who did it…that she'd seen the killer fade through the wall. "Fine," she said again, and hurried back to the nurses' station.

Kyle sat at the terminal, and Tonya leaned on the desk in front of him.

"He didn't make it," Audra told them.

"Seriously?" Kyle shook his head. "That's crazy, huh? Not a sign he was in distress."

"Not a sign." Audra's voice shook.

Tonya shrugged. "Couldn't happen to a more deserving guy."

"Tonya!" Kyle looked horrified. "That's cold. Even for you."

Barely aware of the conversation taking place around her, Audra said, "Listen, I've got to go check on…something. I'll be right back."

She'd have to speak with the charge nurse, fill out incident reports, all the usual procedures, but for now, she had to get some answers the forms couldn't provide.

"Are you okay?" Tonya asked.

"Yeah. I'm good. Thanks."

She backed away and headed down the hall, toward one of the empty patient rooms. As she passed her co-workers, they seemed to all be staring at her, wondering, accusing…

It was probably only her imagination, but she still let out a relieved breath when she reached her destination.

Once inside the unoccupied room, she shut the door. Keeping her voice low but forceful, she said, "Gaylen, can you hear me? I need to see you."

She didn't know if it worked like spirits or a magic genie or whatever, where you could call for them and they'd come. It was worth a shot.

"Gaylen! Please. I need to speak with you."

If he came, would he give her the answers she wanted? And, if he did, what then? If he told her he took Mr. Neufeld and there was nothing she could do about it. What would she do? What if he then said, *"And now, I'm going to take you…"*

She shuddered and wrapped her arms around her body. Dimitri said the person had to be in jeopardy. She was healthy. Recovered from her beating, and not even a cold at the moment. Gaylen surely couldn't hurt her. Not if Dimitri was telling the truth.

Dimitri…

Even if she couldn't reach Gaylen, Dimitri should have the answers she sought.

"Dimitri!" The shout came out a little louder than she planned. She looked at the closed door, which in itself would seem suspicious if anyone noticed. Maybe they'd think she just needed a few moments to herself.

Raising her voice, she again called out, "Dimitri! Where are you? I have to talk to you."

"What is it?"

She whirled. Dimitri stood a few feet behind her. He once more wore the leather jacket. His brow was drawn into a frown.

"Dimitri. You came."

"What's wrong?"

He moved closer, lowering his head to stare into her face. Her breath caught when the electric spark reached out to her.

"I didn't know how it worked," she murmured, her mouth suddenly dry. "I wasn't sure you'd hear me."

"Of course I heard you. You were yelling loud enough to wake the dead. No pun intended."

She didn't smile. "Gaylen. Do you know where he is?"

He shook his head. "Not at the moment. Did something happen?"

"Yes," she whispered. "My patient. Mr. Neufeld. I think Gaylen…killed him."

Dimitri reached a hand out as if to take hold of her arm. Although he couldn't physically touch her, somehow it seemed as though he did. His hand hovered near her elbow, and she let him lead her to one of the visitor's chairs. When she was seated, he took the other chair. Leaning forward, he rested his clasped hands between his knees.

"Tell me what happened." His voice was low, mesmerizing…soothing. Not what one would expect from a dealer of death.

"Mr. Neufeld was scheduled for gall bladder surgery tomorrow. Nothing life threatening. I was with him only moments before, and he was fine. Then…" She looked down to where her hands rubbed back and forth over her thighs. "I saw Gaylen. Outside my patient's room. He went in. Walked right through the door. By the time I got to him…"

"The man was dead."

She lifted her head and nodded. "Gaylen was standing there, looking…satisfied, happy even. He killed him, didn't he?"

Dimitri sighed and unclasped his hands. Resting an elbow on the arm of the chair, he rubbed his temple. "It seems so. I should have been there. I didn't know."

"You could have stopped him if you'd been there?" He nodded. "Then why weren't you? Can't you just follow him around? Make sure he doesn't do things like this?"

He grinned, dimples appearing briefly. "I can't just follow him around. For one, I have duties to perform. For another, I don't always know when he's up to his…shenanigans. Occasionally, I get a feeling…a premonition of sorts. Sometimes, I arrive just a few seconds behind, like at the mall, too late to stop him. There are times when I arrive ahead of him. In that case, he can't do anything, because another reaper is already there. But it's all just random and luck and timing. No pattern, no rules to follow, nothing I can do to ensure he doesn't continue taking souls before their time."

She wasn't entirely convinced he spoke the truth. Dimitri was a reaper, too. He took lives, just like Gaylen. But there was something different about Gaylen. He seemed to delight in what he did. Then again, maybe Dimitri did, too, but he was just better at hiding it.

"So, you get a sense when people are in jeopardy, and sometimes it's their time, but sometimes it's not? If it's not their time, you won't take them, but Gaylen will? If, however, their number's up, you have no qualms about ripping their souls from their bodies?"

His expression darkened. He sat forward so quickly, she thought he was going to lunge at her. She gasped and drew back.

"I told you. It's my job. I do what I'm here to do. If you refuse to understand, I can't make you." He stood. "I'll leave you to your duties, as I must attend to mine. You should be aware that I won't always be around when you're in trouble. You can't just fetch me any time you please."

She rose to her feet, keeping a non-electricity inducing distance between them. "But you came."

"Not because you called. I was in the vicinity." Another grin crossed his face, this one wicked. "You know, the job and all."

She didn't respond.

"Hey," He lifted his hands and shrugged. "It's what I do, right? Soul stealer extraordinaire. What can I say?"

He tipped his upper body slightly toward her in a mock bow and headed toward the wall.

He was leaving. By the same method Gaylen had used in Mr. Neufeld's room.

Walking through walls.

*Shit.* Was this really her world now?

"Dimitri?"

He paused, his shoulders squaring, but didn't turn around.

"I hate death."

He faced her, crossing his arms, his expression now amused instead of angry. "Not many humans list it on their top ten favorite things. It's one of those inconvenient realities of life. Everyone dies, Audra."

"I know. But I mean, since I was a little girl, I've hated death. Really hated it. Wanted to understand it, but at the same time, wanted to stop it. I've fought it my entire adult life."

"Hence your profession."

She nodded, staring down at the floor before raising her gaze to his. "When I was three, my mother died. She and I were alone in a cabin—we fled there when my father threatened to kill us—and my mother became ill."

Her mind went back to that time. Her mother lying on the floor…Audra shaking her shoulder, trying to wake her…crying when she wouldn't respond…begging, *Mommy, please. Please wake up!* Some of the memories were fuzzy, but the feeling was as crystal-clear as if it were happening now. Tears rose in her throat. She swallowed them back, but her voice was still hoarse when she continued. "I was in the cabin with her dead body for three days before we were found. I didn't really know what was happening, but I knew my mother was gone and would never come back."

Dimitri's eyes narrowed, became glittering slits between dark lashes. "I'm sorry. That must have been horrible."

"*Death* is horrible," she said quietly. "So I hope you'll understand why I don't think much of your *duty*. Why—whether it's Gaylen, you, or some other reaper I've yet to meet—death is death. And it sucks."

She didn't wait for a response. She walked out of the room, not bothering to watch him fade through the wall. She'd been away too long. If she wasn't careful, the staff would think she was up to no good. Maybe killing another patient.

Who else could they blame?

Because, she couldn't tell anyone the truth. Couldn't tell them her life had been invaded by a couple of Grim Reapers whose sole purpose was to create havoc, end lives, devastate those left behind as they barreled through the world, carrying out their lethal tasks—minus the black robe and scythe—but just as chillingly evil.

****

Audra had never needed a drink more than she did after work that night. Between the paperwork, the interview with Mary Lou, and speaking to Mr. Neufeld's family, her shift ended much later than planned. Finally, she was free to leave the hospital. She headed straight to the bar down the street.

The Red Door was crowded, mostly with hospital employees. She should have chosen a different place. Somewhere she wouldn't be known. So she could drink in peace.

She settled wearily onto a barstool. “Hey, Ron. Can I get a Chardonnay?”

“Sure,” he said, congenially enough, but his face was set in forbidding lines. He didn’t offer his usual friendly smile.

“You okay?” she asked.

His eyes locked onto hers, and he smirked. “Finally, someone is asking me. You know, it never seems to occur to people that bartenders might have problems, too.”

The anger in his tone unnerved her. There was something a little off about his expression. A faraway light in his eyes. A *creepy* light. She shivered.

“I’m sorry,” she said. He set the glass in front of her, and she took a grateful sip of the wine. “If you want to talk about it, I’ll listen.”

“Nah. It’s okay. You wouldn’t understand. You seem troubled, though. Why don’t you tell me what’s got you so upset?”

She shrugged. “Nothing. I’m fine.”

“Ah, come on. Tell the bartender your problems.” He backed away and spread his arms wide, as if in invitation, his voice rising to a shout. “After all, I’m just one big, fucking cliché.”

She glanced over her shoulder. A few puzzled looks were cast their way, but Mariah Carey bellowing from the jukebox mostly drowned out his words.

As Audra was about to turn back around, she spotted a young girl sitting at a table alone. A *very* young girl. She considered telling Ron, but the mood he was in, he might rough the child up for daring to enter his bar underage.

The waitress, Shanda, came over and cast a worried glance at Ron. Shanda was tall and lithe, with dirty-blonde corn rolls and piercings in her lip, eyebrow, and tongue. She also had large breasts and emerald eyes and somehow made the whole 'look' work.

"I'm sorry," she said to Audra. "Was he an asshole to you?"

"He wasn't his usual jovial self."

"It's my fault. We were seeing each other. I dumped him."

"Ouch."

"Yeah. Working together now is a real treat."

"He doesn't seem to be taking it very well."

Shanda gathered empty glasses in her fingers and tiptoed to set them on the sink behind the bar. "Didn't help matters that the guy I'm seeing is a doctor. Ron thinks I dumped him because my new guy is successful, and he's just a lowly bartender." She called out, "Two drafts and a whiskey sour," then grinned at Audra. "Truth is. My new guy is hung like a friggin' stallion."

Audra managed a grin. She peeked back over her shoulder at the teen who sat sipping on a straw from a glass of something that didn't look like fruit juice. Why had Shanda served her? Maybe she and Ron were too wrapped up in their *Young and Restless* drama to pay attention.

Ron slammed the glasses on Shanda's tray. She grimaced before picking up the drinks and disappearing in the crowd.

Audra slid from the barstool and headed to the girl's table.

"Hi," Audra said.

The girl lifted her head. "Hey."

Smooth skin, blonde hair with fuchsia highlights, large, round blue eyes. Pretty. And young, just as Audra suspected. No more than sixteen or seventeen.

Audra lowered into the chair across from her. "How old are you?" she said in a loud whisper.

"Seventeen. You?"

Audra ignored the question. "How did you get in here? How did you get that drink?"

"I snatched it off the bar." The girl shrugged. "People don't pay much attention to me."

"Maybe not yet, but they'll notice, and you'll be in all kinds of trouble." Audra glanced around the bar. "Not to mention the likelihood that one of these guys will take advantage of you. What's your name?"

"Cassie."

"Cassie, I'm Audra. You really need to get out of here, need to go home. I don't want you leaving on your own. Tell me where you live, and I'll take you."

At her hesitation, Audra pulled out her hospital ID. "I'm a nurse. I work at St Anne's, just down the street. You're safe with me. I just don't want to see you hurt or in trouble."

Cassie studied her like she might study a difficult math problem in school. "You're a really, really nice person, aren't you? How did you get that way?"

Audra blinked in confusion. "Excuse me? How did I get that way?"

"I mean, the world is a pretty mean place. It's easier to survive if you're mean too. But you're not. What made you the way you are?"

Audra frowned. Not the conversation she'd expect from an underage lawbreaker.

"I don't know exactly how to answer that. But let's talk about getting you home."

"Hey, pretty lady, how about a dance?" The voice came from behind Audra.

She looked up to find a large, looming, hairy man hovering over her. A T-shirt with a headless stick figure and the words *Need Head* stretched over his big belly. A tattoo of a dagger on his neck was partially hidden beneath his thick beard.

"No, thank you." She turned away from him.

He moved over to stand next to her, too close, making her feel smothered, even in an overcrowded, smoky bar. "Aw, come on. If not a dance, maybe we can just get to know each other. Is this seat taken?" He pointed to Cassie's chair.

"Is it taken?" Cassie was sitting in the chair. Was he so drunk he couldn't see?

His teeth flashed amidst a thatch of unkempt facial hair. "You're a pretty little thing, but dumb as a bag of rocks. And not even blonde." He held out his hands as if in surrender. "No offense now, I like my women dumb. I think me and you will get along just fine."

Cassie said, "Jesus. I bet you do prefer your women dumb. That's the only way you can get laid."

Audra expected him to spring at the girl and spew some poetic line, maybe something like, *"How about I show you another use for that smart mouth of yours, little girl?"* before he knocked her across the room.

Instead, he acted as though she hadn't said a word.

"I been watching you," he told Audra. "No need to sit over here and talk to yourself all lonely and shit when I'm right here. So, can I sit or not?"

Audra glanced at the girl. Cassie jabbed a finger in

her open mouth and simulated gagging.

The guy leaned in close to Audra. "I tell you what, instead of sitting, how about me and you go find someplace quiet?"

"Oh, brother." Cassie rolled her eyes. "This asshole's a real piece of work."

Audra tensed, waiting for his reaction. Sasquatch didn't blink.

"I don't want…you need to…" Audra trailed off, her mind racing.

Something was off here. The guy thought Audra was talking to herself? He acted like the girl wasn't even there. Like he didn't even see her.

*Didn't even see her…*

Audra's eyes widened, and she jerked her gaze to Cassie. "Fuck me," she whispered. "You're a reaper."

## Chapter 9

"What was that?" The guy squinted into Audra's face. "I get the 'fuck me' part. I'm all about that. What the fuck else did you say?"

Audra's heart galloped, and she struggled to breathe as she stared at Cassie. She didn't know why meeting her was such a shock. Reapers had become almost commonplace in her life. But somehow, this young, innocent-looking girl being a reaper was unsettling. Tragic.

"Hey, are you deaf or just stupid?" The asshole again. "I asked what you said."

Audra found her voice, speaking without looking at the man. "Nothing. Just go away. You're starting to piss me off."

"Piss *you* off? You ain't seen pissed off. And I ain't going away. You just said 'fuck me,' and I ain't never turned down no offer like that."

A male voice from somewhere above Audra's head said, "You're turning it down now, pal. Get lost."

Audra looked up to find Ron standing next to Sasquatch. He grinned sheepishly and set her wine glass in front of her. "Sorry about earlier. I'll get rid of this guy. I think dealing with one dickhead this evening was enough for you. I'm just in a piss-ass mood. Shouldn't have taken it out on you."

"No problem." She smiled gratefully.

“Oh, well ain’t this just the sweetest thing.” Sasquatch bunched his fists and put his nose nearly against Ron’s. “You just move along, fuckface. I got this.”

Ron reached out so quickly, Audra didn’t know he’d moved. Neither did Sasquatch, until Ron had his testicles in his grip. The man cried out, his face coloring a deep shade of red. Audra glanced around, but no one seemed aware of the testosterone-laden demonstration.

“Listen, *fuckface*.” Ron’s jaw tightened as he spoke into Sasquatch’s ear. “I haven’t always been a bartender. I was in Special Forces, and I can do things to you that would make you go crying to your momma. I’ve had a very bad week. So don’t fuck with me. Got it?”

“Got it,” Sasquatch whimpered through clenched teeth.

Ron released him. “Now, let’s let this lady enjoy the rest of her evening. She wants to drink alone. I think it’s time you head on home.”

The man nodded jerkily and lurched away, holding his hands to his crotch.

“Thanks.” Audra smiled up at Ron.

He gave her a little salute and returned to his post behind the bar.

*Drink alone,* he’d said. He hadn’t seen the girl either. No wonder she’d gotten away with being in a bar.

When Audra spoke, she barely moved her lips, so that people around them wouldn’t think she was talking to herself. “Another reaper. Exactly what I needed. Why are you here?”

Cassie shrugged. “We heard about the chick who

could see us. I wanted to check it out for myself. You really can."

"That's just awesome." Audra barked out a sarcastic laugh. "Now I'll be inundated with reapers."

"No. Probably not. I'm a newbie. Still in training. The others are less curious. They'll do their job. Most of them will leave you alone." Cassie leaned forward and sipped from her straw. At least she wasn't *lifting* the drink. Audra was already talking to herself, the last thing she needed was a levitating bar glass.

"Should you be drinking at your age?" Audra asked.

"It's not really an issue. Reapers can mimic human activities, but the effects—pleasure, pain, discomfort, all that stuff—are dulled. We can't quite experience things like humans can. Besides, who the fuck cares? You think I might get in trouble with the cops? My parents?" She looked away, and Audra caught the shimmer of tears in her eyes. "They didn't give a fuck about me when I was alive. Wouldn't now, either."

In spite of being one of the walking dead, the girl was also a troubled teen. Audra reached out to place a hand over hers but drew back. She'd almost forgotten. She couldn't touch her.

"I'm sorry," she whispered. "I know what it's like to have a bad childhood."

That wasn't entirely true. Thanks to Jaxon's parents, she'd mostly had a good childhood. Good, that is, if you didn't count the 'watching her mother die as a toddler and occasional visits by her abusive, sociopath father' thing.

Cassie blinked rapidly, trying not to cry. "Sorry. I didn't appear to you just so I could get all Emo and stuff. I'm okay now."

"Cassie, listen. No offense, but I'm not sure I can deal with another reaper just yet. I kind of have my hands full with the two I've got now."

"You don't want me around?" Her large blue eyes were bright with unshed tears.

Shame washed over Audra. The girl had probably been kicked around enough in life, Audra didn't need to continue the cycle of rejection in death. But, for shit's sake, she couldn't handle much more of the supernatural drama her world had become.

"It's not that. It's just…"

"Don't worry. I'm not going to cause any problems." She stared sullenly into her glass. "I wanted to talk to you about Dimitri."

"What about him?"

Cassie leaned forward, spreading her hands on the tabletop. Her nails were sparkling purple, the tips painted white.

Fleetingly, Audra wondered if her nails had been that way when she died, or if there was some kind of reaper nail shop, maybe a full-service beauty salon with the slogan, *Just because you're dead, doesn't mean you have to look it.*

"Dimitri's good," Cassie went on, interrupting Audra's flight of absurdity. "Trust me. He's like…a legend in our world."

"You must be desperate for legends in the beyond."

Cassie grinned. "Come on, you like him. If you don't, trust me, you will. He's kind of hard to resist."

"I don't find it all that difficult to resist someone who brings death wherever he goes."

Audra took a sip of her wine, glancing around to

see if any suspicious glances were being cast her way. Her eyes fell on a familiar figure sitting on a barstool. A brown ponytail hung down her back, and she wore black scrubs. Audra could just make out the profile, a sharp nose and non-existent chin. *Shit.* Mary Lou. Earlier, Mary Lou had mentioned that her daughter, Camellia, was with her father for the weekend. Her mother probably couldn't stand to go home to an empty house, so she'd come here instead. *Lovely.*

Right now, Mary Lou's attention was on the album she held as she flipped through pages—pages that no doubt held photos of her darling daughter. Ron was her captive audience, and the poor man's expression was that of someone being tortured. Although he'd rescued Audra earlier, she wasn't about to return the favor. She hoped Mary Lou would stay occupied long enough that she wouldn't notice her. Or, at least wouldn't notice that she was 'talking to herself.' Audra certainly didn't need that noted on her recent incident reports.

She pulled her attention back to the conversation, keeping an eye on Mary Lou in her peripheral.

"It's not like that. Dimitri doesn't *bring death.*" Cassie scowled and shook her head. "If it wasn't him, it would be someone else. Death is inevitable."

"So, why all this gushing over the guy? Is he your…" She'd been about to say *lover*. That was just wrong. Sick and wrong. The child wasn't even eighteen. Audra didn't want to know if that were the case. Besides, could reapers take lovers? Only with each other, obviously, but could they even do that?

"Dimitri's my trainer," Cassie said. "He's teaching me how to reap."

"How to reap? It's not just an inborn thing like

eating, sleeping, using a computer?"

She giggled. "No. Before you decide if you want to become a reaper instead of meeting whatever fate waits for you on the other side, they make you go with them to see if you can handle it. It's tough. The people…" Her face took on a faraway expression, and she shuddered. "They don't wanna go. It takes time to learn how to coax them, how to make them feel safe."

"So…Gaylen trains reapers, too? Jesus. That's scary."

"No. He's outside the rules. Since he takes people before their time, the ones he takes aren't given an option to become a reaper. They just go to their destiny. If a soul *is* given the option to become a reaper, they're trained by the reaper who took them. And the only way they'll be given the option is if they have something to atone for, and if they are judged to be redeemable." She shrugged and scrunched her nose. "It's a lot to learn. I still don't understand all of it."

"You said you're a newbie. When did you…die?"

Her face paled. A flash of fear lit in her eyes, then disappeared. "A week ago."

Audra started to ask how, but the look on Cassie's face said it wouldn't be a pretty story. Searching for something else to say, she chose, "I'm sorry you died," and realized she'd never had the opportunity to say that before. Never dreamed she would.

Cassie shrugged. "I'm just glad it was Dimitri. It's his job to reap, but he makes it almost…peaceful. My mom and dad used to beat the crap out of me, then I ran away. I was on the streets when I died." She cleared her throat and knuckled tears from the corners of her eyes, then looked solemnly at Audra. "When Dimitri took me? That was the gentlest anyone has ever treated me in my life."

****

At home the next evening, Audra sat at her dining room table with Sadie in the chair facing her.

"Be still," Audra coaxed the wiggling child as she spread white Halloween paint over Sadie's face. She added black circles around her eyes and streaks of red around her mouth, then dripped it to her chin to give the illusion of oozing blood.

Sadie was going to a Halloween party tonight, and her parents were working late. Audra had volunteered to pick her up from school and help her get ready. She was glad to have something to occupy her mind. Since last night, she'd thought of nothing but Cassie, the dead girl who wasn't a whole lot older than Sadie. Audra pushed the thought aside and finished Sadie's make up by shading the hollows of her cheekbones in with black.

She drew back and looked at the results. "Are you sure you want to be a zombie?"

Sadie nodded vigorously, her infantile exuberance and pinchable, cherubic features in stark contrast to the grotesque costume. "Do I really look like a zombie?"

Audra studied her, from her painted face to the tattered, red-splotched clothing she wore. "You definitely look like a zombie."

"Do you think they'll be scared? Sadie asked. "I bet they'll know it's me." Her eyes widened, giving her a clownish yet fearsome look. "Or maybe they won't. Do you think I can fool 'em? Then they *will* be scared."

"You don't want to scare your friends, Sadie. That's not very nice."

"But it's fun to be scared."

"Not for all kids. You're a bit…different."

Sadie frowned. "Will they be mad at me?"

"No. Just make sure they know it's you. Don't scream and growl at them like a zombie."

"Zombie's really don't make noises. They just sort of go…" Sadie stuck her arms out in front of her and made unintelligible grunts and groans.

"Eeew," Audra's reaction was exaggerated for Sadie's benefit, but she had to admit, the child had created an image that was a little creepy. Her schoolmates would definitely freak. "Yeah. Don't do that, okay?"

"Okay, but that's how zombies go."

Audra laughed and tweaked Sadie's chin.

The doorbell rang as she was ratting Sadie's hair into something resembling the tangled coif of the undead.

"That must be your parents. Go look at yourself in the mirror while I get the door."

Audra headed to the door to let Brent and Riley in.

Brent halted when he saw his daughter. "Good God, Sadie. Are you sure you want to go to a party like that?"

"Yep. I look like a real zombie."

"You certainly do." Brent adjusted his wire frame glasses farther up his nose. Pushing the edges of his suit jacket back, he rested his hands on his hips. "Just like a zombie."

Riley pursed her lips. "Sadie, honey. I don't know…"

"Please, Momma? My recital costume isn't scary at all. Just let this one be scary, okay?"

Riley hesitated a moment, then sighed and shook

her head. "Okay." She turned to Audra. "Am I raising a little serial killer?"

Audra shrugged. "Have any of the neighborhood animals gone missing?"

Riley scowled. "Jesus, Audra."

Brent chuckled. "It's all harmless fun. You worry too much." He picked Sadie up and carefully placed a kiss on her make-up smeared cheek.

She pulled back and looked at his mouth, giggling. "You have white on your lips."

"It's all your fault." Brent tickled her, and she squealed with laughter. "Speaking of recitals." He put Sadie down and turned to Riley. "When is it?"

"The twenty-eighth. I told you that weeks ago. You're supposed to take her."

"I can't. Our CEO is bringing a client into town. We're taking him to dinner."

"But, Brent, I have that fundraising dinner Judge Smithson is hosting. I'll be finished in time to make it to the recital, but not to get Sadie ready and to the auditorium."

"I can help," Audra interjected. "I'll get her ready and take her to the recital. You two can just come when you're done."

"Thanks, Audra," Riley said. "But it's her father's responsibility. He promised." She lifted her chin and glared at him.

"Bullshit. You know how important my job is. I'm up for a promotion, and if I blow off this dinner, there's no way I'll get it." He loosened his tie and ran his hands through his hair. "Dammit."

"Watch how you talk in front of Sadie," Riley admonished.

"Jesus. She watches horror movies and dresses like demented monsters. I don't think swearing is exactly going to damage her."

Sadie's head tilted back as she looked from her mother to her father. Her bottom lip quivered. "Stop fighting. Aunt Audra can take me."

"Yes. I'll take her, and I'll record it in case you two don't make it for the whole thing," Audra said.

Brent glared down at Sadie. "She's not your aunt. She's your mother's friend. That's it." He whirled on Audra. "She's *our* daughter not yours. We don't need you always stepping in and taking over. Riley is going to take her. If you want a kid to dote on, get your own."

Audra recoiled in surprise. Brent could be an ass, but he'd never talked to her that way before.

"Brent!" Riley shouted. "Stop it. Audra doesn't deserve that."

"Well, it's true." Apparently not finished, he turned back to Audra. "Here's a little piece of advice. Next time, go for a guy who isn't, I don't know, gay? Then maybe you could have a kid of your own and leave ours for us to raise."

Riley covered Sadie's ears and in a sharp whisper, bit out, "Asshole. Half the time, I don't know what we'd do without Audra. You apologize right now."

"No," Audra said. Inside, she was seething, but she wouldn't cause a scene in front of Sadie. "He's right. I shouldn't butt in. I mean, I crossed a line by offering to help you guys."

She smiled with feigned sweetness at Brent. His expression went from irritation to embarrassment. Apparently, he hadn't missed the sarcasm.

"Is Daddy mad at Aunt Audra?" Sadie asked,

pulling Riley's hands from her ears.

Brent sighed and closed his eyes. "No, honey. Daddy's cranky. It's not Aunt Audra's fault." He looked at Audra, lifting his brows. "That was uncalled for. I'm sorry."

"It's okay, really," she said.

Unfortunately, there was some truth in Brent's statement. Yes, she wanted a child of her own. But, at thirty years old, with not even a boyfriend, and still carrying a torch for her ex-husband, the prospects were dwindling.

****

Without knocking, Dimitri walked through the front door of the house Gaylen had commandeered.

When he was only a few steps inside, Gaylen strolled into the foyer. "So, I see you've found me. How did you manage that?"

"Word gets around."

"Of course. Just as I found you. No secrets in the reaper world." He turned and lifted a hand, motioning for Dimitri to follow. "Come. See my humble abode. I won't be the ungracious host you were."

Dimitri followed him into a room the size of a concert hall, with expensive but tasteless antique furnishings. The windows were covered in velvet green draperies, making the room dark, other than the glow from a brass lamp.

Dimitri squinted, moving over to an end table that held a marble statuette of the goddess Aphrodite.

"This looks familiar." He lifted it and turned it over. Engraved on the bottom was a scrawled 'S' with a diagonal line across it.

"It should look familiar. It belonged to you."

Dimitri's brows rose, and he turned to face Gaylen. "You're kidding me, right?"

"You don't remember it?"

Dimitri set it back down. "No. Not at all. I recognize the Sarantos crest, but not the figurine."

"Of course you wouldn't. You had so much. One little bauble would go unnoticed. Strange, isn't it? A family heirloom surviving all these years. Ending up in the possession of an elderly recluse in Boon Springs, Oklahoma. Now belonging to me. The irony. Who'd have thought a poor servant boy could come so far?"

"Speaking of elderly recluse." Dimitri glanced around, looking for signs a human lived in the house. "I don't suppose the homeowner is still alive and healthy."

Gaylen grinned and moved over to stand in front of the fireplace. "No. No, he's not. But, in my defense, he wasn't *healthy* when I met him. Alive, yes. Healthy, no."

"So you killed him for his house."

Gaylen's shoulders lifted in a laconic shrug. "I've killed for less. You know how much I enjoy indulging my hobby."

"I do. That's why I'm here. You took Audra's patient."

"Is that a question?"

"Think of it more as a warning. Stay away from her and her patients."

"Exactly what are you going to do if I don't?"

Dimitri shot across the room until he was nose to nose with Gaylen. Emphasizing the warning with his eyes, he said, "I'll make you wish you'd chosen Hell over being a reaper."

Gaylen gave a mock shudder. "When you go all

macho like that it gives me goose bumps."

Dimitri grabbed him by the shirt and slammed his head against the mantel. A loud cracking sound gave him a rush of satisfaction. Gaylen grunted, and his eyes glazed.

"I might not be able to kill you," Dimitri bit out. "But I can make you wish for death."

Gaylen shoved him away, the sudden movement catching Dimitri off-guard. He stumbled back, and Gaylen pounced on top of him. Dimitri's breath whooshed out as he landed on the hardwood floor.

Gaylen slammed his fist into Dimitri's face once, then twice, then a third time. Pain exploded in his jaw. His eyes watered, and his vision blurred. Before Gaylen could land another blow, he landed one of his own, striking out blindly, but making contact.

Gaylen howled, and the punches ceased. Twisting abruptly, Dimitri threw Gaylen off him then leapt to his feet.

As Gaylen struggled to rise, Dimitri dove into him, knocking him against the wall. While he was still dazed, Dimitri gripped a handful of his shirt collar and pulled him upright, balling his fist and upper-cutting his chin over and over. Gaylen's head knocked into the wall with each blow.

Lifting his arms to shield his face, Gaylen panted, "I give. Enough already."

Dimitri elbowed him in the gut, and he doubled over. Bending until he was level with Gaylen's stooped posture, Dimitri spoke into his ear. "Don't ever try me again. You won't catch me unaware a second time. I'll crush you."

Gaylen nodded, gasping as he struggled to draw air

into his lungs. When he recovered enough to breathe, he straightened and looked at Dimitri with a glare of something that went beyond hatred and a desire for revenge, some simmering rage that festered like an infected wound. If Dimitri weren't the stronger of the two, Gaylen would beat the holy shit out of him. The expression on his face said he resented like hell that he couldn't.

Still gasping, Gaylen said, "You can't blame me. For the Audra thing, that is."

"Can't blame you?"

"I'm trying to get her attention." Gaylen's breath was returning to normal, and he tugged at his shirt, smoothing it, then ran his fingers along his eyebrow where a knot was already forming. "You pack quite a punch."

In moments, Gaylen's pain would recede, as would Dimitri's. He didn't let on, but his jaw and spine hurt like a son of a bitch. "Getting her attention? By killing her patient?"

Gaylen shrugged, and the cocky belligerence was back. "You flirt your way, I'll flirt mine. Come on, man. I just want to taste her breath. You understand. You want it too."

Moving in on Gaylen again, Dimitri said, "Last time you tasted a human's breath it didn't turn out so well, did it? Not for the girl and almost not for you."

Gaylen scowled, apparently not liking the reminder of his near demise. Fifty years ago, he'd turned human to taste a woman's breath. He'd kept taking and taking until she lay dead at his feet. Before he was able to turn reaper again, her husband came home and found him standing over his wife's body. The man shot Gaylen, and he'd nearly died. Unfortunately, he turned back to reaper form before he did. If he'd died while in human form, he'd have been dead forever, and Dimitri wouldn't have to worry about him.

"That's ancient history," Gaylen said. "I think I have an idea that will take care of both our problems."

"I'm not interested in your ideas."

"Hear me out, okay?" Gaylen held up his hands and backed away. "But give me some room, would you? I know you were my mentor. We share a special bond, but I can only take so much intimacy."

"That bond was broken the second you went rogue, asshole."

"Ah, yes. That sort of thing tends to drive a wedge between even the best of friends." Gaylen walked over to stand behind the bar. "Would you like a drink? You're a scotch man, right?"

"I don't want anything from you, except for you to leave Audra and her patients alone."

"Right. Which brings me back to my idea. How about if I promise you to not only leave Audra's patients alone, but to stop reaping anyone who's not ready?"

Dimitri's brows drew together, but he didn't speak.

"I see I have your attention."

"What do you want from me?"

"Audra."

"Audra? Are you out of your mind?"

"Hear me out." Gaylen tilted a decanter and poured a golden-hued liquor into his glass. "You let me have Audra. Let me taste her breath. If you do, I swear, I will never reap another soul that's not FDA-approved."

"*Right.*" Dimitri grunted. "For one, I would never

trust you to keep your word. For two, there's no way I'd sacrifice Audra to you, you demented piece of shit."

"I swear I'm sincere. I will go in front of Samuel. Revoke my reaping abilities. He can fit me with copper shackles."

Dimitri's brows rose. Copper was debilitating to a reaper. In ancient times, copper coins were used to prevent the soul from leaking out through the eyes—or being reaped—copper more or less contained a reaper, acting as an immobilizer for whatever length of time it was applied.

"You really want her that badly?" Dimitri said.

The skin on Gaylen's face tightened, and his eyes lit with frenzied hunger. "I do. Desperately. But you know I can't have her without turning human. And that, I would never do again. Not unless you were bound where you couldn't kill me. You could bind yourself in copper and let me turn human just long enough to taste her breath. If you're worried I'd kill her, I swear to you I wouldn't."

"You can't possibly think I'll even consider your diabolical nonsense."

He waved his hand dismissively. "Come on, it's a no-brainer for you. You'd get your wish, and I would no longer be such a thorn in your side." He waited a beat, then said, "I tell you what, I'll even let you have a taste of her. Come on, it'll be just like what Adam did in order to have Eve. Giving in to temptation for a beautiful woman."

Dimitri grunted. "Yeah, and you see how that turned out."

Gaylen lifted his glass in a mock salute. "Adam tells me it was worth it."

In spite of himself, Dimitri grinned. “Fuck you. You never met Adam.”

Gaylen chuckled. “So, you do have a sense of humor somewhere amidst all that tiresome angst. You know, if you weren’t such a tedious perfectionist, we might have been friends.”

“And if you weren’t a psychotic asshole, I might not have to kill you.”

Gaylen shrugged. “Who kills who still remains to be seen.”

“Yes, I suppose it does. Since you’re willing to become human, let’s go right now. You and me. Man to man.”

Gaylen stared at him for a moment, as if considering, then shook his head. “Another time, perhaps. For now, we have a proposal to discuss.”

“Copper shackles? You’re really serious.”

“I want Audra worse than I’ve ever wanted anything in my life…or death.” He rattled the ice in his now empty glass and set it down on top of the bar. “Of course, I know you feel the same. Now is the test of whether you’re really a selfless hero. What will it be, Dimitri? Will you risk sacrificing the woman you love to save the lives of countless others?”

## Chapter 10

After they left, Audra wandered aimlessly around her house for a while, then plopped down on the couch. She turned on the television and found an MLB playoff game. The National league, Reds against Cardinals, in the fifth game of a tied series. Damn. How could she forget about the playoffs? Right now, the Reds were up two-nothing over the Cardinals. She'd only missed a couple of innings. She still had time to enjoy plenty of the game. But then again, the Reds still had time to get their butts kicked.

Two innings later, the doorbell rang, and she groaned in frustration. The Sullivans had provided all the company she could handle for one evening. She didn't particularly want to see anyone else.

When she recognized Shane through the peephole, she amended that a tad. Shane was the one person she didn't mind seeing at all.

She opened the door and smiled. "Hello, Shane. Come in."

"Thanks. I'm sorry to drop by like this." His handsome face was set in bleak lines, and her heart squeezed with fear.

"Is something wrong?"

"No, well, there's always something wrong when you're in my line of work." He gave her a weary grin.

"I'm sure you know the feeling."

"I do. So, tell me, what's up? No one's hurt are they?"

Shane shook his head. "Mind if I sit down?"

"Sure. Sorry." She led him into the living room. Picking up the remote, she muted the television, and she and Shane settled on opposite ends of the couch. "What's going on?"

He pursed his lips and blew out a breath. "There have been a couple of murders in the past few weeks."

Her eyebrows rose. "In Boon Springs?"

"No. One in Tulsa and another in Broken Arrow." His mouth compressed. "Both young girls. Teenage runaways. Looks like the same guy. Law enforcement in both towns contacted me. They wanted to check to see if we had any similar crimes."

"They think it's a serial killer?"

"It appears that way." He frowned. "I want you to be extra careful. Even though the MO is nothing like what happened to you, and the killings took place several miles away, it concerns me. We haven't caught the guys who hurt you. I just want to make sure you're okay."

"Yeah. Sure. Everything's fine."

"Nothing else has happened? Nothing unusual at all that made you even a little afraid?"

"No. Nothing."

He scrutinized her as if she were a clue he had to decipher. "You would tell me if it did, right?"

"Of course." Except for the reapers, that is. After all, who would believe her if she told them? Shane would think she was crazy.

"I mean, not so I can protect you, but so I can up

my solve ratio. I'm Super Cop, you know. Can't have an unsolved on my record."

"So," she said skeptically. "If you don't solve this, it will be the only unsolved on your record?"

"Not by a long shot." He smiled. "But, I like to keep the image, you know?"

She smiled back. "I get you. I'll do my best to stop being a victim of unsolved crimes. For the sake of your career."

"I appreciate that."

A few seconds of awkward silence followed, then Shane stood. "Well, guess I'd better go. Didn't mean to interrupt your evening." He pointed to the TV. "You're a baseball fan?"

"I am. You don't remember that from high school?"

"Not really. I guess I was thinking of other things." He waggled his eyebrows, and she laughed.

"You want to stay and watch?" she asked. "I could make us tea or coffee."

"Coffee sounds great. You sure?"

Her spirits lifted. "Absolutely."

"Need some help?"

"I got it. You stay and keep me posted on the score."

Audra went into the kitchen and brewed two cups of Keurig coffee. When she returned, she handed Shane a mug and settled on the couch beside him.

"You like the Reds?" she asked.

"I do. Became a fan after I moved out there. Since Oklahoma doesn't have a major league team, I was always a Rangers fan. Thought I was supposed to be, since they were the closest team."

"I've always liked the Reds. Love their legacy with the whole Pete Rose, Johnny Bench, Big Red Machine era," Audra said. "Now, *that* was baseball."

"You weren't even born back then."

"I know. But Jaxon's dad and I watched baseball together, and he told me all about it. We watched old highlights. Felt like I was there. Jaxon didn't take to baseball, so I was sort of Hank's substitute son."

Shane grinned. "The whole not liking sports thing should have clued you in before you married him."

Her gaze flew to his face. "You know?"

"That Jaxon's gay? Most people do, in spite of his efforts to be discreet. You knew before you married him, right?"

She nodded. "I did know, but I thought I could give him a chance at the life he thought he wanted. The life his parents wanted him to have. I'm sorry I hurt you in the process."

He blew out a breath and frowned. "It was a long time ago. Don't worry about it."

Although they were speaking about their failed relationship, the expression on his face said he was thinking about something more troubling.

She peered closely at him. "There's something more, isn't there? You look like you're carrying the weight of the world. Is it the murders?"

"Those, and that I can't get a lead on the men who attacked you. They're still out there. I don't like it."

"You know what? They haven't hurt anyone else. You were right before. Probably just drifters who are long gone. Don't beat yourself up over it."

"Maybe," he said quietly.

A shadow of pain came into his eyes, and she put

her hand on his. "Besides, it looks like you're already beating yourself up over something else." His gaze shifted away from her, and he didn't speak. "I see a lot of pain in you. I heard something happened in Cincinnati that made you come back here. Almost made you stop being a cop."

He shrugged. "Cops deal with a lot of bad situations."

"In other words, you don't want to talk about it."

He looked down to where her hand still rested on his. "More like, you don't want to hear about it. Trust me on that one."

"I do. I want to help if I can."

"Thanks, but there's nothing you can do." He took a drink of the coffee, surreptitiously unseating her touch. "You like me, right?"

"I like you very much."

"Then it's best we don't talk about it. Wouldn't want your opinion of me to change."

****

The following evening after work, Audra stopped by Sally's Sundries for coffee. She had coffee at home, but today had been long and grueling. She needed a quick pick-me-up.

After securing a large caramel latte, she headed out the door. A cool breeze blew over her, and she paused to take a sip of the warm, sweet brew. She closed her eyes, savoring that first taste. There was almost nothing that a shot of caffeine and sugar couldn't fix.

"Audra, what a coincidence," a voice said from behind her.

*Gaylen.*

She choked on the hot liquid, scorching her mouth.

She tensed and slowly turned to face him. "What the hell do you want?"

"Hey, now. That's no way to greet a new friend."

"Friend. *Right*. I've had about all I can take of reapers. If I run into one more..." She shook her head vehemently. "Just go away and leave me alone."

"Have you met another reaper? Is some other fella trying to move in on mine and Dimitri's girl? Or, are you just referring to him and me? Because, if you're already tired of having us around, you're in for some unpleasant times."

"I met another reaper. They're apparently roaming around, willy-nilly, invading my life whether I like it or not."

His brows arched. "Who is it? Anyone I know?"

"I have no idea if you know her or not. Listen, just tell me what you want and get the hell away from me."

She glanced around. A few people occupied the downtown sidewalks, but none of them seemed to have noticed the crazy lady talking to herself.

"So, it was a female?" Gaylen asked. "What's her name? I must know her. The reaper community is pretty tight."

Jesus. He acted like they'd just discovered they'd been members of the same fraternity.

She opened her mouth to speak, then closed it. She didn't know why, but she was reluctant to tell him Cassie's name. Not that he could do anything to her, could he? And not that Audra should care. The girl was a reaper. And she was dead. Audra's concern lay with those still living.

"Why did you kill my patient?"

"I beg your pardon?" He cocked his head.

"You killed Mr. Neufeld."

"Mr. Neufeld…ah, you mean the perverted, smelly old dirtbag crybaby? Uh, yes. I killed that one." He didn't even bother to look abashed.

"Why? Why would you do that?"

"Don't tell me you're sorry he's dead. You despised him."

"That's not the point, and it doesn't make it right. He was an innocent man. *My* patient. I was responsible for his care, and you took him, on some kind of whim, for some kind of sick thrill. Don't pretend you did me a favor. I guess now it's pretty clear your smarmy civility was all an act. You're evil."

He shrugged. "Sorry, Audra. Taking souls is what I do."

"It's not your job to take them before their time."

"Ah, I see Dimitri's been schooling you. No, it's not my *job* to take them before their time." His full lips spread into a dazzling, teeth-baring smile. "That part I just like."

She shuddered as icicles formed in her blood, and the flesh on her arms tingled in fear. She backed up a few steps and turned away, but he moved with supernatural quickness and was in front of her once more, only this time closer. A wave of air wafted over her, but unlike Dimitri's that set her pulses racing with a mixture of anticipation and apprehension, Gaylen's was a smothering, tepid blast.

He dipped his head and stared at her. In his golden eyes, there lurked an unmistakable spark of twisted pleasure. The hairs on the back of her neck bristled. His heart-stopping good looks, his Nordic-godlike angelic features masked a depraved monster.

"Please just stop," she whispered. "Just go away and leave me and my patients alone."

He slowly shook his head. "That, I can't do. Even for the lovely Audra. Meeting you…connecting with you, has given me a whole new purpose."

"The purpose of destroying people's lives? What is it that you want?" She huffed out a sigh, and he stared at her mouth. His expression tightened, and he lowered his lids.

"Beautiful," he nearly moaned.

She frowned and stepped back. "What's wrong with you? What do you want from me?"

"The same thing all reapers want. The sweet taste of human breath."

"What?" She didn't like the odd twist this conversation had taken. "Human breath? Why?"

"How can I explain?" He looked heavenward and sighed blissfully before turning his gaze back to her. "It's like the best food you've ever tasted, the best high you've ever had, the most amazing orgasm you've ever experienced, all rolled into one." He winked. "Come on, can you blame me?"

"And you think you'll get to taste my breath by killing people?"

He spread his hands out in a 'you got me' gesture. "I didn't say my plan was perfect."

"All reapers want it?" She had an image of Cassie and others converging on her, jonesing for a dose of her breath. God. What a nightmare.

"Of course. Didn't Dimitri tell you? He wants it too."

"Dimitri said he's trying to stop you. That's all he wants. To follow the rules and do his job."

"He's just trying to make a good impression. Doesn't want you to see the real him."

"Ha! Seems like an epidemic with reapers."

"No. I'm here. I'm showing you the real me." He spoke softly, but menace was woven into every word. "I took that man, and I'll take more until I get what I want."

She swallowed back fear and forced bravado into her voice. "Well, what I want is for you to tell me what the hell I can do to get rid of you. All of you."

He glanced around at the people still milling about. "Right now, it's a little too congested for a private chat. We'll talk soon. I'll explain what I need from you then."

"And after that, I can be rid of you two?" *And Cassie*, she added silently, feeling a smidgen of guilt at the thought.

He laughed. "It's not quite that simple, but things will be better all-around if you do what I say. I offered your boyfriend, Dimitri, a chance to strike a deal, and he refused. You don't want to make the same mistake."

"Are you threatening me?"

"*Warning*, sweetheart. Warning you." He tipped an imaginary hat to her. "I'll be in touch."

She stared at him for a moment, then dropped her gaze and skirted around him.

Behind her, he spoke, his voice taunting. "Oh, by the way. You won't get rid of Dimitri easily, either. He has an additional agenda."

She paused and slowly faced him. "What does he want?"

He grinned. "Dimitri's in love with you."

"In love?" she scoffed. "You're ridiculous."

"You couldn't tell?" He shook his head as if in regret. "Sometimes I forget how stupid humans are. See you around."

He sauntered away, leaving Audra gaping after him.

Dimitri in love with her? Preposterous. Good Lord, the man…the *thing*…wasn't even alive, wasn't even human. Didn't even *know* her.

But sometimes…the way he looked at her…

For God's sake, no. She neither believed nor cared how Dimitri felt about her. She had enough relationship trouble with real men. She damned sure didn't need to get mixed up with the undead.

She slammed her now-cold coffee into the nearest trash can and picked up her pace, hurrying to the sanctity of her home.

A rain forest bubble bath sounded amazing right now. Perhaps another evening of relaxation and wine were in order. This time, as much as she loved her friend, without Riley's company. She felt as though she hadn't really been alone since Dimitri and crew entered her life.

Her house came in sight, barely visible in the dusk falling over her neighborhood. The white frame bungalow with its burgundy shutters and colorful flower garden gave her a sense of calm. She let out a relieved breath. Yes. Solitude was exactly what she needed.

She was a few feet from the porch when she saw what appeared to be a discarded pile of clothing on her doorstep. Who would have left clothes for her? Frowning, she moved closer.

Light from her porch light shone down and

illuminated a swath of dark hair…a smidgen of pale flesh…a woman's face.

## Chapter 11

"Dear God." Audra dropped to her knees next to the figure, flinching when her bad leg folded beneath her.

The woman lay on her back, her face turned to the side, dark hair obscuring her features. Audra touched two fingers to the side of her neck. The pulse was steady, strong. Gently, she placed a hand on each of the woman's cheeks and turned her head. The hair fell away, and the features came into view. One side of her face was bruised and bloody. That same eye was black, nearly swollen shut. Blood trickled from a split in her lower lip.

"Maria," Audra gasped.

Maria moaned and slowly opened her eyes. "Audra. Didn't know where…else…to go." Her eye closed again, and tears poured from them.

Audra fumbled her cell phone out of her purse. "Hang on. I'm calling for help."

"No!" Maria's eyes shot open, and she waved her hand feebly at the cell phone. "Please don't."

"You're hurt. You need to see a doctor."

"Hurt, yes. Call for help, and I'm dead." The words were spoken calmly, but the terror in her expression was anything but.

Audra hesitated. She could at least wait, get Maria inside, check her over herself, and determine if she should be seen. If her injuries were severe, then in spite of her protests, Audra would call. She dropped her cell phone back into her purse.

As she was about to help Maria to her feet, a sickening thought struck her. "Where are the girls? Are they okay?"

"With my mother. She's…hiding them."

"Thank God." Audra wasn't certain if Scott had ever hurt the children, but it damned sure wouldn't be a good idea for them to be around when their father was in this state of mind. Audra peered into Maria's eyes. "Can you stand? Did he hurt you internally? Anything broken?"

"Nothing broken. I can stand."

Audra held Maria's arm and helped her up. They took a few steps before Maria stumbled. Audra steadied her, holding her upright with one hand while she unlocked the door with the other. She pushed the door open, then helped Maria into the house.

She led her to the couch and lowered her onto it. "Here, let's get your coat off." The brown wool coat that had first appeared to be discarded clothing.

Audra shuddered. What if she hadn't come home when she did? What if Gaylen had discovered an injured Maria on her porch?

Banishing those thoughts, she sat next to her patient, feeling along her jaw. "Does this hurt?"

Maria shook her head. Audra continued her examination of her injuries, moving to her neck, her shoulders, down to her belly, gently probing, asking at each point if her exploration hurt. Each time, Maria claimed it didn't, but she winced when Audra pressed against her ribs.

Audra lifted her blouse. A deep, red, angry welt ran down one side of her body. Hot fury pumped through Audra's veins. "Son of a bitch," she muttered. "I think you might have a broken rib. Maybe a couple. We need to call for help."

Maria took her shirt from Audra's hand, tugging it down over her injury. "No broken ribs."

"How do you know?"

Her smile was bitter. "Trust me. Experience. I've had them plenty of times."

Pity clenched Audra's gut. "Good point." She knew the woman spoke the truth. Audra had treated her at the hospital for a few of them. "Let's get you cleaned up. You've had the hell beat out of you, but you don't appear to have any life-threatening injuries. I'll get the first-aid kit. Be right back."

Audra left the room and retrieved the kit from the medicine shelf in the bathroom. When she returned, Maria's fist was clenched against her mouth, and tears flowed down her cheeks.

"I hope you're not crying over that asshole." Audra snatched a couple of tissues from the box on the coffee table and pressed them into Maria's hands.

She used a tissue to wipe tears away, but more took their place. "We fought because I filed for divorce. He went ballistic. I really thought he loved me. This isn't love, is it?"

"Not by a long shot." Audra sat next to her and began gently cleaning the blood from her face and applied anti-biotic ointment to her cuts. "Why were you still living with him after you filed the papers?"

"I didn't know where else to go. For now. I was hoping if I filed, he'd see I was serious about leaving him if things didn't change."

Audra pressed her lips together, but didn't comment. Surely Maria didn't really believe that was the way things worked with a violent abuser like Scott? Running fast and far, making a clean break was the only way to get through to assholes like him.

"Where is he now?" Audra asked. "How did you get away?"

Maria's lips quirked, but there was no humor in the gesture. "He was finished. He went to the store for beer. You know how guys like to unwind after a workout."

Nausea coiled in Audra's belly. "So, when he gets home and finds you gone…" She glanced at the door. Had she locked it? "Be right back."

She hurried over to lock the doors, sliding the deadbolt home as an added precaution. Before returning to the couch, she grabbed the fireplace poker and brought it back with her. Maria eyed it, but didn't say anything.

"I thought I was going to pass out, but I knew I couldn't stay there. I can't let him keep doing this." She sniffed and dabbed her eyes with the tissue.

"I didn't see your car. Did a friend bring you?"

"Friend? I have no friends. I'm not allowed. I walked."

"For God's sake, Maria. It's over five miles!"

She nodded. "By the time I made it here, everything went black. I must have passed out."

"Why did you come here instead of to a hospital?"

"I knew I could trust you." Maria put her head down. "I'm sorry I've been cold to you lately. I couldn't stand for you to see my shame. See what a weakling I am." She paused. "I couldn't stand to see you hurt…knowing…”

Audra lifted her brows. “Knowing what?”

Maria was silent for several seconds, then said, “Just knowing everything Scott’s done. And I still stayed with him.”

Audra pressed an ice pack to Maria’s side. “Lie back and keep this against your ribs.”

Maria leaned into the corner of the couch. “I’m an idiot.”

“That’s not important. What’s important now is what you do next. We need to call the police. He needs to be in jail.”

Maria looked up. “He was in jail before. It only helped me for a few months, and now it’s starting all over again.” She gave a bitter laugh and lowered her voice to a near whisper. “Didn’t help you at all.”

“What was that?”

Maria squeezed her eyes shut and shook her head. “Nothing. Forget it.”

“What did you mean?”

Beneath her closed eyes, tears brimmed and coursed down her cheeks. Her chest heaved, and sobs wracked her body. “I’m sorry. Oh, God. I’m so sorry.”

“Maria? What is it?” Audra asked, although she knew. Somehow, in spite of her claims of, ‘But he was in jail,’ she’d known all along. “Scott had something to do with me getting hurt, didn’t he?”

Maria didn’t answer. She continued to cry.

“Calm down. You’re going to make your injuries worse.” Audra took her by the shoulders. “Look at me, Maria. Stop crying and talk to me.”

Maria opened her eyes. “You’ll hate me. I should have told you.”

"Tell me now."

"Will you promise me one thing? Don't call the police?"

"I can't promise that. First of all, Scott beat the hell out of you, again. Secondly, if he had something to do with what happened to me, the police should know. He can't get away with this shit, Maria. Stop protecting him."

Maria tossed the ice pack onto the cushion next to her and sat forward, dropping her head into her hands. "I'm not protecting him," she said. "I'm protecting everyone else. He will kill me." She lifted her head. "And he'll kill you."

Audra pressed the ice pack back to Maria's side. "All the more reason to stop him. Tell me everything."

Maria considered for a moment, then leaned back once more. "Scott was in jail, but he put his buddies up to it. I don't know if they were supposed to kill you, or just hurt you."

She went cold inside. "If those men hadn't stopped them, I might be dead."

Maria winced. "You're probably right."

"Who all was involved? I need names."

"You're going to call the police?"

"Of course I am."

"We're both dead then."

"For Christ's sake, Maria. You're a walking dead woman as long as that bastard is free." Audra pushed off the couch and paced across the floor. "You might as well tell me everything you know. If you don't, I'll give the police what I know, and the investigation will turn up the whole truth. If you tell me everything, I'll ask them to keep your name out of it. If you don't…" She shrugged. "You're fair game. Scott will find out you talked…if he's out on bail…"

"Okay. Okay." Maria brought a hand to her forehead, fingers shaking as she rubbed them along her skin. "God. I can't believe this is happening. I'll tell you everything."

"Let me call Shane first. He should hear it from you."

"Shane?"

"Sheriff Dunham. He's looking for the men who hurt me. I want you to tell him what you know."

"Please. No police. Not yet. I can't stand the thought of all the questions…being bombarded with cops. Please."

"I'll just call Shane. I'll ask him to come on his own. Initially. But the entire force will become involved. These are serious crimes your husband committed, Maria."

Audra wasn't sure if Shane was at the station, so she dialed his cell. He answered right away, saying, "Audra?" in a cheerful tone, like he was happy to hear from her.

She felt a flash of guilt that she wasn't phoning for personal reasons. "Are you working tonight?" she asked.

"No. Off duty. You need something?"

"Could you come over here, please? I have a—situation."

"Are you hurt? What's going on?" The lightness left his voice.

"You remember Maria? She's the one who's…hurt."

"Did you call an ambulance?"

Audra drew in a deep breath. He could have been here by the time he asked all those questions. "Please, Shane. Can you just come? I'll explain everything when you get here."

"Sure. On my way."

Audra hung up the phone. Maria had been watching her, wide-eyed with hope, and maybe a bit of dread. "Well?" she asked.

"He'll be here soon. I'll make you some hot tea."

Audra went into the kitchen and microwaved a cup of tea. As she returned to the living room and handed it to Maria, someone banged loudly on the front door.

Not Shane. He wouldn't have gotten here that quickly. Or, at least she didn't think so. Of course, she didn't know where he'd been when she reached him.

An angry voice shouted through the closed door. "Maria? You in there? Open the fuck up!"

Definitely not Shane.

Maria choked on the tea and jumped to her feet, nearly dropping the cup. "Scott!" The word came out in a strangled whimper.

"It's okay." Audra placed a hand on Maria's arm, removing the cup from her trembling fingers and setting it on the coffee table. "We won't let him in. It will be okay."

Maria nodded but yelped out a scream when the banging became louder.

"I'll cut you and that whore. Open the goddamned door!" He let out a guttural war cry. The room erupted with the sound of shattering glass as the picture window next to the door imploded.

****

Dimitri tossed the last of his meager belongings

into the duffle bag. Veronica stepped away from the closet, her arms loaded down with dresses.

"Where are we going next?" she asked as she tossed clothes into her suitcase.

Dimitri didn't respond.

"D, honey." She took hold of his arm and tugged until he faced her. "What's the matter? Don't you have another place picked out for us?"

He clenched his jaw, then shook his head. "Not…*us* exactly."

"What do you mean? Not us?" She dropped to the bed and put a hand to her mouth, releasing a dramatic sob. "You're replacing me, aren't you?"

"Replacing you? I don't have to replace you. I don't need anyone."

"You have to have a woman to share your bed. It's better than the torture of being alone, isn't it, Dimitri?"

"That's ridiculous."

"Is it?" She stood and walked over to stand beside him. "You can't bear the quiet, the time with your own thoughts. Can't stand what you were. What you are."

"I was alone for over two hundred years before you came along."

"And how was that, huh? Memories? Nightmares? Regrets? I know what you were. Why you became a reaper. That all you want now is to redeem yourself." She took hold of his arm again, this time with a gentle touch, and looked into his face, her voice softening. "You need me, darling. I can help take away the bad memories." She tightened her grip. "And for God's sake. I need you. I love you. You're the only reason I'm here. The only reason I exist."

In the time they'd been together, she'd taken

dozens of other lovers, so it was unlikely *he* was her reason for existing.

"Veronica, please. Knock it off. It's over."

"It can't be." Her voice was raw with pain. She shook his arm. "Dimitri, listen to me. I'll do anything. Just tell me what you want."

"All I want is for you to leave."

She flinched as if he'd punched her. "You can't mean that."

He jerked from her hold. "Trust me. I most definitely mean that."

"You'll be sorry." The anguish in her voice was gone, replaced by cold rage. "I vow to you, Dimitri. You'll be sorry."

"I'm already sorry."

Hope lit in her eyes. "Sorry about what?"

Flashes of memories assaulted him…a lifetime of feeding his urges, taking what he wanted with no thought for others, driven by lust and greed. Then the night it all culminated in tragedy…waking to flames and a woman's agonized screams…

Pain shafted through his chest, so severe it paralyzed him. All the strength left his body. Dropping his head, he whispered, "Everything I've ever done."

## Chapter 12

A large stone from Audra's flowerbed lay among the broken glass. Chilly air blew in through the shattered window.

Maria screamed, and Audra put an arm around her shoulder. "Come on," she hissed in her ear, just as Scott hurtled through the window. A teenage boy came in behind him, looking confused and miserable. The boy was slightly taller than Scott, good-looking with longish, dark blond hair, and barbell earrings in both ears.

"Joel?" Maria said, but Audra was pulling her out of the room and toward the kitchen. At least she had knives in there. Why hadn't she grabbed the poker? Her cell phone was lying on the table, out of reach. Besides, why call 9-1-1? She'd already called Shane. He'd be here soon.

Before they made their destination, Audra heard Scott approach and felt Maria being yanked away from her. Maria cried out in pain. Scott had ahold of her hair and had nearly jerked her off her feet.

"Where do you think you're going, bitch?"

"I'm sorry," Maria sobbed.

"Hey, please let her go," the kid said from behind them. "She's had enough." He rushed to Maria's side. "You okay, Aunt Maria?"

She nodded, tears leaking from her eyes.

"Let her go and get out of my house!" Audra shouted.

Scott shot a look at her. "Who the fuck you think you are? You're already on my bad side. Don't go making it any worse." He released Maria and shoved her away. She stumbled and fell to the floor. The boy started toward her, but Scott stopped him with a fist to his chest. "You're a pussy, boy, you know it?"

The kid dropped his head and didn't respond.

Audra started toward Maria, but Scott got there first. He grabbed his wife's arm and hauled her to her feet. Pointing a finger in Audra's face, he said, "I'll deal with you later, cunt." Then, to Maria, "Come on. We're going home." Maria looked miserably from Audra to Scott, then nodded. "Okay."

"No!" Audra shouted. "Are you out of your mind? You can't go with him."

"Please, miss. Just go along," Maria's nephew said quietly. "It's better this way."

Audra frowned and turned to study him. That voice. There was something familiar about it…

*Please, miss, don't fight 'em…it'll be better that way…*

That night…a voice whispering in her ear…sounding almost regretful…while he and his buddies beat the shit out of her. Or maybe he hadn't actually thrown any punches? But it was him. Or was it? She looked at the navy blue Adidas hoodie he wore. One of them had worn a hoodie that night. She'd seen some kind of emblem but hadn't been able to make out details. She shook her head. Now wasn't the time to think about it.

"You can't go," she repeated to Maria, ignoring the

boy.

"I have to." She seemed deflated, fatalistic. *This is my life. It's all I'll ever have.*

Audra hardened her voice. "If you go with him, all bets are off. Every deal we made is null and void."

"Please. You can't!" Maria cried.

"Don't go with him."

"What deal?" Scott cut in. "What the fuck you hens cackling about?" He released Maria and started toward Audra. "I've had enough of your butting in. Your smart mouth. Time you learned to keep it shut."

Audra circled around—her limp hindering her progress—but managed to stay out of his reach as she backed toward the center of the living room…toward the fireplace poker resting against the couch, waiting for her.

"Come on, man," Joel said. "Let's just get the fuck out of here."

"Keep your mouth shut, too, boy. You're about to learn how a real man handles a woman."

The backs of Audra's legs hit the coffee table, and she knew she was close enough.

Scott grinned. His prey had nowhere else to go. He lunged toward her. She felt behind her until her fingers gripped the poker. Swinging upward, she caught him on the side of the head. He shouted a hoarse, pain-filled curse and went to his knees.

Maria screamed and rushed to his side. "Are you okay?" she cried, dropping down next to him.

Blood leaked from the side of his head. Audra's heart pounded in fear. Had she killed him?

No. He wasn't dead. He was still upright, cursing and holding his head, blood pouring from his fingers, tears pouring from his eyes.

"I'll kill that fucking bitch." His voice was a mix of rage and weeping. "Swear to God. I'll kill her."

He lurched to his feet and whirled toward Audra. She gasped and skirted around the coffee table. Eyes bulging in fury and one side of his face red with blood, he looked like a deranged accident victim. He slowly came toward her, menacing and purposeful. Her heart crawled into her throat.

*Shane will be here soon. Shane will be here soon. Please, God. Let Shane be here soon.*

"Scott!" Maria shouted. "Don't."

"Stay the fuck out of this."

"The cops are on their way," she said quickly.

He halted, glaring at Audra, then turned to Maria. "You called the cops?"

Maria pointed at Audra. "She did. Please. Just go. I promise, I'll come home. Just get out of here while you can."

Uncertainty crossed his face, then fury. "You have no idea what you're in for, calling the cops," he said softly to Audra. Oddly, the quietly spoken words were more chilling than his blustery threats had been. "Come on, Joel. Maria. Let's get the fuck out of here."

"I'll be home shortly," Maria said. "Let me smooth this over with the police."

"No way. You're leaving with me."

"Scott, please. They'll be here any second."

Audra wasn't sure if Maria was protecting herself and Audra, or Scott, by insisting that he leave. She actually hoped he was still here when Shane arrived. Let the son of a bitch try to screw with Shane.

Scott shot one last intimidating look at Audra, then

left, using the door this time, leaving it ajar.

Audra started to shut it but didn't. The bad guys were gone. Shane would be here soon. Nothing to be afraid of now. Besides, the house still wouldn't exactly be secure. There was that gaping hole where the window used to be.

She turned to Maria. "Why did you warn him? Protect him?"

"I had to."

"As long as you keep protecting him, you'll never be safe." She threw her hands up in frustration. "None of us will."

"I wasn't protecting Scott."

"Your nephew. He was there that night. I recognized his voice."

"That's who I'm trying to protect. I can't let him go to jail."

"But he was involved."

Maria groaned miserably and dropped to the couch. Tears shimmered in her eyes, running down her battered cheeks. "He's a good boy. He doesn't want to go along with Scott, but he can't say no. Scott's like a father to him."

"Yeah. Father of the fucking year."

Maria glanced up at her but didn't respond to her jibe. "Joel's my sister's kid. She was always gone, looking for a fix or a lay or both. His dad skipped out when he was a baby. Me and Scott practically raised him. He worships Scott. Scott has a lot of control over him."

"There's no excuse for—" She stopped at the sound of a car pulling into the driveway.

In a few seconds, she heard footsteps on the porch.

"Son of a bitch. Audra? You in there? You okay?"

Giddy with relief, she rushed to the door, smiling when Shane pushed it open and stepped through, crunching over the broken glass.

She went into his arms. "Thank God you're here."

"What the hell happened?" He looked over her shoulder at Maria. "Your husband did this?"

Audra released him and stepped away, immediately missing his warmth, his strength.

Maria didn't answer.

"Yes," Audra said. "He beat the hell out of her then came here looking for her."

Shane cupped Audra's cheek and stared into her eyes. "Did he hurt you?"

She shook her head. "Not much. I hurt him, though."

His brows rose. "What?"

"He was coming at me. I hit him in the head with a poker." She pulled away from his touch and pointed to the drops of blood on the carpet. "See?"

He laughed. "Seems you can take care of yourself." Moving over to the couch, he sat next to Maria. "You need to file charges. Provide a statement that he hurt you so we can lock him up."

A bitter smile twisted her mouth. "Lock him up like before, then let him go so he can do this again?"

"We'll do all we can. He needs to be put away."

"How long would he go away for assault and battery? Attempted murder? Conspiracy?" Audra asked.

Shane turned to look at her. "What are you talking about?"

She focused on Maria. "Tell him."

Maria grimaced. "I—don't know. I…"

"Tell me what?" Storm clouds gathered in Shane's dark eyes. He pushed to his feet. "Is he the one who beat you up? He was in jail that night."

"He was behind it," Audra said. "He put his buddies, his ne—"

Maria jerked her head up and shook it violently from side to side.

Audra sighed. "Uhm. He put his…ne'er do well cohorts up to it."

Shane frowned. "Ne'er do well?"

"You know. Thug friends. Anyway. Maria can tell you all about it."

He nodded. "We should go down to the station so you can answer some questions."

Maria's eyes widened. "No, please. I don't want to go anywhere. Can't I answer questions here?"

"You have to stay somewhere tonight where you can be protected. Your children. Are they at home?"

"No. At a relative's house. Scott has no idea where they are."

"We'll take you down to the station and when we're done, you can go stay with the children."

"She's been injured," Audra said. "I need to keep an eye on her. The kids are in a safe place. Maybe she should just stay here."

"*You* can't stay here." He pointed to the broken window. "Not exactly safe. In addition to her maniac husband, there might be a serial killer on the loose."

"I can stay with Riley."

"And put her and her little girl in danger?" He stood. "For now, you can come to the station with us. We'll take statements from you both, then figure out where you'll stay tonight."

"I have to go home," Maria insisted.

"You can't go home to that asshole. Especially not after what happened tonight," Audra argued.

"I have to eventually. He'll hurt my children."

The skin on Audra's face tightened. "Does he abuse the girls?"

Maria shook her head. "He never has. But if I leave him, no telling what he'll do. I should withdraw the divorce papers."

"So, that's it? You just stick by him and let him use you for a punching bag? Big bad Scott gets his way because no one can stop him?" She turned to Shane. "You can arrest him, right? Put him away? Keep Maria and the girls safe?"

"I can. He'll most likely post bail and be back out on the streets in no time." He took Audra's hands and looked into her eyes. "But, if he ever hurts you again, I'll kill him." He turned to Maria. "You need to do something. We can't put him away forever, but the longer, the better. You have to tell us everything you know that will go against him. The asshole's not going to stop hurting you until you're dead."

She rose slowly to her feet and rubbed a hand over her face, giving a bitter laugh. "If it wasn't for my babies, I'd pray for death."

****

The next morning, Audra moved around the hospital in a daze. She'd been at the police station most of the night, and by the time they finished, she only had a few hours before she had to be at work, so she'd gone to Riley's to shower and grab a quick cup of coffee. Shane promised to have her window replaced and the mess cleaned up by the time she got off work. She was more grateful than words could say. Not only did it save her the trouble—the last thing she wanted was to go home to a visual reminder of last night's events.

She carried her tray holding a grilled chicken sandwich and potato salad through the cafeteria, feeling eyes on her, seeing the condemnation, the speculation. She hadn't actually heard anything, but she'd engaged in hospital cafeteria gossip herself often enough to know when it was happening.

She chose an empty table and kept her head down as she ate.

"Can I sit?"

She looked up to find Wilton standing next to her. So much for solitude.

"Help yourself."

"Thanks." He took the chair across from her, forking a huge mound of spaghetti and shoving it into his mouth, almost before he was completely seated. He aimed the fork in a circular motion around the room and spoke with his mouth full. "If you're wondering if they're talking about you, they are." He chewed for a few seconds, then said, "Talking about how you almost died, now two patients in a week. Saying you got a black cloud hanging over you. Either that, or your accident made you nuts, and you're offing your own patients." He finally swallowed. "Depends on who you talk to."

"I'm not really interested in gossip."

That wasn't entirely true. She'd been sucked in by gossip about others before; she just didn't want to hear it about herself.

"Sorry. Won't say another word." He ate a few more forkfuls and shook his head, pointing across the room with his fork again. Audra twisted in her seat to find Mary Lou a few tables away. "Man, Nurse Ratched is still busting my balls. Every day."

"Maybe you should slow down and try to stop forgetting things," Audra advised gently. "We have people's lives in our hands. She's just doing her job."

"Look at her," he went on like he hadn't heard her. "Bet she's showing a picture of that daughter she's so proud of. All she talks about. She think anybody cares her kid's a cheerleader?"

Audra grinned. She had to agree with him on that one. Camellia was all the woman talked about, when she wasn't 'busting someone's balls.'

"*Head* cheerleader," Audra corrected, and Wilton's mouth split in a smile. Bits of spaghetti clung to his teeth. She pushed her plate away. The man was not the most charming lunch companion.

Audra was about to excuse herself when Jaxon walked over, sliding into the seat next to her.

He jerked his head toward Wilton. "Hey, buddy, you have spaghetti on your teeth."

Wilton's chubby face flushed, and he scrubbed at his teeth with his forefinger. Scowling, he shoveled in the rest of his food and stood. "See ya later, Audra. Doctor Maroney."

Audra turned to Jaxon as Wilton weaved his way through the tables and out the door. "That was kind of mean."

"Yeah. Got rid of him, didn't it? You're welcome."

She bumped him with her shoulder. "Thanks."

He narrowed his gaze on her. "You okay? You look exhausted."

"Rough night."

A wicked light danced in his brown eyes. "You and Marshall Dillon?"

She shoulder-bumped him again. "Stop calling him that, and no. Well…yes."

His eyebrows rose. "Really? I thought I was kidding."

"It's not what you think. Maria came to my house last night." She glanced around to make sure the gossip mongers were not in earshot. "Scott beat her up again."

"Asshole," Jaxon bit out.

"Tell me about it. I called Shane. While we were waiting for him, Scott and his nephew showed up to force Maria to come with him."

Jaxon scrutinized her closely. "Did he hurt you?"

She shook her head. "Other way around."

"You hurt him?"

"Yeah. Poker to the head. He was coming after me."

"*Damn*, girl."

Audra narrowed her eyes. "You sounded just a tiny bit gay when you said that. Rare for you."

Now he shoulder-bumped her. "Back to your story. So, did Shane arrest him?"

"No. Scott left before Shane got there. We took Maria to where her kids are staying. Then I went to the station with Shane. Filled out reports, answered a bunch of questions, ended up spending the night there, or what was left of it."

"Romantic."

*Kind of*, she almost said. Shane had treated her like she was made of glass. Well, not the kind that was shattered all over her living room floor, more like one of those blown glass figurines that had to be handled with special care.

Jaxon took a bite of his burger and, unlike Wilton, waited to swallow before he spoke. “So, are they going to arrest the asshole or what?”

Audra debated telling him about Scott’s involvement in her attack, but thought better of it. He would be enraged and frustrated that he couldn’t do anything about it. It would come out soon enough, once Scott was finally caught. “The police are looking for him. He’s on the run.”

“Good riddance.”

“Yeah. As long as he doesn’t find Maria and the kids.”

“Or come back and hurt you. Maybe the sheriff should put a police detail on you. You know, just to make sure you’re safe.” He winked. “Bet he’d volunteer himself.”

“You sure are pushing this me and Shane thing. What gives?”

Seriousness replaced his amused expression. “I don’t know. I just think you two would be good together.”

“We haven’t seen one another in years. We had a mild high school thing that didn’t last. Not what you’d call a classic love story.”

“You know, I was an ass for letting you choose me back then.”

“You didn’t *let* me. I just chose you.”

“I was selfish. Because of me, you lost a chance at something real.”

She saw true anguish in his face, true regret. She put a hand over his. “It’s okay, really. My choice. I wouldn’t change things.”

"I would. I wouldn't have been such a dick."

She squeezed his hand before releasing it. "Don't be so hard on yourself, Jaxon. That's not the only reason you're a dick."

He chuckled. "Thanks. You always know how to make me feel better."

She looked at the clock on the cafeteria wall. "Break's over. I'd better go check on Trevor." She slid from her seat. "See ya."

On the elevator ride, she thought of Shane. Could they have something together? Was she even interested in finding out?

She liked him. A lot. Liked the way he was so caring, yet macho at the same time. Sort of like a mix between Mother Teresa and John Wayne. And, he was not at all hard to look at. Big, manly, strong…those sexy laugh lines around his dark brown eyes.

Another pair of eyes flashed in her mind. Blue. Deep blue and ever changing, like a tumultuous sea in a raging storm. A shiver ran through her. *Get Dimitri out of your mind.*

She had to stop thinking about him, stop recalling that odd, shivery, cool spark that somehow made her feel warm and tingly…

*Stop it!* She shook her head to clear it.

When the elevator doors opened, she stepped off, stopping by the desk to pick up Trevor's chart, perusing it for changes as she made her way down the hall.

She looked up from the chart as she entered the room. At first, her mind didn't quite process what she was seeing. He'd been in her thoughts only seconds before, and now, he was standing in Trevor's room.

How could that be? *Why* would that be?

And, worse, Gaylen stood next to him. Dimitri's expression was fierce, angry. Gaylen's looked like someone who'd won the lottery.

Cold wind chilled her insides, and dread settled in the pit of her stomach. She didn't want to, but she turned to look at Trevor. He was slumped in the bed, jaw slack, eyes staring.

She let out a wail and rushed over to his side. "Trevor!" She punched the emergency button and pressed her fingers to his wrist, then to his neck.

Over her shoulder, she glared at Dimitri and Gaylen. "What have you done?" she screamed, not caring if anyone heard. "What in God's name have you done?"

# Chapter 13

As Audra trudged down the hospital corridor, voices around her surged and faded. The people she passed seemed to look at her differently. As if she knew something. As if she was part of this. As if she had seen the monsters who'd taken Trevor.

Somewhere in the hubbub of the code team trying to save the boy's life, of trying to undo what *they'd* done, the reapers had disappeared. Good. She didn't want to look at them. Not ever.

*Like she had a choice.*

She snorted a laugh, drawing the attention of an orderly passing by. He gave her a puzzled look. Before this was all over, she'd surely be committed.

A sound like the howl of a wounded beast rose. At the end of the hallway, near the nurses' station, Dr. Blasingame, Trevor's doctor, was speaking to Cheryl. She gripped the doctor's arms, shaking her head over and over. Her mouth moved, but Audra couldn't make out what she was saying. She could guess, though. *Please, no, it can't be true. My baby can't be dead. Oh, God, please...*

Audra changed her course, heading toward the elevator, her goal the exit door at the back of the hospital. She needed some air. Needed to get away from pain and death and doom.

"Audra?" The word came out as a choked wail, a

blend of shattered hope and disbelief.

She drew in a breath and turned. Cheryl approached, quickly, unsteadily. Her face was a tortured mask—mascara smeared, the flesh of her cheeks quivering, her eyes a window of despair.

"Cheryl, I'm sorry," Audra whispered.

"What happened? I don't understand. I just went down to get a cup of coffee. He was fine." She brushed a hand across her face, then held it out in front of her, let it hang there for a moment as if unsure what to do with it, then let it drop. "He was fine when I left him. What happened?"

Audra opened her mouth to answer, although she wasn't sure exactly what to say.

Cheryl didn't give her the opportunity. "I shouldn't have left him. I'm his mother, and I shouldn't have left him. He was all alone." A noise similar to the one she made earlier exploded from her. "Oh God, my baby died all alone, and now I'll never see him again."

She sagged, and Audra grabbed her shoulders, helping steady her as she led her to a nearby chair. "Here, sit. Let me get you some water."

Audra looked toward the nurse's station and caught Tonya's eye, then made a drinking motion with her hand to her mouth. Tonya nodded.

"I'm so sorry," Audra said gently. "He was a great kid. I can't imagine how you must be feeling."

Tonya brought a cup of water, and Audra pressed it into Cheryl's hands. She lifted it to her lips, then paused, looking up at Audra. "Wait. He wasn't alone."

"I beg your pardon?"

Dear God, had she seen the reapers? Did she know what happened?

"You were there. You were there with my Trevor when he died."

Audra's heart seized. She'd been there all right. And hadn't been able to help him. She'd perhaps been the cause of it, although she wasn't sure how this whole soul-taking thing worked. Had they done it to punish her, to send her a message, to impress her? What?

Her insides trembled. This was all too fantastic, too beyond the scope of reality. She needed air.

"I'm sorry, but I wasn't. Trevor was already…gone by the time I got there. We still tried to save him, but it was too late."

Cheryl might have said more, but her family arrived, and Audra slipped away as they surrounded her, hugging, consoling, offering useless words that brought no comfort.

At the end of the day, her son was still dead.

Audra rode the elevator down, then headed to the exit. The door opened onto a railed sidewalk, which led to a delivery bay. No one ever came out here. She would be alone.

The night was quiet. Peaceful. The full moon hovered in the evening sky, its brilliant glow putting the streetlights to shame. A beautiful evening. The kind Trevor would never be able to enjoy again.

She gripped the cold railing and finally allowed herself to cry. Sobs poured from her body, hurting her chest and straining her throat. Poor, young, funny Trevor. His life cut short. His dream of football and girls crushed. His family left with an empty hole that would now be filled with a lifetime of grief.

"I apologize."

She gasped and whirled to find Dimitri standing

behind her. Her pulse jumped, and it took a moment to get her breathing under control. The fear quickly turned to anger.

"You apologize?" she choked, brushing furiously at the tears on her face. "You just killed a seventeen-year-old boy, a kid I was responsible for helping heal, and you *apologize*?"

"I didn't take him."

"Bullshit. You were there. I saw you." She barked out a laugh. "*Take*. That's sort of a benign word for what you and your psychotic buddy do, isn't it? Maybe I can help you come up with something more fitting. How about execute, annihilate, slaughter? Wouldn't one of those be more accurate?"

"It wasn't me. It was Gaylen. I didn't get there in time to stop him."

She brought her hands up and clasped them over her ears like a child. "I don't want to hear it. Don't care. You're both evil. I shouldn't even know you exist, let alone be seeing you, conversing with you. Can't you just go away and leave me alone?"

"I'm sorry. Now that you can see us, there's nothing I can do. I can't make you *un*see us."

She crossed her arms over her chest and turned her back to him, speaking over her shoulder. "You're not here to reap right now, are you? I mean, unless you're going to take me. So what the hell are you doing here? Can't we leave it to where I only have to see you when you arrive to do your dirty work?"

"We could. Or when I arrive to stop Gaylen."

"How do I even know you're telling the truth? How do I know Gaylen is the one who took Trevor? The evil one who takes people before their time?

Maybe you both do it."

She didn't hear him move, but she felt that chill of electricity on her back and knew he'd come closer. She straightened, her body tensing.

"Look at me," he said softly.

She hesitated before slowly turning to meet his eyes. They were even more vivid than she remembered. The moonlight made tiny little moonbeams dance in the blue irises. She drew in a shaky breath.

"Audra, I didn't take him."

Incredibly, she realized she was starting to believe him. Was this some kind of reaper trick? Could he get inside her mind and influence her thinking? Because, beyond all rational thought, she actually believed he was sincere. She had a certainty that, in spite of what he was, he wasn't lying to her.

"I don't…I just can't…" She shook her head, suddenly aware of how cold it was outside. She hadn't brought a jacket, and the wind nipped at her flesh. She hugged her arms around her body and shivered.

"You're cold." He grinned sheepishly. "Wish I could give you my jacket."

She frowned up at him. "So, how does that work? You're not solid. I can't touch you. You float around Earth like some kind of ghost, yet you appear solid, like a living being." She pointed toward his jacket. "You obviously change clothes. I assume you shower? Eat?"

He chuckled. "You need to go inside. You'll catch your death."

She gave him a sharp look. "My *death*?"

He lifted his hands. "I meant that figuratively. Sorry."

"I want to know. If reapers are going to be

hovering around all the time, screwing with my life, I want to know how it all works."

He sighed. "There's so much to explain. A lot to it that I'm not up to going into and I don't think you're up to hearing right now." He shoved his hands in his pockets and cocked his head. "Let's just say reapers exist almost like humans, but on our own plane. We're among you. Walking, eating, making love—" His eyes locked on hers, and a trill of warmth rushed through her that she tried to ignore. "We can't feel things on the same level, but in our own plane of existence, we experience many of the things humans do."

"Where do you live? Do you have your own reaper houses that we can't see?"

His lips twisted. "We occupy homes that are currently unoccupied for one reason or another. The owners could be away on a trip, the house could be empty, on the market, but those kind of suck because they typically aren't furnished."

"So you use the occupants' things? How can you use objects when you're not even solid?"

Why was she asking such inane questions? Maybe it was to keep her mind off what had just happened, what he really was. Besides, truth be told, she was curious as hell.

"We use their furniture, some of their items, but bring our own clothes, personal belongings. We can make contact with objects, just not people. Part of the whole plan to keep our overlapping worlds apart to some degree." He scrubbed a hand over his face. "Is this really what you want to be talking about? Do you really want to hear the mundane details of the life of a reaper?"

"No. I really want to know why you took Trevor. Was it really his time? He'd just fallen ill again. We could have helped him. We've fought the cancer before."

"Come on, Audra. You're too intelligent to continue asking a question to which you're getting the same reply. For the last time, I didn't take him."

"But you would have, if it had been his time."

He tilted his head forward and shrugged. "Sure. That's my job."

"Well, your job sucks, and I want nothing to do with you."

"You're judgmental."

"I'm what?"

"Judgmental. You criticize, berate me for what I do—which follows the natural order of life and death—yet you work so hard to save people, even when doing so will only prolong their suffering. Rather than letting them go, where they're free of pain and misery, free of suffering, you struggle to save them. Are you any better than I am?"

"Are you serious? Did you really just ask me if I'm better than a *reaper*?" She shook her head. "You rip peoples' souls from their bodies. Take lives. *I* try to save them."

"Right. You fight to save people and doom them to a life of pain, dependence on others, lost dignity. What's so much worse about death?"

"I can't believe you expect me to answer that."

"And what about you, Audra? What about your own life? Is this what you had in mind for your future?" His lips twisted. "Working, having friends, but no one special to love…to love you. Borrowing someone else's kid since you have none of your own? You're so afraid of death you never learned how to live."

Each word was like an arrow to her gut. She didn't know how this…this monster had the power to hurt her, but he did.

"I guess you know all that because you're some kind of sick, twisted, supernatural psychotic stalker, right?" Her voice shook with tears and rage. "Well, you know what, Dimitri? Screw you and your reaper world." She brushed past him, although she supposed she could have walked right through him.

"Audra, wait."

"Go to hell, Dimitri. Don't come near me again."

"I can't make that promise, Audra." His voice carried to her on the chilly night air, but she didn't turn back. "You work around humans in peril. You'll be seeing a lot more of me."

****

Dimitri lounged in the easy chair, his ankle crossed over the opposite knee.

Another rented room. The guy had to spend a fortune in motel bills. He watched as the man leaned into the mirror, carefully peeling the beard from his face. Odd. Normally, he left still wearing the disguise.

He halted before completing the task, the fake hair hanging half off his face, and clutched his chest. Ah. That must be the reason. He wasn't feeling well. Maybe he worried he'd end up in the hospital and would have a lot of explaining to do if he didn't get rid of the beard.

"Damn. You're here."

Dimitri flicked a glance over his shoulder. "Gaylen. I wondered if you'd show up."

Gaylen gestured to the body on the bed. "You

already take care of her?"

"Cassie did. Her first time to fly solo. I just observed."

"How did she do?"

"She did well. Got a little emotional for a second. Hesitated like she could keep the girl alive if she didn't reap her. But she recovered quickly."

"So, she's a full-fledged reaper. Hard to believe that little slip of a girl can stop me from taking souls now. *If* she happens to arrive first." He cocked a grin. "She doesn't have the instinct you do, so I'm probably safe from her for the most part."

"Don't underestimate her."

Dimitri's attention was drawn once more to the killer, who was now gasping audibly, fumbling through his pants pockets. He pulled out a pill bottle.

"The guy's ripe for the picking," Gaylen said. "Thanks for hanging around to spoil my fun."

"Why don't you go reap someone who's ready?"

Gaylen moved closer. "Because *I'm* ready for this one. That's what matters. Come on, let me take him."

"I can't let you screw with the natural balance."

"What if that was Audra lying mutilated on the bed? For shit's sake, man. They'll never catch this asshole. He *lives* in Boon Springs. Audra could end up being one of his victims."

Dimitri's chest tightened, but his voice was steady as he replied. "Then it would be fate."

"Fate, my ass. Audra's sad enough about the boy. You really want to watch her gutted by this asshole?"

"Shut up."

"You don't like to think about it, do you?" Gaylen smiled. "You might actually show some human emotion if something happened to Audra. Am I right?"

The killer shook pills out into his hand, then tossed them into his mouth and swallowed them dry.

"Come on. It's going to be too late soon. Just walk away. Let me take him. Audra knows about the killings. She'd be happy if this guy was history. She'd feel safe. She'd know other young girls wouldn't have to suffer. Don't you want to make her happy? I know you don't like to see her sad."

Dimitri thought back to the tears glistening in her hazel eyes as she wept over the boy's death. It hadn't been easy. Listening to her gut-wrenching sobs…watching her heart break.

He placed his hands on the chair arms and pushed himself upright. "You're right. I don't like to see her sad." The admission was difficult—especially making it to Gaylen. But no use trying to hide it. The asshole knew Dimitri had an unwanted, uncontrollable affection for Audra.

"So, you're out of here? He's mine?"

Dimitri slowly shook his head. "No way. There's something I can do for Audra, but it doesn't involve feeding your twisted urges."

****

The next evening at the beginning of Audra's shift, Mary Lou called her in to her office. When Audra was seated across from her—eye-level with Camellia's smiling face in her cheerleading picture—Mary Lou slid the incident form across the desk. "You should be getting fast at completing these by now."

Audra nodded, but didn't meet her eyes as she leaned over the paper, filling in the information.

"You know." Mary Lou picked up the photo of her

daughter. "I can't imagine losing a child. We see it often, but it's never easy when it's a child, you know?"

"Yes. I know." Audra tried to keep the hoarseness, the guilt, from her voice.

"You can't really know, though, can you? Not being a mother yourself." She shook her head and went on as if she hadn't just added salt to a wound that had been open in Audra for years. "No one can understand until they have a child of their own. I wouldn't want to go on if something happened to Camellia."

Audra slid the paperwork back to Mary Lou and stood. "I'm sure you wouldn't. It's unthinkable."

Mary Lou nodded, but her attention was still riveted to the photo, and Audra slipped from the office.

At the nurses' station, Wilton patted Audra's arm, and Tonya clucked sympathetically. "Are you going to be okay? Three patients in less than a week. Tough."

Audra nodded. "I'll be okay. I'm just sick about Trevor. Poor kid. Never got a chance to live."

Wilton said, "Can't believe the mom's still hanging around. Some people just can't let go, I guess."

"Hanging around?" Audra asked. "Cheryl's here?"

Tonya nodded. "Right now, she's in Trevor's room with the priest. Good thing we don't need the bed yet."

"Priest?"

"The one who was with Trevor when he died."

"But…no one was with—" Something wasn't right. Her heartbeat stuttered. "Excuse me."

She moved quickly down the hallway, stopping when she reached Trevor's doorway. Cheryl sat in her usual chair. A man's black-clothed back was to Audra. Cheryl's face seemed to glow. Not exactly with joy, but with something like contentment…calm.

When Audra entered the room, Cheryl's head rose. "Audra." She smiled through tears. "I want you to meet Father Sarantos."

Audra held her breath as she waited for the man to face her. When he did, she gasped in shock. He wore a white collar, black priest garb, and his face was assembled in a properly pious expression. But those piercing blue eyes were the same. *Dimitri.*

"This is Audra Grayson," Cheryl said. "The nurse who took such good care of my son." She looked at Audra. "I thought my baby died alone, but Father Sarantos came to see me, found me here in Trevor's room. He told me he was with Trevor when he…passed." She let out a sob and lifted a hand to her mouth. "I'm sorry. I'm just so…happy. No. Happy's not the right word. I'm at peace. I'm relieved that this kind man was with my baby."

Cheryl could see him? She clung to Dimitri's sleeve. She was touching him?

Dimitri held out a hand. Fear locked Audra's muscles for a moment, and a frown creased Cheryl's brow. "Everything okay, Audra?"

"Yes, sure. I—I'm just so surprised. I didn't know anyone was with Trevor." She reached a hand out, and Dimitri closed his over hers. She caught her breath at the warm contact. The tendrils of electricity were there again, but this time, they were warm, human tingles. She tugged her hand away.

"I heard about his mother's grief." Dimitri's rich timbre was smooth, comforting. "I thought I should pay her a visit."

Audra narrowed her eyes. What was his end game?

"Thank you," she forced out through stiff lips.

"That's very kind of you."

Dimitri's mouth quirked in a grin, and he inclined his head. "Anything I can do to help. After all, that's my calling."

****

It was after midnight before Audra got home. Having a harrowing experience and being blind-sided by tragedy and grief didn't mean an RN could clock out early. She'd had to finish out her shift, even though she could barely concentrate on her duties.

As if Trevor's death wasn't enough, she had the encounter with a now human Dimitri to wrap her mind around. How could he do that? Just turn human?

She let herself in the house and went straight to the kitchen, trying to decide between a glass of wine or warm milk.

The wine was edging out the milk by a nose.

When she flipped on the kitchen light, a figure moved toward her, and she let out a scream. Then she recognized Dimitri and closed her eyes, shaking her head. "You have got to be kidding me."

"Sorry," he said. "Didn't mean to scare you."

"You just pop in any time you want? I have no privacy now? What if I'd been in the shower or something?"

A lazy grin came over his face, and his gaze dropped down her body. "That's just something I'd have to try to get over."

She stalked to the counter. Wine had definitely kicked milk's ass. She took a bottle down from the cupboard and grabbed a glass, filling it to the rim.

"So, is your last name actually Sarantos?" she asked after a few unladylike gulps. "Or is that just an alias you use when posing as a priest? Oh yeah. And let's not forget, posing as a *human*."

"Sarantos is my last name."

She emptied the remaining wine in her glass and tossed the bottle into the trash can.

"You don't recycle?" Dimitri asked.

She whirled to face him. "What? Did you just ask if I recycle?"

He frowned. "Uh. Yes. You really should, you know."

"Please tell me you're not lecturing me about recycling after all the bullshit you've done."

"Listen, if you'd seen the way the earth has changed over the past few centuries, you'd understand how important it is. I mean, the landfills have gotten way out of hand."

"Jesus," she muttered. She bent into the trash can and retrieved the wine bottle, slamming in on the countertop almost hard enough to break it. "Happy now, Mr. Green? Anything else I can do to make Earth a better place for you to hang out while you destroy human lives?"

"Come on. Back to this? I wanted to come see you, talk to you. I'm sure you have a lot of questions about what happened earlier tonight."

"Uh, yeah." She refilled her glass and threw back another slug of wine. This time, it made her a little woozy. Sent a warm, languorous, yet numbing feeling through her body, to her legs. *Yes. That's more like it.* "Newsflash. You can become human?"

"We can. Once in a twenty-four-hour period and only for a limited time."

"Why is that?"

"It's one of the abilities we were given to keep us somewhat…emotionally balanced, for lack of a better term. If we're allowed to turn human occasionally—and for a brief time—it enables us to continue to feel empathy for the human state. If, however, we were allowed to stay human for as long as we wanted, we would be tempted to set aside our reaper nature…remain human indefinitely. So, we have the ability to turn human, but it's not without risks…consequences."

"What consequences?"

He sighed and shook his head. "It's complicated."

She moved toward him, but not too close, pointing a finger at his chest. "I'm sick and tired of you answering every one of my questions with *it's complicated.* Do you think I'm a freakin' moron? Why were you in Trevor's room today? Why did you become human and pose as a priest? What the hell kind of game are you playing?"

"It's not a game, Audra. You were sad because his mother suffered at the thought of her son dying alone. I wanted to calm her. I couldn't stop Gaylen from taking her son, but I could stop her from thinking he'd died alone. That's it. That's all."

"Whatever." She harrumphed. "Like the hero Cassie says you are. *Right.*" Her words were starting to slur. She set the half-empty wine glass on the table.

"So, you met Cassie?" Dimitri's mouth split in a grin, and Audra saw what could only be affection in his expression. She felt an unwanted and unreasonable twinge of…something. Jealousy? No. No way. She must be drunk.

"Yeah. I met her. All kinds of reapers in my world

now." She wagged her finger in his face. "Oh yeah, and your buddy, Gaylen? He asked me a favor. Has some kind of plan. Wants me to let him taste my breath."

Dimitri's jaw clenched, and his eyes darkened like an indigo sky. "He what? You know you can't let him, right?"

"Would it be that big a deal?"

"It would be a very big deal. Trust me. You don't want to even consider whatever insane notion he has."

"I don't want to consider anything either of you have to say, but the two of you aren't leaving me a lot of choices." She lifted a hand and rubbed her fingers across her forehead. "I'm tired. I feel a headache coming on. Can you please just leave now?"

Sighing, he gave a slight nod. "Fine. We'll talk later."

He moved to the back door. Would he open it and exit? Or just fade through? She leaned a shoulder against the wall as she waited to find out.

He paused before doing either. "If you never listen to another thing I tell you, you must listen to me now. You absolutely cannot trust Gaylen. Whatever he suggests, you must refuse. Listen to your head, and be very afraid of him."

"Hmmm." She tapped a finger on her chin. "But I shouldn't be afraid of you? I'm not sure your advice makes a lot of sense. I'm a big girl. I'll make my own choices, thank you very much."

He growled, and before she knew what was happening, he was no longer at the door. He was right in front of her, so close she could see her reflection in his eyes. His face twisted in fury.

She gasped and pushed herself against the wall.

"Dimitri? What are you doing?"

He slapped a hand against the wall on either side of her head. Even though she knew he was transparent, that he didn't really have her trapped, she froze in place, her heart pounding like it might fly from her chest.

"Yes," he gritted through clenched teeth. "You should be afraid of me, too. I'm a fucking reaper, got it?"

"Got it," she choked out.

His heavy-lidded eyes dropped to her lips. "You're panting. Your breath is coming out in puffs that you can't see, but I can. Did Gaylen tell you I want to taste you too?"

She tried to regulate her breathing. Tried to think straight. What was happening? Dimitri had spent all this time convincing her he meant no harm, and now he was trying to terrify her?

"What are you doing? Stop—"

"What if I can't stop, Audra? Just like Gaylen wouldn't be able to." He lowered his head and his lips were a mere hairsbreadth from hers. "If he starts, if he tastes the sweet nectar of your breath, he'll lose control." His voice was husky, and the wine combined with the fear made her insides do funny things. Things that weren't entirely unpleasant. "Is that what you want, Audra? For him to take, and take, until you're breathless?"

She shook her head, too breathless now to respond. Her legs turned to rubber. His eyes locked on hers, so close she could see nothing but midnight black pupils surrounded by fiery sapphires. Even if she wanted to—and she didn't know that she did—she was unable to look away.

"Are you afraid of Gaylen?" His low, husky tone now held a demanding edge. She nodded. "Are you afraid of me?"

She hesitated, but the quivering in her gut, the sparks shooting through her bloodstream had to be fear. She nodded again.

"Good," he snarled. "Be afraid. And stay that way."

He pulled away and before she had time to realize he'd moved, before she had time to draw air into her lungs, he disappeared.

## Chapter 14

Audra loaded groceries into the trunk of her Impala, trying to focus on the mundane task so she wouldn't think about poor Trevor. Or Dimitri.

Dimitri…becoming human to pose as a priest to comfort a grieving mother. Big deal, right? Probably just a con.

Then, Dimitri threatening her…warning her. Or was it really a threat? She thought of his smoldering ocean eyes, the tingles he sent out…the way her breath sped up, but not necessarily with fear. Even as he menaced her, as she admitted to being frightened, some small part of her felt protected.

*Ludicrous.*

She stashed the last of her bags, holding onto the eggs so she could keep them up front with her. As she started to close the trunk, a wave of cloying air washed over her, heavy with energy that was almost painful. She sucked in a breath, knowing it was Gaylen before he spoke. Still, the too-smooth, melodious voice sent quivers of revulsion down her spine.

"Audra. We never finished our chat. Remember what I asked of you?"

She gritted her teeth, slamming the trunk lid before facing Gaylen. "You were the one who took Trevor."

"Well," he drawled the word out slowly. "That's kind of your fault. You had a chance to stop me. I only asked for one little thing. Now, do you see how serious I am? What's it going to take before you give in, Audra?"

"You want to suck the life from me? Maybe kill me? Right. Just *one* little thing. No way."

"At least hear me out," he said. "I think you'll like what I have to say. You want me to stop taking people, right? Your patients? Co-workers? Friends?" The smile he flashed rivaled the sun shining above their heads, but now she saw the evil in its beauty. He lowered his voice. "Your loved ones."

*Loved ones...*

She had no family, really. Her friends were her loved ones. Riley, Sadie, Jaxon. She had to protect them, but she couldn't trust this monster. Tears tightened her throat. "You can't hurt anyone else. Please."

"Then let me taste your breath. I won't kill you. I just want a taste."

"You can't. I won't just let you—"

"If you don't, I keep taking people. Each time, it will be someone you care about more."

She tightened her grip on the eggs, nearly crushing them. "You're insane."

"Insane with wanting you."

She tried to move around him, but he stepped in her path. Even though she knew he wasn't solid, that she could walk right through him, she halted. She didn't want to feel him that close. Didn't want to experience the sensation she'd experienced with Dimitri. Somehow, she knew it wouldn't feel the same.

She glanced around. The parking lot was crowded with vehicles creeping along, looking for a space, shoppers pushing their carts, some heading inside. Had anyone noticed she was just standing behind her car like a dolt?

"What do you want me to do?" she asked quietly.

"Let's get inside your car. You always seem to be surrounded by people." He glanced around. "Such a tempting array of victims. But I want you to feel free to converse with me, so we'll talk in your car. You'll seem less like a candidate for a mental hospital that way."

The last thing she wanted to do was sit in a confined space with Gaylen. But then again, she didn't want to stand out in the open, appearing, as he said, like a candidate for a mental hospital.

She slid into the driver's side while Gaylen materialized in the seat next to her.

Staring ahead out the windshield so she wouldn't have to look at him, she said, "So, what? What kind of crazy plan have you hatched?" Reluctantly, she turned her head to look at him.

"First of all, this has to be done in a safe place. Somewhere we won't be interrupted. I have to turn human, but I have to be sure Dimitri won't show up and stop my…" His eyes dropped to her mouth. "…feast. I need your cooperation."

"How?"

"Has Dimitri told you the effects copper has on reapers?"

"Copper?"

"It's paralyzing to a reaper. If you bind a reaper in copper, he can't move. He loses all his strength."

She stared at him incredulously. "You want me to somehow immobilize Dimitri with copper?"

"Exactly. That way, I can safely turn human, take

your breath." He stopped, and his eyes glazed over. He seemed to zone out momentarily, then he shook his head as if breaking a trance. "When I'm finished, I go away. You release Dimitri. Your patients and loved ones are safe. Happily ever after and all that bullshit."

As if she was even considering his insanity, she said, "How do I get the copper...*on* Dimitri?"

"That's a tricky one. He'd most likely have to turn human first. A human applying copper to a reaper would be a nearly impossible feat."

"I can't get him to turn human."

"He's done it for you before, when he posed as a priest. I don't think there's much Dimitri wouldn't do for you." He lifted a brow. "You could use your womanly wiles, seduce him."

Her cheeks heated. "I don't know. Even if he were human, I don't know how I'd bind him in copper. This is all too much." She pressed her palms to her eyes and shook her head. "I just can't."

"At least think about it. You know, it won't be so bad for you. What's that song? "Take My Breath Away?"" He grinned. "Makes it sound...pleasurable."

She drew her brows into a frown. "Oh yeah. Having you suck the breath from me would be the ultimate pleasure."

"Thing is, your choices are limited. I don't think you like option two, am I right?" He leaned toward her across the console, and she scrunched against the driver's door. "I tell you what. I'll give you a little time to think about it. *Very* little time. I'm not a patient reaper. I'll lay off your people for a brief while, but I'll need an answer soon. The only reason I'm giving you a window is because I know it's a big decision. I know it's a lot to take in. You don't make the right choice, however, you, and everyone around you, will wish you had."

****

The air was cool, but the sun was bright in the sky, shining through the sparse trees above Audra's head. She leaned into the crook of the fallen oak and closed her eyes. Now, *this* was the way to spend a day off. Away from people, away from problems, away from death. Too bad she couldn't also get away from her thoughts.

She had a decision to make and either option made her stomach clench with terror. Gaylen. As a human. Being at his mercy while he sucked the breath from her. She shuddered. He promised he wouldn't hurt her, but she didn't trust him. God. What do to? Whichever choice she made, she had a feeling it wouldn't go well.

A shadow passed over her, and she blinked her eyes open. "Ah, hell." She sat upright. "It's you."

Dimitri stood above her, wearing a charcoal grey Henley and faded jeans. Her seclusion was shattered. She was going to have to find a different getaway spot. This one was becoming entirely too populated.

"What do you want?" She shaded her eyes as she frowned up at him.

He lowered himself on the tree, straddling it as Jaxon had. Only so many ways one could sit on a fallen tree. Somehow she couldn't picture Dimitri doing the crisscross-applesauce thing.

Before he could answer, she said, "Are you here to threaten me again? Because it's not necessary. I get the message. Reapers are badass."

"That's not why I'm here."

She let out a snort. "You know, I don't get it. Almost since the day I met you, you've done everything you could to convince me you don't harm people. Then you terrorize me, try to convince me how dangerous you are. Really? You should make up your mind."

"I didn't mean to upset you."

She snorted again. "Too late. Upset has been my constant companion since you came into my life."

"I *am* dangerous. We all are, to a degree. I just don't want you to get too complacent. I'd never hurt you on purpose, but I can't be trusted when it comes to taking your breath. I would hope I could stop, but I can't guarantee that I could."

"I don't recall offering you my breath." The words sounded so strange coming from her mouth. But that was her world now.

"No, but I'm afraid when Gaylen comes to you with his deal, you'll think it's a good idea. I need you to understand that it's absolutely not."

She shifted her gaze away, afraid he'd read in her expression that Gaylen had already come to her with a plan. She didn't want him to know just yet. Especially since the plan involved an attack on Dimitri himself.

When she turned back to him, her breath stalled in her chest. His eyes were…magnificent. They'd somehow captured the sunlight, shining like brilliant blue prisms with a light of their own.

*Impossible*. No one could have eyes that color. She swallowed against the dryness in her throat.

He squinted. "Are you okay?"

She nodded jerkily. When she could speak, the words came out strained, as if the pounding of her heart hindered their release. Searching for a topic to take her mind off his knee-buckling good looks, she said, "You know, there's an old wives' tale about this creek. It's called Fertility Creek. They say if you bathe in the water, you'll have a dozen kids."

His mouth crooked in a grin. "I think if you bathe in it right now, you'll have hypothermia." His expression turned serious. "Is that what you want, Audra? A dozen kids?"

She gave a small smile. "Well, maybe not a dozen. But, yeah, I'd like children. I'd like the whole corny package…kids…two-car garage…growing old with the man I love while we sit on the porch together, watching the neighborhood go dark." She shook her head. "Wow. Did I just say that? Corny as hell."

"Not so corny." His voice lowered. "Is that why you come here so often? Why you have since you were a child? Because of the old wives' tale?"

"No, I just like it here. It's peaceful." She looked at him sharply. "How do you know I came here as a child? You watched me back then?"

He hesitated, clearing his throat before speaking. "I've observed a lot of people over the centuries." He stared past her shoulder. "I remember one time you came out here, your Walkman hanging from your ear. You stood right over there. All by yourself. Dancing."

Her face heated. "You saw that?" She laughed to cover her embarrassment. "I was listening to Elvis Presley music. It made me feel better somehow. I guess that makes me a dork."

He shook his head. "No. Your goofy dancing made you a dork."

"Hey!" she said with mock indignation. Then she shrugged. "It *was* kind of goofy."

"Elvis, though. Not a bad choice. He was a talented guy. Nice guy."

"You knew him?" A horrifying thought struck her. "Did you…"

"No. No, I didn't take him. I took someone at one of his concerts. Afterward, I was curious. I followed Elvis around for a few days. I was awed by the effect he had on people. They were so drawn to him."

"I can see why." She cocked her head. "I bet you've met a lot of famous people. I never really thought about that. You can go anywhere, can't you?"

"I've met—well, been in the company of—most of the U.S. Presidents. During the civil war, I was with Abraham Lincoln, Robert E. Lee. In the 1920s, I watched Babe Ruth play baseball."

Her brows rose. "Really? Oh my God. That's amazing. I can't imagine what a thrill it must have been to actually see him play."

He laughed. "You're impressed that I saw Babe Ruth? The presidents…nothing?"

"Oh, yeah. That's cool too." She grinned.

He grinned back, and they sat in silence for a few moments, the only sound the wind rustling through the trees. Maybe because things were going so well between them, maybe because at that moment, he seemed almost human, almost trustworthy, she blurted, "Gaylen came to see me with his plan."

His jaw tensed, and his eyes narrowed to slits. "Did he hurt you?" She shook her head. He studied her for a moment as if trying to gauge her truthfulness. "And what was this plan of his?"

She didn't dare share the details of what Gaylen wanted her to do to Dimitri. "He wants us to find a safe place, somewhere he can taste my breath without being…interrupted."

He laughed without humor. "Gaylen's playing it from all angles. He asked me to help him taste your breath. Promised he'd quit taking people before their time."

Her heart crawled into her throat. "What did you tell him?"

"I refused. He would kill you."

"Kill me? He said he just wants to taste my breath."

"He wants both. If he gets a chance to sample you, he'll be satisfied for a while, but ultimately, he'd like to be the one who takes you." Dimitri closed his eyes, and she momentarily felt cheated, robbed of the opportunity to view their beauty. "I have to destroy him. No one is safe until he's annihilated."

"And how can you do that?"

He opened his eyes. "The only way I can destroy him is if he becomes human. The only way he'll do that is for you."

"You want me to offer myself?"

"No!" The word came out in a sharp bark. "It would be much too dangerous."

"But you're saying I could tempt him to turn human? That he would do it for me?" Funny how they both claimed the other would turn human for her.

"The only way he can sample your breath is to become human. And that is probably the one thing he'd feel was worth the risk." He frowned. "But I'll take care of him without your help. No more innocent lives should be lost. This has to end. Once I'm rid of him, not only will your loved ones be safe, but I can then serve out the remainder of my sentence in peace."

"Your sentence?"

He nodded. "Reapers are required to serve for a hundred years."

"But you've been a reaper for much longer."

"Yes, well. When we go against reaper rules, they add time to our sentence."

No surprise that he'd broken rules. "What happens when your sentence is done?"

"I go away. Really go away. Forever. To whatever destiny awaits me. But, if I've served well, it will be better than the one that awaited me in my human death."

A splinter of dread entered her chest at the thought of him disappearing from her life, forever. But that was ridiculous. That was precisely what she wanted. If she never encountered another reaper, she'd be beyond thrilled.

"Trust me," she said. "I'd be willing to take the risk if it meant getting rid of Gaylen. If I knew for sure it would work, and I would survive."

"I can't involve a human in this. It's my responsibility."

"So, if he did become human, what then?"

"I become human, and I kill him."

"What if he kills you?"

His lips tilted in a grin. "That's not going to happen."

In spite of the cocky bravado, she saw a flicker of something in his eyes. Uncertainty? Fear?

"But what if it does?"

"Then you'll still be rid of me."

She didn't like the slight ache his words brought.

"But Gaylen would still be around. More destructive than ever, because you wouldn't be here to stop him, right?"

"Right."

"Not exactly a win-win situation for me. No matter what, I'm stuck with one of you."

His expression darkened, his eyes looking wounded for a moment, then it was quickly gone. She couldn't have hurt his feelings, could she? He didn't have feelings, right? Before she could decide whether to apologize, her phone rang.

She smiled when she saw Shane's number on the display. "Excuse me," she said to Dimitri before answering the call.

"Hi, Audra," Shane said. "Just checking in with you. Letting you know I heard from Maria."

"Did you? Is she okay?"

"She's good. Still at her friend's. I told her it's best not to contact you, or anyone else here, in case asshole's watching or listening. I figured speaking through me would be safe."

"Thanks for letting me know she's okay."

"I didn't want you to worry."

"That was thoughtful of you."

His voice turned husky. "I have a lot of thoughts. Want to hear more?"

"Are you flirting with me, Sheriff?" She flushed as her gaze shot to Dimitri. His face was averted, but she could see he wore a scowl.

"Guilty," Shane said.

She laughed, feeling lighthearted and liking it. A nice change compared to the darkness and death surrounding Dimitri.

"I'm kind of in the middle of something," she told Shane. "Maybe we can continue this another time."

"Sure. But before I let you go, would you like to go to the costume party with me?"

"The hospital party?"

"Yeah. Unless you already have a date."

"No date."

"Then?"

"I'd love to."

"Pick you up at seven. You'll have to tell me what you're going as, though, so I won't take the wrong girl."

She laughed. "When I figure it out, I'll be sure to let you know." She hung up and drew in a deep, fortifying breath. Back to Dimitri and the surreal discussion of how to destroy a reaper.

****

The girl clawed at Barney's hands, to no avail. He held on tight as he rode her. She tried to scream, but his grip restricted her throat, and no sound came out.

*Yes.* God, yes. This was it, the ultimate. Not just a street-worn runaway, this one. She was someone's darling, pampered…protected. She would be missed. His breathing sped up, and he pumped harder, squeezing her neck more tightly with each thrust. Tears streamed down her perfect cheeks. Her big green eyes widened with pain and terror. Her white-blonde hair was drenched in sweat. He'd never seen anything more beautiful.

Too soon, it was going to end. The pressure was building, and he wouldn't hold out much longer. Nothing had ever felt like this, nothing had given him such a rush…such a high…

There. Yes. He felt the life drain from her body as he drained inside her. He went limp, dropping down on her corpse while he struggled to catch his breath. Not an easy task. He felt as though a boulder was pressing against his midsection.

He rolled off her and clasped his chest. His heart was pounding too fast. That could be dangerous. But so worth it.

For now, he'd rest. Then he'd go through the ritual of erasing his presence. Not the usual procedure this time. No motel room for this one. He hadn't been able to lure her with promises of a nice, warm bed like he had the others. She had that at home.

He had no fingerprints to wipe away, not out here in the woods. Nowhere to flush the condom, either. Not to worry. He'd get rid of it another way.

For the first time, he'd actually killed someone, right here at home, in Boon Springs.

Risky. Exciting. The thought brought a sharp pang to his heart. He fumbled for his pants and the pill bottle in the pocket.

Swallowing a couple of the small white tablets, he lay back on the grass, waiting until the nitro did its magic.

He turned his head so he could stare at her, while she stared up at the night sky. His chest filled with the wonder of it all. He hadn't expected to run into her. Hadn't expected such an opportunity to present itself. But, when offered a gift, you don't question it. You just accept it.

****

"Sorry," she said. "Where were we?"

"Gaylen," he nearly growled the word. "No one is

safe unless I figure out a way to stop him, permanently."

"There's no way other than him turning human?"

Dimitri shrugged. "Or binding him with copper indefinitely. But that's not a guarantee. Another reaper can come along at any time, turn human, and free him."

"What if your sentence ends, and Gaylen is still around?"

"Then it will be up to someone else to end him."

She shivered, imagining Gaylen free to take souls at will, without Dimitri to slow his demented quest. "How much time is left on your sentence?"

"Forty-eight years."

"Oh." Much longer than she would have thought. She didn't like the relief that information brought. Relief that wasn't entirely due to Dimitri's ability to protect innocent souls from Gaylen.

What was wrong with her? She didn't need reapers in her life. Not even ones with glorious sapphire eyes, killer smiles, and the ability to incite tingles in every region of her body.

"I know that being aware of our existence has thrown your world into chaos," Dimitri said. "You don't deserve this. If I can destroy Gaylen, I'll get out of your life. I can't promise it now, because he's stalking the people around you. I have to be here."

"But once he's destroyed, I'll stop seeing reapers?"

"Not entirely. I can't make that stop happening now that the door is open. But you'll stop seeing me. I'll make sure I'm not assigned to anyone around you."

"How can you do that?"

"The guy in charge owes me."

"God?"

He flashed a smile. “No, not *that* guy in charge. The one who oversees reapers. I’ll tell him not to assign me to anyone near you.”

“And no more pop-in visits?”

“No more.”

“Great.” She tried to infuse the word with enthusiasm, but it sounded flat to her ears.

“Admit it, you’ll miss me.”

She tilted her head and a lock of hair fell on her forehead. Dimitri reached up as if to smooth it back. His touch hovered just beyond her flesh, but she could still feel the energy from his nearness.

“Your hair does that a lot,” he murmured.

She nodded. “Yeah.” It was all she could manage. He was too close. His eyes gazed intently into hers, glittering with an emotion she couldn’t identify. Gaylen’s revelation came back to her.

*Dimitri’s in love with you...*

Before she could consider the wisdom of the words, she blurted, “Gaylen said you’re in love with me. Is that true?”

His jaw tightened for a moment, then he shrugged and cocked a grin. “Come on, Audra. Does Gaylen ever tell the truth?”

“So, you don’t love me?”

“Love is...” He sighed, shrugged. “Let’s just say it’s an emotion I’m not familiar with.”

She nodded, feeling foolish and strangely disappointed. “Oh. The reaper thing. You can’t love?”

A brief, indefinable emotion came into his eyes, and he shook his head. “It’s not a reaper thing. I wasn’t capable of love when I was human.”

## Chapter 15

The night of the costume party, Audra was inexplicably nervous. She wasn't sure if it was because she had a date for the first time in a long time, because a reaper was on a mission to steal her breath, or because another reaper had the ability to steal her breath without even trying.

She eyed herself critically in the mirror. Headband, sequined mid-thigh green dress with fringe hanging from the hem, a blonde bob wig. She wasn't sure she could pull off the flapper look, but it was too late to change her mind.

She was applying thick, black eyeliner when the bell rang. Finishing it up, she opened the door to Shane. He wore a black tux with a crisp white shirt. His dark hair was slicked down, the hints of gray glinting beneath the porch light, making him look debonair.

"Wow." They said at the same time, then laughed.

"You look…amazing," he said. "Great choice. The outfit suits you."

"Thank you. You look pretty handsome yourself. But who are you supposed to be? Aren't you really just wearing a fancy tux?"

He looked offended. "You don't recognize me?" He squinted and lifted a brow. "Bond. James Bond."

She laughed. "I see. Maybe it's because I've never seen any of the Bond movies."

“You what?” He clutched his heart. “Please tell me you’re kidding.”

“I’m afraid not. That good, huh?”

“Not just good. A necessity. I’ve got them on DVD. We should get started right away. We need to fix you.”

“I tell you what, I’ll think about it. Deal?”

“Deal.”

He led her to his car and they drove to the Wyandotte mansion. It was the oldest home in Boon Springs and had an interesting—if tragic—history. The leader of the bandits who’d led a massacre on the area settlers had had the home built.

Not long after moving his family into the mansion, each and every one of them had been found dead. Back then, autopsies weren’t performed and no one knew how they’d died. It was assumed they’d succumbed to an illness.

Over the years, other families had lived in the house. Many of them had met a tragic end, others had simply moved out after staying less than a year. Fifty years ago, the town had purchased the home and now used it as more or less a community center, allowing townspeople to rent it out for special occasions.

Tonight, the spacious ballroom was filled nearly to capacity with hospital employees and their guests—which was most of the town, considering every resident was related to or friends with someone affiliated with the hospital.

Spider webs drifted from the ceiling with big, fat, authentic-looking spiders dangling from them. Scattered along the walls and throughout the room were pumpkins, life-size Frankensteins, witches, and other creatures. Sadie would be enthralled. In each corner of the room was a cash bar, along with a refreshment table holding a variety of food choices and large punch bowls with fog rising from them. "Werewolves of London" blared from the speakers.

Next to one of the bars, Audra spotted a group of her co-workers and went over to say hello.

Jaxon looked miserable, trapped by Tonya, who wore an ill-chosen mermaid costume. Wilton wore a blond wig and a shirt with metallic, bronze and black braided designs. Around his ample waist was a belt where a large, blue-bladed sword was sheathed.

"Who are you supposed to be?" Audra asked.

"Eragon." At her confused look, he said, "From the book? Then the movie in '06? Eragon."

"Sorry. Never heard of it."

He shook his head as if disgusted with her ignorance.

Audra turned to Jaxon, who looked magnificent. The gladiator costume showed off his sculpted chest, and he wore it like it was made for him. She could picture him riding in on a steed to rescue a damsel, or brandishing a medieval weapon in a coliseum battle while a princess looked on, hopeful he'd reign victorious and claim her hand.

In spite of how handsome he looked, Audra suddenly realized the sight of him didn't affect her the way it once did. Somewhere along the way, unrequited love had vanished, making way to deep, intense affection and loyalty, a different kind of love, maybe even beyond what she would have felt for actual family.

"You look fantastic," she said. "But it's kind of a cold night for such a…revealing costume."

"Yeah. Did *not* think that one through." He brought his hands up to his chest. "I swear, my nipples could cut glass."

"*Friends* and *Larry the Cable Guy*," Audra said automatically.

Jaxon scowled. "I wasn't doing the movie quote thing. My nipples could literally cut glass."

The group laughed.

Audra took hold of Shane's arm. "You guys remember Shane, right? Sheriff Dunham." After the handshakes and greetings were over, she said, "I haven't seen Mary Lou. Is she here?"

Tonya shook her head. "There's some problem with her daughter. They've been fighting. She wouldn't come home from her dad's. Something uninteresting like that."

"Mary Lou's absence is no big loss, if you ask me," Wilton put in.

The music changed and "I Put a Spell on You" began.

"Are they playing anything other than Halloween-themed music?" Audra asked.

"They're mixing it up some, but not nearly enough," Jaxon said, grimacing. "Shane, mind if I steal your date for a dance?"

"Not at all."

Jaxon led Audra to the dance floor. "Sorry to drag you away from Marshall Dillon. I had to escape Tonya. She's brutal."

"You poor thing," she said with mock sincerity. "You'd think a big, strong warrior could defend himself against a woman."

"Yeah, you'd think, wouldn't you?"

She grinned, relaxing in Jaxon's arms, relieved that she was free of the emotional grip he'd had on her all these years. She would like to attribute it to her budding relationship with Shane, but she was concerned there was someone else who'd replaced Jaxon in her affections. But she wouldn't think about him tonight. She wanted just one reaper-free night. Was that too much to ask?

"By the way, I've been meaning to ask you something," Jaxon said. "Will you be my date for the award ceremony? It's November seventh."

"Award ceremony?"

"Yeah, I'm nominated for a humanitarian award."

"For your work in the free clinic? That's great. It's about time you received the recognition you deserve."

He blushed. "I think they were running out of options for nominees. I was an afterthought."

"Whatever," she said. "You're too modest. You deserve to win. Of course I'll be your date. I'd be honored."

The song ended, and Jaxon said, "I'm going to let you rejoin the group on your own. This is my one opportunity to escape."

"Not a problem. I can find my way back. Good luck."

When she reached the group where Shane still stood, Tonya craned her neck, looking around and behind Audra. "What happened to Doctor Maroney?"

"He saw someone he knew. I'm sure he'll be back soon." *Not*, she added silently.

Over the speakers, "It Hurts Me" by Elvis played.

"Would you like to dance?" Shane asked. "If I recall, you like Elvis."

Audra smiled, pleased and touched that he remembered. "I'd love to."

****

"Hard to watch, isn't it?"

Dimitri didn't acknowledge Gaylen as he appeared beside him. His gaze was riveted to the dance floor, where Dunham held Audra so close a straight pin wouldn't fit between them. The Elvis song ended and, "I Can't Make You Love Me" began. Shane and Audra remained glued together.

"Come on," Gaylen prodded. "You can tell me. Must really hurt watching the woman you love with another man. Hey, I get it. Happened to me once, you know?"

"This again?" Dimitri flicked him a glance. "After two-hundred and fifty years, I'd have thought your lamenting would cease."

Gaylen's face reddened. "Spoken like a man who's never loved a woman like I loved Louisa."

Shane led Audra off the dance floor, his hand resting on the small of her back. Like it belonged there. A band of steel squeezed around Dimitri's chest. It *did* belong there. After all, it wasn't as if he could touch her like that. Not very often, at least.

"I wouldn't think you capable of love, Gaylen."

Gaylen laughed. "I was, back then. I've learned my lesson since, but then I was human…gullible. You took that away that night. I lived another three years, but my humanity died with Louisa. And she died because you had to have her."

Dimitri tried to ignore the truth in his words, but it was impossible. Louisa's death was his fault. He'd stolen her from Gaylen—literally stolen the man's wife—and she'd burned to death in Dimitri's home. The fire had started from a candle he'd knocked over in a drunken stupor.

Speaking of getting drunk, he wanted a drink in the worst way now, but with all these people around, it would be nearly impossible. How to explain glasses floating in the air, tilting, the liquid disappearing into nothingness?

Gaylen didn't have the same restraint. For the first time, Dimitri noticed he held a glass. He lifted it to his lips and drained the liquor. Dimitri perused the room, but no one seemed to notice. It was a Halloween party, after all, maybe they'd think it was some kind of trick.

He scanned the crowd until he once more spotted Audra. She and the sheriff were talking to another couple. Dimitri sighed in unwanted relief. At least they weren't touching. If he had to watch much more of that, he'd throw caution to the wind and have a drink—maybe several—himself.

"That was a long time ago," Dimitri finally said.

"True. Very true. We're in the here and now. No use dwelling on the past. No use thinking about Louisa." Gaylen pointed the glass in Audra's direction. "Our focus should be on the lovely Audra. Another woman we both want, admittedly for different reasons. Let's see how you feel when I take her the way you took Louisa."

Dimitri's spine tensed. "You'd take Audra just to punish me for Louisa?"

Gaylen threw his head back and laughed. "Come now, my friend. Such a simplified analysis of my reasons for wanting Audra. We both know there's much, much more. Unlike Louisa, once I take Audra, she'll be with me forever." He backed away, tipping the glass to Dimitri.

Dimitri just barely prevented himself from diving into him and beating him senseless. What was the use? It would only provide temporary satisfaction. The problem—the threat to Audra—would remain.

His eyes once more found her, and this time she was alone. A quiver moved through his gut. She was so damned beautiful. He couldn't let Gaylen destroy her, couldn't let her spend eternity with a depraved sadist.

Without even realizing he'd moved, he found himself standing in front of her. Her eyes rose to his. Tonight, the emerald dress she wore turned her hazel eyes to a deep, rich green, like the dense foliage in a forest. His body hardened in response to her nearness. He drew in a deep breath.

"Dimitri?" A smile creased her lovely mouth for a moment, then disappeared. "What are you doing here?'

How could he answer that? How could he tell her that he was here because she was? Because every moment he spent away from her felt like dying all over again.

****

"I came to enjoy the party." He inclined his head toward her. "You look stunning."

Audra's pulse sped up, and pleasure shot through her bloodstream. She was here on a date with another man—with an *actual* man—and this was the first time tonight she'd felt that giddy soaring of her heart, the thrill of expectation and new love.

Love? *Love*?

Irritation at the unwanted emotions coursed through her, making her want to lash out. "Really?

Enjoy the party? What, Dimitri, are you going to socialize? Eat, drink? Dance?" She twisted her mouth. "Oh, wait. You can't do any of that, can you? You can't partake of all the normal festivities, because you're not even real."

Dimitri flinched, and Audra experienced a moment of regret, before she soothed it with the thought of what he was. What he had done to her life.

"You're right, Audra. I can't enjoy all that like you can. Like your date can. Speaking of dates." He shoved his hands in his pockets and surveyed the room. "Where did yours run off to? That sharp tongue of yours scare him away?"

"I don't use my tongue on *him*." Heat shot to her cheeks. The words had sounded much better in her head than they had coming out of her mouth.

Dimitri quirked a brow and laughed. "Pity for him. No wonder he abandoned you."

Her mouth tensed. Through clenched teeth she said, "You know what I meant. He went to get drinks for us. Would you please just go so he doesn't return and see me talking to myself?"

"Sure. I'll leave you two lovebirds alone." Dimitri's intense gaze worked its way from her feet to the top of her head. "He's a lucky man."

Audra was searching for a response when a tortured scream—a male scream—ripped through the room.

She jerked her head toward the open patio door where the sound had come from. "What was that?"

"I'm not sure." Dimitri looked over his shoulder and Audra followed his gaze. Gaylen stood to their left, leaning a shoulder against the mantel, drink in hand. He shrugged as if to say, *don't look at me.*

Most of the party-goers had obviously heard it too. They surged through the doorway, spilling outside.

Audra followed and saw a group of people gathered near the small wooden bridge that went over the stream at the back of the property. The night air was cold. A half-moon shone above, partially obscured by a thin line of dark clouds. When she got closer, threading her way through the throng, she recognized Shane. He stood over two figures, one kneeling, the other lying prone on the ground. He turned when the party guests approached.

"Back, people, stay back." His eyes found Audra's, and he gave her a small, reassuring smile, but in it, she detected concern. "I need all of you to stay back. The ambulance is on its way."

Gaylen and Dimitri had followed Audra, but she ignored them. She wouldn't let all these people see her talking to air.

Audra now saw that Jaxon was the one kneeling over the woman lying on the ground. He was giving her chest-compressions. Audra could just barely make out a streak of blood on the woman's forehead, glistening like black oil in the light of the moon. Nearby, a man stood, trembling, crying, his words nearly incoherent.

"She fell," he whimpered. "We were crossing the bridge, and she stumbled in the dark, fell, and hit her head. I told her to wait here. I'd get her some ice." He looked wildly around at the crowd. "She seemed okay. She was barely hurt."

Audra pushed through the throng and rushed to Jaxon's side, kneeling next to him. "What can I do?" she asked breathlessly.

He shook his head, not taking his gaze from his patient. “Nothing. I got it.” His voice lowered to a whisper. “I don’t understand. She’s not breathing. Her injury doesn’t appear life threatening, yet…” He shook his head again as his voice trailed off.

Shane came over and bent toward Audra, placing his hand on her arm. “I’m sorry. I’ll be a while. You want to find another ride home?”

She shook her head. “I’ll wait for you.”

“You sure?”

“Absolutely.”

He gave her arm a squeeze before releasing it, then headed toward the distraught man.

“Calm down, sir,” he said, his tone firm but comforting. “I’ll need to get a statement from you. Let’s walk over here while they’re taking care of your wife.”

“I can’t leave her. I left her once. Look what happened. I can’t leave her again.”

“When the ambulance arrives, you can ride with her to the hospital.”

Audra looked at Jaxon, who’d stopped his ministrations. He didn’t speak, but she knew by the expression on his face. The woman was gone. Dead. Here at a party. After a minor accident?

Audra stood and moved back, allowing room for the EMTs when they arrived. She shot a glower at Gaylen, then shifted it to Dimitri.

“We were inside,” Dimitri said. “I can’t even pin this one on Gaylen.”

“Could have been a fluke,” Gaylen said, shrugging. “Maybe it was just a good old-fashioned, regular, freak accident death. They’re boring, but they do happen.”

Audra glared at him, wishing she could retort.

"Then where's the reaper to take her?" Dimitri asked.

Gaylen frowned. "Good point."

A throaty female laugh rose, sounding like it came from across the stream. Audra's gaze searched the tree line on the opposite bank. She spotted a woman with skin so pale it was almost translucent, and long, thick copper-colored hair. She wore an unbuttoned white fur coat, all black clothing, and shiny black boots.

"Son of a bitch," Dimitri breathed.

Gaylen laughed uproariously. "Looks like you created a monster."

Audra wanted to ask what the hell was going on, but all she could do was raise her brows expectantly at Dimitri and tighten her lips, silently demanding an explanation.

He stared at her for a moment, then shook his head without speaking. Sirens screeched in the distance, becoming louder as the ambulance approached.

Audra glanced back across the stream at the woman. Even from this distance, she could see her blood red lips spread in a wide smile. The woman gave a little finger wave, then faded back into the trees.

****

*Veronica.* Curse her wicked soul to hell. Dimitri had left the party and searched for her, but with no luck. The bitch was hiding from him. She knew what was in store for her.

He'd trained her. Mentored her. Instilled the rules, the guidelines, the ethics of being a reaper into her. How could she have gone rogue?

He knew the answer. Anger and revenge. He'd also

cast her aside and stomped all over her heart. Or, at least, the shell of the heart she'd had when she was human. Reapers could still feel, though. He, among all, knew that to be true. And he'd crushed her feelings like they meant nothing to him.

In spite of his two-hundred plus years trying to atone for his human mistakes, he'd managed to hurt someone. Still. Veronica was responsible for her own actions. There was no excuse for her scorned woman rampage. He feared this might be only the beginning. With her temper, no telling what she was capable of.

Audra… What if she went after Audra? After all, Veronica blamed Audra for Dimitri's defection. What she didn't know was that he'd been weary of her for years. It had just been easier to keep her around than to deal with the drama and theatrics dumping her would bring. But now, getting this close to Audra, he had no other choice. He could barely *look* at Veronica without comparing her to Audra, let alone touch her without wishing he was touching Audra.

He should go check on Audra. She would be home by now. She deserved an explanation. Plus, he needed to make sure she was okay.

He arrived at her house and hesitated. He wouldn't just materialize inside. She'd had enough scares for one night. He'd look inside first, see what she was doing, approach slowly, so as not to spook her.

He scowled at the sheriff's car in the driveway. Of course, he was her ride home. He'd been her date. But it was three o'clock in the morning. Why the hell was he still here?

Unless…

No. They'd gotten home late from the party.

Dunham had stayed to process the scene. They'd probably only been home a few minutes. Audra was just now getting reacquainted with the guy. She wouldn't jump into bed with him on their first date.

In spite of his self-reassurances, a knot of dread opened up in his gut as he stepped onto the porch. Taking a deep breath to fortify himself, he looked through the living room window.

Relief washed over him. Dunham was seated on the sofa, Audra at the opposite end. She tugged the headband and wig off and fluffed her fingers through her thick, dark hair. They were talking, their expressions troubled.

Dimitri watched for a moment, feeling like a stalker. Maybe he should just leave. He could talk to Audra tomorrow. Or, he could just wait it out. Dunham would probably be gone soon, and he could give Audra a quick explanation, then be on his way.

But how much to explain? Did he really want to tell Audra what had happened between him and Veronica? Why the bitch was now on some kind of jealous, deadly rampage? Well, rampage was too strong a word. She'd only taken one victim that he knew of. Perhaps she was just pouting and had gotten it out of her system.

Right. Like he really believed that.

He frowned as he noticed a change in Audra's expression. Her face softened and a small, coy smile appeared.

She scooted toward Dunham on the sofa. Right *next* to Dunham.

Then she moved closer…closer still. Her eyes drifted shut, and she leaned forward, touching her mouth to Dunham's. Dunham pulled her in, getting to enjoy the feel…the taste of Audra's lips.

*No.* Dimitri nearly groaned aloud. His breath left him like a fist had landed in the center of his sternum. He flinched and drew back, quickly retreating.

He wouldn't remain here, ogling them like some perverted voyeur.

Besides, maybe if he stopped watching, the knifing pain inside his chest would go away.

## Chapter 16

The kiss was nice. Pleasurable.

And that was all. No fireworks, no rushing of her blood, no pounding in her ears, no tingling in her nether regions.

It was just nice.

What was wrong with her? The kisses she and Jaxon shared had been more passionate, and he wasn't attracted to women.

She pressed more tightly to Shane, revving up the kiss, moving her hands over his shoulders, trying to incite that rush of uncontrollable passion that was missing from their embrace.

Still nothing.

Shane broke the kiss, pulling away and staring into her eyes. "You're not feeling it, are you?"

"What do you mean?"

"No fireworks, no urge to rip my clothes off and carry me into the bedroom."

She laughed, grateful for his humor to break the tension. "I don't know what's wrong. You're good-looking, sexy, sweet. You're warm and strong, and I feel safe when I'm with you."

"But you're not swooning. Your body's not singing with desire for me."

"Swooning? Body singing? Have you been reading romance novels or something?"

"Would I admit it if I had?" The smile faded from his eyes. "It's okay, Audra. We can back off. Take it slow."

"Slower than fifteen years?"

He brushed a thumb along her cheekbone. "Most of that fifteen years has been spent apart. We need to get to know each other all over again, work on being friends, then we'll see where it takes us."

"What about you? Did you feel the toe-curling passion?"

He looked down at his lap. "Let's just say my toes weren't where I was feeling it."

She smiled. "Yet you're willing to be patient. Try the friendship thing. You're one of the nicest guys I've ever known."

"You know what they say. Nice guys finish last." He grinned and wiggled his brows. "Speaking of finish. I probably need to head home."

"Shane!" She lightly punched his shoulder.

"It's either that or a cold shower." He stood and pulled her to her feet, planting a quick kiss on her forehead. "Good night, sweet Audra. Sleep well."

****

The next day, Riley arrived at the hospital under the guise of having lunch with Audra. In truth, it was to be the bearer of distressing news.

"Maria dropped the charges?" Audra let her fork fall to the plate, suddenly losing the little enthusiasm she had for the pre-made Caesar salad.

"I'm afraid so."

"Is she still at her friend's house?"

Riley shook her head. "I think she went back to Scott."

"Shit. What's wrong with her?"

"I think she just felt she couldn't hide out forever. That going back to Scott was inevitable." Riley sipped from the straw in her Diet Coke. "Doesn't Shane have enough to arrest the asshole?"

"He arrested him, but Scott posted bail. The trial won't be for months. In the meantime, he's free to beat the hell out of his wife as often as he pleases."

Riley reached out and patted Audra's hand. "I'm sorry. We'll just hope for the best."

"Right."

"What about that girl at the Halloween party? She died?"

"Yes. I'm afraid so."

"Wasn't it just some minor accident? A fall or something?"

Audra nodded numbly. She couldn't tell her friend the woman's death was assisted by a ghoul from the beyond.

She'd wanted to ask Dimitri about the woman across the creek. She had to be a reaper. Had to have caused the victim's death, but when she looked back to question him, he and Gaylen had both disappeared. Audra knew, though. Knew the woman was involved and that Gaylen and Dimitri knew it too.

From a few tables away, Audra heard Mary Lou's voice rise. "What? Where is she?"

Audra looked over Riley's shoulder to see that her boss was talking on her cell phone. She looked stricken, fear and shock evident in her expression. She jumped to her feet and screamed into the phone. "No! It can't be. Oh my God, no!"

Audra rose and rushed to her side. "Mary Lou,

what is it? What's happening?"

Dazed eyes stared at Audra from a stark white face. "That was my ex-husband. Camellia's missing. She's been missing for two days, and the bastard just now bothered to tell me." She swayed, and Audra reached out to steady her. "Oh God," The agonized wail trembled through her body, vibrating to Audra's hands. "My little girl. Where could she be?" She took Audra's arms in a painful grip. "Get Sheriff Dunham. Make him find her. He's your friend. *Make him find her.*"

****

Audra stayed with Mary Lou until Shane came and took a statement. Tonya drove Mary Lou home after Shane assured her he'd do all he could to find her little girl.

A sick feeling wound through Audra's gut. Too much was happening. Way too much. Did Camellia's disappearance have anything to do with the reapers? Didn't every awful thing that had happened lately have something to do with the reapers? *Everything* to do with them?

Now, in addition to Gaylen, there seemed to be another evil reaper on the loose. Who was the mystery woman at the Halloween party, and was she, indeed, a reaper? Had she killed the woman? Audra didn't have the answers, but she knew who would.

She went home and paced while she waited for Dimitri. No need to shout for him this time. She had a feeling he'd arrive soon enough.

Her intuition was well founded. Half an hour after she got home, while she was making her umpteenth trek across the living room floor, he appeared in front of her.

He wore a black, button-up shirt, and part of her

mind noted dark stubble on his jaw. Did reapers actually have to shave? She wouldn't think about that. Too many other, more important questions were pressing now.

"Tell me what's happening," she demanded. "Who was that woman at the party? Does Camellia's disappearance have anything to do with reapers?"

"Who's Camellia?"

"Mary Lou Jenkins' daughter. Mary Lou is the charge nurse at St. Anne's. Her daughter is missing."

"I know nothing about that. Reapers aren't really into kidnapping. They mostly leave their victims out in the open for all to find. And, no longer breathing."

"Like the victim at the party?"

He sighed, and his jaw clenched. "That *was* the work of a reaper."

"The red-haired woman?"

Dimitri nodded.

"Who is she?"

He didn't answer.

"Dimitri, who is this woman? What's going on? I thought Gaylen was the only demented reaper out there. Now we have someone new to worry about?"

"I'll take care of her. This is my fault, anyway."

"How so?"

He pursed his lips, then said, "She's a jilted lover."

"*A* jilted lover, or *your* jilted lover?"

"Mine."

A sliver of pain pricked her. She'd expected him to say that, but hoped he wouldn't.

"I thought you told me you couldn't love," she said, noting the almost resentful tone in her voice.

"She was my fuck buddy, okay? And now, she's

been scorned and, you know…hell hath no fury."

"Why did you dump her?"

He held her gaze for a moment. "I just tired of her."

She sensed there was more to it but didn't press.

"With her and Gaylen out for vengeance, we're really screwed," she said. "There's no way we can get two of them to turn human. What are we going to do?"

"Don't say 'we.' I told you I'd handle this. Gaylen's the one I need to concentrate on. He's the most dangerous. Veronica was just sulking."

"That's the way she sulks? Jesus."

A muscle ticked in his jaw, but he didn't respond. He seemed deep in thought. Maybe contemplating a plan to end this. Maybe thinking about how much he'd miss the sex.

"So…reapers can…" she faltered. "I mean. Your lover. You had sex with her?"

"Even reapers have urges."

"So, you can…do it. But only with other reapers?"

"Not necessarily."

"You mean with humans, too? How?"

His eyes caught hers and wouldn't let go. The expression in them stole her ability to breathe. She might as well have said, '*Show me…*'

"There are ways."

The air in the room was hushed with expectation as she waited.

He lifted his brows, then slowly approached as if accepting a silent invitation. She swallowed audibly, her mouth going dry.

"Audra?" he whispered when he was close enough that she could feel his chilling electricity. "Are you asking me for something?"

She started to shake her head, but didn't. She *was* asking him for something. She just couldn't say the words. She stared up at him and wet her lips with her tongue. His gaze flicked over her, and a slow, lazy smile appeared, etching dimples deep in the scruff on his face. She lifted her chin, meeting the challenge in his eyes. Still silent. Waiting.

"Ask me, Audra."

She couldn't breathe, let alone speak.

He tilted his head toward her, as if he might kiss her. She let her eyes drift shut and somehow, she felt the pressure of his lips on hers. It was more a sensation, a sizzling coolness that quickly turned to warmth.

"There's this," he whispered.

She felt that same sensation on her neck, and her eyes flew open. He was so close, the startling ocean eyes delving into hers. His hand stroked slowly down her neck, and she could swear she felt his touch. She nearly moaned in impatience and anticipation as she waited for the touch to travel lower, waited to feel it all over her body. Desire scorched over her, puckering her nipples and settling hotly between her thighs.

"Lie back," he commanded.

She realized her knees were against the couch, which was good. She wasn't sure how much longer her legs would support her. She sank onto the cushions and leaned back. Dimitri settled next to her, keeping his gaze locked on hers as he let his hand travel over her breasts. Her nipples tightened, and she gasped.

"Take your clothes off for me," he ordered softly.

"No." She shook her head in a quick jerk. "I can't."

"You can. I want to see your beautiful body.

Undress for me, Audra."

He could have said, '*Roll around naked on a bed of burning coals,*' and she'd have been powerless to deny him.

Slowly, she unbuttoned her blouse. His eyes followed her movements, glinting with blue-hot passion as she undid her bra, exposing her breasts. She lifted her hips so she could slip off her jeans. His eyes flashed, and his breathing sped up as she hooked her fingers in the band of her panties and slid them down, over her legs, letting them fall to the floor.

His gaze dropped downward, along the length of her legs, then lifted slowly to settle back on her face. She shifted nervously as he drank her in with his eyes. "Just relax." His hand moved lower, and her thighs parted. "We can also do this," he said with a husky growl.

Crazy. *This is crazy. Stop it now*. But she couldn't. Didn't want to.

Heat gathered between her legs. She wanted to reach up and grip his shoulders. Wanted him to turn human…to make love to her. Dare she ask him? No. She should stop this. Stop it now before…

A searing cool-warm friction between her legs caused all thoughts to cease.

"Oh. Yes," she gasped.

"Yes?" he whispered, still holding her gaze.

She nodded, twisting her head back and forth against the cushions as sensation tightened between her thighs, moving upward into her abdomen…her breasts. Her back arched. Her hips moved like they had a mind of their own, back and forth, into the soft give of the couch beneath her, then into the thrill of his touch.

"If I were human right now, I'd bury myself deep inside you. I'm so hard for you right now, Audra. Do you know that?"

Her eyes traveled downward, to the bulge in his jeans. Amazing. How his body could have the reaction of an aroused, human man, yet she couldn't actually touch him, feel him. God, she wanted to feel him.

"I want you…inside me," she bit out.

"I want to be inside you," he answered back. "But for now, this will have to do."

His hand continued to stroke. She could almost feel the touch of his fingers. An urge tugged from deep within her belly.

"I can't…oh my God. I think I'm going to…"

Dimitri kept his gaze fastened on hers as a satisfied smile spread across his face. "Yes, I think you are. Come on, baby."

He dipped his head, and his lips hovered near her breast while his hands worked their magic below. She could feel him…the tingles of his nearness on her breasts and between her legs. Her climax built to a crescendo, rocking her as wave after wave shuddered through her, throbbing and tightening with sweet, blessed release. Hot, heavy languor spilled through her, easing her back down to Earth on a sigh.

She closed her eyes and fell limp into the cushions. "Wow," she panted, trying to regulate her breathing.

Eyes still closed, she heard a deep, throaty chuckle from Dimitri. Reality set in, and her face heated with embarrassment. What had she done? What had she let him do *to* her? She didn't want to look at him, but she couldn't avoid it forever.

She slowly lifted her lids. He was still next to her

on the couch, but now leaned forward, his hands clasped loosely between his knees. "That's how," he said.

She snatched her clothes up and tugged them on as quickly as she could, all the while working up anger to cover her humiliation. "*That's how?* What was that? Some kind of lesson or something? A teaching tool you use to induct humans into the world of reaper seduction?"

His brows drew together. "What are you talking about? I thought I was making you feel good. That's it."

"Right." She shifted away from him and stood. "It's some kind of trick. How did you do that?"

"Do what?"

"Make me…you know." Her skin heated, and the blush moved up her cheeks. "Without even touching me, you made me…"

"Orgasm?"

She nodded jerkily, and he laughed.

"You're a passionate woman, Audra. No reaper tricks involved. You found me desirable—or at least the potential of what I could do to you pleasurable—and it happened. That's it."

"What about you?"

"What about me?"

"You didn't get…satisfaction. What's in it for you?"

He chuckled. "Don't worry about me. There was some measure of satisfaction."

"What? Proving a point of some kind?"

He sighed and shook his head. "Audra, why do you keep trying to hold onto the anger? It was a gratifying experience for us both. That's it. Don't be a drama queen."

"Drama queen?"

"Look. You asked me a question. You were curious. I satisfied that curiosity."

"Yeah? Well next time I ask a question, how about you use your *words* to answer."

"Sure." He tilted his head toward her. "My apologies."

She clenched her hands in her hair and squeezed her eyes shut. She was being completely unreasonable. She had the chance to stop him and hadn't. Besides, what was she pissed about? Truth be told, it had been amazing. But the truth would *not* be told to him. The best she could do was to apologize.

"I'm the one who's sorry. It was my fault, too." She cocked her head as she stared at him. "But seriously, what was that all about? It couldn't have been as…satisfying for you as it was for me. Why did you?"

He smiled and lowered his voice. "Because you're an achingly beautiful woman, and you looked at me so longingly. I wanted to pleasure you." He moved closer. "Besides, your smell drives me wild."

"My smell?" She tamped down the desire building at his proximity. As pleasant as their little interlude had been, she wouldn't humiliate herself like that again.

"Mmm-hmm," he murmured. "I haven't smelled anything like it in years."

"What do I smell like?" she asked softly.

He leaned in, his face next to hers, and inhaled, closing his eyes. "Life," he whispered against her hair.

## Chapter 17

Audra had just ordered coffee at Sally's Sundries when Cassie came into the shop. She acknowledged the girl with a slight nod, and Cassie smiled and waved vigorously.

What was she doing here? Did she think they could carry on a conversation in an even slightly populated public place? They'd managed it at the bar because it was loud and everyone was drinking. Here wouldn't be so easy.

When her coffee was ready, Audra took it and made her way to a nook in the corner where three cushy chairs were grouped around a small table, facing a TV hanging in the corner. Only one person occupied the space—a man who'd thrown his briefcase and jacket on one chair, sat in another, and had his feet propped in a third. Audra paused in the doorway, and he looked up at her, then went back to reading his paper.

Next to her, Cassie bit out, "Asshole."

Audra was looking around for another place to sit when Cassie headed over to the man. Audra cringed as Cassie stuck a foot out and gave the man's footrest a shove. The chair went flying, and his feet came off. He sat up, his head swiveling in all directions. "Hey, hey, what the heck was that?"

Since Audra was the only human in the vicinity, his gaze landed on her. She shrugged. "I didn't see anything."

"The chair? You didn't see the chair fly across the floor on its own?"

"I thought maybe you shoved it away," she said innocently.

He glowered and gathered his briefcase and jacket. "Whatever. Don't need this bullshit."

When he left, Audra settled in one of the chairs while Cassie perched on the other.

"You really shouldn't do stuff like that," Audra said.

"I know. Dimitri would kick my ass." Cassie folded her hands in her lap and lifted her brows. "So, how are you and Dimitri getting along?"

Audra flushed at the memory of what had happened between them and took a drink from her cup to hide it. "We're okay. For, you know, a living human being and a not-so-living reaper."

"I heard what he did for you. It's the talk of the reaper community."

Audra whipped her head to Cassie, eyes widening. "You…heard?"

Had Dimitri told everyone? Kiss and tell didn't seem his style, but she didn't know him all that well. Why would he do that? In the reaper world, was it some kind of accomplishment to bang a human?

"Any time a reaper turns human, it's a big thing. Pretty cool that Dimitri did it to help that woman." Cassie gave her a sly smile. "He really did it for you, though. He's got a thing for you."

Oh, the priest thing. Relief flooded through her. "It was nice of him, yes. Surprising. I didn't even know you guys could turn human."

"I can't, yet. You have to be a reaper for, like, a few years or something. Wouldn't anyway. No freakin' way. Too dangerous."

"Dangerous? Dimitri said there were consequences, but he didn't go into detail."

Cassie shook her head. "Sounds like Dimitri. Downplaying what he did."

"What do you mean?"

Cassie scooted to the edge of the chair and leaned forward. "Turning human is the most dangerous thing we can do. If we die while we're human, then…that's it."

Audra glanced around to make sure no one was paying attention. So far, she and Cassie were still alone in their cubbyhole. "*It* how?"

"We'll be cast into this bleak, torturous eternity, with nothing but darkness. Rather than earning our reward, we'll be destined to wander with nothing but our memories and pain. Forced to relive every horrible thing we've done, every horrible thing that's happened to us, over and over. Indefinitely." Cassie visibly shuddered. "I know I only lived seventeen years, but enough bad shit happened to me in that time, I wouldn't want to relive it even for a second."

"Wow," Audra breathed. "But, really. It's not likely he'd be killed during that brief time he turned human. He was in a hospital. He was safe."

"You'd think so. But there are a lot of defectors out there. There are other reapers who want him dead. If they got wind he turned human…"

Audra couldn't believe it. Dimitri had risked a lot. "Why? Why would he take that chance?"

Cassie smiled. "You don't get it, do you? Dimitri

would do anything for you. He's in love with you."

Audra flushed. "No, he's not. Gaylen said the same thing, but trust me, he's not."

"How do you know?"

"I asked him."

Cassie threw herself back into the chair, howling with giggles. "You asked him? I bet he about shit. He's not going to admit it to you. Good grief. A reaper in love with a human? That's, like, the worst. I mean, where do you go from there, right?"

"Exactly." A sense of hopelessness came over her. Where indeed? Dimitri might have feelings for her—he'd taken a huge risk to please her—but none of that mattered. They were literally worlds apart.

"So, how do you feel about him?" Cassie asked.

Good question. One for which she didn't have an answer. If she did, she wouldn't share it with this rumor-loving teen. "Doesn't really matter. As you said. Where do we go from here? It's not like we can have any kind of future together."

"You never know. Sometimes miracles happen. Even in the reaper world. You just have to believe."

Audra cocked a brow. "That doesn't sound quite like the jaded, street-wise kid I met a few nights ago."

Cassie grinned. "Maybe being dead has softened me." Her head tilted back as her attention riveted to the TV. The grin faded.

Audra looked up to see what had caught her interest. The newscaster was talking about the serial killer who had now claimed five victims in Oklahoma towns, mostly in the northeast. A witness had seen a man believed to be the killer leaving a motel room. A brief description rolled across the bottom of the screen.

The man was average height, stocky, wore a hat. The witness hadn't seen his hair or eye color. The only other identifier was a partial tattoo on the suspect's upper arm. The witness could only see the bottom part, but he said it looked like a creature of some kind, maybe a seahorse or a dinosaur.

Audra thought of Mary Lou's daughter. She hoped this deranged monster hadn't gotten her. Hoped the girl was just rebelling against her obsessive, overprotective mother and would be home soon.

Audra looked at Cassie. Her face was pale, tears swam in her eyes, and her lips trembled.

"Cassie? What is it?"

"I know who killed them."

"How do you know?"

Eyes still glued to the TV, Cassie whispered, "Because, he killed me."

A chill shot down Audra's spine. "Cassie…I'm so sorry."

Cassie nodded, still not looking at Audra.

"Do you know who he is?" Audra asked.

Another nod.

"Tell me. I'll tell Shane. He'll find him, and he won't be able to hurt anyone else."

"I can't."

"Why not?"

"There's a code we have to follow. No interfering with the human world. If I told you, you'd have to tell Shane how you know. Then, all kinds of questions would have to be answered. Everything would come out."

"None of that matters, Cassie. You have information that could stop a killer. Just tell me who he is. I won't tell Shane how I found out. You could stop him by just telling me."

"Yeah. Sounds like a simple plan. Too bad things aren't that easy, huh?"

****

Audra hadn't been able to convince Cassie to tell her who the killer was. She almost felt culpable herself, like she should be able to glean the information that could stop a killer, but she hadn't. No matter how hard she tried, she couldn't convince Cassie.

But Cassie *had* told her where to find Dimitri. She couldn't stop thinking about what he'd done…the chance he'd taken for her. She had to see him. Had to let him know what it meant to her.

She knocked on the door, and he opened it. His brows rose in surprise. "What's going on? How did you find me?"

"Cassie told me where you were." She stepped inside, and he closed the door.

"Ah, Cassie. So, what's up? Do you need something?"

"I found out how dangerous it was…what you did."

"What I did?"

She moved closer to him in the small foyer. "You turned human to comfort Trevor's mother, in spite of the risks."

"So…I…"

Moving a smidgen closer, she said, "You did that for me."

He gave a nervous laugh. "You're getting close."

"I know." She held his gaze.

"I thought you didn't like to be so close."

Now they were nearly touching. He sucked in a breath.

Her stomach tensed, and all rational thought fled. She moved forward until their bodies meshed.

The same sensation she'd experienced before washed over her, a scary, thrilling…sexual tingle. Could he feel it too?

"Does that feel good to you?" she whispered.

"Audra," he groaned, letting his head fall back, his lids shuttering over the blue of his eyes.

"I want to touch you," she said softly. "I want to make you feel the way you made me feel…before. Can I, while you're a reaper?"

"Just being near you almost does it for me."

"But, to really be satisfied, you'd have to turn human?"

He opened his eyes, nodding, but didn't speak.

"And that could get you killed. Permanently. You can't risk it. Turning human isn't safe."

A tight grin emerged. "You're right. But not for the reasons you're thinking. This thing between us…it isn't safe, period. You belong with someone like Dunham. Someone who can give you the life, the future you deserve. Kids and all. You should probably leave."

She blinked rapidly, suddenly feeling hurt and foolish. His words shafted through her soul.

"Future?" she scoffed. "I didn't ask you to marry me. I just wanted to get you off. You know, sort of like paying a debt." She grabbed her purse and whirled toward the door. "Never mind, though. I won't mention it again."

"Audra…wait."

She halted, her hand on the knob.

"I didn't mean to hurt you. This whole thing is just…complicated. Impossible."

"I'm aware of that. I didn't ask you to come into my life. Not you, and certainly not your reaper entourage. I might be handling it badly, but I have no idea how I'm supposed to handle it."

"I know. And if I could protect you from it, I would. If I could take away everything that's happened, I would. Well, most everything. Not that thing yesterday. On your couch. That, I would keep."

In spite of her humiliation, she smiled. The tension in her shoulders eased, and she turned to offer him an apologetic smile.

"You're right. It's an impossible situation. I suppose you're not to blame. You're the only one keeping a level head." She sighed, brushing a lock of hair back from her face. "I overreacted. My emotions have been a little close to the surface lately. I'm sorry. I really just wanted to thank you. For what you did for Cheryl." She shrugged. "I didn't mean to bring sex into it."

He cocked a grin. "There are worse things you could bring into it."

She laughed. "Yes. I suppose there are." She opened the door and gave a little wave. "See you around, Dimitri."

****

The next night, Dimitri stood in a hospital room, waiting for a woman to die. At least she wasn't one of Audra's patients. Audra would be spared that. Pity he had to take her, though. She hadn't even seen her twenty-fifth birthday.

He paused, taken aback by the sentiment. When

had he started to think like that? It was a job. There was no room for emotions or what-ifs. Regardless of age, when it was time to die, you died. Plain and simple. He would have to disregard this new and unwelcome tug of guilt.

Movement behind him caught his attention, and he turned to find Gaylen in the room.

"This one was yours all along, I suppose," Gaylen said. "They're no fun when it's legal."

"Sorry it's been spoiled for you."

"You don't really mean that. I can tell."

Dimitri ignored him.

"Hey, check that out."

"What?"

"The guy out in the hallway."

Dimitri followed his gaze to the back of a heavy-set guy just outside the room. "Yeah, what about him?"

"He's the killer. The one we watched in that motel room."

Dimitri frowned, waiting until the man turned around to get a look at his face. When he did, Dimitri's insides froze.

"Shit," Dimitri bit out.

"That's him, right?"

"Yes. He also killed Cassie."

"Hmmm, and he works with Audra. Interesting."

Dimitri tried to ignore the tightening in his gut. "Why is that interesting?"

"Well, I mean. It puts her in a great deal of danger, don't you think?"

Dimitri didn't answer.

"You know, the guy has a heart condition. You saw him struggling for breath until he popped those pills."

"So."

"He's here. He's in jeopardy. Let me have him. You arrived first, but you can walk away. Leave him to me."

Dimitri glanced back to the bed, at the still-breathing woman. "Can't do it."

Gaylen shook his head. "You're here to take a young, innocent woman in the prime of her life. Hell, you took *Cassie*. Yet you won't let me take a killer? Some hero you are."

"My task is not to seek justice."

"He's a murderer. Remember what he did to that girl? Remember how he marred her flesh? Tortured her? What if that had been Audra? What if he'd raped her like the grunting pig that he is? Squeezed the life from her until her soft, warm flesh was cold with death?"

"Drop it."

"Let me have him. Think about what he would do to Audra."

"That's a chance I'll have to take."

"You'd really let him slaughter Audra the way he did those other girls?"

The lie churned in Dimitri's gut as he nodded. "I would."

"Liar."

"It's the natural order of things."

Gaylen let out a roar of laughter. "Who are you kidding, asshole? There's nothing *natural* about the way you feel about her."

****

Audra sat at the nurse's station, entering patient notes into the computer. She was nearing the end of a twelve-hour shift, and she dreaded it coming to a close.

When she wasn't working, she had time to think. Too much time. Time to think about the deaths, about the ones still to come, about the crazy, mixed-up, irrational desire she had for Dimitri. How he'd made her feel. How, without touching her, he'd brought her to heights of passion no living, human man ever had.

So? What now? What possible kind of future could there be with him?

Not that he'd said anything about a future. He wanted to serve his sentence and go away. He'd promised to go away sooner, if they could stop Gaylen. For the first time, a small part of her almost wished that day would never come. Which was ridiculous. And self-centered. What kind of person wanted a murderous demon to thrive just so she could grab a cheap, physical thrill? She didn't *really* want Gaylen to succeed. Of course not. But she also didn't want Dimitri out of her life.

"You're an idiot," she muttered.

Kyle walked up, coming behind the desk to take his place at the terminal. "Thanks for covering for me while I took a leak."

"Not a problem."

"Were you just talking to yourself?"

"It's been a long day."

Wow. Even when reapers weren't around, she was a raving lunatic. A lunatic who was carrying a torch for a Grim Reaper. A non-human who took souls. And she thought she'd made a poor choice when she'd fallen in love with a gay man.

There was that word again. Love. No. It couldn't be love. She wouldn't let it be.

Why couldn't she feel this way about Shane? Like Dimitri said, Shane was someone who could give her the future she wanted. The future that was quickly slipping from her grasp.

Her cell phone vibrated in the pocket of her scrubs, and she pulled it out, looking at the display. A smile creased her mouth. Shane.

"Hello," she said into the phone. "How did you know I was just thinking about you?"

"I didn't. Any other time, I'd be thrilled," he said, his tone flat.

"What's happened, Shane? Has someone else died?" As she waited for the answer, her mind screamed, *please, no. I can't take much more.*

"We found a body. A young girl. Her mother just identified her. Rumors will be circulating around the hospital in no time. I wanted you to hear it from me. It's your friend's daughter, Camellia. She's been murdered."

****

The night after Camilla's body was found, Audra was scheduled to work a double. Mary Lou wouldn't be in, and they were short-staffed. Audra had stopped by her house after her shift ended yesterday, to offer her condolences. The woman barely even recognized her, she was so deep in her grief. Never had Audra seen a person so destroyed.

Who could have done something so horrific? Most likely, the same psycho who'd killed those girls in surrounding towns. It was inevitable his evil would come to Boon Springs. The town was a freakin' magnet for tragedy and destruction.

Toward the end of her first shift, Audra slipped

into the break room to recharge for the evening ahead. Dropping coins into the soda machine, she punched the Mountain Dew button. Not her usual choice, but she'd need the caffeine jolt for what lay ahead.

A few minutes into her break, Kyle stuck his head inside the room. "You have company."

"Who is it?"

"Your friend. The one with the little girl."

"Tell her I'll be right out."

When Audra saw Riley, she immediately knew something was wrong. Riley's porcelain skin was blotchy from tears. Her suit jacket was askew, her blouse untucked, and her normally sleek silvery blonde hair was mussed as if she'd been running her hands through it.

"Riley? What is it? What's happened?" Audra's heart sped up. Had Gaylen gotten to Sadie? No. Riley would be a hysterical mess if that had happened, not just unkempt and distraught.

"It's—Oh, God." A visible shudder ran over her body.

Audra took Riley by the arm. "Let's go over here and sit." She led her to a lounge area where they settled on chairs next to one another. "Tell me. What's wrong?"

Riley took in a shuddering breath before speaking. "I don't know if you noticed lately how Sadie's been tiring easily. Her skin has looked a little…ashen. I took her to the doctor, and he ran some tests." Riley's stricken eyes rose to Audra. "She has Dilated Cardiomyopathy."

Audra's gut clenched. The condition wasn't necessarily fatal, but it could be if not caught quickly enough, or properly treated. "Which doctor did you take her to?"

"Doctor Gunderson."

"Good. He's the best. What did he say, exactly? How progressed is it?"

Riley shook her head. "He's confident we caught it early. He said with the right treatment, right medications, she'll be fine. He said we might be able to avoid surgery. I wanted to ask you, because I knew you'd know. And you'd tell me the truth." Tears choked her voice, brimming and spilling down her cheeks. "You love Sadie, and you'll tell me the truth. Is my little girl going to be okay?"

Audra scooted forward to take her into a hug, stroking her back. "Yes, she'll be okay. He's right. All we have to do is make sure she gets the care she needs, and she'll be fine."

Riley pulled away. "But that's just it. I'm a terrible mother. What if I let something happen to her?"

"Terrible mother? What are you talking about?"

"I work so much. I'm hardly ever around. I mean, I don't even know if it's okay to take her trick-or-treating. Is she strong enough to handle it? I didn't even ask the doctor. I didn't even bother to think about it. All I think about is work." She ran a hand through her hair. "I'll cut back. Get a partner or give away some of my cases. I have to be there for Sadie."

Audra held onto her hand and squeezed. "She should be fine to go trick-or-treating. Just watch for signs she's getting tired. And, you'll do great. I'll help. We'll both be there for Sadie. And Brent. He's a good father. You're a wonderful mother. We'll take care of her. Don't worry, okay?"

Riley nodded and wiped her tears. “You’re right. She’ll be fine. Thank you.”

“Of course.” Audra forced a reassuring smile, but a knot of dread sat like a boulder in her chest.

Yes, the condition was manageable in the early stages. Yes, they would take good care of Sadie. Yes, everything should be fine with treatment. But, what Riley didn’t know and what Audra couldn’t tell her, what sent a wave of terror rushing through her soul was that, now, Sadie would always be in jeopardy. The illness had given Gaylen a weapon. The most powerful weapon he could possibly wield.

****

Dimitri wandered down the hospital corridor, looking for the killer. Just to see what he was up to, he told himself. He wouldn’t take action, no matter what. He just wanted to keep an eye on the sick son of a bitch. No need to worry about Audra, though, even if he had a right to, which he didn’t. It seemed the sicko’s taste ran to younger girls. Sweet, vulnerable innocent teenagers.

For the most part, they’d been runaways, untraceable phantoms that few would even miss. And, he’d confined his murderous rampage to other locations. But this last girl had been different. She’d been a beloved child of someone the guy knew. Someone he worked with. And she’d been killed right here in Boon Springs.

What was happening? Was the guy spiraling out of control? Changing his MO? If so, what other changes might he make? Might he not be so specific when it came to victims? Might he start to go after older women? Women he worked with, maybe?

Dimitri put a halt to that line of thinking. No matter

what the asshole did, it wasn't Dimitri's job to stop him. What the hell was he, a cop? Speaking of cops. What was it with Dunham? Maybe if he'd concentrate on his job instead of Audra, he could catch the bastard.

He spotted the killer at the end of a hallway, just outside a door. Was there a potential victim on the other side?

Meandering closer, Dimitri saw it was a locker room. That didn't mean there wasn't a victim inside, but the likelihood that he was stupid enough to kill someone right here in the hospital was pretty slim. He *looked* that stupid, but that didn't mean he was.

Dimitri followed him inside. The guy strolled casually—too casually—between the rows of lockers. He was up to something, no doubt.

He stopped in front of a locker, spun the dial, then opened the door. The way he was acting, it wasn't his locker, but he'd known the combination. Maybe whoever owned it didn't keep anything valuable inside and wasn't cautious about keeping the combination secret.

Dimitri's suspicions were confirmed when he pulled a pair of lacy, black women's panties from the locker. Actually, they *could* belong to him. Who knew what the freak was into? Dimitri's curiosity brought him closer, and he peeked over the guy's shoulder inside the locker.

A sudden hot rush of rage almost made him turn human, just so he could tear the guy apart with his bare hands. He recognized some of the items in the locker. A pink canvas book bag. A gray Rock Louie T-shirt he'd seen her wear.

He knew whose locker it was, even before he saw

the cocksucker bring the panties to his nose and inhale, murmuring as if in the throes of passion, "Audra…Audra…"

****

As predicted, the night shift on Halloween was insane. Audra was sent to the ER to help out. Although they'd scheduled extra staff, it still wasn't enough to handle the flood of whack-jobs. The last patient she treated was a college student who'd tried to high jump over a bonfire. She was certain alcohol was involved in his decision. She most definitely hoped that was the case, otherwise, things didn't bode well for this generation of college graduates.

Finally, the excruciatingly long night came to an end. For her, anyway. The eleven to seven shift would have their share of crazies, too.

Just after Audra arrived home, Cassie materialized in her living room.

"I need a favor," the girl said quickly. "I need your computer, and then I need you to do something for me."

"I'm exhausted. What do you need me to do?"

"I'll explain later. Where's your computer?"

Audra sighed heavily, then led Cassie into the computer room. Cassie perched on the chair. Her hands began to fly across the keyboard. In a few moments, the printer whirred, and Cassie plucked a sheet of paper from the tray and handed it to Audra.

Audra looked down at the photo Cassie had printed. A young guy sat atop a large blue dragon, brandishing a sword.

"What's this?" she asked Cassie.

"I need you to give it to Shane. But, I need you to sneak it to him and not let him know you're the one who gave it to him."

"Why?"

"Because, that would just start a bunch of questions about your involvement, how you knew. I need him concentrating on the facts, not getting all clouded with what you know and how you came by the information."

"But I don't know anything."

"Right."

Good Lord. A reaper speaking in riddles. That was exactly what she needed tonight.

"Okay, fine." Audra sighed. "I'll take it to him tomorrow if it means that much to you."

"No! It has to be tonight."

"Tonight? I'm not even sure if he's working."

"He is. I already checked. I really need you to do this. Tonight."

Audra frowned. "I'm sorry, Cassie, I—"

"Please! I'm begging you, please. Can you please just trust me? Just help me?"

Because Audra knew that the girl needed to be trusted, and so few people had helped her in life, she said, "Yes. Of course. I'll trust you. I'll help you. I'll take it to him tonight."

"Thank you," Cassie said fervently, crossing her hands over her chest. "Thank you so much. If I could, I'd give you a hug."

Moved by the intensity of Cassie's gratitude, Audra had to blink back tears. If she weren't careful, she would get attached to the girl. If she were honest, she'd admit that she already had. "You can't even give me a hint what I'm doing? What this is all about?"

"Remember what I said before?" Cassie said. "About miracles? Sometimes, they really do happen."

****

Another dimly lit motel room. Another young girl. This one was fighting with all her might, begging and pleading. Her wide brown eyes poured tears. Her pale skin glistened with sweat.

"Shut up, little girl," the man panted as he plunged into her. "It'll all be over soon. Just shut your damned mouth."

Dimitri clenched his fists. He was there to take the girl, unfortunately, not the murderous deviant. He thought of the first time he'd seen Cassie. In a room not unlike this one.

*Stop it. Those are human thoughts. Stop it.*

"Again this soon? The guy is definitely out of control."

Dimitri glanced over his shoulder, not surprised to find Gaylen hovering behind him.

"Go away."

"You haven't changed your mind? Come on. What's your deal?" He snapped his fingers. "I got it now. Maybe you want Audra dead? Maybe you figure she's got a shot at becoming a reaper. You can train her. Replace Veronica. She'd be a better fuck, I'm sure."

"Shut up," Dimitri growled.

"Even if you want her dead, do you really want her to die like that?"

The guy's hands tightened around the girl's throat. Spittle flew from his mouth as he cursed her, even while she lay dying beneath him.

"Why do you want this guy so bad?" Dimitri asked.

Gaylen shrugged. "The prick thinks he's

invincible. I'd like to show him he's not."

Suddenly, the killer paused, loosening his grip on the girl so he could clutch his chest.

"Now's my chance," Gaylen said. "Come on, man. Let me have him."

Dimitri's lips clenched, but he didn't speak.

"The girl's still alive. If I take him now, she survives. He's gone. No more dead girls. No more threats to Audra." Gaylen clutched Dimitri's shoulder. "Come on. Let me have him. *The guy works with Audra*."

Dimitri flashed to the image of the pervert's face buried in Audra's panties. Audra wasn't necessarily his type, but the guy definitely had an unhealthy fascination for her. No telling what might be going on in the asshole's twisted mind.

Dimitri looked to the girl on the bed, wide-eyed with terror, struggling to free herself from beneath the killer's weight. He held her down while he fumbled for his pants. Going after his pills. The man had murdered Cassie, filled her last few moments with pain and terror…

"Will you leave the girl alone?" Dimitri asked.

"Yeah, sure."

"You won't take her? If I let you have him, you won't take her while she's fighting to survive?"

"This one's a freebie. I won't touch her. I give you my word."

Normally, Gaylen's word didn't mean shit, but for some reason, Dimitri believed him. Gaylen had been gunning for the killer for some time now. He'd most likely be satisfied with this one conquest.

"You gave me your word," Dimitri persisted. "The

girl doesn't make it, you'll have me to answer to."

"Okay, okay. Now what's it going to be? He's got the pills, man. Make up your mind."

Dimitri lifted his hands up in a gesture of surrender. "He's all yours." he said, backing toward the wall. "Make him hurt."

****

Audra felt foolish when she told the deputy at the front desk she was there to see Shane. She felt even more foolish when he led her to Shane's office, and Shane's face lit with pleasure.

"Audra. What a surprise. Is everything okay?"

"Yes. Everything's great. I just came by to see you. To see if you had any leads on Camellia's murder." She suffered a twinge of guilt for using the poor dead girl in her ruse.

Shane's expression darkened. "No. Not a clue. The bastard's killing young girls all over Northeastern Oklahoma, and I don't have a damn clue."

"Don't worry. You'll catch him. I'm sure of it."

"Yeah?" Shane lifted his brows. "Like I caught the guys who nearly killed you?"

"Hey, you did your best. I wasn't any help. I didn't give you any information. Not until the thing with Scott." And they still didn't know who'd actually committed the crime. Scott was still on the loose.

He pointed at a chair across from his desk. "Have a seat. You want something to drink?"

"Sure. That would be great." She didn't. She was still bouncing off the walls from the three Mountain Dews she'd consumed at the hospital, but he'd given her the perfect opportunity to slip the picture to him. "Diet Coke, please," she said as she took the offered seat.

As soon as he left the office, she pulled the sheet of paper from her purse and slipped it on his cluttered desk.

Shane returned and handed her a can of Diet Coke, then settled in his chair. They made small talk for a few moments, and Audra's nerves began to fray. She was exhausted and confused and anxious to get this over with. It was all she could do not to shout, "Just look at the damned picture already!"

Almost as soon as she had the thought, he did. He frowned and picked up the sheet of paper, studying it. He looked at Audra. "What's this?"

"I don't know."

"Where did it come from?"

"How would I know?"

"It wasn't here when I left."

"Oh, that." She swallowed some of the Diet Coke. "Well, I found it on the floor and put it there. I have no idea where it came from. I thought maybe it fell off your desk."

"No. I've never seen it." His brows drew together as he studied the picture again. "Odd. The witness who described the partial tattoo said it was a bluish color. Looked like some kind of monster or dinosaur. Or…it could have been a blue dragon." He tapped the paper. "Someone left this as a clue to the killer. But why does it look so familiar? I've seen something like this lately…" He lifted his head and stared wide-eyed at Audra. "Your friend. At the Halloween party. The nerdy guy with the sword."

"Wilton? What about him?"

"Do you know where he lives?"

"Yes…I've been there a few times. But—"

Then it struck her. The guy on the paper had looked familiar to her, too. She was exhausted and her brain so tired she couldn't place it exactly, but the outfit he wore looked familiar. Now she remembered why.

It was a photo of Eragon. Wilton had worn that costume at the Halloween party.

## Chapter 18

The next day at the hospital, the entire staff was buzzing about Wilton. About how they'd had a killer in their midst and hadn't even known. About how he'd murdered Mary Lou's daughter. About how he could have murdered any one of them.

Audra and Wilton hadn't exactly been best friends, but she was fond of him. Learning the truth about him had hurt—knowing she should have figured out something was wrong, maybe even helped save a young girl's life—was devastating.

She couldn't believe it. Even as she'd given Shane the address, she'd been trying to come up with another explanation. Another reason why the tattoo in the witness's description had matched the Eragon costume Wilton had worn to the party Why, although she couldn't tell Shane this part, Cassie had used her to give Shane a photo of the guy riding a blue dragon. Nothing else came to her, though.

She'd wanted to go with Shane, but he wouldn't allow it. She'd heard the details after the fact. Shane had been on his way to Wilton's house when a call came in that redirected him to a motel. A desk clerk had heard screams coming from the room and called 9-1-1. In that room, Shane discovered Wilton dead. Initial findings suggested he'd died of a heart attack. He hadn't been alone. A young, naked, traumatized girl had been there. Now, that girl—Jessica—was Audra's patient.

When Audra went into the girl's room, her heart constricted with sympathy. Jessica looked so tiny in the bed, so lost and wounded. Her physical injuries weren't that severe. She had some damage to the cerebral vessel and minor laryngeal injuries from being choked. She'd also been raped. Her mind and soul were more damaged than her body.

"Hey, sweetie," Audra said. "How do you feel today?"

The girl's brown eyes were glazed with bewilderment. "Good, I guess."

"We have a therapist coming to see you soon. She wants to talk to you. Make sure you're okay. You can tell her anything you want. You're safe now."

Jessica looked down to where her small hands kneaded the edge of the blanket. "He worked here. You knew him." Without waiting for Audra's confirmation, she continued, "How could you not know what he was? What he was doing?"

Audra flinched, guilt blooming in her heart. "I don't know. I've asked myself that a dozen times. Monsters don't always look or act like monsters." She thought of Gaylen. He definitely didn't look like a monster. But he was one of the worst.

"I don't think he died from a heart attack," Jessica said softly.

"You don't? Why's that?"

"It was…he was…" She sniffed and swiped her hand over her cheeks. "He was screaming. Like he was being tortured or something. It seemed to go on forever…the screaming. Then, he just stopped. His face…it was frozen in this look of…I don't know…pain, fear." Her gaze rose to Audra. "You know what? While it was going on? While he was dying? I was scared because I didn't know what was happening, but mostly, I was glad."

Audra swallowed back a lump of tears. What this young woman…this child must have gone through. She reached out and patted her hand. "I understand, Jessica. It's okay that you feel that way. He was a bad, bad man."

Jessica nodded. "Do you know when my parents will be here?"

"This afternoon. Their flight lands at three-thirty. They were worried out of their minds about you." Jessica had run away from her home in Eugene, Oregon two weeks ago. Audra didn't even want to know how she'd made it here to Oklahoma—what she'd seen and done in between.

"I thought I had it bad at home. Mom and Dad fighting all the time. Being too strict. I turned sixteen in July, and they wouldn't let me get a car." Jessica shook her head and snorted. "Man, was I ever a dufus."

"Sometimes life's like that. We have no idea how good we have it until something worse happens." Audra checked her IV. "You need anything before I go?"

Softly, her voice filled with sorrow, Jessica said, "I just need my momma."

Audra brushed the girl's hair back from her head, then quickly turned away so she wouldn't see the tears. Fury at Wilton, at herself for not realizing, shot through her. The sorry, piece-of-shit, sick, perverted bastard. If he hadn't died, she'd want to kill him herself. Odd what Jessica had said about the way he died. She wasn't sure, but something told her Gaylen had a hand in it. If so, it was the only thing he'd done that she approved of.

****

That night, Audra was changing for bed when Gaylen appeared in her room. She hurriedly jerked the sleep shirt down over her body.

"Asshole," she bit out. "Couldn't you knock or something?"

"I could, but this way's more fun."

She scowled. "What do you want?"

"Just a chat. You've had quite a couple of days, haven't you? Helping to catch a big, bad killer."

"It wasn't me."

"Well, it was Cassie, through you. She blew the whistle on Starkley. Pretty clever, but it was all for naught."

"Because you'd already taken care of it?"

He tipped his head toward her as if acknowledging a compliment. "I had, but that's not what I'm referring to. She went about her little scheme circuitously in order to avoid punishment for interfering in fate…in the human world. She thought if she did it indirectly, it wouldn't count, but alas, she was mistaken."

"Punishment? Cassie's being punished?"

"Oh, don't get your panties—your very lovely panties—in a bunch. She won't be harmed. The worst that could happen is she'll have a hundred years added to her sentence. Not such a bad thing. You see how much fun Dimitri and I are having."

"If that's all you came to tell me, you can go now. I'm tired."

"All I came to tell you? Don't you wish." He smiled, his entire face beaming with evil delight. "No, my dear. I'm afraid not. Your time is up. I've come to put my plan in motion."

"What plan is that?"

He sighed impatiently. "Don't play dumb, Audra. I told you. I want to taste your breath. I need Dimitri out of the way."

"Whatever the plan is, my answer is no. I won't help you."

"Won't you?"

"Absolutely not."

"Even to save those you love?"

"You can't take people unless they're in jeopardy."

"Ah, yes. Jeopardy. Somewhat like the jeopardy your little friend is in now that she's got that awful disease."

Her heart stilled, her body going numb as a rush of icy wind swept through her. "You wouldn't. You can't hurt Sadie."

"I won't. If you agree to help me."

"What do you want me to do?"

"All you have to do is trick Dimitri so that you can bind him in copper. Then I take your breath." A satisfied grin spread across his face. "While he watches."

Nausea wound through her gut at the image of Dimitri, bound and helpless, watching Gaylen take her breath. She brushed the thought aside. "And if I do, you'll stop taking people?"

Gaylen shrugged. "People you know, perhaps."

"That's not good enough."

"How about a promise then? A promise if you don't, it will never stop."

"You could kill me while you're taking my

breath."

"I won't kill you. You will get dizzy, breathless, maybe lose consciousness. Just pretend it's really amazing sex."

"Right." She rolled her eyes. "But how do I *know* you won't kill me?"

"I give you my word."

She barked a humorless laugh. "Not even close to good enough."

"I swear on Louisa's memory, on her soul, that I won't."

"Louisa?"

"She was my wife. Dimitri took her from me. He was my master, and I had no choice but to let her go."

"Your master?"

"I was a slave. He owned me."

"He owned slaves? *You* were a slave?"

"An indentured servant. It was in the mid-1700s. I traded my freedom for passage to America. My wife and I were approaching the end of our seven-year sentence when we were sold to Dimitri. We were going to serve out our time, then we'd be free to start over." He grunted a harsh laugh. "Only we never got that chance. Just a few months shy of paying off our debt, the bastard who bought us destroyed it all."

A tightness in Audra's stomach told her the worst was yet to come. She didn't want to think of Dimitri that way—a cold, impervious ruler, owning slaves and taking what he wanted with no regard for others. She couldn't reconcile that with the gentle man who'd risked his life to pose as a priest. Who'd coaxed her body into a mind-blowing orgasm, expecting nothing for himself in return.

When she didn't speak, Gaylen went on with the story. "Dimitri wanted my wife, so he took her from me. I had no choice. I didn't even fight that hard. I knew my punishment would be severe. Back then, I was weak, beaten down. I just let her go. Two nights later, while I tossed and turned alone in my quarters, I smelled smoke. I ran outside to see the main house aflame. I ran as fast as I could, broke inside to search for Louisa. But the smoke, so heavy, thick, overcame me. I wasn't able to save her."

Moisture appeared in his eyes, rendering Audra in shocked silence. Gaylen, crying?

"When I awoke, Louisa was dead. I learned later that Dimitri was drunk, had knocked over a candle, and set the house on fire. He died that night, too. But the only thing his death did was infuriate me. I wanted to kill the bastard myself. But I had to wait until my death came. I've been trying to make him pay ever since. If she'd been at home with me, she'd have been safe, would have lived. But Dimitri is ruthless when he sees something he wants. He'll take it and damn the consequences."

Bile rose in her throat. This wasn't the Dimitri she'd come to know. Had his years as a reaper changed him, or was she just seeing the side of him he wanted her to see?

No wonder Gaylen hated him. Not that what he'd done since was justified. But she could see where the rage, the desire for revenge had come from. For a fleeting moment, she felt sorry for him.

"I'm sorry for what happened to you. But, I can't do what you ask. I can't betray Dimitri, let you take my breath. I don't trust you."

His brows rose. “Oh? But you trust Dimitri? Has he told you about the first time we saw you?”

She blinked, letting his words sink in. “Wait…we? You were together?”

“We were. You were a small child. A very small child. It was in a cabin up in the hills of the Ozarks.”

The Ozarks. Where she and her mother had fled to get away from her father. Where her mother had died.

“You were there? When my mother died?”

“Dimitri and I both were.” His eyes glinted with victory. “He didn’t tell you, huh? Didn’t tell you about how we watched your mother take her last breath? Watched you struggle to save her, sobbing and terrified. That we continued to keep an eye on you, when you were stuck with her dead body for days, until you were finally rescued?”

She shook her head, her insides crumbling. Dimitri had witnessed the most traumatic time in her life.

Then, a horrifying thought struck her. There could be only one reason for Grim Reapers to be there at that particular time. She stared at Gaylen. “Did Dimitri take my mother?”

Gaylen shrugged. “I think that’s a question you should ask him. Now, how about our deal? You in? Or should I go pay your little friend, Sadie, a visit?”

Numbly, Audra nodded. “I’m in,” she choked out.

She knew she was taking a chance, risking her life. But, if she could save Sadie’s, it was worth the risk. All she had to do was betray Dimitri. And it wasn’t as if he hadn’t done the very same to her.

****

The next night as Audra waited, guilt and dread weighed like a stone in her gut. If Gaylen was true to his word, Dimitri would arrive shortly.

Gaylen had set the time for his own arrival at eight. She looked at the clock on her DVR. Seven. She had one hour between the time Dimitri arrived and when Gaylen would show up. In that time, she had to immobilize Dimitri. One hour to carry out the plan that would betray him.

She took comfort in the fact that, helpless or not, Dimitri wouldn't truly be in danger. Gaylen couldn't harm him while he was in reaper form, and she would get the copper on him without his turning human. She had to keep reminding herself that Dimitri had deceived her about being there when her mother died. That—even if he hadn't taken her mother—he could have helped them somehow. Maybe prevented Gaylen from taking her. And, most importantly, if she didn't go through with this, Sadie would die. She had no other choice.

She was flipping through a magazine, unable to comprehend a single word, unable to concentrate on a single photo, when he came. One second she was alone, the next, he was standing in her living room.

"Dimitri?" She hoped she sounded surprised. "What are you doing here?"

"I was worried about you. Gaylen was making all these innuendos about you. About wearing you down, making you change your mind…give him what he wants." He came over and lowered onto the couch next to her. His gaze locked on hers. "You're not, are you? You can't possibly consider playing into his hands."

She lowered her lids over her eyes so he couldn't see the lie in them. "No. Of course not. I wouldn't take that chance."

"Promise?"

She nodded. She wanted to confront him about her mother, but she wasn't sure she'd believe whatever he told her. She'd grown to trust him to a degree, but there were too many things she didn't know about him. Too many things she'd learned that frightened her. Her gaze slid to the clock. Seven-fifteen. There wasn't time for a lengthy discussion about what he had or hadn't done twenty-seven years ago.

"Would you like a drink?" she asked, trying to make the offer sound casual. "I have beer, wine…scotch."

"No, thank you. I won't keep you from your evening plans. I need to get back to Cassie. She requires a little more training than we realized." He grinned. "That stunt with the photo almost cost her an extra hundred years, but Samuel decided to go easy on her since she's still in her probationary period."

"Samuel?"

"The one I told you about. The gatekeeper who oversees reapers."

"Ah. Yes." She chewed on her lower lip, her mind working on a way to keep him here. She would *not* try seducing him as Gaylen suggested. She didn't have the stomach to make love to him, then screw him over. "Listen, I'm feeling a little creeped out tonight. You know, the whole thing with Wilton, not to mention everything else that's happened lately. Can you please stay and have just one drink? I really don't want to be alone right now."

Her heart constricted at the pleased expression that came over his face.

"Of course I'll stay with you, Audra. I can spare a

few minutes."

"Thank you," she said, barely able to get the words out. "I'll get that drink."

Her feet moved like they were mired in quicksand as she went into the kitchen. *He likes scotch*, Gaylen had said. She'd gotten the inside scoop on how to carry out the plan that would debilitate Dimitri.

*You can't be doing this. You can't seriously be doing this.* The refrain beat over and over in her mind. Not only what she was doing to Dimitri, but the chance she was taking with her own life. Had she actually agreed to let a depraved, vengeance-seeking reaper take her breath?

He wouldn't kill her. She had to believe that. Had to believe he was sincere when he vowed not to. He'd sworn on his dead wife. If there was any emotion at all in Gaylen, she'd seen it when he spoke of Louisa, the woman Dimitri had wanted so badly he'd stolen her from Gaylen. His *slave*. Dimitri had owned slaves, had cruelly snatched a wife from her husband, simply to satisfy his own lusts. She shuddered. What kind of horrible things must he have done, both as a human and a reaper? How could she have feelings for him?

Because, as she'd proven time and time again, when it came to men, her judgment sucked.

She opened wine for herself and the scotch for Dimitri, then poured a liberal amount of Rohypnol into Dimitri's glass, stirring until it dissolved in the amber liquid. Gaylen had acquired the date rape drug for her. She didn't know how. Didn't want to know.

It would take a lot of the drug to affect Dimitri, much more than it would a human. And she didn't have to worry about overdosing and killing him. He was already dead.

When she returned to the living room, Dimitri stood and took the scotch from her. He tipped it to her wine glass, and they both drank.

"Are you going to be okay, Audra? I can stay for a while. I have duties I must tend to, but I'll stay as long as I can. I want you to feel safe."

*I want you to feel safe…* Would he still want that when this was all over? Unlikely. He would probably reap her himself when he learned what she'd done.

"I'll be fine. I just wanted a little company so the evening didn't seem so lonely."

He narrowed his eyes, searching her face as if looking for the meaning behind her words. Did he think she was asking him to make love to her again? Would that be such a bad thing?

Yes. Considering he was about to pass out from the drugs she'd given him, it would most definitely be a bad thing.

Wait. She studied him. *Was* he about to pass out from the drugs? He appeared perfectly fine. Perfectly in control. The copper wire was coiled and waiting in the front hall closet, but if the drugs didn't start to work soon, it would be useless. What then? Would Gaylen go after Sadie? If Audra couldn't carry out the plan, would he immediately go on a soul-reaping rampage?

Her pulse sped up in fear. Maybe she hadn't given Dimitri enough. Maybe she would have to coax him into turning human after all—even if it meant trying to seduce him—and drug him in his human state. By the time he woke, he'd be back in reaper form, and the copper would then be effective.

If he turned human, though, he'd be at Gaylen's

mercy. A drugged, human Dimitri would be vulnerable enough for Gaylen to finally exact his revenge. Murder Dimitri and doom him to an eternity of torture…

"Ahhh…" A groan from Dimitri caused her to jerk her eyes to his. He swayed, his lids closing while he fought to stay upright. "What the…"

His body went limp, and he dropped face first onto the couch.

It had worked. He was out. Now all she had to do was bind him in copper. Yep. That was *all* she had to do. Nothing to it.

Quickly, she retrieved the roll of copper wire from the closet, waiting for Gaylen to show. She was beginning to think he wouldn't…hoping he wouldn't…when he appeared.

"Good work," he said gleefully. "I'll make a villain out of you yet."

"Just shut up and help me. Let's get this over with."

Gaylen shot her a grin and went over to Dimitri, rolling him onto his back. "I'll lift him while you wrap."

The copper was stiff, not as malleable as she'd hoped, but she worked until she managed to wind it round and round Dimitri's body. It was odd, she couldn't touch him, feel him as a solid presence, but she was able to slip the copper beneath and around his body.

Regret and indecision pounded at her with each wrap she made. What if this went wrong? What if Dimitri somehow died? What if Gaylen killed her?

Nothing to be done about it now. She'd gone too far to back out. Hoping for the best was all she had left.

"So, are you going to turn human or not?" Audra asked irritably once they were finished.

"Not yet. I can only stay human for a thousand breaths. While I'm anxious to enjoy what you have to offer, I want it to last as long as possible. And, I want Dimitri to be awake for every delicious second. We'll wait."

Audra tightened her lips and crossed her arms. What had she gotten herself into? Dimitri would be furious. Once this was all over with, she might be wishing Gaylen had killed her.

A groan sounded from the couch. Dimitri blinked his eyes open. "What the hell?" He looked first to his bindings then up to Gaylen and Audra. "What the fuck's going on?"

Gaylen's face spread into a wide smile. "Your little girlfriend here did me a favor. She slipped you a mickey."

Dimitri turned to Audra. The look of betrayal in his eyes stole her breath more than Gaylen ever could. "You did this?" His voice broke. "Why?"

"I'm sorry," she whispered.

"It was my idea, really," Gaylen said, nearly preening. "I wanted to partake of Audra's sweet breath, but I knew you'd use the opportunity to kill me. This way, I can enjoy her without worrying about that pesky little detail."

"You agreed?" Dimitri said to Audra. "You're going to let him take your breath? Are you insane? He'll kill you."

"I had to. He said he'd hurt Sadie. It was the only way."

"And what's to stop him from hurting Sadie once

you're dead?" Dimitri's bewilderment morphed into rage. "What in God's name were you thinking?" He shook his head, seemingly the only party of his body he could move. He let it drop back to the couch. "Fuck."

"He won't kill me. He swore on Louisa."

"I won't," Gaylen said. "I want to enjoy this for a long time to come. Besides, I'm not completely insane. I know what you'd do if I hurt her. I just want to sample her. Be a sport and watch. You might learn a thing or two."

"No!" Dimitri shouted.

Gaylen smiled, then his human transformation began. Audra wasn't sure how she knew, but there was a subtle difference. Although reapers appeared solid, they had sort of an otherworldly appearance she wasn't even aware of until she compared them to their human form. She couldn't put her finger on it, but there was a difference.

"It'll be okay," she told Dimitri, but she wasn't sure she believed it.

"You don't understand. He'll lose control. Even if he doesn't mean to kill you, he won't want to stop. Let me loose Audra. It's not too late."

She thought of how fragile Sadie was. How ruthless Gaylen was. "I'm sorry. I can't."

Dimitri's jaw clenched, and his eyes smoldered with fury.

"Ignore him," Gaylen said. "This is about you and me."

Gaylen stared down at her as though she were the last filet mignon on a banquet table laden with Brussels sprouts. He reached a hand out and brushed it along her cheek. She shuddered, swallowing back revulsion.

Slowly, he began to circle her. “My God. I can’t believe it. I’m really here with you. Human. I can do whatever I want.”

“Just get this over with.”

“Oh no, sweetheart. I have maybe an hour. More if I breathe slowly. I’m going to savor this as long as I can.”

He stopped circling, his back to Dimitri, and moved closer to her. He ran his hands up and down her arms. “I can’t believe I’m really touching you.” He tipped his head forward and rubbed his lips along the skin of her neck.

Nausea rose in her throat. His hands were smooth and dry, eliciting none of the pleasure Dimitri’s touch did. Human or reaper, Dimitri made her go weak in the knees with just a look. Gaylen made her want to hurl.

“Stop!” Dimitri shouted. “Stop this now. Audra, you can’t do this. Let me go.”

Audra couldn’t look at him. She would weaken and do as he asked. And Sadie might die.

She lifted her face to stare into Gaylen’s eyes.

“Tell me, Dimitri,” Gaylen taunted. “Have you touched her like this? Been this close to her while human? It’s better than you can imagine. Her skin is so smooth, so warm.” Dimitri let out a howl of rage, and Gaylen laughed. “You’re beautiful,” he whispered. He leaned forward and sniffed her hair. “You smell so…delicious. Open your mouth for me.” She didn’t comply. His voice lowered huskily. “Open for me, Audra.”

She glanced at the clock. What time had this started? Not long after eight, she believed. Only five minutes had passed. He had an hour or more? Dear

God, she couldn't do this. Panic set in, and she backed up a step.

His grip tightened on her arms, and he shook her. "I said, open your mouth. I can make this hurt a lot worse than it has to."

Audra squeezed her eyes shut and opened her mouth. She felt Gaylen move closer, felt the heat from him. She opened her eyes, and he was right there, his mouth hovering centimeters from hers.

He breathed in deeply, closing his eyes, moaning in ecstasy. "Yesssss." He let the word out on a sigh.

Over his shoulder, she met Dimitri's eyes. They'd turned a deep, dark, sapphire. He scowled at her, pain etched across his features.

"You can't do this," he moaned. "You've got to stop it now."

Gaylen let a breath out, sighing in satisfaction. "Maybe she's enjoying it, my friend. Maybe she wants me to touch her…to taste her."

A knock sounded on the door, and Audra's eyes widened in surprise.

"Who's that?" Gaylen barked. "You were expecting someone?"

Audra shook her head. "No. No one. I have no idea."

"Ignore it."

"Audra?" Shane shouted from the other side of the door. "Are you in there?"

"Answer him," Gaylen said. "Tell him to go away."

"I can't tell him that. He'll know something's wrong. I would never do that."

"Then just don't answer."

She nodded. Shane banged more loudly. “I’m worried about you,” he shouted. “I wanted to check on you after all that happened with Starkley.”

She didn’t respond.

“Audra! I see your car outside. If you don’t answer, I’ll break the door down.”

“Answer,” Gaylen bit out. “Tell him you’re okay, but he can’t come in.”

“I’m okay, Shane,” Audra called out, her voice shaky.

“Can I come in?”

“I’m sorry. I’m in the middle of something.”

Silence for a moment. Shane was a cop. He wouldn’t go away that easily. With the men who’d attacked her still free, he’d worry that someone might be holding her hostage. In a sense, that was the truth.

“Okay, then. I’ll head out. Give me a call later.”

He was lying. Audra knew it, and when she looked at Gaylen, she could see he knew it too. Shane would probably circle the house, look for another way in, one that would take whoever might be holding her by surprise. Too much had happened lately for him to be put off that easily.

“He’s not leaving.” Dimitri’s tone was smug. “He’s worried about her. He’ll probably come in another way. Take you by surprise.”

Gaylen’s eyes darted around the room.

“You need to get out while you can,” Dimitri said. “You have a good half hour before you’ll be back to reaper form.”

“Shut up,” Gaylen growled.

Dimitri went on, “You’re human. He’s human. He has a gun. Do the math, asshole. What’s it gonna be?”

Chapter 19

Gaylen glared down at Audra. He lowered his head and drew in a long pull of her breath. "One for the road." He closed his eyes, relishing for a moment, then opened them. "I wasn't delivered what you promised. We're not finished."

"I did as you asked."

"I didn't get satisfaction. Trust me, this is far from over." He reached out and gripped her neck, pulling her to him, placing a firm kiss on her lips. She nearly choked on the bile that rose to her throat. "Tell me a way out of here where Super Cop won't see me."

Audra tugged loose from him. "Out the back door in the kitchen. Hurry."

He gave her a hard look. "You owe me. Don't forget it," he said before disappearing through the kitchen door.

Shane had gone silent. If he were worried someone was holding her against her will, he'd be figuring out a way for a furtive entrance. And he'd see a coil of copper on the couch. And ask questions.

She hurried over to Dimitri. "Before I let Shane in, I'll get this off you," she said as she unwound the copper.

A muscle ticked in his jaw. His voice was steel. "You sure you want to do that? You might want to keep me bound. For your own safety."

She paused and looked into his eyes. Sparks of fury shot from them. "For God's sake. I had to do it. There's no time to discuss it now."

She finished uncoiling the copper and shoved it under the couch. Ignoring Dimitri's glare, she went to the front door, but before she reached it, she heard Shane's voice behind her. "Audra? What's going on?"

She whirled. "How did you get in?"

"I came in through a window. I was afraid someone was in here with you. Making you say those things." He looked around the room. "You're alone? Everything's okay?"

Dimitri stood up from the couch, crossed his arms, and glowered at her. She shifted her eyes away from him. "Everything's fine. Thanks for being concerned, but that was a bit of an overreaction."

"Your voice sounded strained, like you were in distress. Sorry if I worry about you."

He sounded offended, hurt. She was two for two tonight. Super.

She tried not to look at Dimitri as she spoke. It was odd having this conversation in front of him, her being the only one aware he was in the room. "I'm sorry, Shane. I didn't mean it like it sounded. I was…I was getting sick in the bathroom, and I was embarrassed and felt like shit."

His features softened into concern. "Are you all right now? Can I get you anything?"

She smiled. "I'm fine. Just a stomach bug."

"Get rid of him," Dimitri bit out. "You and I need to talk."

*Screw you*, she wanted to say, but Shane would think she was talking to him.

"Okay, then. I'm on duty so I better take off. Just wanted to stop by and make sure you're doing okay. Things have been a little rough on you lately."

Her heart constricted. He was such a good man. Why couldn't he give her the rush of euphoria Dimitri did?

"Thanks for caring," she said.

He stepped closer and lifted a hand, brushing his knuckle down her cheek. "Always have, always will." He placed a kiss on her forehead and headed to the door. "Call if you need anything."

"I will. Thanks."

"Sure." He smiled, but she detected sadness in his expression. "That's what friends are for, right?"

She held his gaze for a moment. He was asking an unspoken question. Would they ever move forward, or was this all there would be between them?

She shot a quick look at Dimitri. In spite of how insane the very idea was, Shane didn't inspire the same response, the same thrill Dimitri did. A man who wasn't alive himself made her feel more alive than she ever had in her life.

"Right," she answered softly. "That's what friends are for."

Shane nodded, then he was gone.

She turned to Dimitri. An enraged Dimitri. He swooped toward her, halting inches in front of her, breathing heavily, his eyes shooting cobalt sparks. "What in God's name were you thinking?"

"I just wanted to make him stop."

"You thought that would do it, huh? You thought opening yourself to him, sacrificing yourself to him, would do the trick? You're out of your mind. He won't stop until he gets what he wants. Now that he's had a taste of you, he'll be even harder to control."

"He wasn't going to kill me. He swore."

"Even if he meant that, saying it is one thing, actually stopping himself is entirely another. The only thing Gaylen wants more than to reap you is to taste your breath. You were taking a big chance that he would kill you. Suck the very life from you. He's done it before."

"Done what?"

"Years back, he was tasting a woman's breath…he couldn't stop. He killed her."

She hugged herself tightly. "I'm sorry. I was trying to help."

"You risked your life. Right in front of my eyes."

"I'm sorry," she said again.

"Do you have any idea? Any idea what that would have done to me to watch you die?"

"No." She could barely speak. He was so close…again…doing that tingly thing that made her struggle for breath. "What would it do? And why would it be so hard, Dimitri? You watch people die all the time."

He clenched his jaw, not speaking as his gaze roamed over her face. Finally, he said, "I can't watch Gaylen kill someone right in front of me again. Anyone. Can't watch him win."

"Oh," she said, hoping her disappointment didn't show. Had she actually been expecting some kind of declaration of how special she was to him? How much he loved her? Just because Gaylen told her he did, that didn't make it so.

"Promise you'll never do it again," he demanded.

"I promise."

Her words seemed to only mildly placate him. "I'm not sure I can trust you. You tricked me. Betrayed me."

She thought of what Gaylen had said. About that day in the cabin all those years ago. Anger heated her blood. "You're one to talk. About betrayal."

"What do you mean?"

"He told me you were there. When my mother died. A little detail you left out when I was unburdening myself to you."

His face paled, and he stepped back. "He told you."

"Did you take her?"

"No."

"I don't know if I believe you."

"Gaylen took her. He was going to take you, too, but I arrived in time to stop him. Not in time to save your mother."

Dimitri had saved her? Gaylen had killed her mother? Her legs turned to rubber. He and Gaylen had been intertwined in her life all these years. A much bigger part of it…of her destiny, than she could ever have imagined.

"What about his wife? What about the way you took her away from him, then let her die?"

Dimitri flinched. "He's right about that. I've done a lot of things in my past I'm not proud of."

"I guess we both made mistakes."

"*Your* mistake almost got you killed. Don't let it happen again."

****

The phone rang at the nurse's station, and Kyle picked it up. Audra was heading down to check on a patient, when Kyle hung up and called out to her. "That was the ER. They said you might want to come down."

"Why? What's wrong?"

"Maria Bellafonte was brought in. She's asking for you."

Dread settled in the pit of her stomach. "Is she okay?"

"It doesn't sound like it. You might want to hurry."

The emergency room was three floors down. Audra didn't bother with the elevator. She ran to the stairwell and down the flights of stairs.

She burst into the emergency room hallway and ran to the desk. The receptionist looked up at her. "Room three," she said when she saw Audra. "I'll buzz you in."

Audra burst through the doors leading to the ER ward and into room three. She gasped when she saw Maria. There was barely a place on her face that wasn't covered in bruises. A white bandage enveloped her forehead and wrapped around her dark hair. Jaxon stood next to the bed. He looked up when Audra entered, then walked over to intercept her in the doorway.

He kept his voice low. "We've done all we can for her. We're waiting for a room, but it's not likely she'll be using it."

Audra's panicked gaze flew to his face. "No," she whispered. "She can't…"

"The damage was too severe. He beat the holy hell out of her. Now all we can do is try to lessen the pain. She wanted to see you."

Audra nodded and made her feet take her to Maria's bedside.

Maria's eyes fluttered open. Audra thought she tried to smile, but in the battered, nearly unrecognizable face, it was difficult to tell.

"Hi. I'm here. It's me, Audra."

"Thanks…for coming," Maria croaked. "He got me good this time."

"What happened?"

"Told him what…I said to police. That I'd…testify."

"Maria? Why did you do that?"

"Guilt. Couldn't live with it anymore."

"Guilt? Why? You did nothing wrong."

She was silent for a moment. "I'm dying," she said softly.

"No. You'll be okay," Audra could barely get the lie out, but she had to, for Maria's sake, for her to have a modicum of peace in her last hours…maybe minutes.

"I-I know…I deserve to die. But…still scared."

"What do you mean deserve to die? It's not your fault."

She coughed, squeezing her eyes shut briefly, then looked back up at Audra. "It is. I knew. I helped."

"Don't try to talk."

"Have to. You have to know. That night they hurt you, I helped. I asked you to…meet me so they could…get to you. Didn't want to. Scott made me."

Shock rendered Audra speechless for a moment, but she tried to cover it. The woman was dying. She wouldn't hurl condemnation at her.

"You're disgusted," Maria said. "Don't blame you. See? I deserve to die."

"No. No, you don't. You made a mistake. I forgive you."

"Don't…deserve your forgiveness. Just wanted…you to…know. It wasn't Joel's fault. He's a…good boy. Scott made him do those…things."

"Okay. It's okay now. Everything will be fine."

"No, I can feel it. Please make sure he doesn't…get…my babies. Please."

"You're not going to—"

Maria reached out with surprising strength and gripped Audra's hand. "Promise me," she hissed.

"Yes. All right. I promise. Just hang in there, you're going to—"

Maria gasped, her eyes rolling back in her head.

A strange man materialized in the room. He was tall with thin brown hair and a stooped posture. He didn't look at Audra. Instead, his solemn gaze was fixed on Maria. Audra's heart sped up in panic. She knew why he was here.

Maria's grip on Audra's hand tightened, then fell away completely.

****

Three days after Maria's death, Audra took Sadie to dance practice. Riley had a trial and Audra had been happy to volunteer for the errand. She needed to do normal things, needed to be with Sadie. Maria's funeral had been tough, especially seeing the three little girls sob over their mother. Shane was there. He promised he wouldn't stop looking until they found Scott. Audra hoped they found him dead.

She smiled as she watched Sadie through the glass window. The heart medications had been working, she was starting to look and act like her normal, healthy self. Her chubby little tummy strained the tight leotard. She stumbled and went down on her rump, then rose immediately, a beaming smile on her face. Audra laughed, affection swelling in her heart. What the child lacked in coordination, she more than made up for in enthusiasm.

Suddenly, a tingle moved over Audra's skin and her pulse rate sped up. Dimitri was here. He hadn't spoken to her since the copper incident. But he was here now.

She turned to find him leaning against the wall on the opposite side of the hallway.

She gave him a bright smile, but refrained from speaking. A few other spectators were watching their children, and they'd surely notice. He cocked his head, and she followed him down the hallway, into an alcove.

"I'm glad you came," she whispered. She almost said, *I've missed you*. But that would be too much of an admission.

He didn't respond, and she noticed his expression for the first time. He was frowning, his mouth drawn into a tight line. He wouldn't meet her eyes.

"What happened?"

"Nothing's happened." Unspoken was the word 'yet.'

"But something is going to happen."

He looked past her, toward the room where the children were practicing.

"You're here to reap someone? Not one of those children. You can't do that."

His eyes misted over, and in that moment, she knew. Panic raced through her heart. "No. Not Sadie. You can't."

"I have to. I have no choice."

"There's always a choice."

"No. It's the way it has to be. The natural order."

She gritted her teeth in rage. "Fuck you and your

natural order. You can't take her."

His expression turned stony. "I'm sorry."

"If you do this, I'll hate you forever."

He lifted a brow. "Yours or mine?"

"What? Yours or mine what?"

"Your forever or my forever? Because, if it's your forever, it's really not a big deal. Yours isn't all that long, comparatively speaking. After all, you're human."

Tears filled her eyes, fury merging with terror for Sadie. "Yeah. I'm human all right, and you're nowhere close."

"You knew that from the beginning."

"You can't take a child," she insisted.

"It's her time."

"She's *five* years old." Her voice rose to a screech, and she forced herself to lower it. "How can it be her time?"

"Death is no respecter of age."

"You sound like some freaking robot reciting philosophy. I don't care about rules and nature and meant to be. You can't take her. Please. For me."

"You don't know what you're asking."

"If there is anything human left in you, you won't take this child. If you have any feelings for me at all, you won't take her."

"I have no choice."

"I don't believe that." Something flickered in his expression, and she knew she was right. "You do have a choice, don't you? There's another option."

He let out a long sigh. "I can walk away. If the designated reaper isn't here to take the soul, the person will live."

Hope fluttered through her chest. "Yes. Then that's

it. You can go away. You don't have to take her."

"You don't understand. There are ramifications, it's just not done."

"Why? Because you'll have another hundred years added to your sentence? You've risked yourself for less. This is Sadie, for God's sake."

"That's not all. In addition to my punishment, failing to take an assigned soul screws with fate. Although we can't know exactly what they'll be, there will be consequences."

"Nothing's worse than losing Sadie."

He seemed to consider for a moment, then gave a quick, jerky nod. "So be it. Don't say I didn't warn you."

"Thank you," she whispered, then reached out as if to touch him.

He let her fingers hover near his chest for a moment, then swallowed and looked away. "Whatever happens, it's on you."

He turned and strode down the hallway and out the front door. Audra rushed to the glass to check on Sadie. She was still there. Awkward, not exactly sure-footed, but that snaggle-toothed smile was on her precious face. Sadie was fine. Nothing else mattered.

## Chapter 20

That night, Audra was slipping on a robe after her shower when she walked into the hallway and almost collided with Dimitri. She gasped, her heart knocking inside her chest, even when the fear subsided. He lowered his head, his eyes so intent, they seemed to be drinking her in.

"Dimitri. I'm glad you're here. I didn't thank you."

He crossed his arms and stared at her broodingly. "Don't thank me. We still don't know what that decision will bring. That's why I stopped by. I wanted to caution you to be careful. We have no idea what might happen now."

"It will be better than Sadie's death, I assure you." She moved closer to him. "I'm very grateful."

"I don't need your gratitude. It's not necessary."

"But it is," she whispered. The narrow hallway with its muted light provided a cocoon of intimacy, as if they were the only two people on Earth. She stepped closer to him, savoring the delicious tingle his nearness brought. "You have no idea how much what you did means to me. I want to find a way to show you."

He cocked a brow. "Are you offering sexual favors, Audra?" He attempted a derisive laugh, but the sound died in his throat. His eyes glittered as they stared into hers.

Desire uncoiled deep in her belly, spreading

warmth and longing through her limbs. "If I was?" she murmured huskily.

"I don't need you to…*repay* me."

"It's not that. I want to feel you, Dimitri. I want to really touch you." She closed her eyes. "Please," she whispered.

She waited breathlessly, afraid to move, afraid to open her eyes in case she found him gone. But he was still there. She could feel his cool sizzle.

Then, after a few seconds, she couldn't. The sensation fled. She'd offered herself to him, and he'd declined. Her heart sank in disappointment. She opened her eyes.

Blinking rapidly, she frowned in confusion. "Dimitri?" He hadn't left. Then why could she no longer feel the…

He lifted his hand, letting his touch rest on her cheek. A warm, rough, human touch.

Her eyes widened as she stared into the deep blue of his. "I can feel you."

He stroked his forefinger over her bottom lip. "I've wanted to do this for so long," he said. "Wanted to touch you."

"Touch me, then."

His lids shuttered his eyes, and his head swooped down, his lips claiming hers in a searing, knee-weakening kiss. She breathed out a sigh, wonder and joy moving through her blood. The kiss was masterful, glorious. At first, it was just lip to lip, then he coaxed her mouth open and his tongue slipped inside, tasting, plundering, sending shivers of longing down her spine. She lifted her hands, gripping his shoulders, squeezing and kneading the cool leather. A moan escaped her throat.

Dimitri pulled back and shook his head disbelievingly. "This can't be happening."

"What can't be happening?"

"Us…this."

She smiled. "I know. But it is."

His eyes roamed over her face, and he tenderly brushed the hair back from her forehead. "Yes, it is."

"How long do we have?"

"A thousand breaths."

"How long is that?"

"Normally, about an hour, but the way you've got me panting, it will be half that."

"Then we'd better hurry."

His crooked grin made his dimples appear. "I've waited too many lifetimes for this moment. I don't want to hurry."

She stood on her tiptoes and planted a hard kiss on his mouth. "I can't stand it another second," she said against his lips. "I want you."

He groaned, and his arms came around her, crushing her to him. Even through the barrier of their clothing, her sensitized breasts rubbing against his hard chest spiked her blood with desire. She pressed more fully to him, marveling at the feel of his hardness against her belly. He wanted her. *God, yes.* He wanted her.

He broke away long enough to lift her, cradling her in his arms while his mouth devoured hers in a fierce, demanding kiss. He strode down the hallway and through the open doorway of her bedroom, then gently laid her on the bed. She rose to her knees at the edge of the mattress and ran her fingers over his chest.

He sucked in a breath. Dipping his head, he trailed kisses along her shoulder, nudging the robe aside to gain access to her flesh. She threw her head back while his warm, firm mouth explored the curve where her neck met her shoulder. She shuddered as his thumb stroked along her collarbone, then plunged into her robe to brush across her taut nipple.

"I can't believe I'm here with you," he whispered. "Of all the times I watched you…imagined touching you, I never dreamed it would feel this good, that your skin would be so soft…so alive." He lifted his head, his gaze reverent as he worshipped her with his eyes. "I want to inhale you," he ground out.

She put her hands the sides of his face and stared into the cobalt eyes that gleamed with desire. "Can you feel things fully when you're human? Or is it like when you're in reaper form and the effects aren't the same?"

"Sensations are still dulled," he told her absently as his hands continued to skim her flesh. He worked them over her ribs, sliding up to gather her breasts and gently massage. "Why?" he murmured as he skated his lips over her breasts.

"I want you to taste my breath."

His exploration ceased. His head snapped up, the blue gaze alive with shock. "What? No. I can't do that."

"Please," she entreated. "I know it makes you feel things more intensely. I want you to really experience it, to feel what I'm feeling now."

Dimitri's expression softened as he rolled his thumbs over her nipples again. His hips pressed into hers, his erection rubbing her just right. He let out a shaky laugh. "If I felt it any more intensely, I'd shatter into a million pieces."

"Don't you take my breath when we kiss?"

"It's not the same. I need to actually breathe it in, take it inside me. And I won't do that." He touched his forehead to hers, his eyes glued to her mouth. "It's not safe. I'm not sure I would be strong enough to stop."

"You would. I know you would."

"Trust me, sweetheart, being with you, even with the sensation filtered, is more than plenty. Just relax. Enjoy. Don't worry about me. I want to please you." Again, he pressed his hips forward, emphasizing his husky confession.

She bit her lip, but his mouth slanted over hers, and she forgot about wanting him to taste her breath, forgot about everything except the feel of him, the storm of desire brewing inside her.

She pulled back far enough to say, "Should we worry about…" then trailed off in embarrassment. Protection wasn't likely an issue for the undead.

He cupped a hand to the side of her face. "Worry about what?"

"Uhm…birth control. Safe sex."

He chuckled. "No need. I don't have a disease. Couldn't transmit it if I did. And I can't get you pregnant."

That thought brought on despondence, but she brushed it aside. She wasn't in this for a fairytale happily-ever-after. She wanted whatever she could have of Dimitri. Now.

"Then what are we waiting for?" she asked.

His gaze delved into hers for a split second before he clenched his fingers in her hair, and fused his mouth to hers, snaking his tongue inside, plundering and stroking. A whimper started in her throat, but he captured it with his mouth. Shoving the edges of her robe open, he swept his hands down her side, along the curve of her hip. A tremor moved over her flesh, stirring hunger in her bloodstream.

He lifted his head to stare at her. "Audra," he said brokenly. "You're so....so..." His brilliant blue eyes shimmered. "...so beautiful," he ended on a ragged sigh.

She stroked her fingers along his jaw. "So are you."

He laughed softly, then bent his head. She moaned in ecstasy when his warm mouth latched onto her nipple, tugging as he flicked his tongue over the hardened peak.

Impatiently, she reached down and unfastened his jeans. "I want to feel you," she whispered.

He hurriedly slipped off his jacket, jeans, and shirt, while she opened her robe and tossed it onto the floor. Oddly, she was totally at ease baring herself to him. The room was dimly lit, but not dark enough that he couldn't see her. And it didn't bother her a bit. Especially when his gaze raked hungrily down her body and he went to her, taking her in his arms, gliding his lips over her skin, starting at her neck, working his way lower.

She sucked in a breath at the feel of him...his hot mouth on her flesh. He lifted a hand and kneaded her breast, his lips gliding along her neck, her shoulders. She reveled in the sight of the dark head bent to his task.

Her heart pounded so loudly, she was sure he could hear it as he journeyed tantalizingly close to the hard peaks of her nipples. She waited...anticipating his tongue closing over them. When it did, she nearly came out of her skin. Sparks of desire shot through her, wrenching a heated response from between her thighs.

"Dimitri," she panted. "I need you inside me."

"I want to make this last," he muttered against her breast.

"We don't have much time." She took his face in her palms, tugging until he was looking into her eyes. "I need this right now. Please."

She saw surrender in his face, in the upward tilt at the corners of his perfect mouth. He eased her back onto the bed, then joined her.

His nearness elicited a need, tight and scorching, so strong it was beyond her control. Tremors vibrated through her, and she pulled on his shoulders, urging him to satisfy the craving he'd started.

He held her gaze for a moment, then his head lowered. His firm lips moved over her heated skin, trailing down to her breasts. His tongue did delicious things to her nipples while his hand slid down her stomach and lower…lower still. Her muscles tightened in response. Tingles of anticipation thrummed between her legs as she waited, breathlessly. His touch whispered along the skin of her inner thighs, and she parted for him, allowing his seeking fingers access.

*Sweet mercy.* Audra arched her back, craving more.

"Oh—my—God," she choked out.

*Dear God…nothing had ever…how could he…*

She couldn't think, could barely breathe as he magically brought her to mind-numbing ecstasy. She could hold out no longer. A guttural scream started at the base of her throat, then tore from her mouth as an orgasm rocked her, pounding through her body in long, pulsating tremors. Her fists knotted in the sheets as she gave into the quaking explosion.

"Mmmmm." He kept his mouth locked tightly onto her nipple as the tremors slowed and eventually subsided.

"Wow," she breathed.

He kissed her, deep and hard, his tongue darting into her mouth, sliding against hers. "I want to be inside you," he murmured against her lips. "I've dreamed of this for years."

A slow, satisfied smile curved her mouth. Heady with the power she held over him, of his desire for her, she nodded. "I'm all yours."

He flipped her on her back, then slid on top of her, his eyes capturing hers as he braced a hand on either side of her head. "I can't believe…this is…incredible," he panted.

She gripped his shoulders, hungrily arching her hips upward, kneading the skin of his chest, his shoulders, enraptured with the feel of him…smooth, warm, alive.

He lowered his hips until she felt the tip of his erection prod her inner thighs. She opened to him on a sigh of bliss. He slipped inside her, and she gasped his name on a cry. Then, he was filling her, stroking back and forth. Her eyes locked onto his, and a connection passed between them, breaching the chasm between her world and his. He represented death, yet never had anyone or anything made her feel so alive.

She clasped her hands on his tight buttocks, holding her to him as she ground against him, panting his name, her mind numb with the sensations jarring through her.

"Audra. Oh, Audra. I'm going to…"

"Yesssss," she hissed through gritted teeth.

Her heart swelled with emotion, with the wonder of the feel of him, the look in his eyes before his lids shuttered over them. She writhed beneath him, her insides tightening and spasming as friction built and his movements increased in tempo. The feel of him nearly drove her insane with need.

****

How many breaths did he have left? Dimitri had lost count, had no idea, but he pushed the tormenting thought aside. Now that he'd actually touched Audra's velvety skin, kissed her perfect, soft lips, he couldn't imagine never doing it again.

The feel of being draped in her warm softness was like nothing he'd ever experienced before. The muscles in his shoulders bunched as he delved in, then out of her, as he tried to drag the moment out, tried to control the urge to release his seed into her. It took all the willpower he possessed to hold off…to make it last…just a little while longer, because he knew, this was it. This was all he would ever have of the exquisite creature writhing beneath him.

The pleasure on her lovely face filled his chest with lightness and bliss. Her hazel eyes shone with the inner beauty of her soul…with passion for him. He didn't examine why someone as perfect as Audra could feel anything for an immoral being like him. No, he would simply bask in the wonder of it all. He would carry this moment with him through eternity, however long his eternity was to be. But now, every second of it would be wrought with the agony of knowing he would never have this again. Never have Audra again.

He was ashamed to feel the beginning of tears gather in his throat. What had she done to him? Never in his nearly three-hundred years had he so desperately missed being human. How could he go back to his torturous, spectral existence after touching and tasting her living, breathing essence?

He pushed the emotion aside, concentrating on the primal, animalistic pleasure of the climax he could no longer stave off. Blood roared through his system with the force of a tidal wave. *Please let this last forever...* He didn't know to whom he was entreating, but he knew it was a useless request. He had this moment…this now…this…

*Oh, Christ...*

His body tensed. "Audra…I…" he clamped down on the words. He'd been about to say, *I love you.* But he wasn't worthy of her love. What could he offer her except a future of living on the edge of something real? Nothing, that's what. Instead, he moaned her name once more as he pulsed within her, the tremors growing, then subsiding, over and over, until they finally stilled.

In that instant, he finally knew perfect contentment…could almost believe he'd someday earn absolution. If someone like Audra could feel any sort of affection for him, then surely, all was not lost. He went limp, staying inside her, using his elbows to hold most of his weight. This was where he wanted to remain…eternally wrapped in Audra's sweet body.

****

The sound of her name sliding off his lips incited her ecstasy to a near fever pitch. Teetering on the precipice of another orgasm, excited beyond all rational thought, she undulated her hips, rubbing against his groin. The pressure built and pulsed, shooting through her nerve endings, into her veins, heating her blood as it rushed to her head. When she could stand it no longer, her own climax shuddered through her, eliciting small moans of delight as waves of pleasure crested over her, carrying her somewhere she couldn't define, buoying her in its rocky turmoil, until it finally ebbed and she settled into the safe harbor of Dimitri's warm, perspiration-slicked body.

Satisfied lethargy stole through her limbs, leaving her weak and sated.

Dimitri groaned his contentment as he gazed down at her, wonder and joy dancing in his glorious eyes. Lowering his head, he placed a tender kiss on her lips, then rolled off her, staying close, pulling her into his body. "That was unbelievable," he said breathlessly.

"Most definitely," she agreed. She was chilly, but too relaxed to summon the energy to slide under the blankets. Instead, she snuggled into Dimitri's warmth.

He turned his head to stare into her eyes, then looked down her body and ran a finger along a scar at the top of her rib cage. "I remember this. You were sixteen. You and your friends were swimming, jumping into Grand Lake from the cliffs. You miscalculated and hit against the jagged rocks. I nearly lost my mind. I wanted to rescue you." His gaze rose back to hers. He frowned and shook his head. "What kind of reaper does that make me?"

An emotion frighteningly close to love tugged her insides, a tender ache resting along the edges of her heart. She felt the sting of hot tears. To think he'd been watching her all these years. Had witnessed so many moments in her life. A bond like nothing she'd ever known.

She smiled up at him. "It makes you a reaper with a touch of humanity."

He grinned and kissed her softly. "You meant that as a compliment, but in our world, it's not." His expression turned solemn. "It's almost time. I'll turn back soon."

She nodded and lifted her hand to his jaw, letting it rest there, wanting to touch him for as long as she could. "Thank you."

"For the sex or for Sadie?" he said, his mouth quirking in amusement.

"Both."

He pulled her closer, brushing his hand along her hairline while she kept her touch on his face.

All too soon, she felt him fade beneath her palm. Despair opened like a chasm in the center of her chest. Was this what life with Dimitri would be like? An hour of companionship—of mind-blowing sex—then back to amorphous nothingness?

Yes, it was precisely what life with Dimitri would be like. But why was she worried about it anyway? He hadn't said anything about a future. She hadn't asked. She knew now that she had fallen hard for him. That any future with Dimitri was better than no future at all. But he hadn't said any more than that she was beautiful, special, and he'd wanted her for a long time. Not exactly the foundation for a lifetime of bliss.

"I'll go now," he said as he left her bed. "Sleep well."

Suddenly freezing without his warmth, she slid beneath the blankets.

"Good night," she whispered.

He winked, then disappeared through the wall. She snuggled down into the covers. She wouldn't allow the hopelessness of the future to mar the contentment she felt now. Her night with Dimitri had been amazing. Sure, he couldn't stay and cuddle with her, but a lot of men didn't do that anyway.

She smiled at the thought and was just drifting into sleep when the ringing phone jarred her awake.

"Hello?" She sat up, not even bothering to look at the caller ID before she answered.

"Audra? Oh, God. Audra," a distraught Riley screamed.

"What is it? What's happened?"

Sadie? Had she died after all? Was this the consequence Dimitri mentioned? You can have her a few hours longer, but she's still going to be snatched away?

"It's Brent." Riley was sobbing so hard Audra could barely understand her. "He's dead, Audra. Brent is dead."

# Chapter 21

Audra took Riley and Sadie to her house after Riley was released from the hospital. The car accident that took Brent's life had left Riley with nothing more than a few scratches and a bump on the head. But Riley didn't want to be alone in the house she'd shared with Brent. And Audra didn't want her to be left alone with a head injury, regardless how minor.

Once Riley and Sadie were settled in the guest bedroom, Audra went to her own. She couldn't get the image of Riley's shell-shocked face out of her mind. The white bandage on her head, the pretty features haggard with agony and disbelief. Riley hadn't cried once since that first hysterical phone call. Shock. The tears would come again. Anger would be in there somewhere. Audra would be with her during every stage of the process.

Audra had just changed into her sleep shirt when Dimitri appeared in her bedroom.

He stood near the window, his face partially in shadows. "I'm sorry," he said softly.

"You know about Brent?"

He nodded.

"Are you the one who took him?"

"No. Not me. But I was afraid something like this would be the result."

"Result of what?"

"Messing with fate."

Exhaustion and sadness made it difficult to think clearly, but realization dawned, and she stared at him in disbelief.

"Was that the consequence for sparing Sadie?" She stalked across the floor until she stood directly in front of him. "Did you make a trade?"

"It doesn't work like that. Not exactly. It's somewhat like the butterfly effect. One little alteration can set off a whole new chain of events."

"Of course," she said quietly. "Sadie's parents went out to dinner that night, after you came to dance practice. If you'd taken Sadie—if Sadie had died that day—they wouldn't have gone. Her father died because *she* didn't."

It all made sense in a tragic, nonsensical way. If Riley and Brent hadn't gone to dinner that particular night, at that particular restaurant, at that particular time, then that particular drunk driver would never have careened into Brent's side of the car, crushing him beyond recognition. Stealing his life. These were the consequences of Dimitri sparing Sadie's life. *Ain't that just a hoot?*

Dimitri frowned and dropped his head. "I told you there would be consequences."

But she'd never dreamed they would be of this magnitude. Grief made her lash out. "This is bullshit. I convince you to save a child so you take her father? What the fuck kind of tradeoff is that?"

"I didn't take her father. It was fate."

"But you knew. You knew he would die."

"No. I knew something could happen, but I had no way of knowing what. I did as you asked, Audra. I told you, whatever happened was on you."

The words landed like a punch to her gut. "You're saying it's my fault Brent's dead?"

He stared at her, but didn't respond.

Tears sprang to her eyes. She couldn't even argue. He was right. It *was* her fault. He'd done as she asked. For her, he'd spared Sadie. As a result, the child lost her father.

She was so weary of this odd and dangerous world she'd been exposed to. Weary of reapers, even though she was pretty sure she'd fallen in love with one. She suddenly had no strength left to argue. No foundation for her rage.

"Let me ask you this," Dimitri said. His eyes bore into hers, barely illuminated by the light coming in through the slit in the curtain. "Had you known this would be the result, would you have chosen for Sadie to perish?"

She couldn't answer his question. But for a split second, she hated him for asking it.

"Please leave," she choked out. He gave a slight nod. She watched him go, waiting until she was alone before breaking down in tears.

****

Sometime in the wee hours, Audra heard Riley sobbing. The sound was muffled, but since Audra hadn't been able to sleep, she heard.

Did that mean Riley had heard her speaking to Dimitri? No. They'd kept their voices low, and Riley would surely have come in to investigate.

She rose from bed and found Riley in the kitchen, sitting at the table, her head in her hands, shoulders shaking violently.

"Riley, sweetheart. Come here." Audra folded her friend in her arms, stroking her back and murmuring comforting words as she poured out her grief.

"I can't sleep," Riley said when she finally reined in the tears. "I keep seeing Brent lying there, broken. I keep hearing the sounds of the crash."

"Didn't the doctor prescribe you sleeping pills?"

Riley nodded. "I didn't get them filled."

"Why not?"

She shrugged. "I didn't think it was fair. That I should be able to rest. After…after what happened to Brent."

"Come on, that's not right. You need your rest. Sadie needs you." Audra gripped Riley's hands in hers. "It won't be selfish to find a little bit of peace, of escape."

Riley gave a reluctant nod.

"Where's your script? I'll take it to the hospital pharmacy. They're open twenty-four hours."

"You don't need to do that."

"I do. I want to. It's the only way either of us will get any sleep." She smiled to soften the words, and Riley managed a brief smile in return.

****

Audra drove to the hospital and parked in the visitor's lot since she wouldn't be long and didn't want to bother with her employee garage key. Once she had the prescription, she headed back to her car. She hoped the pills would help Riley sleep. She needed to forget what happened, even for a little while.

As she reached the car, she experienced an odd sensation that something was wrong. She couldn't put her finger on it, but something felt…off.

She glanced around the nearly deserted lot but saw nothing. Shrugging it off to the effects of all that had happened lately, she thumbed the key fob and reached for the door.

The attack came from behind. She was standing one minute, the next, a blow slammed to the back of her shoulders, and she went down to her knees. She barely had time to notice the pain of her impact with the cement before she was grabbed from behind and hauled to her feet.

Her attacker whirled her around to face him, and her insides froze. *Scott.*

He shoved her against the car and put his face a few inches from hers. "Finally. I been following you and I finally get my chance. You fucking cunt," he spat. "It's your fault. All your fault Maria's gone. You destroyed my life."

Audra's insides quivered, the blow making her woozy. "My fault? You killed her, you insane piece of shit."

He punched her in the jaw, and her head snapped back so hard, she thought it would sever from her neck. Pain exploded, far worse than the ache in her shoulders, or the sting in her knees.

*He's going to kill me. He killed his wife. He'd think nothing of killing me. It's what he's wanted all along.*

Panic fueled her, and she tried to shove against him. He didn't budge. She brought her knee up and jammed it into his groin. He grunted and doubled over. She pulled free and was about to run when his hand reached out and snatched her hair, jerking her nearly off her feet.

"Scott, no!" A young, male voice penetrated her

consciousness. Audra turned her head as much as Scott's grip would allow, finding Maria's nephew, Joel, standing a few feet away, fists clenched, chest rising and falling. "Let her go. You killed Aunt Maria, you son of a bitch. I won't let you hurt anyone else."

"What are you going to do about it, you pussy?" Scott snarled.

Joel lunged toward him, and Scott released his hold on Audra. She stumbled to the ground, but gained her footing. Her gaze shot around the parking lot, to the entrance of the hospital, but no one was around. How could there be no one around?

She fumbled for her cell phone, hoping Joel could keep Scott occupied long enough for her to summon the police. Her trembling fingers latched on to the phone, but before she could retrieve it, she heard a shouted grunt. Her gaze flew to the two men. They seemed to be locked in a lover's embrace, suspended, frozen in mid-motion. Then, she watched in horror as Joel slid to the ground, a knife protruding from his chest, eyes staring up at the night sky.

"No…" she gasped, her hand flying to her mouth to cover the sound.

Scott whirled toward her. His face was streaked with tears. The moon reflected in his eyes with an insane light.

"See what you did," he sobbed. "Everyone I love is gone because of you." He reached down and yanked the knife from his nephew's chest. It made a popping, sucking sound that brought a wave of nausea to her throat.

He staggered toward her, and she dropped the phone, stumbling backward, a strangled cry wrenching from her throat.

He was almost upon her when a blur of darkness flew into his path. Scott halted, letting out a cry of surprise.

Dimitri stood between her and her attacker. Her relief turned to terror when she realized that Scott had seen him too. That meant this was the human Dimitri. The vulnerable, easy to kill Dimitri. And Scott had a knife.

She was afraid to cry out, afraid to distract Dimitri as the two men circled one another, Scott enraged and armed, Dimitri protective and weaponless.

"Come on, mother fucker," Scott taunted. "I have nothing left to lose. First I do you, then the bitch. Her, though, I'm gonna fuck her in half before I kill her."

Dimitri lunged, and Scott brought the knife up. Audra yelped, her heart stalling as the knife hit its mark. Dimitri grabbed his side.

Blood poured from beneath his hand. The nurse in her knew a wound like that could be fatal. A lung might have been punctured. Dimitri would die, right here in front of her eyes.

Scott was moving in to aim another blow when Dimitri straightened, bringing a fist up into Scott's chin. Scott reeled from the impact, staggering backward. Dimitri swayed, but stayed upright. Scott gripped the knife, thrusting outward, but Dimitri grabbed his hand, twisting. Audra heard the undeniable snap of bones breaking, then Scott's howl rent though the night as the weapon clattered to the cement. Dimitri scooped the knife up and plunged it into Scott's gut.

Audra gasped. Scott slid to the ground, then went still.

Dimitri turned to face her, doubling over, his hand cupped to his side. Red streams painted his clothing, the ground beneath him. *That's a lot of blood*, she thought dumbly, before rushing to him.

"Dimitri! Oh God, Dimitri. Hang in there. We'll get you into the hospital. I'll call for help." She couldn't think straight. She wasn't sure if, this close to help, she should still dial 9-1-1. Could she get him inside in time?

She let him lean on her while she searched frantically for her phone. Wait, she'd dropped it earlier. It must still be around here somewhere.

"Hang on," she whispered, easing Dimitri's weight off her to lean him against her car. "I'm going to grab my phone. Call 9-1-1. Help will be here soon."

"No. Can't."

"Can't? Are you crazy? You'll die."

"I'll be fine. Just help me into your car. Another forty-five minutes or so, and I'll transform."

"You might not live that long. I need to take you to the hospital."

"Then what?" he panted. "We make it there, they're treating me, the thousand breaths come to an end, and I disappear right in front of their eyes?" He lurched around to the passenger side. "Just open the damn door."

She slid into the driver's seat. Searching for something to stanch the flow of blood, she dug a gym towel from her duffle in the back seat. She pressed the cloth against the wound, cringing when she saw the amount of blood it quickly absorbed.

"Dimitri, please." Tears coursed down her cheeks, the terror of watching him die clawing at her chest. In spite of everything, in spite of what he was, she loved him. She might never be able to have him, but she couldn't let him die. "Please, Dimitri. I can only do so much for you myself. Let me get you help."

"If you did get help, what then? How would you explain me away?" He rested his head against the back of the seat. "I can't put you in that position, Audra."

"What?" Her voice rose in fury. "You're going to die to keep me from explaining a tricky situation?"

He grinned, clenching his eyes shut for a moment, then said between gasps, "It would be a little more than a tricky situation. A lot of strange things have happened around you lately. Who knows what this would lead to?"

"But, you can't—"

"Jesus Christ, woman. If you'll shut up, I'll breathe faster and turn sooner. No more arguments. Please." He reached a hand out and she took it, closing her fingers over his. "No more crying, okay? Just hold my hand."

Sniffing back tears, Audra held on, praying with each breath he took. *Dimitri can't die, please don't let him die.*

How could she live with herself if he died saving her? How could she live if he died at all?

****

Veronica strode across the living room, agitatedly throwing her hands in the air. "The bitch. He's so besotted with her, he can't even think like a reaper anymore. Stupid fool nearly got himself killed to save her."

Gaylen strolled to the bar and poured a drink. "Yes, but he didn't. He turned back to reaper form before he could die. The white knight to the rescue, safe and sound."

"We have to get rid of her. I can't rest until she's dead. And not in the fun, live-forever way we are. Dead and out of the picture." She turned to him, her eyes wide with frenzy. "You can take her. You can reap her, and she'll be bound to you forever."

"That's been my plan all along."

"I want in."

"I don't need a partner, thanks anyway." He brought the glass to his lips and drained it.

"You owe me." She stormed over and slapped the glass from his hand. It skittered across the carpet, then thunked against the far wall. "You owe me, dammit."

"What the fuck are you doing?" Gaylen grabbed another glass and filled it. "Calm down. What do you mean I owe you?"

"Because, you son of a bitch, you're the one who got me into this mess in the first place. Fifty years ago, when you sucked the life from me."

****

The newspapers carried the story about Joel's and Scott's deaths. Speculation was that Joel had attacked Scott because Scott killed his aunt. How they both ended up dead was a question the police had been unable to answer. Audra felt guilty that she couldn't go to Shane, that she couldn't explain and solve the mystery for him, but there was no way she could come clean about what happened that night.

She was just happy—so deeply relieved and grateful—that Dimitri had survived. Those seconds she'd waited, watching, hoping he'd hold on until he regained his reaper form, were the longest of her life. God, if he'd died, if she'd had to *watch* him die…

With a shudder, she tried to put it out of her mind. For now, she needed to focus on the awards ceremony Jaxon had invited her to. Pride filled her heart as she watched from the audience while Jaxon walked onto the stage.

She'd almost forgotten about agreeing to accompany him to the event. Brent's funeral had been today, and she was hesitant to attend a social function hours after her friend had buried her husband. But Riley insisted. And, Audra owed it to Jaxon. He'd always been there for her.

In spite of all that had happened lately, she was glad she had come. Seeing him win the award was almost enough to take her mind off all the bad stuff. He was handsome and beaming in a white tuxedo with a black, silk shirt and tie as he accepted the award.

"This night wouldn't have been possible," he said into the mic. "Most of my successes, large or small, would not have been possible without the love of one special person. My best friend, the love of my life, Audra Grayson."

Applause exploded in the room. Those who knew them were probably wondering why, if she was the love of his life, they were divorced. They couldn't know he hadn't meant it in a romantic way. Jaxon did love her completely, just as she loved him. Finally, her love for him was no longer romantic, but it was deep and lasting. He was really her only family.

When he returned to the table, he leaned forward and placed a kiss on her cheek. Pulling back, he stared into her face. "You're crying." He laughed. "What's wrong?"

"I'm just so happy for you. And what you said, that

was beautiful. Thank you."

He pulled her to him for a tight hug. "No. Thank you."

After the ceremonies were over, and seemingly everyone in the room had approached them to offer their congratulations, it was finally time to leave.

Audra was glad they'd valet parked when she stepped out of the Wyandotte mansion to find rain pouring from the evening sky. Jaxon slipped an arm around her and pulled her under the awning. "Don't want your pretty dress ruined. You look gorgeous."

She looked down at her ruby red floor-length dress. She'd been a little self-conscious about the way it hugged her body, the way it dipped low in the front, revealing more cleavage than she was accustomed to showing, but Jaxon's approval made her less self-conscious. He had an impeccable sense of style, and his compliment wasn't based on sexual attraction. Maybe she looked okay after all.

Jaxon's Lexus pulled up to the curb, and the valet got out, handing over the keys.

"Come on," Jaxon shouted above the noise of the rain. "We'll make a run for it."

He took her hand and was pulling her to the car when a roar sounded above the clattering rain. Audra looked up, her eyes widening in terror as a dark-colored car jumped the curb, careening directly toward her. Before she had time to do more than scream, Jaxon shoved her out of the path of the vehicle.

She flew to the sidewalk, landing with a bone-jarring thump. Through the downpour, she looked up to see what had become of Jaxon and the car. Her heart leapt to her throat. Icy fingers trailed down her spine.

The car sped away, but Jaxon lay still on the sidewalk.

"Jaxon!" she screamed. She scrambled to her feet, nearly tripping over the hem of her gown. Stumbling over to him, she dropped to her knees. "Jaxon, please!"

He lay on his back, eyes squeezed shut, grimacing. *Thank God.* He was alive.

"Jaxon, hang in there. I'm getting help."

He opened his eyes, staring dazedly around. For the first time, she noticed that the liquid on the cement next to his head wasn't all rain. It was a deep, rusty color. Blood. *Oh, God.*

"Help!" she screamed at the crowd that gathered. She tore off a piece of material from the hemline of her dress and pressed it to Jaxon's head. "Call 9-1-1." In the panic that ensued, she wasn't sure anyone had heard at first. Then a man called out, "They're on their way."

Looking up, she spotted Dimitri standing next to Jaxon.

Relief swept through her. "Oh, thank God. Dimitri, help me, please. He's hurt."

She wasn't sure why she asked, wasn't sure what he could do. She was a nurse and was doing all she could until the ambulance arrived. But she was desperate, panicky, she needed to know something, someone was helping.

"I'm sorry, Audra."

"Don't be sorry. He's not dead. Just help me." She held the cloth tightly to Jaxon's head and touched his face with her free hand. "Look at me. Hang in there. You'll be fine. Help is coming."

"Audra?" Jaxon panted. "Who are you talking to?"

"Don't worry about it. Just hold on. We're getting help—"

He nodded, then his face clenched. His eyes rolled back, and his features relaxed. His body went limp. He gazed blankly up at the sky. Rain poured into his eyes.

But it didn't matter now.

He couldn't feel the rain. Couldn't feel anything anymore.

A sob tore from her chest as a crushing weight settled into her bones. "No, Jaxon. No!" she wailed.

She looked around wildly, her gaze falling on Dimitri. "Help him. You have to help him. You can save him."

But he ignored her. He stood, arms outstretched, focusing on something only he could see. Then he crooked his hands, beckoning.

****

Audra had ridden in the ambulance with Jaxon to the hospital. They didn't turn on their sirens. There was no need.

She stayed with him until the morgue took him, stroking his hand, thanking him for being her friend, for always having her back. Apologizing for not having his.

By the time she left the hospital, dawn was approaching. She stepped outside just as the sun broke through the murkiness of the night. An array of orange, purple and pinks melded into a glowing ray as the sun crested over the downtown buildings. So gorgeous. How could something so beautiful still exist in a world without Jaxon?

The agonizing, ripping hole in her gut had closed for the moment. Now all she felt was numb. And fury. Dimitri had taken him. Damn him to hell. He'd taken Jaxon.

She let herself into the house, too drained to be

surprised to find Dimitri waiting for her.

She tossed her keys onto the end table and lifted her chin to stare at him. “There’s no one here to take except me. Unless you’re here to do that, get the hell out.”

“I had to see you.”

“I don’t want to see you. I don’t ever want to see you again.”

“I had to make sure you’re okay.”

“I’m not. Now you’ve seen. Get out. You bring nothing but death and destruction. I want you out of my life.”

“Something has to be done about Gaylen. Things are escalating, and it’s got to end.”

“This had nothing to do with Gaylen. It was an accident.”

He didn’t respond, just stared at her, jaw clenched, arms crossed over his chest.

She peered suspiciously at him. “Wasn’t it? How could Gaylen be involved? You’re the one who took Jaxon. They haven’t found the driver of the car. Whoever it was didn’t even stick around to find out how he was,” she spat out.

“She couldn’t.”

“She?” Audra realized she never heard what had happened after she and Jaxon had left. She didn’t know if the driver was hurt, what made them do what they’d done, if they’d been drunk or what. Apparently, Dimitri did know. “Who was she? Is she all right?”

“She’s fine. Not long after the accident, she transformed.”

Audra stared up at him, eyes widening. “Transformed? Oh my God. Veronica!”

"I'm sure she and Gaylen planned it. I swear, I'm going to do something to stop him. I can't let him keep hurting you. I promise, I'll take care of this."

She didn't answer. Her mind was clicking on a plan. The only way to destroy Gaylen was for him to turn human. She'd have to figure out a way to make that happen. Then kill him.

"Something has to be done all right," she said. "But you don't need to do it. You've tried for nearly three-hundred years. Where has that gotten you?"

He flinched, but didn't defend himself. "You can't do anything, Audra. There's no way you can stop Gaylen. You can't even try. It's too dangerous."

"I can't let anyone else I love die."

"Neither can I." His voice lowered, and he stepped closer.

It took a moment for the words to sink in. When they did, she wasn't sure he meant what she thought he meant. She looked up at him. "What?" she whispered.

His eyes glistened with emotion. "I love you."

She curled her lips into a bitter smile. "*Now* you tell me that you love me? You just took my best friend from me, and you want to declare your love? Great timing, Dimitri. Don't say it after we've made love. Wait until you've ripped my soul to shreds."

"I told you I was sorry. I had no choice. It's who I am. It's what I do. I don't know what you want from me, Audra. I can't die for you, I'm already dead."

Her heart cried out for her to forgive him, to tell him that she loved him, too. But she couldn't erase the image of Jaxon's broken, bloody body. Or, of Dimitri reaching out to take him away.

"What I want," she bit out. "Is for you to leave me

alone. Forget you ever knew me."

He barked a humorless laugh and shook his head. "Wish I could do that, Audra. But dying would be easier."

****

Audra lay in bed, but sleep eluded her. She couldn't quell the screaming in her mind, the anguish in her heart.

Gaylen had to be destroyed. She'd have to figure out a way to tempt him to turn human. In order to do that, she had to pretend to give him what he wanted, which was to reap her. Of course, she'd have to be in jeopardy for him to reap her. A plan was formulating, she just wasn't sure of all the details. It would take a little bit of acting, a lot of subterfuge, and a hell of a lot of luck.

The opportunity to put her plan in motion presented itself sooner than she expected. She roused herself out of bed and went into the kitchen for a bottle of water. She was closing the refrigerator when Gaylen appeared.

Supernatural beings materializing unexpectedly in front of her no longer scared her. Just showed what constant exposure to terror and tragedy could do.

She sighed. "What are you doing here?"

"I wondered if, now, after what happened to your friend, you'd be ready to cut a deal."

"You had nothing to do with it. Dimitri took Jaxon."

Gaylen smiled. "Yes. But I made him ripe for the taking. Veronica was there at my bidding."

Sick realization wound through Audra's soul. Just as Dimitri suspected. Gaylen—and that bitch,

Veronica—were the reason Jaxon had been in jeopardy.

Gaylen moved closer. "Do you get me? No one is safe. Not unless you make it stop. I swear to you, the little girl is next. And she won't be as much work. Not with that heart thing she's developed."

Audra took a deep breath. She couldn't cope with this right now—but she had to find a way to stop him. "Okay. I can't fight any longer. Can't let anyone else die. So, in order to allow you to reap me, I need to be in jeopardy, right? And Dimitri needs to be out of the way so he can't stop you from reaping me."

"Correct."

"What if you turn human? You could harm me, then reap me, right?"

"No. That won't work. If I turn human and harm you, then I won't be in reaper form to take you. You'll have to harm yourself."

Nausea tightened in her throat. She'd hoped Gaylen would agree to turn human, that she could take him out, and that would be that. She should have known it wouldn't be that easy.

She'd have to adjust the plan just a bit. Bottom line, she had to coax Gaylen into turning human. She couldn't allow him to remain in the safety of his reaper form and just *take* her. No way.

"Harm myself?" she asked, her voice cracking.

"Yes."

"Like, attempted suicide? An overdose?"

"Right. And it is unlikely Dimitri would coincidentally show up at that second." He nodded slowly. "This could work. Dimitri's stopped me many times, but there are many, many times he hasn't." A slow, chilling smile split his face. "Maybe Veronica can keep him occupied at just the right moment."

Audra nodded, although she was hoping for the opposite. In order for her plan to work, everyone had to do what she needed them to, at precisely the right time. Otherwise, she was doomed to eternity with a sadistic lunatic.

"Then the people I love will be safe?"

"You have my word. They'll be safe." He frowned down at her. "This has to be done correctly. There's no room for error. When you take the overdose, you can't kill yourself. You just need to make yourself very, very ill. Close to death. Don't rob me of my joy."

Her blood chilled. She was actually having a conversation about how to almost commit suicide? She infused her voice with as much confidence as she could muster. "I'm a nurse. I know how many pills to take."

A faraway look came into his eyes, and he rubbed his hands together. "Can't wait to see Dimitri's face when he realizes you belong to me forever. Bastard should have let me die the night he killed Louisa."

"Let you die?"

"Yes. He pulled me from the house just before he succumbed to the smoke and died. He let her burn alone."

"Wait. Dimitri lost his own life saving yours? You hate him for saving your life?"

"He killed the woman I loved. All he did by saving my life is guarantee I could never be with her again."

"I doubt that was his intention," she said dryly.

"Intention or not, here we are. It is what it is. And now, he'll pay for everything."

She shuddered. If one little thing went wrong, she'd be the one paying. Paying with her eternal soul.

## Chapter 22

Audra stood in her bathroom, watching the door, holding a bottle of water in her right hand, a colorful array of pills in her left. Randomly, a scene from Burt Reynolds' movie, *The End*, popped into her head. His character tried to commit suicide by swallowing a handful of pills, but when he washed them down with spoiled milk, he spit them all over the coffee table, then said, "Looks like Walt Disney threw up."

She giggled. The giggle turned into a full-blown laugh that wouldn't stop. Taking a deep breath, she sucked it back down. She couldn't lose it. Couldn't become hysterical. She had a plan to execute. Grief wound around her heart, expanding in her chest. Why hadn't she put a plan in motion before Jaxon died? She could have saved him. Now she had to save Sadie. She couldn't let her go the way Jaxon had.

The pills were gripped so tightly in her damp palm, she'd no doubt have to swallow them all in one moist sticky ball. As long as she convinced Gaylen she was attempting to follow his plan, that was all that mattered. Once he realized the only way to reap her was to turn human himself, he would surely do it. He had to. Then, she could kill him.

Her heart pounded, slowly and loudly. The beat reverberated through her ears as she watched the clock tick over to eight fifty-four. She'd told Cassie to have

Dimitri here at nine, although she wouldn't tell her why, or allow her to tell Dimitri that Audra had asked him to be here. She wasn't even sure Cassie could pull it off, but Audra had impressed upon her how important it was that she succeed. She hadn't told her that if she didn't, Gaylen would reap her, and she'd spend all of eternity as his companion, at his mercy.

Gaylen was due to show up a few minutes after nine. Very small window, but it was a window nonetheless.

The clock ticked to eight fifty-five, and she tossed the pills into her mouth, washing them down with water.

*Get here, get here, get here,* she prayed.

Heaviness stole through her limbs. Her head felt disconnected from her body. Her vision blurred, but through the haze, she heard someone say, "Audra? Audra, dear God."

Dimitri. He was here. She tried to smile, but she was sinking to the floor. What was she supposed to do? Something to keep from dying…?

Oh yeah. She stuck her finger in her mouth, aiming for the back of her throat, but having trouble reaching her target. What was wrong with her hand? It wouldn't obey her mind.

"Cassie, what the hell is going on here?" Dimitri's voice again.

"I don't know. She didn't tell me. She just said to get you here."

"Fuck," Dimitri bit out. Then she felt his hands on her, lifting her, holding her. He was human? No. She hadn't thought about that. How could she not think about that? How could he stop Gaylen from reaping her if he was human? "You need to vomit, Audra."

Dimitri jammed a finger into her throat and tilted her head forward, over the toilet. She threw up, all the while thoughts merging one into another. Dimitri human. Saving her life. But he wouldn't be able to stop Gaylen. Gaylen would appear any second. He would reap her. This was all for nothing. He could still go after Sadie.

"I'm sorry," she moaned when the spasms subsided. "I'm so sorry."

"It's okay, baby." Dimitri cradled her in his arms. "I called an ambulance. Help is on the way. It's okay."

"No, you don't get it," she mumbled. "It's not okay at all."

"What—" Dimitri began, but something drew his attention away, then she saw Gaylen looming over his shoulder.

"Audra. Damn you," Gaylen roared. "You promised."

"I—I tried…" She frowned up at him. Why wasn't he reaping her?

"Promised what?" Dimitri demanded.

She didn't answer.

"You're fucking with the wrong person, Audra," Gaylen ground out. "You won't like the consequences."

The wail of sirens split the air.

"What's going on?" Dimitri asked. "What did you do?"

"Why didn't he reap me?" she asked in bewilderment. "You can't stop him while you're human."

"No, but I can," Cassie said.

Audra looked up at Cassie. Her vision was growing

dimmer. In spite of regurgitating the pills, traces of them were still in her system. She couldn't stay awake much longer.

"You stopped him? How could you? You're new."

"Doesn't matter," Cassie explained, but the words were getting lost in the hammering in Audra's head. "As long as another reaper is around, he can't take someone when it's not time."

Blackness shut her voice down.

****

Audra lifted her eyes to discover she had a pounding headache and a visitor.

Riley sat next to the hospital bed, but rather than concern, her faced was scrunched in anger. Her cheeks were pale, and stress lines were etched into the skin around her eyes and mouth.

"How could you?" she whispered hotly.

"What?"

"How could you try to leave me?" Riley shook her head. "After losing Brent like that, I need you. Sadie needs you, and you were just going to check out? How could you?"

"I'm sorry. I didn't think—"

"No, you didn't think. You might have lost Jaxon, but there are other people who care about you. You weren't thinking of us at all. I'm not sure I can forgive you for this. Ever."

How could Audra tell her she'd done it for Sadie? That she hadn't meant to die? There was only one way to convince her. The truth. Riley would either believe her and forgive her, or have her committed. Either way, she had to try.

"There's something I should tell you, Riley. It's

going to be hard to take in, but you know I've never lied to you. I'm not crazy, and I'm not lying now."

Riley frowned. "What's this all about?"

"You remember those ghosts I mentioned to you? That day we were drinking wine at my house?" Riley nodded. "They weren't ghosts, as it turns out."

"What were they?" Riley's voice held a note of skepticism and fear. Like she didn't really want to know.

"Reapers," Audra said. Riley's eyes widened, and she opened her mouth, but Audra held up a hand. "Let me tell you everything. Then you can tell me how insane you think I am. For now, just listen."

Audra began speaking, relaying the events that had taken place since Dimitri and Gaylen appeared to her. She ended the story by explaining that she hadn't really tried to kill herself. That her plan was to show Gaylen she'd tried to put herself in jeopardy. She wanted him to believe she had panicked and made herself throw up, and that Dimitri had unexpectedly shown up, and now the only way he could reap her was for him to put her in jeopardy himself…by turning human.

Riley sat staring at her, blinking slowly, shaking her head from side to side. Audra wasn't sure if it was because she indeed thought Audra was insane, or that she just thought she was lying. That she'd woven the story just to get out of the whole suicide thing.

"Aren't you going to say anything?" Audra asked. "Call me a liar or a lunatic?"

"Neither." Her voice was hushed, cold and trembling.

"Why not?"

"I believe you."

"You do?"

Riley nodded. "Yes. I mean, I still think it was foolish, dangerous to do what you did, but I believe you about the reapers. I think I've seen them too."

Audra's heart sped up. "You've seen reapers? Gaylen and Dimitri?"

Riley shook her head. "No. The night of the accident. When Brent…died. I thought it was my imagination, but he was so real. I saw him there. Before I passed out."

"Who did you see, Riley?"

Riley's green eyes were luminous with tears. "Steve," she whispered. "I saw Steve. He was there when Brent died."

****

In the two days since Riley's revelation, Audra hadn't let herself think about the fact that her friend could see reapers, too. Had seen her dead former lover.

Steve had most likely reaped Riley's husband. That was a lot to take in, but for another time. She needed to concentrate on the issue at hand…stopping Gaylen before Riley witnessed a reaper taking her child.

She was forced to take leave from work after her suicide attempt. They wanted her to get counseling before she came back. Little did they know, she needed a hell of a lot more help than a counselor could provide.

She was sitting in her living room, staring at the turned-off television, when Gaylen showed up.

"You really have no idea what you've done, do you?" His voice was as cold as the block of ice sitting in her chest. "I told you what would happen if you didn't let me take you. Now, the little girl will die. You like living so much, live with that."

She came to her feet, forcing sincerity into her tone. “No, I meant to, really. I freaked out at the last minute. Couldn’t go through with it. I’m just too chicken to do it myself. But you can do it.”

“Do what?”

“You can put me in jeopardy, then reap me.”

He lowered his brows over his golden eyes, seeming to consider her proposal for a long time before he finally said, “The only way to execute your plan is for me to turn human. As I’ve told you, I can’t do that. Dimitri will be all over me.”

“What if I convince him to turn human just before? Then he won’t be able to turn for another twenty-four hours. You’ll be safe.”

“Do you really think I’m going to fall for your tricks again? Fool me once, Audra…”

“No. No trick. You’ll know whether or not I was able to get Dimitri to turn human, right? I can’t trick you. If you don’t see that he turned human, then we don’t go through with the plan.”

“And the little girl dies,” he said matter of factly.

Audra swallowed hard. “And Sadie dies.”

Gaylen pursed his lips and nodded. “This might not be such a bad idea. I like the way you think. But then again, if I’m human, I can’t reap you until I turn.”

Right. She’d forgotten about that little detail. She intended to kill him while he was human, so she wasn’t worried about his lack of ability to reap her. That was actually a bonus.

“Although…” he said. “If I time it just right, wait until I have only a few breaths left, I can hurt you, take those last breaths, turn reaper, then take you.” His face lit with joy. “It’s a deal. But don’t screw it up this time.

You won't like how it ends."

She tried not to cringe at the calm recital of his plan to dispose of her. "Okay. I promise."

His mouth stretched into a satisfied leer. "So, when do we do this?"

****

Dimitri banged on Veronica's door. "Let me in, Veronica. I know you're in there. Let me in now!"

The door swung open, and Veronica stood there, wearing a flowing lavender gown. She tossed her long auburn hair over her shoulder and smiled like a satisfied cat. "Dimitri. What a lovely surprise. Please come in."

He stormed inside and gripped her shoulders. "What did you do?"

"What are you talking about?"

"Audra's friend, Jaxon. You killed him. I've been looking for you ever since. What the hell are you up to?"

"Why do you care? He was just some human."

"He was Audra's friend. A doctor. He was a good man."

"Yeah, well. She was also in love with him, and now he's out of the way. You should be thanking me."

"You're out of your mind."

She looked up at him, tears filling her eyes. "You never loved me."

"I don't love."

"Don't you?"

He narrowed his eyes.

"You love her," she said.

"I don't love her."

"Right," she scoffed. "You're so blinded by your love for her you don't even know what's about to happen."

"What's about to happen? What are you talking about?"

Her lips stretched into a pleased smirk. "You'll know soon enough."

He huffed a sigh and released her with a shove. She wasn't worth his time and effort. "When you see Gaylen, tell him I'm looking for him."

"Why don't you tell him yourself?"

"What—"

Before he could finish the sentence, a blow landed to his right kidney. He went down on one knee, trying to catch his breath. As he was staggering to his feet, another strike smashed into his head.

Gaylen circled around, stopping in front of him. Something hard slammed against the back of his neck. He twisted his head to find the leering grin of the man he'd stabbed to death less than a week ago.

Dimitri looked up at Gaylen, panting in pain. "So, I guess you found a running buddy."

Gaylen grinned. "We're like-minded. It was only a matter of time before we connected."

"A match made in hell."

Gaylen smiled widely. "Hell is where you'll be when I get through with your little girlfriend."

"Fuck you," Dimitri growled. He struggled to his feet, but just as he was regaining his strength, another shot landed, this one with more force than the others. He went to his knees once more, then turned in time to see Scott lifting a bat over his head, aiming for another blow.

His ears rang, and pain exploded from his shoulders through his back, but he summoned his waning strength and wrenched the bat from Scott's hands. He pulled the bat back over his shoulder, preparing to swing for a home run. A crack like fireworks sounded, and a searing pain burned through his midsection.

He whirled to find Veronica—a human Veronica—holding a gun. He dropped in a dizzying, pain-filled heap to the floor. Damn her. When he recovered from the bullet wound, there'd be hell to pay.

He lay on the ground, sucking in gulps of air. Veronica loomed in his vision, holding a roll of copper. "Lift him up for me," she said to Scott.

Scott tugged him upright, and Veronica rolled the copper around him while Dimitri gasped for breath.

After several moments, the pain subsided. The bullet wound had healed. But he was as helpless as before. More so now. The copper insured that.

"What are you going to do?" Dimitri demanded. "You can't kill me."

"No," Veronica said. "But we can keep you here while Gaylen finishes it. Finishes her."

Panic welled in his chest, but he forced calm into his voice. "You must really want this badly, to turn human like you did."

Veronica bent down and put her lips to his. He couldn't feel her, but just knowing she was that close almost made him gag. "I want to destroy her—watch you suffer—more than I've ever wanted anything in my life."

"So, what's the plan? What's going to happen?" Dimitri tried to make the question sound casual, but inside he was screaming with fear for Audra. His mind raced to formulate a plan. But he was as helpless as a newborn. Audra was at Gaylen's mercy.

"What do you *think* is going to happen?" Veronica's full lips curved into a malicious smile. "Gaylen is finally going to have what he's always wanted. Revenge on you. And a woman to replace the one you stole from him."

****

Gaylen was waiting for Audra in her living room when she arrived home from running errands.

"It's time," he said.

She removed her coat and hung it in the foyer closet. Her fingers shook so badly, she almost couldn't get it on the hanger. "No. Not yet. I haven't had a chance to get Dimitri to turn human. You won't be safe."

"Oh, but I will. I decided to take matters with Dimitri into my own hands. With a little help from friends."

"What have you done?" A chill wound through her stomach.

"Not for you to worry about. You and I have our own business to settle."

She took a deep, fortifying breath and inclined her head in a nod. "Okay. Then this is it."

"Any last preparations? You have everything in order?"

"I've written notes to the people I love." She hadn't, because she didn't intend to die. But she thought it made her sound more sincere. "I'd like to freshen up a bit. Change clothes. I mean, if you're going to take me, I want to be dressed properly for the journey."

He laughed. "You're such a delight, Audra.

Eternity with you is going to be fantastic." He patted her on the butt. "Go. I'll give you a few minutes, but don't take too long. I'm running out of patience."

She left the room and went into her bedroom to change clothes. She dressed in black workout pants and a Brett Favre jersey. She wanted to be comfortable, loose, and free to move quickly. From the nightstand, she retrieved a switchblade and slipped it into her bra. It wasn't likely Gaylen would search her. He was so egotistical, so beyond the scope of reality, it would probably never occur to him that she herself might try to harm him. In his mind, if Dimitri was out of the way, he was home free.

Dimitri…what had Gaylen done to him? He hadn't killed him, surely. Dimitri wouldn't let himself be caught unaware, as a human, and killed by Gaylen.

She couldn't think about that now. She had other issues to deal with.

When she returned to the living room, Gaylen ran his gaze up and down her attire. "Are you kidding me? I thought you'd wear something sexy for me."

"This is comfortable. I'm nervous. I thought wearing my favorite jersey would help me relax."

He lifted his shoulders in a shrug. "What do I care? I'm not after your body. Although…" His eyes once more swept over her. "I must say, you do have a lovely body." He stepped closer and brushed her hair back from her face. She felt it…he'd turned human. With the tip of one finger, he stroked her neck. "This, however, is my favorite body part. So soft, so delicate." He cupped his hand around her neck. "Pardon me if I seem distracted, but I have to keep track of my breaths, so I'll know when I'll turn back to reaper form. Just before, well, you know what happens then. In the meantime, let's have some fun."

His touch felt clammy on her skin, repulsive. He reeked of some cloying cologne, although she didn't know how that was possible. He surely hadn't been wearing cologne when he died. Maybe it was from the last time he turned human? However it had happened, the smell made her want to puke. She swallowed the urge and said, "Just tell me what you want me to do."

"Don't worry, sweetheart. Just leave it all up to me. All you have to do is stand there and look beautiful. And, open your mouth."

She shuddered and closed her eyes, letting her mouth open slightly. Still holding onto her, he dipped his head and inhaled deeply. "Ah, yes. Your breath is warm, sweet, exhilarating." He tightened his hold on her neck. "This is going to be the best night of my existence."

****

Veronica had turned back to reaper form. That meant nearly an hour had passed. That meant Audra was in deep trouble while Dimitri sat, helpless, useless. He clenched his eyes shut. There had to be a way. Had to be something he could do. He couldn't let Gaylen take Audra.

Veronica bent toward him, stroking her fingers along his jaw line. "You could have had it all. I'd have loved you forever. You didn't need to get mixed up in the human world. There's nothing for you there but heartache. I wasn't enough for you, though, was I?"

When he didn't answer, she reached down and took hold of his shirt, tugging until the buttons popped. She raked her fingernails down his chest, gouging his skin, drawing blood. He flinched at the stinging pain.

Scott slowly circled him, his face twisted in a malicious smile. "You and that bitch will finally get what you deserve. She made me kill Joel. He was like my own son."

Dimitri laughed. "Even after death, you're blaming others for what you did, you sick fuck."

Scott bent down next to Veronica, attempting to infuse menace in his voice. "The only thing I hate is that you don't get to watch her die. I would really like that. If you had to watch your woman die."

Dimitri stretched his mouth in a humorless smile. "When I get loose, asshole, you'll be my first."

"First? What are you talking about, first?" He looked to Veronica, whose lips were pursed in amusement. "What's he talking about?"

"You'll be the first one he goes after, darling. And in your novice state, he'll be able to truly make you suffer."

Scott's face blanched, and he swallowed audibly. "You didn't tell me that. He won't get loose, will he? Can't we just keep him like that forever?"

Veronica opened her mouth to reply, but there was a commotion at the door, and she looked over Dimitri's shoulder. Her fair skin paled even further. "Oh, no. It can't be."

Dimitri twisted his head to find Cassie and Samuel barging into the room. Relief coursed through him. Samuel was impervious to copper. Help had arrived.

"What the fuck is this?" Scott asked. "What's going on?"

"I'll tell you what's going on," Veronica spat. "We're screwed."

Cassie shot over to Scott and shoved him hard. He went flying backward and landed with a thud against the wall.

"What the…? How did she do that?"

"You're still in training," Cassie said. "I just graduated. You're mine, bitch."

Scott looked to Veronica. "Can't you do something? You can handle this cunt, can't you?"

"I can," Veronica said. "But Samuel here…he's a different story. It's over, Scott. Let's just hope Gaylen has taken care of his little task. Then, none of this will matter."

Dimitri glared up at her. "You better hope, for your sake, that's not true."

Samuel frowned at Scott. "I'm not sure how you made it into the program. Not sure how they decided anything in *you* was redeemable. Maybe it was your love for your children. You're still in the probationary period. It's not too late to revoke the offer. One more misstep, and I'll send your ass straight to hell."

Scott glowered but didn't respond as Samuel went over to Dimitri and began unwinding the copper.

"You okay?" Samuel asked.

"Yeah, fine." The wounds Veronica had inflicted were already starting to heal. "How did you find me?"

"Cassie knew you were looking for Veronica. When she couldn't reach you, she became concerned. She came to me. For a little slip of a girl, she has a lot of tenacity."

Dimitri smiled. "She does, indeed. What will you do with those two?" He jerked his head to where Veronica and Scott looked on.

"Some punishment fitting their transgression.

They're so fond of one another, maybe I'll bind them together in copper for half a century."

"I wouldn't mind seeing that." Dimitri smiled. Once he was free of the copper, he stood, then stuck his hand out to Samuel. "Thanks for coming. I guess this makes us even."

Samuel returned the handshake. "You saved my wife and daughter from a horrifying death. I don't think unwrapping you quite equals that."

"If I get to Audra in time to save her, trust me, it will."

****

"Five-hundred ninety-two. Five-hundred ninety-three." Gaylen rubbed his lips along Audra's cheek. "Did I tell you how I'm going to do it? How I'm going to put you in jeopardy?" He slid his hand up and gripped her neck, then stroked his thumb along her skin. "I'm going to squeeze the life from your pretty, silky smooth neck. I've fantasized about that for years."

Audra shuddered. She'd been waiting for an opportunity to pull the knife, but so far, Gaylen hadn't given it to her. He'd stayed glued right to her, counting, touching her, giving her the heebie jeebies. She had to figure out a way to distract him, to gain some distance.

"Hey," she whispered. "I heard everything is better, more intense, after you've tasted human breath."

"That's right."

"You should take advantage of this moment. Have a drink, now that you can really enjoy it. I still have some scotch left."

He lifted his brows. "A drink actually sounds fantastic. I like the way you think." He stepped back. "Don't move. I got this. I know where you keep the liquor. Be right back."

As soon as he went into the kitchen, Audra took the switchblade from her bra. Her skin was so damp with perspiration, the blade almost slipped from her hand. She hoped she could hold onto it long enough to plunge it into the asshole's black, evil, human heart.

He returned in moments, a glass of scotch held in his fist. He sipped slowly. "This is amazing. I almost forgot what I'd been missing out on." Releasing a satisfied sigh, he slowly approached her. "Now, where were we?"

Fear uncoiled in her belly. It was now or never. She wouldn't have another opportunity. She brought the knife up and flicked it open. "Right here, asshole."

His eyes widened, then, he smiled. "You don't actually think—"

She thrust her arm forward, plunging the knife into his chest. He let out a *whoompf*, then dropped to his knees.

Her legs trembled. Her entire body shook. *Oh my God.* She'd killed a man. She'd actually killed a man. She sank to the floor, closing her eyes. She should feel some sort of remorse, but she didn't. Just an overwhelming sense of unreality, of relief.

An inhuman growl made her snap her eyes open. Gaylen was coming to his feet, his face twisted in rage. And, he was far from dead.

## Chapter 23

Gaylen staggered toward her, blood pouring from his chest, the knife held in his grip. "You bitch. You tricked me again," he panted. "Our eternity together was going to be fun. Now, I'll spend it making you suffer. After I gut you."

She scrambled to her feet and backed away. How many breaths did he have left? She'd lost count. Maybe if she could stay out of his way, he'd return to reaper form before he could—

He lunged toward her, and she stumbled backward, barely staying out of his reach. Terror thudded through her heart, cutting off her breath. "Gaylen, please. I—"

A crashing sounded at the door, but Audra couldn't look, couldn't take her eyes off Gaylen. If she did, he'd surely kill her.

"Leave her alone!" a voice boomed. Dimitri's voice.

Gaylen whirled. "What the hell? How did you…?"

Thank God, he was here. But what could he do as long as Gaylen was human. Unless…

Gaylen was in jeopardy. Could Dimitri reap him? Would he?

On the heels of those thoughts, a horrifying realization dawned. Dimitri hadn't just *appeared.* He'd slammed the door open. She looked at him and could tell…he was human.

And Gaylen had a knife.

Fear turned her blood to ice. She looked around for something to use as a weapon, but saw nothing. The fireplace poker? Why wasn't it next to the fireplace? *Think.*

A tortured bellow rose, and she whipped her head around to see Dimitri gripping Gaylen's wrist, the one that held the knife. Dimitri's jaw was clenched, his arms trembling from the effort to overpower Gaylen. They battled for dominance for several terrifying moments.

Audra froze, unable to move, to think.

Shaking her head, she cast her gaze around the room, rushed to the fireplace, frantically searched for the poker. What had she done…

She spotted it, lying on the carpet next to the hearth. Snatching it up, she raced to where Dimitri and Gaylen still struggled. "Let him go," she shouted.

Dimitri flicked a glance at her, but Gaylen ignored her. She lifted the poker, aiming for Gaylen's head, but the two men crashed into the coffee table, Dimitri on top. No way she could hit Gaylen without hurting Dimitri. Tears filled her eyes. Who was the stronger of the two? Gaylen was bigger…could Dimitri possibly overpower him, especially when Gaylen held the knife?

She headed toward the men, looking for an opening where she could…

The knife thrust upward, and she gasped. Dimitri sliced the blade across Gaylen's throat, and her knees weakened with relief. A gaping wound appeared, and Gaylen's hands flew to his neck. Blood spurted from between his fingers. He swayed, eyes wide, then crumpled to the floor and went still.

Dimitri let the knife fall from his grip. Rising, he rushed over to Audra. He hugged her to him, his hands sticky with blood that smeared her jersey, but she didn't care. She clung tightly to him.

"What were you thinking," he whispered against her hair. "You could have died."

"I just wanted to stop him." Her voice was muffled in his chest.

He pulled back to look into her face. "And you thought you could do that on your own?"

"I almost did."

"Yes, you almost did." He stroked a hand down her cheek, and she shivered at his warm touch. "You were pretty incredible."

"So were you."

His gaze roamed over her face. "I'm just glad I made it here in time."

"Me too," she said. "Everything turned out fine. It's over."

A scowl creased his brows. "Not entirely over, I'm afraid. I have some unsettling news."

"What?"

"While we might have taken care of Gaylen, Veronica's still out there and she has a partner." He frowned. "Scott Bellafonte."

"Scott? Scott's a…" She shook her head. "He's a reaper?"

"I'm afraid so. He and Veronica held me hostage so I couldn't stop Gaylen from taking you. Samuel threatened to bind them in copper for fifty years, but I don't know if he went through with it. Even if he did, it's possible someone might release them." His arms tightened around her. "If Samuel and Cassie hadn't…"

He closed his eyes and shook his head, then opened them to stare down at her. "I don't know what I'd have done if anything happened to you."

He bent his head forward, and her eyes drifted shut as his mouth touched hers. His lips were warm, seeking. She opened to him, surrendering to his kiss. She pressed closer and wound her hands behind his neck.

She knew as she drank in his kiss that, in spite of everything, she loved him. He hadn't *killed* Jaxon. He took Jaxon's soul to a better place, after his body was already dead. She was crushed, heartbroken over the loss, but Jaxon would be gone either way. It wasn't Dimitri; it was Veronica and Gaylen. And Dimitri had taken care of Gaylen. Like he'd taken care of everything else since he came into her life. Doing the best he could. Loving her.

She wouldn't lose him. She wanted him, flaws and all. Admittedly, reaping souls was a big hurdle, but one she could live with. As long as she had him.

"I love you, Dimitri," she whispered against his lips.

He pulled back, his eyes searching hers. "You love me?"

"Yes. I don't care if you're a reaper. Don't care what the future holds. I can't fight it any longer. I love you."

He smiled and brushed her hair back with his fingers, then cupped her face, planting a kiss on her lips. "Hold that thought. I have to go see Samuel and report on what happened with Gaylen. But I'll be back."

She nodded, then turned to look at Gaylen's body. "You'll do something about that before you go, right?"

He laughed. “Of course. I’ll take care of it, then take care of Samuel, and be back in no time.”

Audra nodded, her heart lifting with joy as she reluctantly released him. “See you soon.”

****

Dimitri stood before Samuel, resisting the urge to tap his foot in impatience. That would be a sign of disrespect, and although Samuel was excruciatingly slow, and Dimitri was itching to get back to Audra, he at least owed the man respect.

“You’ve done well, Dimitri. You deserve rest, yet you have over forty years left on your sentence.”

Dimitri nodded. “This is true. But, what can you do? I’ll make the best of it.”

“I’ll tell you what I can do. What I did.” A beaming white smile appeared in his dark skin. “I’ve commuted your sentence. You can finally move on. It’s time for you to have peace.”

“Commuted my sentence?” A crushing weight settled in Dimitri’s soul.

“Yes.” Samuel frowned. “What’s the matter? You don’t seem pleased. This is what you’ve wanted for nearly three-hundred years.”

Dimitri tried to keep the emotion from his voice as he spoke. “I thought it was what I wanted until I met Audra. I’ll never have peace if I don’t have her.”

Samuel sighed and closed his eyes. When he opened them, Dimitri could see sadness in their depths. “I’m sorry, son. It is done.”

****

Audra filled a bucket with soap and water and used a sponge to scrub Gaylen’s blood from her floor. This wasn’t something she’d be reporting to Shane. She couldn't imagine trying to explain that one.

Not only did the task need doing, she had to keep herself busy until Dimitri returned. She thought about calling Riley. They had a lot to discuss. Audra needed to decide how much she should tell her friend about what went down today. Knowing about reapers was one thing. Hearing the violent, dangerous details of the day's events was quite another.

"Hey, I think you got it all."

Audra smiled at the sound of Dimitri's voice. She hadn't heard him come in. She stood and dropped the sponge, then the rubber gloves into the bucket.

"I'm glad you're back." She walked toward him and held up a hand, palm out. Dimitri lifted his and pressed it to hers. The cool sizzle traveled to her and she smiled. "I know we can't touch," she said. "But just being with you will work for now."

"Nothing makes me happier than being with you."

The words were positive, but his tone held a touch of something not so positive. Maybe it was her imagination.

"How did it go with Samuel?"

"Samuel was very pleased. He's rewarding me."

"That's great. What will your reward be?" Hope lit in her heart. "Will he let you become human forever?"

"No. He's given me what I wanted from the beginning."

"What did you want?"

He hesitated, then said, "Do you remember what I told you at the tree that day?"

She thought back. "You said…you wanted peace. You wanted to go on. To meet your destiny." Pain clogged her chest as she remembered. "To die."

"That's right."

She stared at him incredulously. "Dying? Dying's your *reward*? That's bullshit."

"I'm sorry."

"No." She shook her head violently. "Tell him that's not what you want. You changed your mind. You can't leave me."

"It's too late. It's done."

"*No*." Tears crowded her throat. "There has to be something you can do."

"Kind of ironic, huh? Now that I finally have something to live for, I have to die."

"It's not fair," she said, realizing how childish she sounded and not caring.

"He did grant me one last favor. I can turn human once more, and I want to spend that time with you."

"Once more? That's it?"

He cupped her cheek, brushing tears away with his thumb. She could feel him. He'd turned human. That meant the clock was ticking.

She wrapped her arms around him and laid her head on his chest. "One lousy hour? That's all we'll ever have?"

"I'm afraid so." His words rumbled against her ear. "But we'll make the most of it. You remember what you told me you wanted? You said you wanted to sit on a porch swing and hold hands with the man you love. Grow old with him."

"Right." She sniffed back tears. "And now, that's not going to happen."

"I can't do anything about the growing old part, but I can take care of the rest."

She pulled back to stare up at him. "What do you

mean?"

"Come on." He took hold of her hand and tugged. "It is the middle of the night, but I think this could still work."

He led her outside. The sky was black except for the smattering of white-blue stars and the glow of the moon. Cool air nipped her flesh. She should have brought a jacket, but Dimitri's hand in hers provided all the warmth she needed.

They walked down the block, past a few houses, until he stopped in front of one and led her to the porch.

"There," he said, pointing proudly at a wooden swing.

"This isn't my house. We can't just—"

"They won't mind. They're not even home."

She followed him, and he settled on the swing, then pulled her down with him. Putting his arm around her, he tucked her into his side. "This is all we have now. Let's enjoy it for however many breaths I have left. We're too late to watch the neighborhood go dark, I'm afraid."

Anguish squeezed the breath from her, and all she could do was nod. She tried to blink back tears, but they ran in warm streams down her cheeks. Her heart was breaking. She had to hold onto these last few moments, wanted to enjoy them, but she couldn't stem the flow of tears. She couldn't believe this would be all she had left of Dimitri.

Feeling his warmth, the comforting weight as he rested his chin on her hair, she snuggled in close to him and whispered, "Breathe slowly please."

****

"It's almost time." Dimitri's words were soft, but

the message ripped a jagged wound in her heart.

She nodded, unable to speak around the tears blocking her throat. He stood and took her hand, pulling her to her feet.

They walked in silence, halting when they reached her yard. She looked up at him. "I can't believe this is it. That I'll really never see you again." Her voice choked on the words, and tears spilled down her face.

Dimitri kissed the moisture from her cheeks and tucked a strand of hair behind her ear. "You'll see me one day. When you cross to the other side."

Cross to the other side? Did he think that was *comforting*? She shook her head in disbelief. "That's not good enough. I can't live like this. I'll still see reapers, but none of them will be you. How can I deal with that?"

His lips tilted in a sad grin. "Because, you're strong and brave. You have a lot of living to do, Audra. You'll find someone to love, and he'll give you the children you've always wanted."

Her breath caught on a sob. "I'll never love like this again."

Narrowing his eyes, he cupped her face in his hands. "I'll carry that thought with me. And it will sustain me through eternity."

Pain wrenched her gut. Her voice dropped to a tortured whisper. "No, please. I can't let you go."

"I'm sorry." The anguish in his expression mirrored that in her soul. "I only have a few seconds left. Goodbye, my beautiful Audra." He placed a tender kiss on her lips.

She gripped his shoulders, kissing him back. Then, she felt him fade. Away from her hands…her lips. She almost cried out, almost begged him to stay, but it would be useless. Besides, she didn't want his last image of her to be that of a hysterical, sobbing mess.

He turned and headed into the dark night, looking back at her briefly and flashing the smile that brought out his dimples and made his cobalt eyes glitter. She watched until his silhouette merged with the blackness and she could no longer see him. Then, she dropped to the ground, clawed her hands into the damp grass, and wept while her soul splintered in pieces.

****

Hours after Dimitri vanished, Audra was still pacing the floor, clenching her hair in her hands.

"It's bullshit," she muttered. "Nothing but bullshit."

The tears had dried long ago, and she let anger sweep away her grief. Anger, she could deal with. The grief would destroy her.

A figure appeared in front of her, and she halted. "Cassie? What are you doing here?"

Cassie wore a pair of frayed jeans and a white, Old Navy hoodie. She tucked her blonde-pink hair behind her ears, then gazed warily at Audra. "I wanted to check on you. Are you okay?"

"Am I okay? Does it *look* like I'm okay? Dimitri's gone. So much for your miracles."

Cassie blew a breath out between pursed lips. "This bites big time."

"That's an understatement." Rage shook through her. "I mean, come on. We destroyed Gaylen. After all these years, that monster is gone, and *this* is our reward? I'd given up on love, decided it wasn't in the cards for me. Then, I met Dimitri."

“I told you he’d grow on you.” Cassie tried a smile, but when Audra glared at her, it faded from her face.

“Tell me, Cassie. I really want to know. What kind of bullshit miracle is that?”

“You can’t *make* miracles happen, they just do. Sometimes. But not all the time.”

Audra rolled her eyes. “Thanks for clearing that one up.” She crossed her arms and resumed pacing. “Listen, Cassie. I’m not really in the mood for company right now. Can you please just go?”

“Sure. Yeah. I just wanted to tell you I’m sorry.”

Audra nodded, feeling like an ass, but unable to work up the ability to do anything different. She knew she’d get better. One of these days, she’d learn to live with the pain. But not today. Today, agony was clawing out her insides, and it felt as though it would never end.

****

Dimitri stood with his eyes closed, arms outstretched, waiting for death to claim him. This time, he’d move on to his eternal rest instead of serving as a reaper.

Funny. He was finally getting what he wanted, and it was the worst thing he could imagine. He’d died once before, but it hadn’t hurt like this.

Tightness seized his flesh. His body began to shut down. He could feel the breath leaving him. Blackness crowded in. It was happening. He’d never see Audra again. What the hell was he thinking? Falling in love with a human? For nearly three-hundred years, he’d gotten by just fine without giving in to emotions. Now, he understood why he’d avoided them. Feeling was excruciating.

The blackness took him completely, and he felt a

floating sensation. There was no excited anticipation about what awaited him on the other side. Whatever it was, Audra wouldn't be there.

Suddenly, the floating sensation ceased. Cassie's voice came to him from the darkness. "Dimitri. Hey, Dimitri. I'm here to make you an offer."

"What?" He frowned, opening his eyes to find Cassie standing in front of him, her face alight with a beaming smile. "What's going on?"

"You can choose to meet your destiny, or become a reaper. The sentence is a hundred years." She gave a wink, lowering her voice conspiratorially. "But we both know it can end up being much longer than that."

"What? How did…"

"Samuel…uhm…*decided* you should have another chance. You destroyed Gaylen, something no one has been able to do in hundreds of years. And, even though you broke some rules, they were all for unselfish reasons. To help others. You've beyond redeemed yourself."

Dimitri lifted a brow. "Samuel just suddenly decided this?"

"*Weeellll.*" She lifted her shoulders in a shrug. "I might have said some things that made him realize this whole 'meeting your reward thing' was bogus." She smiled. "Oh, yeah, there's a third option."

"Third option?"

"You can choose to become human."

Dimitri waited to let the words sink in. When they did, he said, "You're kidding, right?"

Elation budded in his chest, but he was afraid to give in to it. Afraid to believe it in case this was some cruel hoax.

She shook her head, her pinkish hair swinging back and forth. "Nope. Not kidding. Come on. I don't have all day." She grinned impishly. "Actually, I do. I have, like, a hundred years. But, I'm kind of anxious to hear your decision. I know someone else who will be, too. So, what's it going to be?"

Dimitri suppressed the urge to shout with joy. Audra. He was actually going to be with Audra. He smiled at Cassie. "I think you know the answer to that." He tweaked her chin, then placed a kiss on her forehead. "Thanks, sweetheart. See you around."

"Yeah. See you around." He was walking away when her voice stopped him. "Dimitri?"

Tamping down his impatience, he turned back to face her. "Yes? What is it?"

Moisture brimmed in her eyes. Her voice wistful, she said, "Enjoy being human."

****

"Be careful, Sadie!" Audra cringed as Sadie crawled over the dome climber. With her heart condition, she sometimes became weak. The medications had helped, but they didn't always keep her from tiring easily. Besides, the child was a natural-born klutz. Audra could just see her tumbling to the ground. Although it wasn't that high up, and Gaylen was no longer around to swoop in and reap her, she could still be injured. Or killed. Audra shuddered, pushing that thought from her mind. She'd lost enough. Too much. She wouldn't even think about losing Sadie.

Although she hadn't slept all night, after Cassie left this morning, Audra had called Riley to see if she could take Sadie out for the day. She couldn't be alone with her thoughts. Her heart felt weighted with lead. Not only had she lost Dimitri, forever, tomorrow was Jaxon's funeral. How would she get through that? And the days following, with neither of them in her life?

For now, she'd focus on what she did have—Riley, Sadie. Thank God for Sadie. She needed her sweetness, her youth and vitality, a reminder that she had something to live for. She'd brought her to the park. It was a warm day for November, typically unpredictable weather for Oklahoma. One day there might be a snowstorm, the next, spring-like temperatures.

Briefly, Audra and Riley had discussed the reaper situation. Riley hadn't seen Steve since that first time. Hadn't seen another reaper, so she was starting to believe she'd imagined it. Audra explained to her that, although she *thought* she hadn't seen a reaper, it was likely she had. She wouldn't always know if the people she saw were reapers.

Besides, what Audra had dealt with the past few months couldn't be denied. Riley might prefer to think Audra had gone insane, but in her eyes, Audra saw she knew the truth. It would just take a while to come to terms with it. Hopefully, when it was all said and done, Riley wouldn't lose her heart to a reaper, only to have him snatched away forever.

A movement near the closed-down concession stand caught her eye. A man walked toward her, his dark hair ruffling in the breeze. He wore a black T-shirt and faded jeans. The walk was familiar. When he drew closer, the blue eyes were unmistakable.

"Dimitri?" Audra breathed. She came to her feet and slowly walked toward him, afraid a sudden movement would make him disappear. This couldn't be happening, he couldn't be real, but she'd enjoy the fantasy as long as it lasted.

"Hi, there," he said.

"It's you? It's really you?"

When she reached him, she lifted a hand to his face, expecting to feel the chilling electricity, or nothing, since he wasn't really there. But, her hand met warm flesh. Rough whiskers scraped her palm.

"It's me," he whispered, snaking his arms around her waist and pulling her to him.

"What are you doing? You're human now? Is this just another visit? I don't understand."

"Yes. I'm human."

"But you were going to meet your destiny. Going away forever. I don't understand," she said again.

While this was exactly what she wanted, even if it was only for a brief moment, she couldn't stop the flow of questions. She had to know what this meant…couldn't deal with another heartbreak. "How long will you be here?"

"How long do you want me here?"

"Forever."

"Okay, then."

"Okay? Really? How is that possible?"

"You can thank Cassie. She's kind of a pain in the ass. She ambushed Samuel, berated, shamed, and harassed him until he undid my reward."

"Undid your reward…You mean, you aren't going to die?"

"Actually, I will die. Someday. Unexpectedly. Like a regular, normal human being. But not today. Not right now."

"Oh…wow." Tears of joy choked her voice. She lifted her lips, and he touched his mouth to hers. She sighed with pleasure. There it was. Dimitri's kiss…the one that made her pulse race, made the blood rush in her veins, the kiss she'd thought was gone forever.

He pulled his head back and looked down at her. "I'm not sure how this is all going to work. How we'll explain me to your friends. How I'll get a job. I have no past. No identification."

She cocked her head and frowned. "Are you really worrying about all of that right now? At this moment?"

He smiled, his sapphire eyes glinting with amusement. "I suppose we can deal with it later."

"Aunt Audra? Who's that man?"

"Uh oh," Audra whispered.

She disentangled herself from Dimitri's arms and looked down at Sadie. Sadie's gaze went from Audra to Dimitri, her face scrunched in curiosity.

"He's a friend of mine," Audra said.

"Are you going to 'vorce him like you 'vorced Jaxon?"

Pain shafted through Audra's heart. Jaxon. She missed him so much. He was the first person she would have told about falling in love. She met Dimitri's eyes.

Sympathy shadowed his expression. He mouthed, *I'm sorry*. Giving a little nod, she sniffed back tears.

Dimitri squatted down until he was eye level with Sadie. "We're not getting divorced, but we might get married. And you could be the flower girl. How would you like that?"

"I would love it!" she squealed.

Dimitri rose and took Audra's hands. "So, you want to get married? Or are you going to crush a little girl's dream?"

Audra laughed, tiptoeing to place a kiss on his lips. “I would never, ever crush a little girl’s dream.”

## A word about the author...

Alicia Dean began writing stories as a child. At age 10, she wrote her first ever romance (featuring a hero who looked just like Elvis Presley, and who shared the name of Elvis' character in the movie, *Tickle Me*), and she still has the tattered, pencil-written copy. Alicia lives Edmond, Oklahoma. She writes mostly contemporary suspense and paranormal, but has also written in other genres, including a few vintage historicals.

Other than reading and writing, her passions are Elvis Presley (she almost always works in a mention of him into her stories), MLB, NFL and watching (and rewatching) her favorite televisions shows like Ozark, Dexter, Justified, and Vampire Diaries. Some of her favorite authors are Michael Connelly, Dennis Lehane, Stephen King, Lee Child, Lisa Gardner, Ridley Pearson, Joseph Finder, and Jonathan Kellerman...to name a few.

You can find her here:
Email: Alicia@AliciaDean.com
Website: http://aliciadean.com/
Facebook:
https://www.facebook.com/AuthorAliciaDean/
Twitter: @Alicia_Dean_
BookBub: https://www.bookbub.com/profile/alicia-dean
Goodreads:
http://www.goodreads.com/author/show/468339.Alicia_Dean

Thank you for purchasing
this publication of The Wild Rose Press, Inc.

For questions or more information
contact us at
info@thewildrosepress.com.

The Wild Rose Press, Inc.
www.thewildrosepress.com

www.ingramcontent.com/pod-product-compliance
Lightning Source LLC
Chambersburg PA
CBHW051130030726
47504CB00004B/790